THE
RENAISSANCE

THE SOKOLOV SERIES

The Russian Renaissance
The Collaborator
Temple of Spies
Kremlin Storm

IAN KHARITONOV

THE RUSSIAN RENAISSANCE

Copyright © 2011 by Ian Kharitonov

All rights reserved. No part of this publication may be reproduced in any form or by any means without the prior written permission of the copyright holder.

Cover design by Hristo Kovatliev.

This book is a work of fiction. Names, characters, places, and incidents either are products of the author's imagination or are used fictitiously. Any resemblance to actual persons, living or dead, or actual events is purely coincidental.

ISBN: 1532964323

www.iankharitonov.com

PROLOGUE

1941

THE SOVIET UNION

Death was the only destination in the train's five-year-long schedule.

Even its name sounded like a shrill omen. The *Felix Dzerzhinsky*, a 137-ton locomotive, was a child of its era—an unstoppable mass of raw power fleshed in metal.

During 1936, its first year of operation, the *Felix Dzerzhinsky* coursed between Russia's faceless stations and towns, hauling cattle. The animals had filled the tidy new freight cars with the lingering smell of their sweat and waste, parasites infesting the cracks between the hoof-dented boards, the feeling of imminent slaughter staying with the train forever.

Soon enough, the cattle was replaced by people. Men and women, old and young, most sick, some bleeding, all filled the freight cars heading to the gulags, towards a fate far more dreadful than that of the animals. The luckiest died on the way.

Now, as the war broke out, the *Felix Dzerzhinsky* carried a special cargo to the safety of Central Asia: hundreds of wooden crates stacked from the secret vaults of Leningrad and Moscow. Special passengers in the form of a six-man Red Army escort occupied the newly-fitted first class carriage.

The single beam of light sheared the night as the *Felix Dzerzhinsky* roared across the vast Kazakh steppe. The train pushed its boilers to the limits, charging to the invisible finish line. Yet its run was cursed by the presence of the treasured cargo.

Death still waited at the other end.

Inside the confines of the single passenger car, the gunshots boomed above the monotonous throbbing. The Red Army soldiers were too slow to react. They had not expected an attack from within. Not from their commander, Comrade Yehlakov of the NKGB.

At close range, Yehlakov blasted the heads of four soldiers keeping watch, each barely eighteen. While the other two fumbled for their bolt-action rifles, shocked awake from sleep, confused, Yehlakov finished them off.

The new car was now also smeared with death.

Yehlakov replaced the empty clip of his TT semiautomatic, and entered the driver's cabin, gunning down the crew. The driver clutched his throat, trying to clog the wide open hole, and the torrent of blood gushing from it mingled with the soot on his hands. He stumbled, gurgling, looking at his black blood. A second gunshot destroyed his face, and he crashed over the corpse of his fireman.

Stepping over thier bodies, Yehlakov pulled the brake handle. The brakes locked onto the wheels and the enormous friction showered sparks in every direction. A piercing screech of protesting metal reverberated around the compartment. The train shook as it tried to restrain its own momentum. Gradually, the *Felix Dzerzhinsky* came to a stop.

Yehlakov climbed down from the cabin and looked around. The gloom was impenetrable. The train's lamp would serve as a position marker.

Leningrad, the origin of the *Felix Dzerzhinsky*, was a city commanded by evacuation mayhem. Fuel, provisions, armaments and entire factories were being relocated from the advancing Germans, and many consignments lost in the process. The disappearance of the train, if it were ever noticed, would be written off to a Luftwaffe raid in Moscow by Army staffers fearful of repercussions. Yehlakov didn't care much. There was little chance of Moscow surviving anyway.

A column of trucks appeared in the distance, their flickering lights drawing closer. The huge ZIS-5 vehicles stopped in front of Yehlakov, washing him in the beams of their headlights. In the blinding light he couldn't make out the faces of the men approaching him.

"Right on time," Yehlakov said, squinting.

"Too bad for you," the man from the lead truck replied. Three figures leveled their machine guns at Yehlakov—the recognizable silhouettes of American Thompsons.

Yehlakov's cry was cut short by a hail of .45-caliber bullets that shredded his body.

"All right men," an order sounded. "Move, move, move!"

The tiny figures of two dozen soldiers scurried to the *Felix Dzerzhinsky* like scavengers ravaging a beached whale.

Reloading all the crates into the trucks proved to be a massive job, but the attackers carried it out with efficiency. Trouble arose only once. A crate crashed, bursting open, and antique icons poured from it onto the dusty ground. Gleaming through the darkness in their radiant halos were the faces of saints. The holy men gazed at the killers with divine serenity, their eyes full of suffering and forgiveness.

After it was all over, raging flames engulfed the empty cars, and the attackers vanished back into the night.

The dead metal beast had completed its final, blood-drenched journey.

20??

KAZAKHSTAN

Over its dynamic 200-year history, the town had gone through several incarnations, renamed and rebuilt with each change of ownership. Originally known as Akmolinsk, it had been a fortress established by Siberian Cossack troops who travelled south, at a time when the Russian Empire explored its own newly-acquired lands populated by nomadic Kazakh tribes. Later it became Tselinograd, a Soviet springboard to deluded ambitions in agriculture. And heading into the twenty-first century it assumed the title of Astana, the capital of independent Kazakhstan.

The word *Astana* meant precisely that—capital city.

James Quinn, the U.S. Ambassador to Kazakhstan, knew that this town still had a long way to go before it could be called a major city. Yet even in his tenure he had witnessed a staggering transformation that Astana was experiencing. Even though the place had a reputation of a huge construction site, Ambassador Quinn had never seen such rapid development as Astana was undergoing now. The man partly responsible for the new shape of Astana was Clayton Richter—an American businessman he was greeting in the VIP hall of Astana International Airport.

Richter had changed little over the years they had known each other. At fifty he was full of vigor and confidence, his gait lithe. He was lanky, a few inches taller than Quinn and a lot fitter, dressed in a silk shirt and designer jeans. Apart from a jacket draped over his arm, Richter carried nothing—in a few hours his private jet would be flying him back to the States.

Behind the casual appearance, traveling unaccompanied by a phalanx of aides and bodyguards, was a man wielding immense power. Clayton Richter was on first name basis with the President of the United States.

The privilege came with the position of CEO at Seton Industries. SI was a corporate juggernaut that exemplified globalization. From a core interest in energy infrastructure, Seton's activities had expanded to transportation and logistics, construction and investment, finance and oil trade. Yet with such influence, SI avoided publicity, dealing in the realm of top-level government contracts. Wherever budgets were allocated, tenders announced, procurement initiated, Clayton Richter was there. Adding to the extensive international portfolio, SI had also scored a significant domestic coup. Through a host of affiliates and subsidiaries, Seton Industries ranked as the seventh largest contractor of the U.S. Armed Forces. For some, business was war, but for Clayton Richter war had become business.

Richter liked to call SI a small company with large resources—and the description was not far off the mark. The list of entities surrounding SI was ever-growing. Lawyers, bankers, manufacturers, and intermediaries all serviced Seton's needs without being fully cognizant of how far its tentacles reached. But stripped of the outer units it commanded, the company remained a compact nexus that was difficult to trace, let alone penetrate. Richter's ingenuity created a mega-corporation that never caught attention. He appreciated the discretion as it gave him more leeway to choose his methods. The ones he often utilized were questionable at best, and mostly corrupt—from aggressive lobbying in Congress to bribery in Third World countries.

Quinn shook Richter's hand cordially. The businessman smiled, but his eyes showed no warmth. His shrewd mind seemed forever occupied, tackling figures and percentages, calculating prices and profit margins. It was a mind which also judged every person as a tool on his way to success, with no capacity for human affection. This emotionless calculation was a characteristic that had always been present in him. Even back when Clayton Richter and Jim Quinn had still shared the executive floor of the SI headquarters in Manhattan.

Ambassador Quinn's own career as plenipotentiary had launched from the offices of Seton Industries. Prior to his assignment as Head of Mission in Astana, Quinn had been Richter's closest associate at the corporation. When Richter had arranged Quinn's posting as Ambassador to Kazakhstan, Quinn understood the importance of the move. Richter needed to have his own man in Kazakhstan, a man loyal to him alone. The company's interests in Kazakhstan far exceeded construction and logistics. After contributing as a donor to the president's successful campaign, assuring a nomination and approval in the Senate had posed no problems.

James Quinn acted as a secret liaison between Richter and the President of Kazakhstan, Timur Kasymov.

Today, Clayton Richter had arrived to Astana incognito following an urgent request for a meeting coming from President Kasymov himself. Quinn was taking Richter straight to Kasymov's residence, as Kasymov had insisted. This way, no outsider would be privy to the arrangement, even among the presidential staff.

Together, the businessman and the ambassador emerged from the private section of the terminal. Outside, they were instantly assaulted by a dry wave of air which was so hot that it might have been coming from a furnace. The embassy's Cadillac, distinguished by the flying Stars and Stripes, already stood idling. The sun made its black body shimmer with elegance. A Diplomatic Security officer held the door open for them. The former Secret Service agent now worked for Blackwood Solutions, a private security company that won the U.S. State Department contract to protect the U.S. diplomatic mission in Kazakhstan. Blackwood belonged to Seton Industries.

Climbing inside, Quinn was grateful that their exposure to a temperature of ninety-five ended quickly. He sank in the seat, its coolness soothing. Richter's complexion was pale, but he wiped a bead of perspiration from his brow.

"Damned heat," Richter said.

"It's the climate of the steppes," Quinn said. "Astana in the summer is hotter than a desert, and then it freezes over during Siberian winters."

As the diplomatic car departed from the Japanese-designed terminal, cruising along the highway, silence fell between the ambassador and the businessman. As a rule, Richter never discussed business while they were in the car, even though an armored polycarbonate partition sealed all sound from the DS driver, and a jamming device prevented electronic eavesdropping.

The airport was located only sixteen kilometers from Astana's southern limits, and soon the effects of the city's booming progress came into view. Skyscrapers, shopping malls and residential blocks formed a glamorous maze of glass and concrete. Unsurprisingly, the most intense construction was concentrated in this area, since Astana's south was the most prosperous part of the city. Entire districts had been built from scratch.

Richter admired the city skyline.

"Look at that, Jim. New buildings are growing by the day. I see true ambition here. The Kazakhstanis are putting their oil revenues to good use. And it's just the beginning. It's going to be a country of fantastic growth, with dozens of cities like Dubai and Doha. The *difference* is that the Arab oil empire is grinding to a halt, while Kazakhstan is reaching its zenith."

"I don't know," Quinn said. "I've never taken a liking to Astana. It's not just the weather that turns me off. The climate is so harsh only because of the terrain. Astana is in the middle of nowhere. The Soviets couldn't have picked a more fitting place for the women's gulag that Stalin set up here. What sort of nation's capital is so remote and desolate that it's hard to access from the rest of the country? I understand the logic behind relocating it from Almaty, the desire for a new start after they got their independence. But they didn't have to take it literally, for God's sake! These buildings are here only because the rulers wished to flatter their egos. A Potemkin town. No matter what you try to do here, it's still a wasteland."

He motioned at the stretching plane that the road cut through. All the way to the city limits the earth was a scorched flat surface covered by low weeds.

Richter laughed at his friend's rant.

"I see that you're getting a bit homesick, Jimmy."

"Sure as hell. It doesn't matter, though. I'll grind it through another year, or as long as it takes to finish what we started."

"A wasteland, hmmm? Funny that you mentioned the word. How very ironic. You'd be surprised if I told you the reason I'm meeting Kasymov today."

In fact, Quinn felt astonishment.

He had always assumed that Richter's latest visit was related to the Caspian. It had been the most important aspect of SI's operation in Kazakhstan, the one Quinn handled personally. It had to be the Caspian. Nothing else could demand such an extraordinary summons.

And yet, something far more sensitive than the oil project was going on, *behind his back*.

There was at least one skill Quinn had acquired from his diplomatic work in order to save face—pretending not to hear the remarks he didn't wish to respond to.

The presidential residence, known as *Ak-Orda*, was also located in the southern part of Astana, taking up a sizable estate on the left bank of the Ishim River. It was a massive granite palace that evoked a mixture of awe and confusion. Ak-Orda's exterior, and especially its semicircular portico, bore a striking resemblance to the southern facade of the house at 1600 Pennsylvania Avenue, Washington, DC.

What made Ak-Orda radically different was a gigantic blue dome crowning it at the center, a feature more appropriate for mosques than government housing.

The name Ak-Orda chosen for the residence also signified Asian tradition—it meant White Horde, a part of the ancient Golden Horde that had ruled this land.

The golden spire topping its Islamic dome was about to come into view.

A quiet neighborhood separated the American car from the parkway that led directly to Ak-Orda. The Cadillac was easing through light traffic, only a few blocks away from reaching the turn to the parkway, when suddenly, from behind, an old Toyota sedan burst forward and cut into their path, braking. Trying to avoid a head-on collision, the DS driver turned the wheel sharply, and pressed the accelerator. Even though the fender battered the Toyota's taillight, metal scraping, the Cadillac was about to drive on, but the maneuver was destined to fail. In the next instant the Toyota disappeared in a tempest of flames.

The force of the roaring blast pounded the Cadillac like a sledgehammer. Shockwaves quaked through Quinn's body. Shaken by the concussion, he shut his eyes. He wanted to scream, but no sound came, agony ringing in his head, the pain deafening.

The ambassador regained his senses, moaning. He saw that the car's inch-thick windshield had disintegrated. Corrugated by the explosion, the hood had bent upward, obstructing the view ahead. The driver's slumped body was held in place by the seat belt. He was dead, the partition painted red with his blood.

Yet the car was moving.

The tires had been blown to shreds, Quinn realized, but the run-flat system made the Cadillac roll forward until the car smashed against an obstacle and came to a stop.

Jolted by the final impact, Quinn turned to see that sitting next to him, Richter was unconscious. A trickle of blood was streaming down the businessman's face from a gash in his forehead. Quinn didn't know if Richter was dead, but he didn't care.

He had to think about himself now. The car was burning; soon he would be trapped inside. Luckily, the gas tank had remained intact, but it could blow up at any moment.

Quinn reached for the door and yanked the handle. Pushing the door open, he desperately crawled out of the car. Dashing a few yards away, he felt his knees buckle. His vision blurred and he tumbled down onto the road. He couldn't pick himself up, his limbs wobbly, so he gathered all his strength to turn around and check his surroundings.

He saw mayhem.

The car of the suicide bomber was a charred frame devoured by fire. Black smoke billowed from the wreckage of the Toyota. Anguished cries filled the street, passersby fleeing the area in a frantic commotion. Shards of glass covered the road, strewn from the other vehicles hit by the blast. All the cars in the vicinity had suffered damage—either hit by fragments, catching fire, or crashing into each other. There was blood on the asphalt, motorists and pedestrians injured or killed.

Swerving into the opposite lane, the Cadillac itself had hit a car parked at the curb, blocking traffic. The ambassador could hardly believe the destruction his car had taken.

Nothing lighter than a tank would survive a similar attack. The entire front of the car had been destroyed, the radiator and the engine gone. The crumpled hood was reaching the roof. Only the additional shell protecting the passengers had saved Quinn's life, or else he would have been mutilated like the DS driver. Absorbing the fragments, the side of the car was peppered with dents and holes. A mesh of cracks netted the windows.

The smoke and blaze was intensifying.

Then, out of nowhere, two running figures appeared, heading for the wreckage. Both were dressed in military fatigues and carried Kalashnikov rifles, but they were no soldiers. In lieu of insignia, they wore green headbands with Arabic lettering. Black bandannas concealed their faces.

One of them rammed a foot into Quinn's gut. He gagged from the pain.

Eyes watering, he saw the man's partner approach the ambassadorial car. The masked guerrilla aimed his Kalashnikov at Richter, still lying prone inside.

"*Allahu akbar!*"

The Kalashnikov rattled, the gunfire cracking like thunder. Hitting Clayton Richter, the bullets tore up geysers of blood that streaked on the leather upholstery.

Without warning, another volley sounded, fired by the man standing over Quinn. The ambassador felt hot slugs corkscrewing through his body in a split-second.

Quinn gaped.

Blood sprouted from him.

His murderer yelled a command at the second terrorist and they ran away.

As he lay dying, their voices haunted him. They were young, still in their teens.

He could not imagine a death more stupid than being killed by some damned brats.

THE UNITED STATES

William Underhill was accustomed to long sleepless nights. Langley lived with no regard to time zones. As Director of Central Intelligence, he had learned long ago that the worst contingencies always broke out at night. Bombings in the Middle East, assassinations in Europe, hostilities in Asia all caught the world's strongest country sleeping. It was broad daylight everywhere else, and disaster seemed eager to strike just in time to be fresh for America's morning headlines. Clayton Richter was killed eleven hours ahead of midnight in Virginia.

Heading for an emergency briefing at the White House, Underhill felt that the last few hours had been more frantic than any he could remember.

He was ushered to the Oval Office, the President expecting him to deliver the full details. As much as he would have liked to, Richter's death was not something he could conceal from the President. But the DCI's report carried omissions even at Top Secret level. The whole truth did not always benefit national security. Underhill had no intention of telling the President that Richter had been a CIA man, or divulging his agenda in Kazakhstan.

The walls of the Oval Office converged in a domed ceiling fifteen feet above the President, who was sitting behind his massive oak desk. The panoramic windows behind him were adorned with velvet olive-green curtains, identical in color to those originally chosen a century earlier.

The President belonged in the Oval Office. He matched the grandeur of his position; he was a leader that this country deserved to have. Over his three years in office, he had united the American public at a time of hardship.

Yet the burden of leading the nation was taking its toll. Challenged by the problems the previous administrations had left him, each victory was harder to claim. He now was a different man compared to the energetic Governor of Iowa who had won the election by a landslide. Even the outward change was notable. At fifty-eight, his blond hair had tinged with grey, and his face had acquired stress lines.

Accepting the classified folder from Underhill, the President placed it on his desk for later study.

"This," he said jabbing his finger at the folder, "is a full-blown catastrophe."

He failed to contain his frustration.

"We have only begun climbing out of recession," the President continued. "Our economy is still a few years from returning to growth, and even then I doubt our recovery will be full, with the strain of our trade and budget deficits. You know as well as I do how much we need the Caspian oil. Every extra dollar per barrel of crude increases our debt. And once the economy has bounced back, the oil prices will soar again. If that happens, we will plunge into a deeper abyss than we've ever encountered. And now we're staring at a very real possibility of that happening."

"I understand your concern, Mr. President. It appears we have lost the Caspian."

With ten percent of the world's total oil reserve, the Caspian Sea was an untouched treasure trove. Development of oil sites has remained deadlocked because of the power struggle among the Caspian states. Essentially, the Caspian Sea used to be the Soviets' inner lake, but after the breakup everyone wanted a slice of the oil pie. For years, Russia, Iran, Kazakhstan, Azerbaijan, and Turkmenistan had been going for each other's throats over territorial claims.

Everybody had their own way of dividing the seabed in their favor. Russia insisted on what was known as Modified Median Line—meaning that the shares would be proportionate to the countries' respective coastlines. That proved completely unacceptable for Iran and the smaller nations; they wanted equal twenty-percent shares. Others added to the confusion by offering their own dubious calculations. Nobody wanted to lose, but the inability to resolve the dispute paralyzed oil production. Time is money, so the negotiations resumed. A compromise was about to be reached.

"I want to know who's responsible for this attack, Bill. The Russians? The Iranians and the Chinese?"

"I doubt the Russians are behind it. Russia, of course, is the world's number one oil and natural gas exporter. They'd never let us into the Caspian. For them, it's a matter of national security. They still consider the Caspian Sea as their private property. But their initiative of the Median Line method is all but accepted. Their share is secure and they don't have to worry about losing it."

"The country with the longest Caspian coastline is not Russia," the President suggested. "It's Kazakhstan."

The DCI nodded. "And Kazakhstan's part of the seabed accounts for almost eighty percent of the proven reserves. The Kazakhs will have more oil than all the Arab nations combined. The Chinese are indeed pursuing their Caspian ambitions through Iran. If the Russians push their plan, the Iranians—and, by extension, the Chinese—miss out with only thirteen percent. They won't settle for that. So naturally, together they are trying to influence the Kazakhstanis. One might think this triple alliance is sensible. Especially from a cultural viewpoint, considering that the Kazakhs are both Oriental and Muslim. And having said that, I don't believe it a viable option. I don't think Richter's assassination can be traced to China or Iran."

"What the hell are you saying? None of the three key players in the region had anything to do with the murder?"

William Underwood cleared his throat.

"Mr. President, we have identified the most probable scenario of Clayton Richter's death. The only person who could sanction the killing was Timur Kasymov himself."

"The Kazakh President? It's inconceivable! Do you understand the gravity of this implication, Mr. Underhill?"

"Sir, my agency does not make such assumptions on a whim. You may find the complete analysis in my report. Suffice it to say, this is the only option backed by current evidence. This act of terror was a signal of intent. A warning. The entire setup of the attack is pointing to the fact. There can be no other explanation for the ineptitude of the police, or the precise planning and execution of the attack. It demanded prior knowledge of Richter's visit, and there could be no chance of a leak. I'm afraid our list of suspects is extremely limited, Mr. President. Only Kasymov had the means to do it. And the motive. We're facing the prime example of state-sponsored terrorism. For years we have been aware that the Kazakh government was supporting radical Islamic groups. Now one such cell has claimed responsibility for the assassination. When all the bits and pieces add up, they make for a very scary picture which is impossible to discount. It's as though Kasymov *wants* us to know that he did it."

"Dear God ... What is the meaning of this?"

"Timur Kasymov is showing us that he's breaking all the rules and playing by his own. He's slapped us in the face, making our own covert plan backfire. I fear it's just the beginning. Kazakhstan is rich with natural resources as it is, but as Kasymov's regime seizes the Caspian oil, he knows he can build a force to be reckoned with. An aggressive force."

The final words lingered in the air.

"The situation you've described is terrifying, but all too real. I hope you're wrong."

"I hope so, too," the DCI replied. "But more often than not the most dangerous enemy is a former ally."

The President reached for the report on his desk and dismissed his advisor. As Underhill walked down the West Wing, his mind was occupied with a different consideration. Perhaps even more essential than its mineral wealth was Kazakhstan's value in geopolitics. This advantage displayed through the U.S. Army's presence in Central Asia during the war on terror. From a military perspective, the location was unique. Not only Iran, Iraq, and Afghanistan, but all of Europe, Russia and China lay within easy reach.

The efficiency of an advanced weapons system based in Kazakhstan would be unrivaled. After Clayton Richter's death, Underhill knew, such a weapon might have fallen into the hands of Timur Kasymov. The true purpose of Seton Industries' involvement in Kazakhstan was a joint military project. William Underhill found consolation in the fact that it was still years away from being functional. At least Kasymov would have no way of using it against the United States.

Inside the CIA, it was designated as Project R.

Renaissance.

PART I

1

FRANCE

Andrei Borisov had his cheek pressed into the grass with relentless force. Traversing the vineyard on the other side of the empty house, he had anticipated trouble, but not such an onslaught of violence. Shamefully, Borisov, an experienced bodyguard, had missed an attack from behind.

To the credit of his assailant, it had come like a lightning flash. A thunderous kick had walloped into his knee, and he toppled to the moist ground, his right arm twisted inside out behind his back, his own gun yanked from under his belt and pushed against his skull.

A knee dug into his spine, with the attacker's body resting on top.

"*Que fais-tu ici?*"

The voice was soft and calm, but by the man's breathing, Borisov judged that his assailant was hyped on adrenalin.

The pressure in his back increased, prompting him to start the explanation.

"I'm looking for—"

The man repeated his question, his tone stronger.

"*Je . . .*" Borisov's mind raced. He fumbled for the appropriate words. His French was poor. "*Je cherche* Monsieur Constantine Sokolov." Now the voice was close to his ear. Hissing with malice.

"*Malheureusement pour toi, c'est une reponse incorrecte. Je m'appelle Jean-Pierre Youdine. Quelques minutes plus tard, les flics vont arriver.*"

Despite what the quiet voice had said, Borisov was certain that it was the man he sought. He had proof in the pocket of his jacket! Inside the house, he had stolen two passports. One was French, in the name of Youdine, the other Russian, belonging to

Sokolov. Both had the photo of the same man. The man holding the SIG-Sauer to his head.

But if the cops were really on their way, there wasn't much time. Abandoning the futile efforts in French, Borisov said the next sentence in Russian. It was a gamble.

"The Metropolitan sends his blessing from Moscow."

At these words, the man's breath was cut short.

That didn't prepare Borisov for what was about to come.

Harshly, the man twisted his arm, turning him face up, crashed the gun against his ribs and pinned him down again with his weight, one hand holding the gun, the other grabbing his lapel.

"You're a *spy*! Who *sent* you?" the man shouted in Russian.

His eyes were as grey as stormy clouds and, full of rage, just as menacing. The sandy hair fell to his shoulders. Week-old stubble had darkened his face. Constantine was clad in a cotton shirt and jeans, simple clothes not dissimilar in style to those worn by the common townsfolk of Blois, except for their tragic black color.

Another knee strike, this one expertly delivered into Borisov's liver, gave the question extra urgency.

"*Je travaille*—damn ... I work exclusively for a Russian businessman. He sent me to relay a message for Constantine Sokolov."

Something evil flashed behind the gray eyes.

"*How do you know my name and address?*"

Borisov's mouth turned dry. "I ..."

The man leveled the automatic between Borisov's eyes. His finger wrapped the trigger.

"*HOW DO YOU KNOW MY—*"

"From the members of Free Action! I was to say the words: *John 19:23*. The Metropolitan told my employer that you'd understand the meaning."

Rage disappeared from Constantine's face, replaced by incredulity. He held the gun up.

And grabbed Borisov's hair with his free left hand. Tearing it away from his scalp, Constantine Sokolov thrust the gun under Borisov's chin.

"Who *are* you?"

"My name is Andrei Borisov! I provide security for Maxim Malinin!"

The businessman's name didn't seem to ring a bell to Youdine-Sokolov.

"Why should I believe you?"

The man was clinical. Borisov groaned. The brutal pull at his hair caused such agony that it felt as though the top of his head was about to peel off.

"My ID ... it's in my wallet!"

"No. Why should I believe that you didn't come here to kill me?"

"Because I *didn't*! I'm *alone*! I'm here to *talk*!"

"Is that why you've brought a *gun*?" A sharp yank at the hair arched Borisov's head back, the muzzle scratching the taut skin of his neck.

Borisov wheezed, "It was a mere precaution!"

"Is that why you jumped over my *fence*? And broke into my *house*?"

"No one answered ... the bell at the gate!"

"Then why didn't you leave? It was a sure sign I'm in no mood for visitors." Then, abruptly, "What does this Monsieur Malinin want?"

"A rendezvous ... The Metropolitan asked him to see you."

"Where?"

"In Paris."

"*Why?*"

"He wants to confess."

"I'm not a priest."

"But you're the only one who can abolish his sins."

Constantine's gaze became unfocused while somewhere in his mind a decision was forming.

He released Borisov's head. A moment later, the fingers patted over Borisov's jacket. Constantine didn't bother about the cell phone, or the wallet. Neither was he interested in the second pistol, a small revolver hidden in a holster on Borisov's shin. He was checking if Borisov had stolen anything from his house. He retrieved the two passports from the inner pocket, and frowned at the treachery.

Then lifted himself off Borisov and got to his feet.

The stormy grey eyes bored into Borisov's face before Jean-Pierre Youdine, also known as Constantine Ivanovich Sokolov, motioned with the gun for Borisov to get up.

"*Alors, on y va,*" he said and walked off towards the wrought iron gate, in the direction from which Borisov had approached. "But I'll keep the SIG-Sauer."

2

Borisov's large Audi sedan was parked on a curb outside Constantine's house, overlooking the ancient stone bridge across the Loire River. With Constantine's permission, Borisov rearmed himself, substituting the SIG-Sauer with a spare Beretta that he stored in the glove box.

All the way to Paris they drove in silence. Their first encounter could hardly serve as a foundation for amicability. But Constantine was grateful for the lack of conversation. He did not want to be disturbed by meaningless words. Too much had happened to him at once—his world had shattered with the intrusion. A storm of conflicting images raged in his head.

Who was the man that he was about to meet?

Maxim Malinin, of whom he only knew that he was a Russian businessman, and that he had earned the trust of Father Ilia, Metropolitan of Kolomna, Constantine's mentor from a time long gone—from a *life* long gone. But the Metropolitan's trust was enough to agree to meet the man. To trust him as well. To hear him out.

"*He wants to confess.*"

"*I'm not a priest.*"

Yet who *was* he? Constantine Sokolov or Jean-Pierre Youdine? In his seclusion, he had lost all identity, becoming a shadow, but he remembered all too well the person he *had* been.

True, he had never been a priest. But he had once been an historian, a confessor of Russia's past.

He had been *son* and *brother*. His father had died live on television, in the most atrocious act of terrorism ever known. Mother had passed away years later. His brother Eugene was back in Russia, separated from him.

What was left of him?

Fugitive? Immigrant? That had been his legal status in France, where he had obtained asylum, and later an EU passport.

Recluse? Hermit? Monk?

All that and much worse. Twelve months of self-induced exile. Penance for the sins of others.

Day after day passed in prayer and meditation, his physical being improved by exercise, his soul cleansed through acceptance of God's will.

He had stayed in the sarcophagus that was his little house in the Loire Valley, shut off from the world. No one outside Free Action knew his whereabouts. Not even Metropolitan Ilia, for his own sake.

Free Action—the very thing he was devoid of. It was the name of a human rights organization in Moscow that had helped the Metropolitan to smuggle Constantine out of Russia and hide him in France. Words of hope that now sounded like cruel mockery.

He was suspended in a vacuum. Just to get away from the horrors, and to keep his brother safe from them.

Ultimately, he was a man lost from home.

But he was alive, somehow. Each day of his survival had increased his moral debt to the old man who lived in a medieval convent in Moscow. Now Ilia was calling for a favor.

3

Immersed in his thoughts, Constantine was surprised to see that the two-hour drive to Paris had flashed by. Constantine was intimately familiar with Paris—but the same didn't apply to Borisov, who relied on a GPS map.

Approaching from the south via the A6 motorway, Borisov drove onto Boulevard Peripherique, the ring around Paris, and then cut inside the 20th *arrondissement* at Porte de Vincennes, aiming for the center of the city.

Borisov took out his cell phone and sent a text message.

As numerous as they were, the *arrondissements* followed each other quickly, because Paris was too small. Borisov's Audi was a ridiculously oversized car for the narrow, one-way streets of the French capital. More than once, the bodyguard cursed out loud, maneuvering the car along the maze of single lanes, huddling between curt cars and pesky motorcyclists. Around them, the low, four-story Parisian buildings still carried century-old grime on their façades.

Paris was a flea market. Everything was for sale—from its proud name on postcards and coffee mugs, to its cultural heritage that attracted busloads of gawpers like a whore in a red-light district. Faded signs and blinking lights and price tags stuck on Parisian life—the overpriced meals, lazy taxis, sprawling pawn shops and trademark designer stores all rolled together in one wrapper. The city was petty; littered with, and by, tourists. It catered to buyers who could not realize that Paris was a caricature of itself, a city reduced to its postcard image.

The cell phone buzzed once, announcing a reply. Borisov glanced at the text, and altered his route. Constantine guessed that he had received directions to the rendezvous site.

Along the constricted streets, the quaint Parisian brasseries seemed immune to change. Constantine could visualize his ancestors, the Cossack cavaliers who had captured Napoleonic Paris, sitting at the same tables and spurning the waiters to *move!* Quickly! *Bistro*, dammit! It was a command that the owners still heeded to, etching the Russian word into the names of their eateries, as if wary that the Cossacks would return two centuries later to check the efficiency of servicing.

In Constantine's mind, the French would forever remain as perfect lackeys. Arrogant with sanctimonious self-importance, and instantly eager to lick boots when lured by a coin.

Only on the cobblestoned Place de la Concorde did the space become more open. The Audi turned around the jutting *Obelisque* and slipped away to the Champs Élysées. The recognizable shape of the Arc de Triomphe loomed ahead. Again, Constantine couldn't fail to notice that the country's main avenue numbered a pitiful three lanes in either direction.

And he noticed a darker side of the city—the one that always appalled him in Paris. A cripple's outstretched hand begging passersby. A homeless woman arranging a thin pillow on the sidewalk. A man urinating in a phone booth.

Paris was oblivious to them all. Nothing could tarnish the sweet postcard reputation.

Rounding the Arc de Triomphe, Borisov took the third intersection to Avenue Wagram, where the road narrowed again. Only a few blocks from the Arc, Borisov parked the Audi on an offshoot named Boulevard de Courcelles, and they exited the car. The bodyguard led the way. Rows of buildings converged at either flank as they turned to a tiny perpendicular side street.

Hidden by Parisian houses, the image appeared with abrupt glory. The sight subdued Constantine's breathing, and enveloped him in a shroud of reverence. Overwhelmed, his mind transcended reality. He was back in Russia ... He was home ...

Ending the street, the Cathedrale St. Alexandre de la Néva towered as it came into view, sparkling with the gold of its domed spires. Constantine felt a pure sensation sweep deep inside, as though he were cleansed by the holiness of what his eyes witnessed.

As his feet carried him to the church, it seemed that the Russian cathedral was out of place amid the glamorous bustle of Paris.

But in truth, Constantine decided, it was Paris that was out of place around it.

4

It was Wednesday morning, and the church was closed until late afternoon. Like any Russian Orthodox temple, the Cathedrale St. Alexandre was shaped in the form of a cross, the main dome surrounded by four smaller candle-shaped turrets. Located in a cul-de-sac, the church was a detached spot in the middle of Paris. Behind the church itself was an enclosed courtyard. Any watcher from the street was unable to see the courtyard, as it was concealed by the body of the church and the canopy of trees that surrounded its perimeter. Scanning the premises for any intruders, Borisov led Constantine along the white walls of the church, to the invisible corner on the far end of the grounds.

A silent wraith sat on a bench in the cool shade of beeches. The short, dry man was close to eighty. The long-sleeved shirt, pullover, and trousers were the finest possible, complemented by his brilliant black shoes and diamond-studded watch. His hair was a white texture cropped on his skull. Brown blotches overran his hands. Despite his body's frailty, the eyes were lively, excited. They shone with warm sincerity that attracted Constantine immediately. The old man smiled, squinting at the sun rays filtered by the canopy.

"Ah, Andrei, I see that someone roughed you up quite a bit." The eyes crackled with youthful mischief. "No doubt it was your new acquaintance here. My, my, Andrei, I worry about your qualifications. I see that the young man also has your gun."

Constantine had concealed the SIG-Sauer under his belt, the loose shirt rendering the bulge almost invisible, and yet the old man picked out the hints of it—a quality of training, not eyesight.

The effervescence vanished, and a tired gaze shifted to Constantine. The old man assessed him.

"I'll wager this martial proficiency comes with your fine Cossack breeding."

"My father taught me how to handle a gun when I was six, and believe me, you don't want to be in the crosshairs if I aim."

Constantine's cocky answer only served to avoid showing that he was taken aback by the businessman's knowledge.

"Good. Now that we've determined you're not afraid of me, perhaps you can sit down? Come on, I don't bite."

Hesitantly, Constantine seated himself on the bench. While he did so, Borisov had retreated to watch the street. Sitting vis-á-vis with the mysterious businessman, the physical closeness was uncomfortable. Constantine's nostrils caught a musty odor coming from him; the kind that always seemed to arrive as a compliment of old age.

"In case Andrei had no chance to tell you, my name is Maxim Malinin."

"Jean-Pierre Youdine."

"A pleasure to meet you, Constantine. So good of you to come. I knew you would."

"I wasn't so certain about accepting your invitation. I still have my doubts. Well, Maxim Malinin, what's your problem? I'm not too keen on charades."

"Speaking in broad terms, the problem is in my head. The incessant migraines. The sleepless nights. The vengeful memories. My shrink called it a mental disorder. Psychosis. Paranoia. I call it conscience. God is punishing me for the sins of my past. But my suffering is fully deserved."

"I don't think you only want my sympathy."

"True. It's your *confidence* that I want. Metropolitan Ilia advised me to seek your help."

"What for, exactly?"

Malinin raised his head, eyeing the cross atop the golden dome of the Church. His voice was barely above a whisper.

"*The soldiers therefore, when they had crucified Jesus, took his garments and made four parts, to every soldier a part; and also the coat: now the coat was without seam, woven from the top throughout,*" he quoted.

"John 19:23," Constantine said. "The Coat of Jesus. Metropolitan Ilia has been searching for it all his life. It perished when the Bolsheviks robbed the Kremlin, which once held an art collection, kept by Russia's Patriarchs for over six hundred years."

"And not just art. The holiest of relics. Antique Christian icons. The sakkos of Virgin Mary, Jesus's garments, and a nail which was hammered through His flesh into the cross."

"So you *are* familiar with the story."

"It is the reason I contacted the Metropolitan." Malinin's eyes reflected desperation. "I know where to find the Kremlin Collection."

Astounded, Constantine struggled to grasp the enormity of the words. It took him several seconds to recover. If the meeting hadn't been sanctioned by the Metropolitan, he would never have believed that Malinin was serious.

"But ... Still ... What can I do to help?"

"The Metropolitan does not trust anyone in Russia. The Holy Synod in Moscow is still rife with KGB infiltrators. Even Alexis II had been an informant before he became Patriarch. "

"All his life, the Metropolitan had been fearful of enemies within the Church," Constantine confirmed.

"As *I* am fearful of *my* enemies. Like you, I'm restless hiding in Europe. Hunted like a wild animal. The people I trust are few. I cannot approach the Metropolitan directly, let alone transfer any papers. But I must share my story before I die. I must pass on the knowledge of the treasure's location. *You* seem to have the Metropolitan's utmost trust."

"And what about Free Action? Your bodyguard told me that you used their network to get in touch with the Metropolitan."

"They were only necessary to find you. Free Action has Ilia's confidence, but not *mine*. The information is too sensitive to be surrendered to any outsiders. Which means you are the only possible candidate."

"What makes *me* worthy of your trust?"

"You're just the way Ilia described you, Constantine. Young, brash ... and hurt. However, I have no faith in you—yet," Malinin said. "I must learn more about you to make the decision."

"Paranoid lunatic." Constantine stood up and turned to leave.

The bodyguard emerged out of nowhere to block his path.

Malinin's voice reverberated around the courtyard, off the walls of the Church, the stone fence, the leaves of the trees.

"*Do you want to reclaim your life? To return to normalcy?*"

Constantine stopped in mid-stride. His jaw was rigid with fury.

"My life will never be normal again."

"I can empower you to change it! The fate of the antiques is petty trivia compared to the rest! The documents in my possession contain the energy of an atomic bomb! What I am about to confide in you will reshape the history of the Second

World War—the entire twentieth century—and the future of Russia! Enough to destroy anyone standing in your path! You can take your freedom into your own hands!"

Ice coursed through Constantine's veins.

Suddenly he was disoriented. Could it be? Was it his chance to break away from hell? Did he dare to believe that something could end the delirium of his existence, that one day sharp sounds would no longer startle him, making him look over his shoulder in fear that the killers had come for him after all.

"Constantine, information can be both a blessing and a curse. It alters the mind. I don't want to make your life a bigger nightmare than it already is. I must know that you are the right man. I want the Metropolitan's choice to be beyond suspicion. *Tell me what made you abandon your home and hole up to rot in the French countryside!*"

It came like a slap, as if Constantine were coerced to admit that his plight could not be any worse, that he was a man reigned by despair, one who had nothing to lose. It pained him because it was perfectly true.

Constantine's chest swelled with bitterness that had boiled inside him far too long. He realized that *he* was the one in need of a confession. If he was ever going to exorcise his demons, doing it at the doorstep of a Russian church was the most appropriate.

He slumped back on the bench. "Three masked men raided my apartment in Moscow. They pulled me out of bed and beat me up, threatening to kill me and my brother if I didn't vanish off the face of the earth. And they promised to kill anyone I would involve to help me."

Constantine paused.

"The President of Russia wants me dead."

5

After the Berlin Wall came down, the decay spread like never before. Embezzlement and corruption had always been present, in one way or another, but by 1990, the Soviet West Army Group was flooded with marauders.

"Our family lived in Merzeburg. My father was Colonel Ivan Sokolov, commander of a MiG Regiment in the 16th Air Army. He saw what was happening around him, especially as the Soviet troops began withdrawal from Germany. The WAG was a massive machine eliminated in haste. Fortunes were made as funds, materiel, and military hardware disappeared.

"My father reported the incidents to his superiors, hoping for an investigation. Instead, the Generals kicked him out of the Air Force. They stripped him of the stars on his shoulders. They took away his honor and dignity. And they did it smiling in his face. He had been unaware just how high up the corruption ran, so his reports went straight into the main culprits. The Generals."

Constantine lowered his gaze, his mind wandering decades back.

"We were forced to return to Moscow, of course. Disgraced, betrayed, and broke. Do you remember what Moscow was like in the nineties?"

"I left Russia in 1992," Malinin said. "But I remember Moscow too well. A city of twelve million, dark and dirty, reeking of desperation. Ruled by gangs, drug pushers, addicts, rapists, bandits, robbers, sold-out cops, crooked bureaucrats, Mohawk-haired punks and serial killers. Walking the streets was a crazy game of Russian roulette."

"The promised miracle of economic reforms was a farce. Father stayed unemployed. He didn't want to choose between washing cars and selling T-shirts on Red Square, but he had to feed us somehow, so he did it, throwing away the last of his pride. I was in my teens then, and Gene was only ten years old. Mother was a teacher, but her salary's value was soon worth less than the cost of paper it was printed on."

"Hyperinflation had rocketed to five hundred percent," Malinin remembered.

The people's accrued savings had been declared null and void, which had catapulted most of the population into poverty, while the government feasted on the clear-out garage sale that they'd turned the country into.

Russia's population had started to decrease by a million each year.

Life expectancy had plummeted into the fifties as death and birth ratios crisscrossed in inverse lines, stretched further by never before seen rates of suicides and infant mortality.

"But at the same time, billions of dollars were claimed overnight by those who'd shaken hands with the right people in the Kremlin. The nouveau riche caste of tycoons, and a scattering of lesser cronies, soaked the emerging markets in the blood of their competitors.

"By that time, the troops had withdrawn from Germany. The real eye-opener for my father was seeing his former brothers-in-arms, who had been pulled back to Russia literally into an open field, with no roof over their heads. The 3,000 refugee families of the 85th Air Regiment joined a mass of over two hundred thousand other homeless military servicemen across the country who had been discarded as human waste.

"It drove him beyond the edge. So he joined the Moscow uprising of 1993."

Painfully, a kaleidoscope of terrifying images played out in Constantine's mind. The views he had seen through the window of the apartment in Presnya district, and the footage of massacre on the television screen in their bedroom.

6

Russia's death wasn't abstract. It had a name.
Boris Yeltsin.

Millions voiced contempt for Yeltsin all over Russia. The Parliament denounced his policies, demanding his resignation.

But the ensuing twenty months of confrontation between the two branches of power ended in bloodshed.

Yeltsin was furious that anyone would question his policies.

He was Czar Boris.

On September 21st, 1993, Boris Yeltsin violated the Constitution yet again by dismissing the Parliament as he signed a decree that transferred all legislative functions into the hands of the government. During a televised speech, Yeltsin also pronounced the current Constitution invalid, so that a new one could be drawn up.

Only this time, it would be tailored to suit his person.

In turn, the sacked parliamentarians refused to comply and leave their building, making a last stand against the rampant head of state.

The Parliament building—a tall white house on the bank of the Moskva River. Broad-shouldered. Defiant. The personification of Russia.

Long into the night, at an emergency session of the Parliament, President Yeltsin was unanimously impeached in accordance with Article 121 of the Constitution.

Early in the following morning, army troops began to pull up in BTR transports.

Thus began a two-week siege of the white house on the riverbank.

Thousands of Muscovites poured into the streets to support their Parliament and Constitution. Over 800 unarmed civilians set up barricades, wrapping the House of Parliament in a human shield. Among those protestors waving Russian tricolors was Ivan Sokolov. He was a dogfighter. Once shot down, he took it to the skies again, seeking retribution.

By the start of October, reports from the provinces attested that the number of people backing the Parliament was growing with each day. The longer the parliamentarians held on, the more momentum the protests would gain. Downtown Moscow had already been paralyzed.

Police and Army forces could not move in, kept at bay by the old stock of Kalashnikovs left over at the Parliament ever since 1991. And the besieged MPs' demands were non-negotiable, echoed by the ever-growing crowd of four thousand supporters that had gathered around them. Yeltsin had to step down. The verdict of the Constitutional Court had already confirmed that he'd broken the law.

The stand-off had to be ended, Yeltsin decided.

Sporadic fire burst out at 7 a.m. on October 4th, 1993. It was impossible to tell which side had started the shootout, but in minutes it intensified into a full-blown urban battle. The civilians were caught in the crossfire, which was soon directed at them by the police units who stormed ahead to occupy the Parliament's ground floor. Army snipers perched on adjacent roofs picked out innocent bystanders below, augmenting the panic. Droning choppers circled the area like vultures.

Utter pandemonium raged as the crowd was riddled with lead in a sickening bloodbath.

Yet no one believed their eyes when a rolling column of tanks took position on the Novoarbatsky Bridge. Their turrets started revolving, turning the fearsome cannons in the direction of the beleaguered white house. The protectors of democracy could not fathom that any of this was real.

Insanity!

But it *was* real.

The T-80's recoiled as their mammoth 125-mm guns blasted HEAT rounds in thunderous unison. Direct hits registered in clouds of disintegrating concrete, setting the building ablaze. Inside, the explosions tore human bodies apart, mingling flesh with shards of glass and rubble. More salvos followed. The armored execution squad gutted the white house. Consumed by flames, it soon turned charred black.

The cannonade continued until the evening, the howling shells tearing through the Parliament's long-dead corpse.

At 6 p.m., the few survivors of the siege surrendered to the police, hands raised as they walked past the bodies that littered the embankment of the Moskva River.

Yeltsin had exhibited his own vision of Russian democracy. No terrorist could have ever conceived such a cold-blooded, bestial attack.

Official reports masked the exact number of casualties, pegging it at 74 dead. Several thousand Muscovites were presumed to have gone "missing" during the unfolding "events."

Ivan Sokolov's body was never recovered. The state refused to admit the death of a citizen it had killed.

As they watched the gory skirmishes and gun battles that had climaxed in a tank barrage live on television, Constantine, Eugene, and their mother had their hearts ripped out and crushed. Their husband and father was no more.

Dead.

They could never overcome their grief ever since. They merely pretended to exist. Misery was their world.

Hollowness.

There wasn't even a grave they could visit.

7

My will to live came back when Gene and I resumed school. One day, we were standing in the cafeteria queue at lunch break. A big fellow was passing, talking to his friend. He said to him that the best action flick he'd ever seen on TV was the shooting of the Parliament.

"I don't know the guy's name. All I can remember now is that he was from grade ten. A pimple-faced heavy metal hooligan that scared even the teachers. He was at least a head taller than me. I didn't care about his size then."

"What did you do?"

"I hit him in the crotch. Hard. He crashed on the floor, but his friend fisted my head. Gene ran at the second guy and bit his arm. A real fight started. Two of their buddies joined in. They thought that they'd mince the two of us, but Gene and I gave them a hard time. We made them chase us around the cafeteria while we toppled tables. We threw chairs at them, forks, knives, anything we could use. Even hot soup."

"How did it end?"

"The principal came in with a cop. Lucky timing, because they had us cornered and the pimple-faced bastard had already taken out a switchblade. So I got away with a swollen eye and a few bumps and bruises. Gene had a split lower lip and a sprained wrist from punching one of them in the ribs. Oh, and the principal suspended us from school for a month."

"And how did your mother react?"

"She was extremely unhappy with us. And more so with herself. She had failed to protect us, and we couldn't protect ourselves. She told us that we must learn to beat the crap out of anybody. Make the others dread the idea of trying to hurt us. So she took us to a karate dojo, which I later quit."

"And after that school fight you found a reason to live on?"

"Mom had the two of us, her boys that were her life, so she lived for *us*. As for me and my brother, I guess we were driven by an urge to right the wrong, in the memory of our father. Each of us did it in his own way. I majored in history at Moscow University, trying to get to the roots of the evil that infested my country. Gene entered the EMERCOM Academy, and enrolled in the Rescue Corps."

Malinin prodded on.

"Was it then that you and the Metropolitan got close?"

"Yes. At one point, theology engrossed me. I attended lectures at the St. Sergius seminary, vying to grasp the divine reasons of life and death. That's how we met. Ilia was my teacher there. I was seeking the comfort of knowledge. And then mother passed away ..."

Constantine's vision dimmed. He had to fight back tears.

Malinin waited.

"At the same time, Gene got badly injured, in hospital, fighting for his life. Father Ilia became ... well, a father figure. The closest person outside my family ... Every day, he prayed for my brother, and for me. After that, we spent a lot of time together, talking. For hours. Eventually, I told him about what had happened to my family.

"One day, during our conversation Ilia told me that he'd learned the name of the person who had ended my father's career. He asked me if I wanted to know.

"Out of sheer curiosity, I asked him. At that time the name was meaningless. I had no idea how important it would become in a few months. The corrupter, the man ultimately responsible for my father's death, was Nikolai Alexandrov."

"*President* Nikolai Alexandrov?"

"*General* Alexandrov back then. He'd returned from Germany, becoming an *apparatchik* in the headquarters staff. At the time, the public didn't know that he would become the heir apparent to the Kremlin throne. Neither did I, of course.

"After I learned the man's name, I detached myself from the world, hollow again, not caring about anything happening around me. Gradually, my heart filled with hatred. I became obsessed with the name. I imagined the beast hiding behind it. The name itself, each black letter of it that I doodled on white paper, gave me no answer. A name is faceless. Like a sign on a locked door.

"When I saw the Metropolitan again, I inquired how he'd been able to learn about the man's identity. Father Ilia, ambiguous in his usual way, said that he respected the anonymity of his sources. I wondered aloud if his sources could tell him more about the man.

"Soon, details emerged. The source shoveled a lot of dirt. Stuff that could ruin the career of an aspiring politician. And destroy a successful president. The scale of the corruption in the Army boggled the mind. I attempted to make this information public knowledge. But one night, the visitors came. They made a point of dissuading me."

"I see hatred in your eyes, Constantine."

"It *is* there."

"A hatred that is bigger than you," Malinin said. "I think you are just the man I need. Because your hatred will serve you well."

Malinin stood up and placed his craggy hand on Constantine's shoulder.

"But you never said whether *you* believe in *me*."

"I believe the Metropolitan. That is sufficient."

Malinin stood up and motioned towards the street. "In that case, may I offer you a ride?"

8

With Constantine and Malinin sitting in the back, the car returned to the Arc de Triomphe, taking a northeasterly bearing.

"Ah, Paris," Malinin breathed. "A horrible city, really. Do you agree, Constantine?"

Despite his own distaste for the town, the question was confusing. "What do you mean?"

"The history, if nothing else, my boy. The torrents of blood, the piles of headless bodies ... That is where the Bolsheviks found inspiration. The original Paris Commune. It was *there*," he pointed his finger, "on the Place de la Concorde, that the heads rolled off the Guillotine."

Constantine turned to see that the old businessman was overcome with emotion. Flickers of memories rekindled inside his eyes. His lips paled and quivered. It was Malinin's turn to dispel his demons.

"The Bolsheviks were always driven by only one cause. Terror. They were nothing more than bandits. Vermin. Stalin was an exemplary Bolshevik—street thug, bank robber, and rapist," Malinin said. "But they never fantasized about ever fulfilling their dreams. About ever returning to Russia. The Provisional Government gave them that chance as they sent the country spiraling into chaos. The February of 1917 stemmed from these Parisian streets as well."

"Kerensky didn't just give the Bolsheviks a chance, he did all the hard work, paved the way for them and handed over the keys to Russia on a silver platter," Constantine corrected him. "Financed by the Kaiser, Lenin rushed back to Petrograd and arranged a scrappy overthrow."

Malinin smirked. "It's almost comical, isn't it, the Bolsheviks and their mythical revolution. Their so-called Great October is a hoax. A mystification. Claiming power in Russia for the Bolsheviks felt like winning the lottery. No one took them seriously at first. All the while, Lenin was hiding in a safe flat wearing a pathetic disguise, fearful of arrest! Their rule didn't seem like it could last very long."

"I'd say they found their feet pretty quickly," Constantine noted.

Malinin shook his head in apparent disgust.

"You're a historian, Constantine. Do you know how many the Bolsheviks killed in the ensuing war?"

"How can anyone *ever* know? Nobody was counting the bodies. The official stats estimate thirteen million killed during the Civil War and another ten murdered by Red Terror. But where does that put the millions who perished due to famine and disease? Officially, within just five years, from 1918 to 1923, Russia had been butchered by *five* Holocausts. Thirty million dead in the blink of an eye. But why not fifty million? It could easily have been a hundred. Lenin declared that he would kill ninety percent of the Russian population as long as the remaining ten witnessed his victory."

Constantine paused, bitterness creeping up his throat. He was conversing with Malinin about genocide carried out against them. Millions of Russians.

But most of all, Cossacks.

It was genocide that no one acknowledged even in the face of archived documents. Two million captive Cossacks sentenced to death by a single note from Lenin to Dzerzhinsky ...

"The bands calling themselves the Cheka marched across the country, exercising their newfound right and duty to instill Red Terror. They became the new Jacobins, entitled with a freedom to kill. Coming to every town and village they captured hostages by the thousands and shot them down with machine guns. But killing en masse was not enough for those pathological sadists. The Chekists skinned and scalped their victims, sawed off their heads, severed limbs and genitals. Their ruthless craze stemmed from their cowardice—for they were afraid of the people they killed. In the merriment of bloodlust, they raped and tortured, confiscating food and possessions, burning homes and churches."

"Churches," Malinin echoed. "Lenin was a mass murderer, but he killed for profit. The call to annihilate the old world and build a workers' paradise was rooted in very mercantile foundations. I'm sure you know that as early as 1918, a massive campaign unfolded to confiscate all valuable possessions from the population."

"I believe Lenin authorized Trotsky to control its progress. That terrorist gang marauded even the remotest villages."

Malinin nodded.

"Here's a fact from history I'm sure they didn't teach you at university. In the pre-war global monetary system, the Russian currency's parity with the existing Gold Standard was 0.774 grams of gold per ruble," the businessman said. "The crown jewels alone, highlighted by the legendary 190-carat *Orlov* diamond, were evaluated at 375 million. By 1922, Trotsky's campaign amassed valuables worth a total of more than one *billion* rubles. The helpless Church proved to be a real treasure trove for the Bolsheviks—jewelry, gems, precious metals and icons. Over 50,000 churches and monasteries were ransacked, hundreds of thousands of priests killed."

Constantine knew what Malinin was getting at.

"The Bolsheviks tried selling the relics abroad, but failed. So what happened to the treasures after that? This disappearance has always been a mystery."

"Indeed. The most priceless items, including the Kremlin Collection, remained locked in the vaults of the Bolsheviks—and vanished in the chaos of the Second World War, during the rise of the Soviet Empire. And the Empire's fall proved to be a turning point in my life as much as it had been in yours. At that time, I stumbled on the trace of the greatest artifacts in Russian history. And like you, I had to pay a price for the revelation."

"What did you have to give up in order to find it?"

Malinin stared in the window.

"My soul. I had to shed blood for that."

The only sound inside the car was the hiss of the tires against the smooth asphalt.

Driving via the Boulevard Peripherique, off the A1 and past the suburb of St. Denis, it took no more than ten minutes to reach Le Bourget airport. Although international and regional airline traffic had been shut down decades ago, Le Bourget operated as a business class airport hosting general aviation.

Alarm bells went off in the back of Constantine's mind.

"Where are we going?"

Malinin cocked his head, amusement on his face. "Why, the only place on earth to store secret documents! An alpine haven of first-rate banking."

9

A pilot's son Constantine knew enough about aircraft to recognize Malinin's business jet instantly. With a maximum range in excess of 6,000 kilometers, the Cessna Citation X was designed for transatlantic flights. The highly swept wings and tail stabilizers made the Citation X the fastest civilian aircraft in production, as the side-mounted Rolls-Royce Allison turbofans on the rear of the fuselage could produce a maximum speed of 965 km/h.

The plane's interior was refined enough to pass for a deluxe hotel lounge—despite its cylindrical shape and porthole-sized cabin windows. The beige leather chair that Constantine sank into had nothing in common with the typical spine-breaking contraption of a commercial carrier. The six club chairs were arranged in doubles, facing each other. There was also a two-seat divan across the carpeted aisle.

"Can I get you anything?" Malinin called from the galley. Borisov was at the controls in the cockpit, waiting for permission from the tower to take off.

"Mineral water, please."

He came back carrying a glass bottle and two bar tumblers, which he set on the hardwood table.

"Special stock," the old man said, unscrewing the cap off the bottle. "You won't find it in your local supermarket."

Having filled the glasses, Malinin popped a handful of pills into his mouth, and washed it down with the water.

"These damned headaches," he said, wincing. He looked queasy, trying to steady his breathing.

The jet taxied out on the runway and halted, as if bracing itself before letting the engines peak their howl. Breezing forward, it challenged the paved strip of land, and beat it, tipping the nose skyward.

"Every revolution kills its own creators," Malinin continued as the Cessna soared into the air. "Once the initial purpose of the revolution is achieved, it takes one person to step in and exploit the results. Assume control before another iteration starts. The Paris Commune drowned in blood and fizzled out. In the end, the Place de la Concorde had claimed Robespierre's head as well. And Lenin's 'old guard' was eradicated by Stalin. The Red revolutionaries became his enemies—he had to protect his power against them. He'd learned the lessons from his teachers in mass murder—Lenin and Trotsky. So Stalin killed them all. Along with sixty million other people ... "

"But he didn't kill Trotsky when he had an easy chance. I always wondered why Stalin had to wait until he escaped to Mexico."

"Because he *needed* Trotsky. Stalin invented a brilliant conspiracy to achieve his end. He claimed that Trotsky had arranged a plot against him. Against the Revolution. So he uncovered evil Trotskyites within the Party's ranks and eradicated them. The Great Purges needed a pretense. And Trotsky was a *living* symbol of counter-revolutionary menace. Yet at the same time he was powerless in exile. So at first, the Trotskyite conspiracy was a stroke of genius by Stalin, utilized against Trotsky himself."

"Wait a minute. What do you mean, *at first?*"

"Every action triggers a reaction. Trotsky knew that one day Stalin would get to him as well. What could he do as he watched former comrades being wiped out on conspiracy charges? *Create* a conspiracy for real. One that Stalin would not expect. In 1938—in Paris, amusingly—Trotsky set up an undercover organization known as the Fourth International. It rose from a group of Trotsky's closest followers living in exile, and those still alive in Russia. At the start of the so-called Great Patriotic War, they set their plan into motion, conning one of the most powerful men in Stalin's empire. During the evacuation, when a secret train run was taking the artifacts to safety, they pulled off the heist of the century."

"How can you know it?"

Malinin's lips curled in a tragic half-smile.

"Because the Fourth International exists to this day. The *real* Fourth International."

This was getting crazier by the moment.

Constantine felt his head swim. His brain was about to burst from his skull. The sensation was physical, too real but

inexplicable, driving him on the verge of panic. But the pressure in his ears was something else, he gathered quickly. It was ...
Descent.

Just then, Borisov announced over the intercom that they were about to touch down at the airport of St. Gallen, Switzerland.

They'd been airborne for a meager half hour. Banking over the still surface of Lake Constance, the Cessna performed a smooth landing at St. Gallen-Altenrhein, a small airfield in Switzerland's northeastern-most canton overridden with peaks and valleys. The town of St. Gallen was among the most elevated in Switzerland.

In the VIP arrivals lounge, a border official waved them through without delay. No visas were required. Constantine showed his French ID. Malinin and his bodyguard carried passports of the proud Republic of Latvia. A European Firearms Pass for each of the three pistols enabled Borisov to bring his weapons unchallenged.

Another car, a sleek Porsche Cayenne was waiting in the reserved parking lot. Borisov continued his chauffeuring duties.

Speeding away from the airport terminal, the black SUV gripped the waving road, playful as it took on the succession of rises and falls.

"What will you do next?" Constantine asked Malinin. "After you hand over those documents to me, where are you going?"

"London is the nearest thing I have to a home." Malinin absently rubbed his eyebrow, pensive. "My bouts of headaches ... Eventually, they became so murderous that I had to undergo a thorough medical check-up. As it turned out, I have a brain tumor. It's inoperable, and chemotherapy would only prolong the suffering, so the prognosis is dire, but certain."

"Oh, my ... I'm ... I'm sorry."

"What? You needn't be. Like I said, I don't want your sympathy." Malinin smiled. "Back in London, I have a very good friend. He's also a very good doctor, one who is quite flexible when it comes to the moral aspect of euthanasia. After my business with you is finished, he'll help me commit suicide."

The nonchalant tone of the old man's comment sent a chill through Constantine, and ended the conversation.

On the horizon, the snow-capped ridge of the Alps was mesmerizing. Constantine watched the road, letting his mind wander—until something caught his attention.

He realized that driving southeast, along the Rhine, they were heading *out* of Switzerland.

10

Lodged between the Alps and the Rhine, on an area of 160 square miles, the Principality of Liechtenstein is one of the world's smallest countries. With 5,000 inhabitants, Vaduz was large enough to become its capital.

Lacking its own army, currency and airport, the Principality relied on Switzerland to provide all of those.

But Liechtenstein's real charm lay in something else. Liechtenstein was a financial sanctuary. What Malinin had called an alpine heaven of first-rate banking. The country's financial sector was destined to be the main driving force of the economy, specifically attracting foreign investors. Above all, Liechtenstein knew the value of discretion.

The trip from St. Gallen had taken another thirty minutes. As they approached Vaduz's famous banking center, the Bankplatz on Pflugstrasse, Andrei Borisov slowed the Porsche. Futuristic, curved buildings scrolled by beyond.

"Which bank is it?" the chauffeur-bodyguard asked.

"It's not here," Malinin replied.

"Not at the Bankplatz?"

"No, not in Vaduz."

Borisov frowned in surprise.

"Continue along the Landstrasse, out of Vaduz. A few blocks from here you'll see the town of Triesenberg. That's the place we need."

Vaduz ended before they could notice. Triesenberg was indeed a short distance away—as was everything in the Principality. The town itself was clustered around a stone church. The dome of the church peaked in the shape of an onion, so much similar in form to Orthodox churches in Russia.

"St. Joseph's Parish Church," Malinin said, pointing.

Malinin ordered Andrei to park the Cayenne on the square in front of the church.

"Wait in the car," the old man said as he climbed out after Constantine.

Standing next to the Roman Catholic church, surrounded by a cloudless blue sky, Constantine appreciated the fresh alpine air.

"One of the few places on earth where what you breathe isn't likely to kill you straight away," Malinin said. "We're about eight hundred meters above sea level. And we're going up." He motioned towards the Alps.

Constantine faced the mountain range.

"Up? Into the *mountains*?"

"Not *into* the mountains. *Towards* the mountains. Up a slope. Come on, we're almost there!"

Constantine threw up his hands in frustration. "But where are we going?"

"There's a small hamlet near the town. You needn't worry, Constantine. Don't you enjoy a pleasant stroll in the green alpine pastures?"

Malinin pulsated with energy. He may have been a dying man, but the closer they came to their destination, the more animated he became.

Constantine followed.

He couldn't stop thinking that from the beginning, it wasn't *him* that Malinin had kept in the dark about their ultimate destination—but rather Borisov.

"You don't trust your own bodyguard?" Constantine asked bluntly.

"But I do. If I didn't trust Andrei, he'd be nowhere near me. It's simply that I never bestow more trust on anyone's shoulders than one can handle."

They traversed the town, and walked along a graveled hiking path that snaked through the lush meadows that were the most intense green that Constantine had ever seen. Against the backdrop of the Alps, the scenery took his breath away.

As they developed a pace, marching wordlessly, the crunch of gravel accompanied their strides.

Suddenly Constantine's instincts kicked in. Preoccupied with his thoughts, he had almost failed to notice that something didn't add up.

His eyes took in the surroundings.

Nothing but the emerald green of the grass, and the blue of the sky. They'd moved away from the town. They were in one of the world's smallest countries—and at the same time, in the middle of nowhere.

Malinin was leading him into a trap! The promised documents did not *exist*! It was an elaborate lie!

Sweat rolled down his spine, slicking the gun handle under his shirt.

He *would* use the gun if necessary.

"There!" Malinin exclaimed. "Take a deep breath now!"

At the same instant, they reached the crest of another hill, accessing a view of a tiny hamlet.

The opposite end of the valley rose, becoming so steep that the hamlet was situated on an almost vertical mass of land. At the apex, it was lined with a dense pine forest. And commanding the limits of vision, were the gargantuan Alps.

Although distant, they dominated the view completely, making everything else seem miniscule—the matchstick pines, the puny breaks in the green valleys, and the houses that looked like matchboxes strewn around casually by a giant hand.

"See?" Malinin pointed his crooked finger. "That's our house."

The hamlet numbered no more than a dozen chalet-style buildings, and Constantine couldn't make out which one of them Malinin was referring to.

But none of them looked anything like a bank.

Following the hiking path, they crossed the valley quicker than he expected.

He could see the place now. A three-story detached house that stood apart from the other buildings in the hamlet. Stone walls and a tiled roof with a protruding chimney, and windows shut out with blinds. Typical alpine dwelling that didn't convey anything businesslike.

But if it *was* a trap, why did Malinin go to such lengths to get him here? Constantine had been at his mercy all the time.

At the door of the strange house, Malinin left him no alternative of doubt. A single moment would decide if it was all fake or not.

Malinin pressed the buzzer.

For several seconds there was no reply.

He pushed the button again.

A woman's voice, distant, called out in a hurry: "*Wer sind Sie?*"

Malinin replied in accented German. "Frau Hasler? Frau Hasler! *Ich bin* Herr Szabics! *Bitte, öffnen die Tür.*"

In the window next to the door, the blinds opened into narrow slits and the woman's puffy face appeared. A wary gaze examined the outside world. At the sight of Malinin, the woman beamed, her eyes growing wide.

She bolted away from the window. Seconds later, Constantine heard the latch unlock, and the wooden door swung open.

Frau Hasler stood on the threshold—she was a stout woman in her mid-forties, with plump cheeks and fleshy pink hands. Benign surprise was written across her face. Her eyes darted back and forth between Malinin and Constantine, with expressions of recognition, and bemusement.

"*Liebe* Herr Szabics!" she said with delight, motioning her visitors to enter the house. "*Hereingekommen!*"

11

The sofa in Frau Hasler's sitting room would have been comfortable if not for Constantine's SIG-Sauer pressing against the small of his back.

He and Malinin were sipping coffee offered by the hospitable lady.

"You were born in the DDR, yes, Herr Klein?" Frau Hasler asked, calling Constantine by the false name he had used for introduction—the very first that had sprung to his mind. Malinin was posing as a Hungarian named Szabics.

"Yes, I'm from Leipzig," Constantine replied, his East German dialect flawless. "My accent betrays me, I guess."

"Ah, but it is natural. The German language is so geographically diverse in phonetics that a man from Munich can hardly understand a word from a Berliner!" the woman chuckled.

"And *I* can hardly understand *any* German," Malinin-Szabics laughed.

"Herr Szabics!" Frau Hasler said. "As always you are too humble!"

Constantine set his porcelain cup on the saucer, wondering what was really going on. After a frenetic dash across the continent, he was whiling away the afternoon in a quaint house in the Alps, engaged in small talk with an aging housewife, drinking coffee in a cozy parlor. It was absurd.

"You don't visit me very often these days, Herr Szabics," the lady said, teasing.

"I'm renting one of Frau Hasler's rooms," Malinin explained to Constantine. "The area is very popular with tourists, so lodging is a good business, isn't it?"

"Yes," Frau Hasler nodded. "For the most part, it's the skiers who are attracted by the slopes of Malbun. But now, in the summer, the season is off. So I'm alone. Thankfully, I have enough income from you, Herr Szabics. You paid for two more years in advance! For that I am truly grateful."

"No need. Your discretion is worth much more."

"Your work is so important, Herr Szabics," a giddy Frau Hasler said. "It's still a secret, yes? But perhaps soon, when it is finished, I will be able to tell everyone that I was involved in Nobel-prize-winning research!"

It hit him. Constantine realized how simple and effective it was—renting a room indefinitely at a daily rate, where the secret cache was safe and sound. And most importantly—no questions asked, no banking paperwork required, no inconvenience of a secure deposit box that left an electronic footprint. Frau Hasler's house was perfectly invisible. And since the lovely old lady largely depended on Malinin's money, her discretion surely topped that of any banker.

"Very soon you will be able to, my dear Frau Hasler," Malinin assured her, playing his role. "In fact, Herr Klein, my assistant, has come with me to review the papers."

Frau Hasler rose.

"Let me guide you upstairs, then," she said.

12

Frau Hasler's house had four bedrooms—two on the second floor, and two directly above them on the third. The second-floor rooms were meant for paying guests. One of the third-floor bedrooms was Frau Hasler's own. And the last was always empty.

It was the room rented by Malinin, or rather the obsessed Hungarian physicist Szabics, who had employed Frau Hasler's simple mind and natural greed.

This room was the smallest in the house, and the slanting mansard walls that met at the roof made the space even tighter. The furniture was minimal—a bed and a chair, and the small easterly window failed to do justice to the Alps.

On the properly vertical wall over the bed, there was a decent copy of Van Gogh's *Starry Night*.

When Frau Hasler tactfully went downstairs to wash the dishes, Malinin asked Constantine to help him remove the painting. Behind it, protruding from the wall, was a hidden safe.

"Can you imagine it?" Malinin said, turning the knob. "Of all the places in the world, I store sensitive documents in an old-fashioned safe behind a *painting*."

"Sometimes the most obvious is also the most deceptive," Constantine said.

The tumblers clicked into place, and Malinin opened the safe. It was long and wide, almost equaling the dimensions of the painting concealing it, but only as deep as the thickness of the wall allowed.

Inside, there was a single object. A Samsonite attaché case slim enough to fit the width of the safe.

"Damn, this thing is heavy ... Help me pull it out ... "

Despite its modest size, the case felt like it weighed a ton. Constantine set the case on the bed, and then locked the safe and replaced *The Starry Night* back on the wall.

"The thing is, I slightly modified the Samsonite. It's waterproof, bullet-proof and incombustible. The combination is triple zero," Malinin informed him as the locks on the case unclasped. "Factory settings. Like you said, the most obvious ... "

Raising the top, Malinin revealed the Samsonite's contents.

Filling all the space of the attaché case were bundles of euro notes, a digital memory disc and a sheaf of yellowed pages bearing scraggy handwritten script.

"Listen to me carefully," Malinin said, his eyes boring into Constantine. "The money is one hundred thousand euros—what I call an emergency survival kit. The *disc* contains everything I know about the Fourth International—member list, cell structure, inventory of assets, past activities, sources of funding, *everything*."

"And the papers?"

"*These*," Malinin wheezed, placing his palm over the pages, "are the missing papers of the late Lazar Kaganovich."

"Stalin's right-hand man?"

"The same. As Minister of Transport, he was in charge of the secret consignment in 1941."

Constantine shuffled through his memory. "Yes, I remember that Kaganovich's memoirs were published in the mid-nineties, but they didn't contain anything groundbreaking. Typical rants about the joys of Communism."

"The *published* memoirs were indeed quite shabby, especially for a man who had basked in the epicenter of Soviet power for a period of *forty* years, and spent *another* forty years writing about it! By the way, do you know the circumstances of his death?" Malinin asked.

"Kaganovich died in 1991, aged ninety-seven, at his writing desk."

Malinin's eyes glistened.

"*Precisely*, at his writing desk! He was in perfect health and continued to work on his memoirs until the last moment. Don't you find it odd that the cardiac arrest killed him only days before the Soviet Union collapsed? Gorbachev's *perestroika* and *glasnost* made the country uncontrollable. The wind of change permitted him to divulge the tale of the missing relics. Lazar committed himself to publishing the story as part of his epic memoirs. The Fourth International could not allow it."

"You mean, the cause of his death ... It wasn't natural? That seems a little too far-fetched, to be honest."

"Oh yes, Kaganovich was *murdered*."

Constantine shook his head. "How can you be so certain?"
Malinin sat on the edge of the bed, shoulders stooping.
"I was the one who killed him."

13

Downstairs, the doorbell rang, distracting Frau Hasler from her housekeeping chores. There were sounds of Frau Hasler stomping her way to the front door and yelling her usual "Who is it?" which was followed by an explanation that unfortunately she had no rooms on offer today, but surely, tomorrow one of her tenants would vacate—

Her scream was harrowing.

The guttural sound of Frau Hasler's death was abrupt, echoed by the crash of the front door breaking off its hinges.

Startled by the commotion, Malinin pivoted in the direction of the staircase. Then he looked at Constantine with realization in his terrified eyes.

"My God, they are *here!*" the old man mumbled. "I've doomed you."

Constantine never lost his composure. He shut the attaché case, grabbed it, and dashed to the window. The latch was jammed, and the couldn't open it. Swinging the briefcase, he hit at the window, disintegrating glass. Using the Samsonite's bulk to clear away the shards jutting from the frame, he yelled, "Come on, we can get out through the window. The second-floor balcony is directly below."

Malinin's reply was a cry: "Take cover!"

Constantine pivoted.

A man rushed into the room, aiming a submachine gun.

With the muffled shots coming from the gun's suppressor, Malinin's body erupted with blood as he blocked Constantine from the line of fire.

Instinctively, Constantine dropped to the floor, his back against the wall, holding the Samsonite in front of him with one hand, pulling out the pistol with the other.

Angry slugs hammered the metal case, but his shield protected him.

He fired two quick shots.

He'd never thought he could do it. The bullets from the SIG-Sauer speared the gunman's abdomen. The gunman collapsed, slamming against the floor, blood gushing out from him in a red fountain.

The pistol's blasts had deafened Constantine. His heart pounded. One part of his brain told him to approach the gunman's body and retrieve the silenced submachine gun. The other part told him to get the hell out of there before anyone else came shooting at him.

The other part won.

His eye measured the balcony below. It was long and wide, extending at least five meters out from the side elevation, forming a portico at the rear entrance of the house.

Constantine dropped the attaché case. It landed on the glass-sprinkled tiles of the balcony.

Tucking the SIG-Sauer under his belt, he swung his legs over the window sill, preparing to jump a level down, and then froze.

Attracted by the fall of the case, another gunman ventured out on the balcony.

Constantine's muscles tensed. This gunman had the same type of submachine gun which Constantine now recognized as a Heckler & Koch. The muzzle of the gun was sweeping a three-sixty turn, searching for targets. It would be seconds before the man looked up and behind him—and locked his sights on Constantine.

Just as the man was turning, Constantine came down on him, pulverizing the shooter's chest with his knees, and they tumbled onto the layer of broken glass.

The impact had knocked the H&K from the man's hands. On the floor, struggling to choke each other, neither of them was able to reach for the weapon. With a sudden movement, Constantine swung his arm back and elbowed the man in the temple, cracking the weak bone, and he went down.

Bullets zinged past. Constantine rolled sideways.

The fire was coming from inside the house, through the open French doors. Constantine's hand found the H&K. Blindly, he unleashed a volley into the room and heard a body hit the floor.

Constantine stood up and let out another muffled shot, more out of fear than necessity. Inside the bedroom, a corpse was oozing blood on the intricate pattern of the carpet.

Squeezing the gun handle, Constantine's hand was slippery with sweat. His heart thumped. Around him, the colors seemed duller, the sounds fainter, the time slower.

But his mind raced like a light beam.

What alternatives did he have? What should he do? Wait in the room like a sitting duck? Or go outside and catch a slug in the head?

No time to think.

He rushed out of the bedroom and ran to the solid oak staircase, gun in one hand, the case in the other.

The second floor was empty. No one was shooting at him.

He hurried down the stairs, each crashing stride resonating in his temples. Reaching the ground floor, he stopped in his tracks, appalled by the ghastly image of Frau Hasler sprawled at the front door. The simple plump face had grown into a rigid mask of terror, features distorted, teeth bared. Mirth in her eyes had been washed off by streaks of blood that ran from a gunshot wound in her forehead. Her white apron had mopped up bright stains of blood as if to undo the damage.

She didn't deserve an end like this, Constantine thought. A languid flow of life defiled and torn off so perversely.

Without warning, a strike came down against the nape of his neck, felling him. His skull thundered with exploding pain.

Before he could begin to recover, a kick connected with his spine.

He half-opened his eyes and saw Andrei Borisov leering at him, Beretta in hand.

"The roles reversed, pal," Borisov laughed. "This is how you met me, and now I'll see you off."

He held the Beretta inches from Constantine's head.

Borisov's finger tightened over the trigger, and his eyes flashed with genuine satisfaction.

In that instant, Constantine swung his leg up in a frenzied kick, hitting Borisov in the groin.

Hard.

The former bodyguard toppled.

Gritting his teeth, doubled over, Borisov still had a firm hold on his Beretta.

Constantine reached for the small holster strapped on Borisov's leg.

He found it and yanked out the revolver.

Thrashing, Borisov kicked him away.

Overcoming his pain, enraged, the bodyguard whipped out the Beretta, Constantine in his aim.

The gunshot opened up a wound in his head as Constantine fired.

14

Liechtenstein was so small that it would be no wonder if the gunshots had been heard in both Switzerland and Austria.

Constantine knew that he had to flee. Fast. Wiping his fingerprints off the weapons was pointless. He had left his prints all over the house anyway, as well as some blood from the gash cleaved on his neck by the Beretta. More than enough evidence for forensic experts.

He grabbed the briefcase. On his way out, he had to frisk Andrei Borisov once more, like he had done in the morning, with the exception that Borisov was now dead. Overcoming the revulsion of close physical contact with the body, he found the electronic key to the Porsche Cayenne. As soon as he had it in his fingers, he rushed away, as if escaping a plague.

He exited the house of death through the rear door, out on the portico, and headed towards the pine forest. Reaching the trees, he followed the edge of the hill, circling the hamlet. When he emerged from the forest, he found the hiking path that led back to Triesenberg.

No matter how fast his legs carried him away from the scene of the massacre, the images chased him. He had crossed the line discerning humans from animals. He had *killed*. True, he had done so in self-defense. He had beaten professional assassins only because his will to survive had been greater than their commitment to murder.

But was he free of guilt?

He had not been forced to kill by circumstance—being in the wrong place at the wrong time—but rather by the contents of the attaché case, and his own urge to use the power of the documents within it.

It was a deadly sin predetermined one year ago, a part of the insanity he had plunged into. He had to end it all.

Do you want to reclaim your life?
Destroy anyone standing in your path!
The documents could help him achieve both ends.

There was no way back for him now. He had to deliver the attaché case to the Metropolitan.

To Moscow.

Ilia's sources were powerful enough to use the material in full and protect him. It had been Malinin's ultimate intention.

The car was still parked near the church, waiting for its master, unaware that it had changed hands. Constantine approached the Cayenne, struggling not to look around for witnesses of his rightful theft, for fear of appearing exactly like a thief, and drawing suspicion. He slid into the seat, threw the briefcase somewhere behind, and shut the door forcefully. The effect of a protective shell around him was reassuring. The stench of blood, the pain, the fear remained outside. He was inside. He was regaining control of his senses, the numbness of shock thawing off.

He brought the key to the ignition, but saw that his hand was shaking so fiercely that he was unable to insert it. Only on his third attempt did he manage it, every iota of willpower required to steady himself. Even though his hand no longer trembled, his mind was reeling.

He pulled out from the parking lot and drove out of town, accelerating on the main highway.

The 4.5-liter engine purred under the Porsche's hood playfully, intruding into his thoughts, calming him as he forced his concentration on the soft sound. The road from Triesenberg to Vaduz was familiar. From then on he relied on the GPS navigation screen. Shortly, the B191 took Constantine out of Liechtenstein, becoming B190 already in Austria. Past Innsbruck, he charged north on the E60. Only a roadside plaque denoted the German border. As he sped over the invisible line separating the two countries, something churned inside Constantine. Apprehension, anxiety, déjà vu? All of that, perhaps.

He had returned to the country of his childhood—Germany. A different *country*, unified and prosperous, but the same *land*. And exactly as decades ago, he was returning from this land back home—to Russia.

A different *Russia*, indeed, but his only *home*.

The German autobahns allowed the Cayenne Turbo S to demonstrate its superiority over conventional transport, breezing along the roads in the rays of a lateral sunset, sometimes giving him the bravery to charge at 250 kilometers per hour. A dark night had settled by the time he reached Berlin—starry like in Van Gogh's painting. The warped sky swirled around the lights, making Constantine dizzy. His vision blurred. He had traveled 800 kilometers from Vaduz and had another 1,600 ahead of him. He had to leave the remainder until tomorrow. In a single day he had crossed France, passed through Switzerland and Liechtenstein, survived a gunfight, and spent six hours behind the wheel of the Porsche, all the way through Austria, and deep into Germany. Trying to battle fatigue was becoming too dangerous. His muscles ached with stress.

According to the laws of the *Bundesrepublik*, all shops would be closed at this late hour, except for those at twenty-four-hour gas stations. He found one, and stopped to refill the Porsche's tank. In the grocery store he bought provisions—sandwiches, chocolate bars, and water. Unwilling to leave more traces of his presence than absolutely necessary, he decided against a motel, so he permitted himself a three-hour nap in the back of the Cayenne.

By noon, he entered Poland. There, on the outskirts of the EU, the countryside was paltry, unable to boast the developed roads and myriad lights, a rural cousin awaiting hand-me-downs from wealthy relatives. In Warsaw, he was surprised to see a touch of France—a Carrefour hypermarket. He chose its multi-level underground parking lot as another temporary stopover, gearing up before the final thousand-kilometer charge to the finish line. A change of fresh clothes bought in the store was more than welcome, as was a paper cup of hot coffee from Carrefour's food court. He needed a clear mind.

So far, his tactics had been holding up well. Even though no news reports of the Liechtenstein killings had appeared yet, it didn't mean that the police authorities weren't keeping a lid on the story while they were closing a dragnet around him. But the odds were on his side. Taking the car had given him several advantages over trains and airplanes. He had avoided the potential traps of departure schedules, security checks, on-board registration and linear movement. And he was less than two hundred kilometers away from the border of Belarus, where he would pass through on his Russian passport.

Frenchman Jean-Pierre Youdine would disappear forever, and Constantine Ivanovich Sokolov, citizen of the Russian Federation, would be on his way to Moscow.

15

MOSCOW

Sun rays beat down on Lubyanskaya Square with abandon. The radiance spilled into every window like it was breaking over the edges of an overflowing vessel, illuminating the office on the top floor of the square's main building.

The workspace testified that its owner was a stickler to order. It was devoid of any personal effects. Standard-issue curtains and a drab green carpet over faded parquet boards. A huge oak desk with a high-backed leather chair; a laptop computer; a stack of files; an old-fashioned, corded telephone set.

Perhaps the only item on the desk that showed any hint of character was a small glass prism that contained two squashed metal slugs. Two tokens of history, dating from the 1930's.

The slugs had been extracted from the skulls of Kamenev and Zinoviev, Stalin's executed rivals. Then-NKVD chief Yagoda, a man fond of sick souvenirs, had kept the bits of metal as trophies. His successor Ezhov, having disposed of Yagoda, inherited the slugs.

Stalin's fiendish irony had it that Ezhov himself was sentenced to death soon afterwards, so the next man took up the slugs, and the post.

The post that now belonged to Saveliy Ignatievich Frolov.

Thus the crystal prism was a perpetual reminder to Frolov of his own fallibility. *Reminders*—that's what everyone needed, Director Frolov kept saying. Reminders spurred self-discipline and motivation.

The door to his office opened, and a tall man in his late thirties entered. He had the privilege of immediate access to Frolov's office at any time. His alias inside the FSB was Victor, the identities he assumed in his field work required a separate list in his file, accessed only by the Director. His real name was a state secret, as was his status within the FSB. Victor's attire—a brown leather jacket and blue jeans—was appropriate for the streets, where he belonged. His body was muscular and agile, his instincts predatory, honed through countless missions, hunting or being hunted.

Frolov raised his eyes from an open file to greet his man.

"Comrade Director."

The Soviet form of address was still official in Russian enforcement agencies.

"Any developments?"

"We have found Malinin and Constantine. They'd made contact."

"Details."

"Malinin showed up as a corpse in a house in Liechtenstein. He was found by the police along with the landlady, and four other bodies that had guns on them."

"Hitmen."

"Professionals," Victor confirmed. "The local authorities think that the shoot-out was the result of a bust-up inside the Russian Mafia, which is a good thing. We can certainly help them stick to this story."

"That's secondary," Frolov reminded.

"The house is covered with Constantine's prints. Malinin had probably taken Constantine to his stash. Someone from Malinin's inner circle was working for our adversaries. As soon as they became aware of the documents' location, they sent a team to take out Malinin and Constantine, and destroy the documents once and for all."

"Where is Constantine now?"

"His Russian passport has been flagged at the Brest station of the Belarus border."

Frolov nodded, as if agreeing with his own prior assumption.

"So he's heading to Moscow."

"It appears so. I believe he also has the documents with him," Victor suggested.

"Yes. Otherwise there would be no reason for him to be coming back," Frolov said. "He's a blind cub seeking protection. Next, he will try to get in touch with Ilia. Keep a close eye on the Metropolitan. We must intercept Constantine, and get the documents. And one more thing. If it was Constantine who killed the enemy hit team, then he is even more resourceful than we have assumed. To the point of being dangerous. Don't underestimate him."

"Don't underestimate *me*, Comrade Director."

"Yes, Victor, I trust you to lead our mission to a successful finale."

Trust. It had been the key from the very beginning.

PART II

1

THE BLACK SEA

She was a gift from the gods. The passionate lines of her white body stirred obsession. With the gentle swells caressing her, wrapping her in foam, the *Olympia* glided over the sea like a reborn Aphrodite.

The luxurious 187-foot-long megayacht had been crafted by Dutch naval architects. A marvel of design and performance, powered by twin 1,500-horsepower diesel engines.

Like any desirable woman, she wore a provocative veil of mystery. In the case of the *Olympia*, her secret was the identity of her owners. Various sightings spawned a myriad of rumors as to who they were and where they kept her.

Around the Mediterranean, be it Monaco, Sardinia or Majorca, she never lingered in one spot for more than a few days. Her port of registry was Georgetown, as evidenced by the flying Cayman ensign. Her crew was reported to be English. She was sighted in the Caribbean several times a year, and there was a photo of her appearing in the vicinity of the Maldives. Still, nothing suggested her possible hideout.

A check of the *Lloyd's* catalogue would provide no clues. Officially, the *Olympia* was owned by a company based in Jersey, Channel Islands, and managed by a Cypriot outfit with an office on Paparigopoulou Street in Limassol.

Only a handful of people in the world knew that both these private companies had their stock in the possession of Sovcomflot, the FSB's maritime cover.

Her home was the Black Sea resort of Sochi. Her nickname was *The Cruising Kremlin.*

She belonged to the President of Russia.

2

At 147 kilometers measuring between its farthermost tips, Sochi was one of the longest cities in the world, stretching out on a narrow ribbon of land between the Black Sea and the Caucasus mountains. Even though it had a population of 500,000, a term as vulgar as *city* would be the last to come to mind when describing it. No, Sochi was a park, an earthly glimpse of Eden.

Because of its unique climate, Sochi provided sanctuary to a most varied plant life collected from across the world, creating a natural botanical garden so vast that it boggled the unaccustomed mind. Here, all that was otherwise exotic was so commonplace as to be considered trivial. Throughout the cityscape, the assortment of flora intermingled in wanton combinations and perfect geometry. One could find alleys of platanus that gave way to palm trees. Scores of cypresses outlined their towering shapes against the crystal sky. Yuccas grew with the petulance of weeds. Along the walkways, neatly trimmed boxwoods stretched as far as the eye could see, overlapped by roses. Seaside, wandering past the colonnades of the embankments, it was easy to get drunk with the aroma of magnolias and camellias in bloom. There is no recipe to emulate the air of Sochi—lazy zephyrs coming from the sea, crispness descending from the mountains, fragrances gifted by the flowers, are all touched by one another, twirling.

Sochi's architecture was palatial, every surface seemingly carved from white marble. The motifs were reminiscent of Ancient Greece—not without homage to myth and local lore, which claimed that Zeus had nailed Prometheus to a nearby cliff up in the mountains.

The style was matched by the *Olympia*'s decor. Polished floors, exquisite furniture and round-bellied vases had managed to stay in fashion throughout millennia.

On the main deck level, four persons sat at the table in the dining room. President Nikolai Alexandrov and the First Lady hosted two guests: an Oriental man in his fifties and a young woman—his daughter.

The Oriental's oversized chest protruded underneath his shirt. He was of medium height, flabby at the waist, but his feline eyes oozed narcissism. In his country, Timur Kasymov had grown accustomed to attention. He was the President of Kazakhstan. Beauty was an attribute of power.

Earlier that morning, Kasymov and his daughter had flown in for an informal visit, honoring the invitation of the Russian President, who spent most of his first summer in office at his Sochi residence. After the Kasymovs had settled in the halls of Bocharov Ruchey, Alexandrov suggested a maritime adventure in the evening, which they duly accepted.

Now, the *Olympia* was anchored two kilometers off Sochi. Distant patrols of the Coast Guard kept a watchful eye for potential attackers, while a mixed security detail attended to the needs of the passengers on board. The *Olympia*'s staff of FSB and FSO officers was complimented from the Kazakh side by Kasymov's security chief, a dark, black-bearded man named Ahmed Sadaev.

From Bocharov Ruchey, their pleasure cruise had taken them on a northerly course, away from the bustling center of the city, to an area guarded from tourists and the media. It was territory under direct authority of the Presidential Staff, belonging to recreational sanatoria that had been built by Stalin for the Party elite. Ashore, access to the beach was restricted, so there was no chance of any casual stroller happening to witness the *Olympia*—nor could any saboteur threaten it.

The evening flowed in a relaxed mood, but the questions that Alexandrov had to settle with his Kazakh counterpart nagged him all throughout the dinner. The pressing issues had to wait until the discussion became tête-à-tête.

"Nikolai?"

"Yes?"

"I want," Timur Kasymov said with finality, "to hire your chef. I'd keep him forever. The dinner was excellent. Like everything on your wonderful yacht."

"The yacht isn't mine. It belongs to the Russian people."

Kasymov chuckled. The First Lady raised her head in laughter. She was a petite woman with a mole-spotted neck, and her gray hair, unwashed, was a mop of poodle shavings.

President Alexandrov dabbed his mouth as an FSB steward took away his empty china plate. "But you're right. The *Olympia* is magnificent. A peaceful setting like this does help ease the stress."

"You still work too hard, my friend, even when you should rest," Kasymov said. "I see the bags under your eyes."

"I keep telling him to see my cosmetic surgeon. After what he did to me, I look ten years younger," the First Lady said.

President Alexandrov almost slipped into confessing that bug-eyed, she looked uglier than ever. Instead, he turned to Asiyah Kasymova.

"You have a gorgeous daughter, Timur. *She* is the one to grace the television screens, not old fossils like us."

Throughout the evening, Alexandrov had been stealing glances at Asiyah.

At twenty-six, her face retained a childish look. She wore no makeup, only a touch of perfume on her neck. She had inherited the high forehead and cheekbones from her Russian mother, who had died when Asiyah was ten months old. Exotic sensuality shaped her rosy lips. But her huge hazel eyes, framed with faint arcs for brows, were the real source of her magnetism, hiding the child in her.

Her proportions were faultless. Mentally, Alexandrov undressed her, his eyes going over the lines of Asiyah's bosom, her flat abdomen and narrow waist.

"Why didn't you ever bring her along with you before?"

Alexandrov's remark made Asiyah lower her head in apparent timidity. A strand of silky raven hair fell over her cheek. Her fingers tucked it back behind the ear. Long, gentle fingers.

For an instant, the hazel eyes burned with emotion. Alexandrov detected what might have been rage, provoked by his attention. It was intriguing.

"Asiyah is a shy girl. I gave her traditional upbringing ... In accordance with the values of the Koran."

"Ah yes," Alexandrov said finally. "The Muslim customs. I find it very disturbing that Islamic extremism is on the rise in Kazakhstan."

"The assassination of Ambassador Quinn is a terrible tragedy, the worst terrorist attack in the history of Kazakhstan. But we are determined to fight against these enemies of freedom and true Islam. I assure you, it was a foreign influence. There can be no tolerance for terrorist ideology in the Kazakh society. We stand by our values of democracy, and we will protect them."

The First Lady sighed.

"A shame you had to bring up this unpleasant topic, dear," she said in a bored tone. "All this talk of politics and terrorism ruins an otherwise perfect evening."

"Perhaps it would be best if we left the men do discuss their affairs in private," said Asiyah.

"A splendid idea," the First Lady said. Her husband's glances across the table were not lost on her.

Asiyah rose from her chair.

"On the contrary," objected Alexandrov. "I trust that the evening has a lot left in it."

The First Lady froze, seething behind her smile.

Asiyah resolved the impasse instantly.

"No, really, I wish to retire early. It's been a long day. I'm still a bit weary from the flight."

"I won't stand in the way of your wishes," Alexandrov said coyly.

The two women, young and not so young, left the table. The First Lady guided Asiyah up the stairs, to the boat deck.

"Good night, Asiyah," called the President of Russia, but she was already gone.

The Russian President walked to the lounge beyond the colonnade.

"I have a fine selection of cognacs in the bar."

"My pleasure, Nikolai. The choice is yours."

Although formally Muslim, Kasymov had no qualms about the vice.

Alexandrov returned with a bottle of aged cognac and two snifters.

"The timing of the attack couldn't have been lousier," Alexandrov said. "Exactly when we expected serious progress for the Median Line agreement in the Caspian."

"It is the work of the China-Iran axis," Timur Kasymov said. "I am sure of it. They are desperate to stop it."

"At least I hope nothing can thwart your initiative that we have dreamed of for so long."

Kasymov brought the cognac to his lips.

"In a week's time, I shall announce a referendum to be held, asking the citizens of Kazakhstan if they want to reunite with Russia."

Alexandrov nodded.

"It pains me to think that we only have to go through this because of the illiterate madman Khrushchev, and Yeltsin who finished off the deed."

For any Russian president, no triumph compared to the possible reunification. The Caspian Sea would return to Russia's control. Reclaiming a land mass five times the size of France would put Alexandrov's name in the history books on par with the greatest Russian rulers. But for President Kasymov, it was something else.

"I also want to rectify the mistakes of the past, Nikolai. But I feel that from now on, it's a question of the country's survival. All sights are set on Kazakhstan now. Only together can we withstand the military threat. Without Russia, the Chinese will crush us. The increased terrorist activity is just the first phase of their strategy. Next, they will attempt a coup d'etat, by which time it will be too late for Russia to intervene. After the Chinese troops flood in, imagine what is going to happen. In many ways we are a single country in all but the paperwork. We share sixty-five hundred kilometers of a completely unprotected, non-existent border. Empty steppes that leave Russia exposed. Before it's too late, the Russian Army must return to defend Kazakhstan. If we combine our resources, we can save the region from chaos. I see no other way but to push the procedure through."

"Of course, it will be up to the people of Kazakhstan to decide if they want to take this course," Alexandrov said carefully.

"I'm sure they'll make the right choice. I need not tell you that Kazakhstan's population is forty percent Russian."

Alexandrov nodded.

"They were the first to suffer from the division, entire families separated. We have always felt a historic duty to support their bond with the homeland."

"And I can tell you that the Kazakh people share a connection with Russia as strongly as they ever did, economically and culturally. Russian is one of our official languages, after all. I am confident about the referendum's outcome."

"If that happens, then nothing can prevent Kazakhstan from joining the Russian Federation," Alexandrov said.

They raised their drinks, toasting the endeavor that would make them immortal.

3

If his calculations were correct, the *Isebek* would be passing the *Olympia* at a point where the two ships would be closest to each other. Oleg Radchuk could not yet see the presidential yacht. Sticking to its designated course, the *Isebek* was travelling far enough away so as to avoid attention from the Coast Guard.

As he stood propped against the rail, wind tried to pick at his long blond hair tied in a ponytail. He had an angular, Slavic face, the nose bent slightly, broken in a fight. Radchuk's arms had the thickness of tree trunks, developed early from his teenage years as a dockworker in Odessa.

He peered over the rail to examine the water beneath his feet. The Black Sea, it could be so different. Scorched limestone near his home, and unrestrained glory of life where it met the mountains. The Germans could never tackle that ridge, and he himself had found shelter in the Caucasus. But he had lived on the other end of the Black Sea, and the other end of the mountains, two worlds apart.

He had made the transition to manhood when he left Odessa and arrived to Grozny, feeling a call of blood when he had enlisted as a volunteer during Russia's first Chechen War in January of 1995.

Oleg Radchuk's grandfather had served in the Ukrainian *Waffen-SS* battalion, being one of the only three Ukrainians who had earned an Iron Cross. Of all of Hitler's collaborators in the Second World War, no one could match the sadistic barbarity of the Ukrainians. The senior Radchuk got his medal by helping out in the mass execution of over 100,000 Jews at the Babi Yar ravine. The grandson, too, had made a prolific career, killing the damned Russians, proud of his part in the death toll that matched the Yar.

Now, Radchuk couldn't help but smile at the irony of fate. For a short span, his former-life's aspiration of seagoing had fulfilled through the lethal skills acquired in the forested mountains. And now, both of his worlds, the Black Sea and the Caucasus, surrounded him in one spot, awaiting his decision.

The *Isebek* was a small ship by tanker standards, measuring 99.9 meters in length, with a capacity of 5,797 deadweight tons. *Deadweight.* More irony. Loaded to the brim, the *Isebek* had a purpose that differed from transporting petrochemical products.

Radchuk raised a radio to his lips.

"Dump it."

The *Isebek* disgorged her water ballast into the sea.

4

Asiyah could not bring herself to face the First Lady in strained small talk, so no sooner than she was up on the deck, she had proceeded wordlessly to her private cabin in a display of unprecedented insolence. The First Lady attempted to be outraged by such manners, but Asiyah ignored her. Throughout the evening, she could smell the bile churning inside that old woman, and thinly-veiled contempt directed at her. Asiyah didn't care.

She slammed the door shut behind her and pressed the lock, letting out a sigh. More so than getting rid of the First Lady's company, she was relieved to have escaped the disgusting attention of the President himself. The playful comments. The lust in his piglet eyes. He was as repulsive as a mud worm; she loathed him unconsciously, on a basic level.

And, too, she was glad to be away from her father.

Days ago, she had asked him why he was taking her with him to Sochi.

"*I want you and Nikolai to pass the time together.*"

With humiliating bluntness, Timur Kasymov had explained every detail of what he meant by that.

Shocked, she had cursed him.

"*All you do is use me!*"

She had paced the room in utter fury, yelling something at him. He had pleaded. He'd said he needed her help, that he was doing it for both their sakes.

"*No—please—don't make me do it! I can't. I won't!*"

"*I need your help, child. Imagine that it's a game. Like in the old days.*"

"*I don't want the old days to return!*"

"*The President likes you. Give in just once. Then I will set you free. I will be gone from your life forever.*"

After she had gone hysterical, he had stroked her hair, telling her through her sobs how much he loved her, and that everything would be fine, and she needed to trust him. He had vowed to forget the whole thing. By that time her resolve had broken, mainly from the knowledge that she had no choice at all.

But she knew her father too well. He would never set her free. He hated to part with property. She felt like a fly trapped in a web of deceit.

For once in her life, she had rebelled against her father's will, locking herself up in the cabin. Perhaps Alexandrov might make further advances back at the residence, but she would have to deal with it later. For now, she had done what she felt was right.

She sat on the edge of her bed, her gaze fixed on the setting sun. The blue of the sky would have been impossible to tell from the blue of the sea, if not for the disc the color of flaming strawberry. It didn't move at all, and yet crept closer to the horizon. Then it touched the sea, immersing in water, dissolving in it. The flaming disc diminished at a staggering rate. The less was left of it, the quicker it disappeared, like the last years of life, until only a sliver was left, and then, where the sliver should have been, there was a shrinking dot—and that was it.

It had taken fifteen minutes. So little of her life, and so much time for the sun to be gone, and for life itself to seep away just like the burning pink shape.

In its absence, isolated sounds grieved for the sun, and for her. The plaintive cries of seagulls. A lone motor, droning away, only to fade as well.

But the vanished sun had left behind a dazzling vista that set the sky aglow with red, and the sea seemed to radiate from the bottom, so again there was no clear line to separate the two. The water carried flaming ripples on its waves, the last sparks of which touched Asiyah's face.

The motion of the sea was lulling her, bringing calmness. A part of her mind wanted to indulge in self-pity, but she snapped from such mellowness, bringing herself back to the reality of her surroundings. She had noticed that she was still wearing her dress, lost in her reverie. Wearily, she flicked her high-heeled shoes free from her feet. As she was heading towards the bathroom door, she unzipped the stifling evening gown at the back, letting it slide down her legs on the carpet, and kicking it aside.

There was a soft rap on the door.

Ice spilled inside her chest. She stood paralyzed, like a deer caught in the glare of headlights. Motionless, she prayed she could be undetectable.

The knock became insistent.

Her breathing sounded amplified in her head, and she thought her heartbeat was too loud. What would she do? Give herself away, or wait silently until the visitor left?

A key scraped in the lock. Too late for thinking. Now her only hope to ward off the intruder was to raise her voice.

"Who *is* it?"

There was no reply.

Instead, the cabin door swung open, and Nikolai Alexandrov stepped in, shutting the door immediately behind him. As he sneaked the key back into the lock, dandruff fell from his white head like snow off a tree branch.

Turning around, he froze as he saw Asiyah standing before him in her black lingerie. There was a shine in his eyes.

"Ah, I see you have prepared for me. I will not keep you waiting."

He moved across the cabin, towards her.

"No, listen, I am not going to—"

"Lovely stockings."

He was close now. Dangerously close. She could feel his reeking breath, a byproduct of consumed cognac.

She backed away, her heart banging in her throat.

The President of Russia reached out, running his fingers over the smooth skin of her arm. He gripped her elbow and pulled her near.

"You're so sweet ... "

The bridge of her free hand knifed away his grey-haired wrist. The sharp blow snapped Alexandrov from his fantasy. His piglet eyes focused.

She glowered at him.

"Get the hell out of my cabin."

Scowling, he pushed her with force onto the bed. Before she could do anything, his crab-like claws pinned her wrists to the mattress.

In a flash, her father's commands raced through her mind.

"*Submission will feel good. Don't think about it. He'll be done quickly. You must ... *"

No.

"Let go of me. Right now."

She attempted to buck him off, but he smothered her spastic jerk with his weight. He stared into her eyes, his face so close to hers that she could hear the air whistling through his nose with each breath.

"Stupid girl ... You don't know how lucky you are."

"I'll scream." It sounded so banal she almost regretted saying it.

"You'll only compromise yourself. Relax."

He drew closer, opening his vile mouth to kiss her lips.

Asiyah head-butted him in the face.

He rolled back, cursing, grabbing his mouth. Blood seeped through his fingers from the bruised lip.

As he looked at her in shocked bewilderment that grew into anger, she kicked him off the bed, and he thundered down on the floor.

"Still miss the point? Go back to your wife."

With amazing agility, he rose to his feet. He was seething, his jaw clenched with rage, eyes wild. Blood covered his chin like smudges of smeared lipstick.

He paid no attention to his swelling face, as his hands were busy unbuckling the belt of his trousers.

"I'll teach you a lesson ... "

The leather sliced through the air, scorching.

The metal tongue of the belt buckle grazed her cheek. Asiyah fell back across the bed.

Alexandrov piled on top of her. His fingers tore away her stockings. Hastily, he raised her leg, placing it on his shoulder, groping inside her thigh.

Her leg seized, he fumbled one-handed to pull down his trousers.

Summoning all her inner force, Asiyah swung her free leg up, level with his head, and her thighs squeezed his neck in a viselike lock.

He tried to brush it off, underestimating her strength. She pressed harder, grunting. Choking, he struggled to break free, but her thighs clamped.

Alexandrov puffed. The veins on his temples bulged. Purple vessels burst in patches on his red face. His mouth agape, he wheezed as if to say something, but she was past listening.

Asiyah drew her arms back, grabbing the base of the bed, securing leverage. Tensing every muscle in her body, she twisted, one knee scissoring over the other, and Alexandrov's head crunched sideways.

She released the hold, and the dead President of Russia tumbled onto the floor. She was panting, her legs dangling from the edge of the bed.

She forced herself to get up, and saw his body. The President's neck was twisted at a grotesque angle. His pants were unbuttoned, to no avail.

Wasting no time to pick a new dress for the occasion, she crossed the cabin and unlocked the door.

5

On the lamp-lit main deck of the *Olympia*, an FSB bodyguard stood waiting. It was the same steward who had attended her in the dining room. There wasn't a doubt in her mind that he was there to dispose of her body once the President had made use of it. It wasn't unlike her father, nor was it beyond Alexandrov.

He sucked on his cigarette to pass the time as his boss entertained himself in the cabin. When he heard the sound of the door, he flicked his cigarette into the sea, apparently glad that Alexandrov had been quick to finish. When he turned, he realized that the President's leisure hadn't gone as planned.

In the doorway, Asiyah stood stripped to her lingerie, her cheek swelling around the gash.

The bodyguard reached for his gun as she dashed at him. He was drawing his weapon out when Asiyah leaped, ramming a kick into his collarbone. As he fell, the bodyguard landed on his shoulder, the crack audible. He roared.

Asiyah ran up to the man sprawled on the deck and drove her foot into his midsection, knocking the air out of his lungs. Kneeling, she clutched a fistful of his hair, raised his head and crushed the windpipe, pinching it with her thumb and forefinger and thrusting.

She retrieved the bodyguard's pistol, assessing her options. Her only chance lay in speed and stealth. There was no way to challenge the rest of the FSB security detail and the six-man crew in an open fight. Armed, she could escape any immediate attack as she made her way to the *Olympia*'s tender.

If she could only make it ... The border with Abkhazia was a stone's throw away, and from then on she had alternatives ... A new identity, a new life ... Too early to hope—she focused on her actions, calling on her survival instincts.

Holding the gun out, she followed the catwalk to the stern, up the steps where the tender garage was set in the bridge deck. To her horror, the boat was gone.

6

Asiyah scurried back along the deck to the corpse of the FSB steward/killer, hurrying before anyone else was alerted to her resistance.

That blasted drone of a motor that she had heard in her cabin! It was the sound of the tender! How foolish of her to miss it for what it had been!

Now she had to face the consequences of that error. She had to escape. The only way out was to jump.

She looked beyond the rail. She threw the gun and it plopped into the black abyss, which was darker than the gloom of the night.

She glued her hands to the rail and climbed up, balancing her weight like an acrobat preparing for a death-defying act, knees pressed to chest.

Hyperventilating, she uncoiled her body and sprang off the rail.

In the weightless euphoria of freedom, she braced herself for impact.

Eyes shut, she wrapped her arms over her head, fingers joined in an arrow shape, taut legs pressed together. Slicing the water like a torpedo, her body burst below in a vortex of bubbles.

When the sea devoured her, it was as though giant fists clapped against her ears as seawater gushed into her head, disorienting her.

Undulating in a wave-like motion, she allowed her body's momentum to carry her as much as possible underwater, but slowing, she felt a downward pull. She arched her back, pointing her hands up, and frog-kicked, heading to the surface. Her lungs pleaded with her to find air soon. She wrestled the mass of water, arms swinging to her sides, her legs kicking—and her head popped over the waterline. She gasped, sucking air, slapped in the face by a passing wave. She brought her arms to the surface now, stroking, breathing.

The lights of Sochi beckoned her.

She worked out a steady pace, letting her legs work up the propulsion, her front-crawl strokes carving the water. She took in air every three strokes, measuring the distance in her mind.

She felt she had cleared a hundred meters—her customary two lengths of a pool lane—when at once, light and darkness, air and sea, became swirling madness.

A roaring tide knocked her legs over, shoving her down, cutting air from her lungs. Its force was pressing her down as she struggled to recover from the abrupt shock.

She bobbed back above the surface, groping for air. Taking in a lungful, she coughed, both from the water in her throat and the thick cloud of black smoke fuming into her face.

The night sky flickered with orange.

She rotated in the water, looking seaward. Distant plumes of black smoke rose from dancing tongues of flame that irradiated the white outline of the *Olympia*. The megayacht was listing on her port side, sinking with frightening speed, carrying those left aboard to a silt-bottomed grave.

The sound of the explosion was still ringing in Asiyah's ears when she resumed her effort, doubling it. There was no time to ponder another near brush with death or bereave the lost souls. She was shaken, but she still had to work for survival, and at the moment all she wanted to do was get away from the cursed yacht.

In each three-stroke window she allowed for breathing, Asiyah eyed the faraway lights before burying her face into the salty water, straightening like an arrow. The glowing shore was her beacon, a promise that fed her willpower the way a mirage made a desert wanderer push on, only to creep away from him with every step he made.

At first, the land did not look as if it were drawing any closer, but she knew that her salvation was real, well within her grasp.

Fatigue was seeping through, her motions no longer filled with energy. Her arms and legs felt burdened by extra weight. She tried to concentrate on the challenge of completing each motion. One more stroke... one more...

She was making good progress, she thought, although her marathon had barely started and she was already losing tempo.

Her legs, thrashing like mechanical screws, experienced build-up of lactic acid. Muscles ached. She tried to stow the sensation into the nether corner of her consciousness, but it persisted, smothering her.

It seemed that instead of moving through water, she was resisting the pull of quicksand. The rolling swells were steeper, every meter of the distance tougher to conquer. She had to suck in air every two strokes now, which slowed her pace further. Soon even that wasn't enough. She leveled her head up to allow steady breathing.

Soreness mounted in her body, but she knew she would be dead the moment she stopped. The pain had to be outraced.

There was no more consideration for her swimming technique—she was paddling in raw, desperate impulses.

Only her sheer will to live made her go on.

The coastal lights had become murky as seawater splashed against her face.

Submission will feel good. Don't think about it. It will be over quickly.

The voice of her enemy, mocking her, forced her to battle against the sea in a frenzy. If she died, no one would avenge her. She had to make it to the shore. Alive.

She sloshed against the water, inching forward, too weak to even cry.

When her face smacked against a wall of spikes, she was certain that she had drowned, hitting the bottom ... or was it hell already ...?

Then she heard herself squeal. Surely, the sound couldn't have come from her if she was dead.

She labored to open her eyelids, as something scratched her face ... sharp ... painful ...

Pebbles.

There was solid ground under her. Rock.

The frothing surf prodded her from behind, urging her to crawl inland. She dragged her knees and elbows through the crunching pebbles, feeling crushed by the sea. Her body wobbled like jelly, vision rocking. She was swallowing air in greedy gulps, her heart rattling with the force of a jackhammer.

Feverish, she managed to squirm for a few meters on her elbows before collapsing.

Through the pulsating agony, she would have laughed with relief had she mustered the strength. Lying on the beach, she released emotion weeping in silence, overcome with joy, realizing her freedom to inhale at will.

She was dizzy. The air was making her drunk.

Then she knew it was something else.

Her body gripped with convulsions, she recoiled and retched violently.

With apprehension, in a succession of gut-raking seizures, she felt blood surging inside her head.

7

Located off Garden Ring Road between the Lubyanka and Theatre Square is the headquarters building of EMERCOM, the world's finest rescue service. Officially known as the Ministry of Extraordinary Situations, it was one of the main agencies in the Russian Government.

It was the only apolitical agency in the Russian Government.

And the only one that wasn't a reworked Soviet relic.

In 1990, a man named Sergei Shoigu and a handful of enthusiasts formed the Russian Rescue Corps. Shoigu's team of volunteers soon earned battle-hardened experience as they faced every known cataclysm, both natural and anthropogenic. Earthquakes, fires, floods, NBC threats or military conflicts—they threw themselves head-on into every emergency, launching humanitarian and search-and-rescue operations. In 1994, the agency was given federal status, and from then on EMERCOM evolved further to devise an efficient disaster-prevention and monitoring system, establish nationwide branches and incorporate all Civil Defense and firefighting units. On average, EMERCOM specialists saved twelve lives each day. For that, sometimes they sacrificed their own.

The unsurpassed expertise of Shoigu's agency was called upon globally by the United Nations and individual countries. From war-torn Yugoslav villages, to tsunami-hit Asian shores, to the streets of New Orleans devastated by Hurricane Katrina, the EMERCOM teams were always there to assist relief efforts, whenever and wherever disaster struck.

The current head of EMERCOM, Daniil Klimov, Minister and General, was a man devoutly dedicated to his job and his country. He could have made a career as a ballet dancer across the street, at the Bolshoi, but in his late teens he had chosen a different path—that of a demolition expert. It was a profession in which he had no equal. Shoigu had personally hand-picked Klimov to join the EMERCOM bomb squad. It was Klimov's skill, dedication and leadership that eventually led to different posts within the agency—first the bomb squad chief, then the leader of the Extra-Risk Team, and nineteen years after signing up, all the way to Minister.

Although he directed EMERCOM with fanaticism, just like the Ministry's legendary founder, he loathed the bureaucratic capacity in the Government that came with the job. Klimov was an action man, so he found the weekly cabinet meetings akin to tussles in a vipers' nest. But it was now part of his managerial duty, and it was the responsibility and loyalty to his men that made him battle the government reptiles for budget funds and approvals of development programs. To Klimov, a suit-and-tie combo was just another battle uniform, like his blue parka of old, albeit slightly more comfortable, and more suitable for his status. At forty-two, he still looked impressive in any attire. His every motion carried underlying grace, and his 190-centimeter frame was gaunt and muscular.

Perhaps the only aspect of his appearance that betrayed Klimov's true age was his hair. Once completely raven-black, it now had streaks of white as intense as the color of pure snow. Klimov joked that his hair was a reflection of his job. Too much black and too little white. He hoped that as time passed, life would improve accordingly.

One of the few top-brass privileges that Klimov was actually grateful for was owning a home close to work, a factor ever more important in the frenetic environment of Moscow. His custom was to leave the office at ten, but not to cease his function. In fact, when he was away from his desk at the helm of EMERCOM, unable to monitor every incident on the planet in real-time, his brain was tuned to work sharper, ready to react against any arising disaster with maximum efficiency. And the worst disaster, he knew from haunting experience, tended to erupt at night.

And so he felt tickling apprehension when the call came, only an hour after he'd come back home. Such a call could only mean emergency big enough to add extra grey locks.

The location he heard over the encrypted line indicated that this was the worst crisis in the history of EMERCOM.

"Sochi."

He was hit not by one, but two unthinkable disasters. Each was shocking in its own right, but their convergence in time and space magnified their scope beyond nightmarish.

The Presidential yacht transmitted a brief distress signal before it vanished without a trace, against a backdrop of reports that described an explosion out at sea that matched the *Olympia*'s last know position.

Horribly, it was as though the sea had gone mad, bearing death. Spreading from the area where the yacht had dematerialized, the waves discharged dead fish in a mass that covered the entire beach.

8

There were several operational Departments within EMERCOM such as Crisis Management, Emergency Prevention and Response, Science and Technology, Logistics, and International Cooperation, all of which comprised the backbone of the Ministry's daily function. At times of catastrophes that required instant deployment of the finest specialists to any corner of the globe, EMERCOM relied on its Rapid Response Teams. They were the Ministry's elite.

EMERCOM's Central Airmobile Rescue Detachment located at the Zhukovsky airbase outside Moscow worked in 24-hour stand-by mode, ready to take off at two hours' notice. Past midnight, when Klimov's Land Rover arrived to Zhukovsky, the technicians were already running final checks on their Beriev-200 aircraft.

The Ministry had a fleet of Ilyushin-76 transports as well as helicopters ranging from Ka-32 to Mi-26 birds, but the park of seven Be-200 multi-purpose amphibious planes was Klimov's pride.

And for good reason. The Be-200 was a beautiful flying machine. Based on the Beriev A-40 "Albatross" amphibious jet, it was the most versatile airplane of its kind, capable of performing cargo and passenger freight runs, or serving as a firefighting, SAR or patrol aircraft. The trademark EMERCOM twin orange-and-blue lines painted along the airframe highlighted the unassuming perfection of its massive size. Two large turbofan engines mounted on the rear of the fuselage, close to the T-tail, were the force that carried the Beriev into the skies. Honeywell avionic instruments allowed the two-man crew to carry out any task in the foulest weather imaginable, day or night. Rough choppy seas were tamed by its curved belly and symmetrical wingtip floats.

A solitary figure was standing on the floodlit tarmac, overseeing the preparation procedure. The man was clad in the uniform of an EMERCOM officer, a Major's golden stars gilding his shoulders. The blue windbreaker could not disguise the man's athleticism. He was as tall as Klimov, but slightly wider in the shoulders, dominant as a lion. Arms akimbo, feet firm on the tarmac, he viewed the airplane while the air current generated by its monstrous engines toyed with his sandy hair. The Major could easily be mistaken for the aircraft's pilot, for there was pride in the man's stance, the romantic aura of someone who called an airfield his home. And although he was comfortable inside a cockpit of any flying vessel, he was not the Beriev's pilot. He was the leader of EMERCOM's primary Rapid Response Team that tackled the worst disasters around the world.

"Gene!" Klimov called out over the engine roar as he strode across the runway.

The man turned around. Klimov wasn't surprised that the Major heard him over the engines' din, for he was notorious for his acute auditory perception. The name badge over his left breast pocket read, SOKOLOV E.

At the sight of Klimov, Eugene Sokolov's face beamed with a sincere smile that gave his azure-blue eyes a twinkle. His handshake was firm and confident, with not the slightest suggestion that some years ago all of his fingers had been broken.

"So how bad is it, Danya?" Sokolov asked. Despite more than a decade's difference in age, and a greater gap in rank, they were the closest of friends. Over the years, they'd saved each other's lives more times than anyone would care to keep track of. "What happened there is not some chemical leak."

"What happened there," Klimov nodded slowly, "is hell for you and me. The President, his wife, and two guests are as good as dead, presumably blown up to bits on their yacht. At the same time, something kills every living creature in the sea within several kilometers. Two dozen late-night swimmers get hospitalized and three of them die. Their condition is difficult to recognize because of the symptoms—headaches, high blood pressure, fever, vomiting, rashes ... all too common for anything from influenza, to food poisoning to subarchanoid hemorrhage. That's the gist of it, Gene. The priority is top secret."

Sokolov stared under his feet and then looked at Klimov.

"Our mission?"

"You need to reach the *Olympia*'s last known position before any of the FSB-Army-Navy bunch can react and crowd the area like vultures. Find out what happened to the yacht, and to the ecosystem. If we know what caused all this, we can save more lives."

"You can count on us."

Daniil Klimov embraced him in a bear hug.

"Be careful."

Sokolov jogged in the direction of the Be-200 that was about to taxi out onto the runway, ready for the flight.

9

The Be-200 completed a smooth climb to 8,000 meters, banking to a southern course to the Black Sea.

As always, Sokolov sat with eyes closed, trying to occupy his mind with the monotone drone of the huge turbofan engines. His imagination projected the scene of tragedy that could await them, but his heart was heavy with the knowledge that reality was infinitely more gruesome. He had filled his teammates in on the details provided by Klimov, and the atmosphere inside the craft had become deathly silent.

The only thing he dreaded during the flights was a sense of helpless inability. That was the only stage of the mission where he did nothing to reach the disaster site quicker. He could speed up the response to get airborne. He could coordinate a quick setup and launch the rescue operation in record time once they landed. But he was powerless in making the Be-200 fly faster than its top speed. All he could do was sit and wait. He used the time to theorize, going over the data repeatedly, assessing their resources, the required actions and the possible risks. Once in a while, he would consult his wristwatch, scrutinizing the minute hand as it crawled in a lazy arc.

If there was one man who was able to push everything out of the Beriev, it was Yuri Mischenko, the head pilot in Sokolov's team.

"How's our flight going?" Sokolov said, poking his head into the cockpit.

"ETA is two hours," Mischenko growled in a deep baritone. He was a heavyset man, big-boned, but by no means obese. Holding the stick with his enormous hand, he took a moment to scratch his short red beard.

"It's your weight that's bogging us down, Yura," came the craggy, tarred voice of Sergei Zubov from the co-pilot's seat. "I think he's been stealing food supplies from our humanitarian relief program. Those poor, starving African kids ..."

"No, it's your cigarette haze that's screwing our visibility."

"Gene, one day we should leave Yuri behind and let me captain the plane. Since you're our commander, I'll let you be my co-pilot."

"One day, I should leave *both* of you behind," Sokolov said.

According to Mischenko, any natural disaster paled in comparison to his partner. They were a mismatched pair judging by Zubov's appearance. A good ten centimeters shorter than Yuri, he was built like a sack of cement. A long nose and dense eyebrows gave his shaved head an eagle's profile. His image would be incomplete without a cigarette in his teeth.

Yura and Serge seemed to be constantly engaged in a battle of wits, each trying to launch opportune taunts at the other. It was a game they both enjoyed. The mental gymnastics kept their grey matter alert. It also saved them from brooding over the nightmares they had witnessed in every corner of the world. Zubov's mouth was sarcastic and cynical, but his heart was pure gold. The two airmen had developed a unique friendship that lasted almost twenty years. They trusted each other with their lives, and Sokolov knew that they would never let him down either.

Sokolov retreated back to the Beriev's aft, where Pavel Netto, the fourth and final member of their compact crew, was snoring peacefully. He had a sharp if somewhat withdrawn mind. No matter what chaos was raging outside, the sinewy tech wizard was cool under pressure and was a quick decision-maker. Sokolov could bet that asleep, Netto was counting the digits of Pi instead of sheep.

Sokolov glanced at the dial of his watch, a Breitling Superocean chronometer.

Time. His best friend and worst enemy. Giver and crusher of hopes. Healer of wounds and cruel sadist.

Breitling SA produced the finest instruments in the world, being the only company to have all of its watches certified as "chronometers" that was awarded to only three percent of Swiss-made watches. Each model was an inspiring achievement in functionality, reliability and precision, crafted with the passion that only aviators possessed. Sokolov's Superocean was no exception—a diver's watch capable of withstanding a depth up to 1,500 meters, or 5,000 feet.

Sokolov looked at the Breitling emblem in the centre of the blue dial—the letter "B" adorned with a pair of wings and an anchor. Involuntarily, he reminded himself that Father, the wings, and Mother, the anchor of his family, were long gone, killed by the bone-grinding mechanism of Russian history. His brother was missing without trace.

But he could save others. Saving lives—the purpose of EMERCOM as well as his personal one.

Saving those that could still be saved.

If the deadly tide in the Black Sea was still reaping more victims, time was his enemy. The ally of death.

Sokolov was lost in studying depth charts and maps of Sochi coast, giving extra scrutiny to the five-kilometer strip in the north affected the worst, but soon he was able to see the effects with his own eyes. Before he knew it, the Beriev was tilting in a pass over the mountains. Since Sochi was positioned at the base of the Caucasus, the only possible approach to Adler airport was seaward, the aircraft then having to make a 180-degree turn back inland towards a runway that projected into the sea. The Beriev, however, glided parallel to the coastline, skimming the waves as it descended on its way to the potential wreck site.

It was a breathtaking view, thrilling with its beauty and the fear for its fragility. The fleeting Sochi skyline of trees and high-rises illuminated against the night sky. Seaside, the beaches were lit brightly as well, but cordoned off. EMERCOM personnel were clearing away the remains of marine life. The most vivid image stamped in Sokolov's mind was a row of dead dolphins awaiting to be driven away, so human-like in their posture, and in the needlessness of their deaths.

"Poor things," Netto murmured next to him.

Sokolov sighed. The Black Sea, named so for the high content of iodine, renowned for its healing power, had become a killer.

The famous breakwaters, jutting a hundred meters out into the sea, and spaced equally apart, raced by like distance markers. In Mischenko's hands, the Be-200 touched down on the water surface like a majestic swan. Once it had set comfortably in the waves, the amphibious jet continued to cruise forward, until Mischenko idled his craft to a stop not a whisker away from where he wanted it.

All around them, moonlight played on the water surface, the waves shining silver.

"Welcome to the Black Sea," Mischenko called as he powered down the engines. "Our current coordinates match the spot where the *Olympia* vanished. The position is about as accurate as we can get given the computer projection of her fall to the bottom."

"Let's get to work," Sokolov said. "Pasha, unleash your midget."

Netto reached for a worn travel case, packed with equipment according to the specifics of each mission. Today Netto carried eighteen kilograms' worth of sea-wreck exploration gear.

Sokolov's 'midget' comment was a tongue-in-cheek reference to a remotely operated vehicle. It had a long, forgettable name that was reduced to an acronym which read GNOM.

The Russian-made ROV was indeed a forerunner in terms of miniaturization and maneuverability. Weighing under three kilograms, roughly the shape and size of a two-liter bottle, it was one of the most efficient units of its kind, able to access a 150-meter depth. The *Gnome*'s movement was limited only by its Kevlar-reinforced umbilical cable.

Interestingly enough, the *Gnome* received commands via a standard Sony Playstation controller. With the video feed from the ROV's cameras appearing on a laptop screen, the entire operation did at times feel like an electronic game.

It took Netto all of four minutes to set up the *Gnome* and make sure that the ROV functioned properly, calibrating the controller's directional sticks whilst consulting the output on the computer monitor.

As Mischenko radioed Klimov to announce their arrival, the right-side door hissed, rising out in gull-wing fashion.

Warm air flowed inside the Beriev, bringing along the smell of algae. In the silence, waves lapped against the fuselage, inviting into the sinister blackness that lay beyond the twinkling surface. Bending over, Sokolov gently lowered the ROV into the water, careful to avoid contact himself.

The *Gnome*, having a slight buoyancy, stayed on the surface, before Netto engaged its motors and it submerged. Then he toggled a switch on the controller, and powerful LED lights bit through the desolate gloom. Breaking suddenly near the Beriev, a brilliant orb permeated the water mass, shrinking and dimming as the ROV drifted lower.

Netto launched the sonar software and squinted at the monitor. Sokolov looked over his shoulder as the depth gauge ticked off descent. Slowly, the sonar was painting a meticulous rendering of the *Gnome*'s surroundings in the screaming colors of a Kubrickan vertigo. The live video feed from the camera was murky. Even with the lights on, visibility was near zero.

It was a painful process to Sokolov, almost physically so. New bits of data presented by the *Gnome*'s sensors stirred hopefulness that bordered on anxiety. The mind wished that each new shape in the emerging picture would be the object of their search, but as detail grew, disappointment gave way to expectancy for the next unknown outline, again and again. It was ... like tuning to human sounds within mountains of rubble ... A frantic patience Sokolov had learned to contain. Only this time, there was no chance of finding survivors.

"There," Sokolov let out, marking their first accomplishment.

The sonar had a range of three hundred meters. At the edge of its reception, a hundred meters from the Beriev's position, the picture showed a hazy V-shaped outline.

It was the *Olympia*.

"We got her!" Netto said. "Yura, you put us almost spot on."

"No sweat."

After they had pinpointed the shipwreck, Mischenko feathered the controls to correct the Beriev's orientation, bringing it closely above the ship's location, within range of the *Gnome*'s video cameras.

She lay askew on her port, elevated on an incline that rose over a trough. The highest point was her stern, starting at approximately thirty-eight meters below the surface. Her nose dipped ten meters lower, resting on a bed of sediment.

Mesmerized, Netto sat unmoving in his chair, transfixed on the apparition. Sokolov, though, seemed to be paying no attention to the breathtaking panorama of the wreck. He tapped his finger on the chart in the upper-right corner of the screen. It showed the water spectroanalysis readings processed by the *Gnome*.

"What do you make of this?" he asked Netto.

"Hmmm ... The chemical sensors aren't picking up anything abnormal."

"Meaning that the water is poison-free?" Sokolov asked.

Netto stuck out his lower lip. "To my own surprise, there's no hint of any toxic pollutants."

"Good," Sokolov said. Then he added, "Are you sure?"

"Positively certain. You doubt the data?"

"No, I'm just double-checking."

"Why?"
"If you're wrong, my restless soul will come back for you."
"Just what on earth are you up to?"
Sokolov shrugged.
"I'm going down there."

10

Every member of EMERCOM's special teams had to be proficient in at least two areas of expertise. While Sokolov possessed versatile skills to handle any crisis, his two primary professions were diving and NBC defense.

He finished checking his scuba gear. "All set. While I'm at it, Sergei can prove his worth to our cause."

"Oh?" said Zubov. "I'm not diving there first."

"I'd never give you the chance. What I want you to do is head over to the mainland and check out the patients. This entire territory belongs to the presidential sanatoria, so with their state-of-the-art equipment, most of the victims were able to receive adequate treatment on site. Perhaps the medical staff may shed some light on what's going on. Look around, see the symptoms for yourself, and get back."

"Will do."

Sokolov had stripped off his uniform, for a moment revealing a scar on his back. Blemishing his skin was the entry mark of a gunshot wound, courtesy of an Islamic terrorist who fired at him in a destroyed school. The bullet had missed Sokolov's heart, but stabbed it with remembrance. Sokolov was quick to hide it under his drysuit.

Together with Zubov, they launched the inflatable. It was an Orion 25S, a top model produced by a military factory in Yaroslavl that built boats since 1936 and had been classified for the most part of its history. The Orion was indispensable equipment for EMERCOM's sea operations, a quick and agile little workhorse. With an overall length of 5.6 meters, it could carry nine passengers, with a maximum payload of 900 kilograms.

As Zubov started the Orion's thirty-horsepower outboard motor, Sokolov strapped on the scuba tank and prepared for the dive.

11

The sea was a cosmic black hole that sucked him in.

Sokolov felt vulnerable in the hostile water. His dive computer told him that he was submerging ever deeper into the very environment that could kill him. As he moved through a blizzard of microscopic plankton, it appeared that his presence was so negligible to the main as to be acceptable.

Sokolov kicked with his fins, following the *Gnome*'s umbilical cable down into the abyss. Like the leash of a blind man's guide dog, it led him to the wreck through the mist. The sound of his breathing resonated in Sokolov's ears, the Nitrox mixture passing through the regulator with a swelling hiss.

The tiny screen of the laptop that received the *Gnome*'s video signal could not reflect the sheer magnitude of the *Olympia*'s proportions. Seeing her reclining form again, this time with his own eyes, just meters away, Sokolov felt amazement.

She was a former queen that had died in oblivion, abandoned by past admirers, and betrayed by her court. Once lustrous, her skin had turned pallid grey. The explosion had mangled her side, ripping it wide open.

Hovering over the *Olympia*, the ROV lit the yacht's sundeck in a ghostly glow. The deck itself was empty, the lounge chairs swept away.

"*I see you!*" Netto said over the comms link.

Sokolov held a thumbs-up into the camera eye of the *Gnome* and pointed in the direction of the *Olympia*.

"All right, show me the way," he said.

Under Netto's control, the *Gnome* whirred and rounded the angled stern, aiming at the teak door of the main deck. Sokolov pushed the door open and proceeded after his robotic attendant into the superstructure.

As soon as Sokolov floated into cavernous space of the main lounge, his mind was jarred by the surreal image. The *Gnome*'s lights played around the walls, casting sinister shadows of debris around the room.

What had once been a lavish lounge/dining area, was now a scene left in the wake of a hurricane. Bolted down to the decking, the furniture that held in place had rotated sideways, the enormous table and chairs clinging abnormally to a vertical surface of metal. The rest was scattered around, heaps of crashed paraphernalia: lamps, vases, paintings, and books among the rubble. Crystals of broken glass glistened on crumpled carpets. Of the two dominant rosewood columns, once proudly separating lounge from dining, one had splintered at the base, and the other remained as a purposeless bar stretched across the cavity.

Bubbles of trapped air rose up. The *Olympia*'s last gasp. As if not fully dead, she let out a coarse croak. It was the pressure of the sea testing her hull.

Sokolov had never experienced claustrophobia, but the overturned walls closed in on him, warping, making him feel sick.

"Where's the bedroom?"

"*Let me think ... The master bedroom is now bottom, far left. The VIP room is starboard, so it should be above the dining hall.*"

He visualized the *Olympia*'s layout in his mind. Each of the two large cabins were accessible either from the open deck, or the anteroom adjacent to the dining hall. With the yacht lying propped on her port side, the outside door to the master bedroom would be blocked.

"*And hurry up, Gene.*"

The luminous dial of Sokolov's Breitling confirmed the caution. To avoid decompression, he had only twenty minutes of bottom time at his disposal.

He finned toward the anteroom and looked around. Realigned, one doorframe was now at his feet, the other over his head. The two flimsy doors had been yanked open, hanging on their hinges. Left and right had become top and bottom.

Sokolov grabbed the edges of the frame above him and pulled himself up, into the open space.

His dive light met with the President of the Russian Federation, Nikolai Alexandrov.

Ex-President. Deceased.

Alexandrov was lying on the now-horizontal bulkhead, eyes bulging out, as if in disbelief at his predicament.

The faithful *Gnome* followed Sokolov inside, and trained its lights on the President's corpse. The bacteria in his stomach had not yet filled the body with gases to make it float.

"Are you recording this?" Sokolov asked Netto.

"*Yes,*" Netto replied, needing a moment to find his voice.

Sokolov found no reason to linger on the grisly sight.

He eased down into the master bedroom. There he saw the First Lady, her body pressed down by debris.

Sokolov drew closer. The First Lady looked like a battered mannequin. Rigor mortis had stiffened her face into a waxen mask. Under her greenish skin, capillaries streaked in bright petechial webs. Sokolov forced himself to reach out and touch it. Even behind the gloves, his fingers pricked with repulsion as he lifted her eyelids.

Her eyeballs were black.

Two glass spheres about to burst with blood.

"I need a close-up here," Sokolov instructed.

The *Gnome* moved in a position to zoom in on the body.

"*I've never seen anything like it. Is this normal?*"

"I don't think so."

Although conjuctival hemorrhaging could be attributed to asphyxiation, what he saw wasn't typical. Also, the patterns on the skin seemed chaotic, too inconsistent, too pronounced for livor mortis. Sokolov's hunch told him that she may have been killed by the unknown agent. The President's eyes and skin showed no such extreme signs. Sokolov was hardly an expert to make an accurate diagnosis, especially in the given circumstances.

"*Gene, time's nearly up. You have to head back now.*"

Sokolov's own schedule confirmed Netto's words. Besides, he did not want to disturb the crime scene any further. He had already broken too many regulations. But he couldn't leave just yet. The mission of his team was to uncover the causes of the mystifying deaths. Unless he broke one more rule, they would lose a vital clue once the wreck was secured by the military.

He unsheathed the knife strapped to his shin.

Originally designed as a heavy dive knife, the Katran had a double-edged blade with serrated teeth on one side, which made it useful for survival and combat.

Bringing it to the head of the dead woman, Sokolov moved the seven-inch blade with delicacy.

He picked a lock of the First Lady's hair and sawed it off.

Pocketing the hair sample, he swam back, in the direction of the exit.

12

Halfway up, Sokolov performed his first safety stop. His hand following the umbilical cable, he craned up to peer through the gloom. Above, he could see the sun rays playing on the other side of the water. Consulting his Breitling, he made one-minute stops every ten feet. At fifteen feet remaining, he raised his body at a minimal rate of ascent, clearing the nitrogen out.

Bobbing in the swells as he broke the surface, he spit out the regulator to taste the saline air. Still holding the umbilical cable he pulled himself to the opening in the Beriev's side. When he was within reach, Mischenko hauled him in. He splashed on the hard floor, water dripping.

After Mischenko helped remove his gear, Sokolov rose to his feet, unzipping the dry suit.

"Any word from Zubov?"

"He radioed in to say he's bringing an interesting find."

Sokolov changed back into his EMERCOM uniform, remembering to extract the damp wad of hair from the Velcro pocket and seal it in an evidence container for subsequent lab tests.

He joined Netto who guided the *Gnome* around the wreck to document the destruction, finding the bodies of the crew. Those who did not die as a result of the explosion shared the horrific appearance of the First Lady.

Sokolov was the first to pick up the faint hum of the outboard motor. With the sun fully up, they could see the Orion's orange hull riding the waves, Zubov piloting carefully.

Zubov wasn't alone.

Lying prone in the Orion, strapped to a stretcher, was a dark-haired woman, the top of her hospital gown visible over the covers that protected her from the spray. She was unconscious.

As Mischenko and Netto pulled the boat's mooring line, Zubov and Sokolov transferred the stretcher inside the plane, and carried her into the medical section of the Beriev. Securing the stretcher atop a fixed gurney, Sokolov placed an oxygen mask over her nose and lips.

Under the glare of the lights, he studied her, looking for signs of trauma instead of admiring her beauty. Her skin displayed no bruises or other marks. No bones seemed to be broken. Sokolov's biggest concern was her loss of consciousness, which could indicate a severe head injury. With relief, he noted that her breathing was even, her head and face showed no swelling, and there were no fluids discharging from her nose or ears. His fingers explored her neck for stiffness or damage to the vertebrae. There was no threat to her life, unless her internal organs had been damaged. Even though the amphibious jet was fitted with complete ambulance equipment, she needed to be diagnosed more thoroughly. Another reason to hurry back to base.

After his teammates pulled the Orion inside the Beriev's hold, they gathered around Sokolov, staring at the young woman on the gurney.

"What's wrong with her?" Netto asked Sokolov in a low voice.

"She's reasonably fine," Zubov replied in his stead. "She woke up screaming, so the doctors had to sedate her."

All eyes turned on him.

"So *she* is your interesting find," Mischenko said. "How did you manage to get her?"

"She has no ID, and no record of ever being there ... She was a burden that the medics were glad to get off their shoulders. I actually did them a favor, sparing the paperwork, the explanations, and the risk of her dying on their hands if her condition deteriorated."

"What I'd rather like to hear," said Sokolov, "is *why* you brought her."

"I'll tell you why. I saw a couple of people at the morgue who looked like their blood boiled inside them. Chemical blood tests showed no toxic compounds. It's not poisoning, and it's not a virus."

"The *Gnome* couldn't find anything in the seawater, either," Netto said. "What could the sickness be, then? Some sort of hypersensitive allergic reaction?"

Zubov shrugged. "Those who are still alive are suffering from fever, vomiting and hemorrhaging. Not her. When they searched for poisoned swimmers, they found her on the beach, passed out. She was wet and had blood on her face, probably after a nose bleed. So the doctors picked her up and put her in the ward together with the other victims. Soon they discovered that even though she had also been exposed to the water, she didn't have any of the symptoms that the rest did. I thought it would be better if we found out why. Either she's been terribly lucky, or maybe—just maybe, she's immune. Whatever struck these waters, it happened yesterday, and it's gone already, but she was right in the middle of it."

"You did the right thing," Sokolov said. "No one knows who she is or where she came from. But *we* do. That beach can be accessed by sanatorium guests only, so the only way she could have approached it unnoticed would be if she had come from the sea."

"And there was only one boat at sea that was within sight of that spot. The *Olympia*," Zubov said.

All the way through the return leg to Moscow, Sokolov's mind was occupied with something else entirely. As he studied the girl, he knew his mind was playing a trick on him, but the likeness was no less frightening.

The jet-black hair ... The big eyes, the youthful face ...

It was as if he had been visited by a ghost from the past. Sokolov imagined a six-year-old girl, wondering what *her* face would look like now if he had saved her life in Beslan.

13

Unnoticed, the oil tanker crept through the Black Sea towards Turkey, holding a ballast of harmless seawater.

Aboard the *Isebek*, the captain's quarters were spartan. Nothing resembled the grandeur seen on the *Olympia*, save for a bottle of twenty-year-old French alcohol placed atop a stained aluminum table. The bottle was all that remained of the *Olympia* above the sea's surface, a souvenir Kasymov could not resist.

Sitting on the rock-hard cot, Timur Kasymov took a mouthful of the cognac from the bottle. By his standards, the celebration was unsavory, but he had every reason to celebrate. First the Americans, and now the Russians were out of his way.

Oleg Radchuk banged on the door, disrupting Kasymov's appreciation of the drink.

"What is it, Oleg?"

The Ukrainian entered, visibly tense.

"I've just received a radio intercept of the EMERCOM aircraft calling Moscow."

"Ah," Kasymov said, waving his hand as if he were brushing away a mosquito. "Their involvement is inconsequential. Our plan was a complete success. High damage and no trace of the substance. Nothing for them to find."

"Quite on the contrary," Radchuk said. "They didn't leave empty-handed."

Kasymov raised an eyebrow. "What did they get? Pebbles from the beach? Seashells, maybe?"

"Not *what* but rather *who*. They picked someone up. A survivor."

Fire seized Kasymov's stomach. "Impossible."

"An unconscious woman in her mid-twenties. Sporty. Black hair. Asian features."

Screaming, Kasymov hurled the cognac bottle against the floor and it shattered into fragments.

"Why—didn't—she—*die!*"

14

Following a sleepless night at the Zhukovsky base that he spent warding off barrages of phone calls from fellow ministers, Klimov was down on the runway to greet the returning Beriev. Together with him, a group of medics waited to rush the survivor to the hospital inside the modern, sturdy structure of concrete and glass. Klimov knew exactly who she was the moment he caught a glimpse of her face as she was carried off on a stretcher. It was Asiyah Kasymova, the daughter of the Kazakh leader.

The setting within the six-storied Zhukovsky quarters was special, even home-like, designed to reduce stress. Here, the Rapid Response teams kept stand-by duty for alerts, rotating in seventy-two-hour shifts.

Sokolov's team assembled in the large recreational area. As Klimov looked at his men during the debriefing, he saw their haggardness. Mischenko slumped in a sofa. Netto buried his face in his hands, stifling yawns. Standing by the window, his posture solid, Sokolov showed few signs of fatigue, and did most of the talking as he recounted their findings, Zubov adding the details of his trip ashore.

"I'm certain that this girl," Klimov concluded after they had finished, "is the daughter of Timur Kasymov. Last night she was aboard the *Olympia* together with her father."

Klimov voiced his concern for their own well-being. After all, they had been potentially exposed to hazardous substances. Their shift was over, so he ordered them to undergo a medical check and take a few days' leave.

The quiet across the hallway was shattered by footsteps—a procession of feet, marching with determination. Klimov rose to face a group of men set towards him, the EMERCOM base commander at their side, protesting their actions. Seeing the Minister, he began an explanation.

"Daniil Petrovich, these people—"

"Don't worry, I can handle them myself." Klimov stood in their way, towering over the pack of officials. "Want do you want, gentlemen?"

Their leader stepped forward while the rest struggled to formulate a response between them. Klimov would have ignored him altogether had he not faced the EMERCOM Minister directly. He was profoundly unremarkable, average in every way—a shadow.

"Mr. Minister, I am here on behalf of the Federal Security Service," he said, holding out his ID. "And my colleagues here serve the public as prosecutors and bailiffs."

"I guess you missed my question. What do you want?"

"Dear Daniil Petrovich, we have come to conduct a search. Here is the warrant. We are looking for a woman named Asiyah Timurqyzy Kasymova, citizen of the Republic of Kazakhstan."

Klimov felt an urge to twist the man's neck.

"I have absolutely no idea why you would be looking for this lady within the walls of an EMERCOM base."

"So you claim that you have no knowledge of her whereabouts?"

"Until a moment ago, I had no knowledge of her *existence*."

The FSB man nodded slowly, and then said, "Dear Minister, that is a lie."

Klimov exploded in outrage.

"Do you know who you're talking to? I'll make sure you regret ever coming here."

"I hope it's not a threat against the life of an officer on duty," he smiled without humor. "Daniil Petrovich, I believe you will not contest the authority of a search warrant issued by court? We have the right to examine every forsaken corner of this fine establishment."

Klimov gave him a cold stare. "You will have no cooperation from my staff. I'll make your job very difficult."

"Asiyah Kasymova is to be placed in custody of the witness protection program. She is vital to a case we're investigating. But if she is unavailable at present, perhaps we could detain other important witnesses?" The FSB officer produced another document. "Summons for Messrs. Zubov, Sokolov, Mischenko, and Netto to appear at the Prosecutor General's office."

Out of the corner of his eye, Klimov noticed Mischenko stiffen in his sofa. Netto blanched.

"I won't let you have my men."

"Let's be reasonable. *My* men carry firearms. Things can get quite ugly. Of course, this procedure may be put on hold, indefinitely, should we find Ms. Kasymova."

Effectively, it was blackmail. Klimov could hardly conceal his disgust.

"I won't leave it at that." Klimov fished out his cell phone and speed-dialed FSB Director Frolov. Only hours ago they had discussed the crisis in Sochi, and Frolov gave no indication that he knew about the EMERCOM team operating at the wreck. Someone at the sanatorium must have tipped the FSB about the girl.

When Klimov described the unfolding intrusion, Frolov confirmed the FSB officer's story word for word.

"Just give us the girl, Minister. It's for her own good. We'll transfer her to a good clinic. She'd be safer under our protection."

Klimov's grip tightened on the handset. In a clipped tone, he said, "Just keep your goons away from my boys, or else you will deal with me personally."

He killed the connection. The FSB envoy watched silently, triumph in his eyes.

In the end, Klimov had to accept defeat, and, in a sense, Frolov's logic. But not the audacity of his methods.

The Minister turned to the base commander.

"Show them to the medical ward where Ms. Kasymova is being kept."

PART III

1

The last ten kilometers were the hardest. Russia's vastness, so cherished to behold some four hundred kilometers ago, when Constantine had entered the country, was piling more frustration onto him with every turn of the Porsche's wheels. The endless plains became a blur.

But closing in on Moscow, he saw hints of an impeding finish emerging in the landscape. The familiar greenery made his heart race again.

The highway swerved through the trees, past the sparse communities of the city's outskirts, towards denser neighborhoods, and finally, through blocks of high-rise towers.

As the M1 punctured Moscow's outer ring, the road fused into *Kutuzovsky prospekt*, the city's main entry point that opened into ten lanes of speeding traffic. The paved space was so wide that the adjacent buildings seemed distant, as if separated by an aircraft runway. Embroidered by jubilant banners and flags, Kutuzovsky was a major venue for Moscow's never-ending carnival of life.

Straight ahead was Russia's own Arc de Triomphe, a mark of supremacy over France. Constantine passed the chestnut alleys of Victory Park, the rising obelisk, and the gushing fountains. On the grassy knoll, the flower clock registered eleven o'clock.

It would still take some time for Constantine to absorb it all—the sights and sounds, the faces, the summer air scented with mixed blooms, and above all, the changes around him. Moscow had become even more beautiful—vibrant, colorful, and rich. The Russian flair for grandeur, backed by petrodollars, burst from every corner, window and billboard.

His Porsche did not stand out here as it did in Europe, for the street was swarmed with luxury cars, making Bentleys and Lamborghinis seem mundane. Kutuzovsky had always been a favorite district of the elite, be it Politburo members or billionaire oligarchs. On the left-hand side was Moskva City, a high tech business center that stood on the banks of the river. Concrete and glass, shimmering in the sun, had evolved over the twelve months he'd been gone, new framework acquiring form. The cluster of corporate towers rose a hundred stories high, showcasing Russia's economical renaissance.

When a different kind of tower appeared in view, the tips of his fingers turned to ice. The mountainous shape poked through the sky. He felt pride in its beauty reigning over the blue, shaded with melancholy surrounding the age of its construction.

Kutuzovsky, built under Stalin, ended as it hit the steepest curve of the River Moskva, reaching the heart of the city. There, gloriously neighboring the postmodernist Moskva City, was a classic monolith of brick and stone, flanked by tiered wings, lavish with spires, balconies and parapets. The Ukraina Hotel, although it was constructed during Khrushchev's reign, was one of *his* seven famous skyscrapers, placed by Stalin's hand atop each of the seven hills of Moscow surrounding the Kremlin.

Constantine parked his Porsche under the trees in a quiet square in front of the hotel and got out, facing the monumental building. Intended to evoke trepidation, it felt as if the stone epitomized the spirit of Stalin. With twenty-nine levels above the ground, and three more below, the Ukraina Hotel was the second-highest of the seven siblings, the tallest being Constantine's native Moscow University.

And so it stood, forever young, crowned by a Soviet pentangle, its visage retouched to be ever more blossoming as time went by.

Arching his head so that his vision could absorb the edifice in its entirety, Constantine became dizzy. He pressed against the side of the Porsche, massaging his temples. The fatigue was killing him. He grabbed the Samsonite and started towards the hotel. As he walked, he glanced over his shoulder at the car one last time.

Windows opened, doors unlocked, engine running.

Within minutes, the Cayenne would be stolen. Within days, it would roam Chechnya or St. Petersburg sporting fake license plates, any link to him erased.

2

Few people realized that of the entire ensemble of the Ukraina, only the main 170-meter-tall tower was dedicated to the hotel itself. Instead, the two low wings stemming from its base housed residential apartments. It was one of these apartments that Constantine was heading for.

Using Borisov's cell phone, he had found the listing on the internet among thousands of other advertisements for typical two-room flats. As the old adage went, Muscovites never worked, but rather made a living leasing their apartments to migrants.

And lease was popular business, indeed. When a few hours earlier he had called to negotiate the terms, Constantine clinched a one-month rent for five thousand euros. Keys and money would change hands, forgoing any written agreement. A verbal deal was in the interest of both parties, allowing to evade taxes and retain anonymity.

Which is exactly what Constantine needed.

As he reached the designated door on the eighth floor and pressed the buzzer, Constantine was greeted by the apartment owner, an elderly woman with red hair and an overly made-up face.

"You must be Constantine."

He nodded, and she guided him inside, providing a perfunctory tour of the property via gestures at closed doors.

When the corridor opened into the main office/dining/living room, she faced him expectantly.

"Well?"

"I'm sorry, but I've changed my mind," Constantine said.

Her penciled eyebrows arched.

"But ... but ..."

Constantine produced three bundles of cash from the Samsonite.

"Three months' pay. Fifteen thousand euros. Surely, you wouldn't mind such alteration to our terms?"

"Your stay here is *assured!*"

"As is my privacy, I hope."

"Most certainly!"

Her eyes, heavy with mascara, were hypnotized by the thick wads of money.

Constantine dropped the money onto the table. "Deal."

Eager to abandon him as soon as she'd stuffed the money into her purse, she wished him a pleasant stay and ran off. Constantine was equally eager to get rid of her.

The elderly lady had left behind only a set of keys and a fleeting reminiscences of Frau Hasler, a continent and a life away.

Constantine shut the door behind her, exhaling.

He walked around the flat like a chased animal that had to become familiar with its new lair before deeming it safe. The apartment had two tiny rooms and a monstrous four-meter ceiling. Although dusted, the furniture was stale, affected by age and use no matter how much the owner had tried to gloss it, just like her face. In the bathroom, the tiles had absorbed stain, and the ceiling exhibited rashes of nicotine rust; but it seemed safe for use, and nothing else mattered.

He settled into the bedroom, which he chose as his anchor point.

What mesmerized Constantine was the bedroom view.

A stunning panorama of downtown Moscow.

Directly in front of him, staring across the river, was the vivid white building that had been executed by a firing squad of tanks. Now it was reborn from the black ashes of its own burning body ... But his father ...

Farther out, Moscow spanned beyond infinity, or so it seemed as the city limits bettered the horizon. More than two hundred churches cast a brilliant glow all over it, the sun rays reflecting off their golden domes. Moscow, Europe's largest and most populous city, a world in itself ... And somewhere in that city was his brother, still waiting for him.

Constantine slumped on the bed. Worn out by his journey, his mind had lagged to register that he was finally there. Now the realization was full. No one could take it away from him.

Moscow.

His jaw ached with the tears he was holding back. His breathing came in gasps, forced and ragged, in and out, until his chest tightened spastically and he could no longer contain himself, sobs breaking out, fingers digging into hair, wailing, screaming, screaming ...

He got off the floor and dragged himself into the bathroom. Washed his face. Took off the clothes. Showered.

The tears had done to his soul what the shower did to the body—it dulled the pain, but didn't absolve him from it. A corkscrew still worked inside his heart. A sledgehammer was still pounding his muscles and bones. Back in the room, he wanted to crash down and dive into sleep. But he stopped himself. He looked at the flat black object. The damning suitcase. The only thing now that separated him from his brother.

He still had something important to do. Something that couldn't wait.

Constantine shoved the Samsonite under the bed, and stormed out, locking the apartment behind him.

3

The Ukraina Hotel was located perfectly. The junction of Kutuzovsky and New Arbat was perpendicular to the flow of the Moskva River. A granite staircase running from the hotel led straight to the embankment and the riverbus station. Constantine paid the fare and sat back, watching the scenery pass by.

The river made a gradual slant to the south before snaking back north in an tight hairpin turn. On the tip of this narrow headland formed by the Moskva, a group of baroque churches reared up beyond a medieval stone wall, crosses topping their onion-shaped golden cupolas.

Fortified by a wall joining twelve towers along its perimeter, the Novodevichy Convent served as an outpost that protected Moscow's south-western borders since its founding in 1524. Ladies from royal and aristocratic families lived here in seclusion. It was the centre of Russia's spiritual life, for it held the Hodigitria— the Smolensk Icon of the Mother of God, which dated back to the beginnings of the Christian religion, painted by the Holy Evangelist Luke himself.

The fortress-convent was dominated by the perfect Smolensky Cathedral and its bell tower, surrounded by four other temples and chapels, and monastic chambers. The Convent's sacred cemetery had long since been converted into a necropolis for Soviet VIPs, and significantly extended. Here, among the 26,000 tombstones was the one that marked the grave of Lazar Kaganovich.

As well as that of Boris Yeltsin, his father's murderer.

And the Novodevichy Convent was also the residence of Father Ilia, Metropolitan of Kolomna, his mentor. Within sight.

So near, and yet so far.

Constantine could not risk venturing to the Novodevichy directly. After the blood-drenched frenzy in Liechtenstein, those who'd attack him would be alert to his determination to bring Malinin's documents to the Metropolitan. The Convent would be under surveillance, easily maintained throughout the day. A cozy park in front of it, with numerous benches circling a duck pond, was a natural position for watchers. Yet he *had* to transfer the documents to Ilia personally!

He hoped his solution would work.

Finally, the riverbus pulled to a stop next Constantine's destination—the great Cathedral, so contrasting with the red stars of the Kremlin visible ahead.

The Cathedral of Christ the Savior stood in all its majestic splendor on the banks of the Moskva River, its image reflecting in the water, its golden dome rising towards the heavens. Russia's sufferings transcended through the fate of the most magnificent church of the Orthodox world.

Construction of the Cathedral began after 1814 to commemorate the triumphant victory of the Russian nation over Napoleon Bonaparte. By 1883, works had been completed and the first service was held on May 23rd to worship the Savior. With the 35-meter main cupola, the temple reached 103 meters in height, being the tallest edifice in Moscow of its time.

In 1931, Stalin ordered that the Cathedral be demolished. The man who had personally detonated the explosive charges under the Cathedral of Christ the Savior was Lazar Kaganovich. It took three blasts to bring down the Cathedral completely. The area was cleared for the future Palace of the Soviets—a gargantuan abomination three times larger than the Great Pyramid of Giza, higher than the Empire State Building, with enough space to hold a mass of 21,000 communists. The scale of the project was so staggering that by the time Stalin died, only the 17-meter-tall podium had been completed atop the foundation and the basement. And that was it; the Palace never materialized.

In the nineteenth century, it had taken almost seventy years to build the Cathedral of Christ the Savior, and another seven decades in the twentieth to start rebuilding it. Sentenced to death by a crazed mob, it was resurrected after the collapse of the atheistic regime.

Somehow, the new Cathedral had never set off any feeling inside Constantine, and looking at it now, he still felt hollow. Or, rather, the *Cathedral* felt hollow. It was artificial, not solely because of the coppery tint to the golden dome. The original Cathedral could not and would not be replaced—ever. What defines a church is not the geometry of its walls, but the spirituality of its builders. The real Cathedral had been shaped by the trial and burden of the Napoleonic war—Russia's Patriotic War, fought in the name, and with the help, of God—and the subsequent elation of victory. A symbol of thanksgiving to the Lord for salvation at the darkest hour.

The fake Cathedral was not a symbol of anything, it was a show. Amid cries for democracy, when all things Soviet were being destroyed with Soviet fervor and insanity, the ideological void left by Communism should have been filled with religion—but instead came a cult. A monetary cult that assumed the appearance of Christianity. Ilia had once told Constantine that faith could not return to Russia, because anyone who could bring it back had become extinct.

The rest were chameleons. Overnight, communists had turned into democrats, atheists pretending as believers.

The Cathedral's colossal structure, though if not the center of Russian Orthodox faith, had become the center of Russian Orthodox bureaucracy. In its present form, the would-be location of the flopped Palace of the Soviets wasn't far off its Communist designation—the Cathedral also acted as the quarters of the Holy Synod, which wasn't too dissimilar to a clerical Politburo.

Under the celestial dome, theatrical, televised services were staged on Christmas and Easter. Uncharacteristically for a place so seemingly divine, most of the everyday work was buzzing underground, in the realm of darkness.

After all, it was Stalin's basement.

It would take decades to wipe out Stalin's curse from everything he had touched.

The podium was so immense that the centrally-placed Cathedral took up only a quarter of its area, at least forty meters separating its walls from any of the podium's edges. That was why the church felt distant as Constantine entered the podium's ground level. Like a flower that had broken through concrete, the new Cathedral was flawed and sickly, its roots planted firmly in the bedrock of the evil past, but Constantine knew that cared for and nurtured, it would blossom again, as it had centuries ago, filling with true faith.

Inside, Constantine found the souvenir store amid the myriad facilities. It offered products ranging from icons and books to multimedia discs and stickers, but he didn't come here for the merchandise. His eyes searched for a single object, his throat becoming parched as he found it. It was a plain-looking donation box, its sign urging to help children suffering from cancer. However, the charitable effort was not made on behalf of the Orthodox Church, and the box also served a second purpose. The name of the fundraising organization was stenciled in small print.

Free Action.

It was his pre-arranged dead drop.

Constantine inserted a folded banknote through the slit in the box. Inside the banknote he had hidden a scrap of paper with a handwritten message for his contacts at Free Action. Constantine was asking to arrange a meeting with Metropolitan Ilia.

As soon as he had completed the procedure, Constantine returned to the embankment, and another riverbus took him in the reverse direction, back to the Ukraina Hotel. Back to safety, and comfort, and sleep. If only all three could last a few hours.

4

The box was taken off at regular intervals, its contents examined.

Constantine's note, together with other bills and coins, genuine donations, was picked out minutes after the dead-drop, and placed in a sealed envelope. A courier carried the envelope several blocks away from the Cathedral, up the Marx prospekt, past the Kremlin, the State Duma, and the Bolshoi Theatre, to Lubyanskaya Square.

The note's ultimate destination was the desk of FSB Director Frolov.

Reading the note, Frolov allowed a rare smile to crease his lips.

Free Action, his own creation, had fulfilled its role. A fictitious organization—mysterious, evasive, backed by truth built solidly around fundamental lies to support the conviction of its authenticity. The perfect conduit to bring the documents to his possession.

5

*L*ightweight, the clouds passed through the sky in nebulous wisps, stretching, swirling ... Stars twinkled like jewels on a satin blanket of dark blue. Below the shimmering yellow moon disc, amid the blue-tinted hills, the tiled roofs stood. He marched towards the hamlet, as gentle drafts of wind fanned his hair together with the ethereal clouds.

He looked at the sky again, breathing it in, letting the night air carry him across the Rhine, to the tiny Principality huddled at the base of the forest-lined summits. Suddenly, his eyes locked on a single house. The large wooden front door opened, and two figures emerged, Maxim Malinin and Frau Hasler, their clothes dripping blood.

The two dead bodies chased him. He crashed on his back. The sky, sparkling blue, plaintive and serene, exploded with fat blotches of crimson red. He got up, his legs struggling to obey, always too slow, and ran to the bridge. The Rhine was black, decaying.

And above, streaks of blood crisscrossed the sky, filling it, booming with last gasps of the dying, threatening to wash over him, and there was blood gushing from his ears, and he clamped his hands over his head, running, trying to escape the blood-red world he was under, but there was no escaping the red sky, and his mind dissolved in a scream—endless and frantic, eyes shut ... running ... blood sprouting through his hands ...

Screaming, Constantine bolted upright in his bed, waking from the nightmare. He was panting, heart drumming in his throat, forehead clammy with sweat. It took him several moments to realize that he was in a bedroom ... Strangely, it wasn't Frau Hasler's.

In France there were nights when he would dream of coming home, taking the elevator to his apartment, opening the door, and as he woke up, finding to his horror that none of it was real. And now, when he was back in Russia, his mind found other horrors to fill his nights with.

He got off the bed and approached the window. Moscow was aglow with lights from neon signs, huge buildings, and entire streets, and the traffic that never thinned. Across the shimmering river, the white house stared right at him. Backlit with a faint blue, it was more beautiful than ever. Constantine felt his eyes moisten.

Sleep was unattainable. It was three in the morning. Midsummer nights in Moscow were fleeting passes of twilight and daybreak; sunrise was already approaching. He could not allow himself to brood in the empty time before his nine p.m. meeting with the Metropolitan.

He had to prepare himself for the meeting. Retrieving the Samsonite, he decided it was too bulky to carry to the rendezvous site. He would leave it there with the money inside while he was away. The disc was miniature, easy to conceal in a pocket. The papers he would tuck under his shirt.

The papers ... Constantine's fingers flipped through the yellow pages. They smelled of age. And death.

He went back to his bed, carrying the final testament of Lazar Kaganovich, written a quarter of a century ago. Constantine held the sheets as Kaganovich had held them, felt the paper in his hands as he had felt it, and the words, made alive as Kaganovich had written them, were about to become alive again as Constantine would read them.

The historian in Constantine was riveted by professional curiosity, and his cultured Russianness demanded to look in the murderer's eye. Whichever side was stronger, it urged to learn more about Lazar Kaganovich. And about the man's Master.

Stalin.

6

Lazar Moiseyevich Kaganovich was born in a poor Jewish family outside Kiev in 1893. Like Stalin, he had no formal education. Like Stalin's father, he barely made a living repairing shoes. Lazar's life took a fateful turn in 1911 when he first attended a Communist meeting in Kiev. The performance of one Marxist theorist at that assembly inspired the eighteen-year-old shoemaker to become a Party member. The fiery, passionate star spokesman of the Revolution was Leo Trotsky.

A local activist during the October Revolution of 1917, Kaganovich was noted for his decisiveness by Molotov who transferred him to Moscow. In the following years, Kaganovich climbed up the pile of corpses towards the summit of the Politburo Olympus, his thick boots crushing the skulls of friends and foes alike—even his own brother.

Trotsky and Kaganovich. One man's dizzying ascension timed with the other's downfall. The man Trotsky had unwittingly introduced to power would see to his demise. With Lenin's death in 1924, Trotsky, the heir apparent, was ousted by Stalin from the top flight of Bolshevik hierarchy. In the same year, Kaganovich became a member of the Central Committee.

After his fall from grace, Trotsky's opposition to Stalin could not last long. He was exiled to Kazakhstan in 1928, and deported from the country a year later.

The rest of Lazar's biography read like a list of crimes, and the early thirties marked the zenith of his career. Minister of Petroleum, Minister of Industry, Minister of Construction, Minister of Transport, Secretary of the Central Committee, Deputy of the Comintern.

Like any other of Stalin's men—Molotov, Beria, Malenkov—he functioned as filler for government posts. Only *one* man wielded all the power in the country, the man who had replaced

God in a godless country. The Politburo was a stack of faceless cardboard cutouts that Stalin used through—and for—terror. Each of them knew that when they acquired actions of their own, voices of their own, and their own *thoughts*—their own *deaths* would follow instantly.

For Stalin, Lenin's style of giving out written orders to execute millions was an idiotic waste of authority. The Master never implicated himself, putting his puppets in charge of the purges.

So formally, it was Kaganovich who conducted the repressions of the 1930's, and proving his worth, he hunted for Stalin's enemies with wild-eyed zest. The bloodletting wasn't limited to Party ranks alone. Ferocities in Ukraine brought that land to a famine that claimed two million lives. Under his supervision, a local hard-hitting cadre by the name of Nikita Khrushchev emerged as the most remorseless headsman. In rural Russia, thirteen million people were terminated by the agricultural collectivization that Kaganovich commandeered. The Cossacks were annihilated as a nation that endangered the Communist cause.

Orchestrating the mass murders, Kaganovich felt that his own time would soon come. The words in his last testament poured across the pages in waves of relived desperation, the anticipation of doom. There was the horror of witnessing Molotov's wife betrayed by her husband, and Lazar's own brother, Mikhail, betrayed by himself. And throughout all the treachery, the bestial scramble for self-preservation among killers, no one felt remorse or regret. A son would kill his own father; a mother would strangle her child. They were fighting for a just cause. No form of insanity was unacceptable if the Master demanded it, if the *enemies* within were still plotting against their Soviet Motherland. Those who were branded as enemies pleaded guilty and begged to be shot, if only their deaths could benefit their great country.

Night after night, as Kaganovich returned from Stalin's drunken parties, he expected to see visitors in a black NKVD car pulling up to his house to arrest him. When the Master was especially cordial, everyone knew it was a bad sign, his last goodbye to a dear comrade he was about to dispose of.

But no one came for Kaganovich then, as everyone around him in the Party list dropped dead before a firing squad, their relatives, wives and children freighted to Siberia in his trains. Only the war had come.

Kaganovich's description of the wartime effort amazed Constantine—

not by what was written there, but rather, what *wasn't*. His account of the first days was shockingly brief, disjointed, *irrelevant*. Constantine knew why. *No undue elaboration, no self-implication.* Something had happened—something too frightening for Kaganovich to mention in a secret diary forty years later, as if Stalin would come back from the dead and crush him.

After the war ended, fear needed to return to the triumphant country. It was coming: new terror, new purges, new blood. Unlike anything seen before.

As Constantine finished reading the last pages, what he learned about Kaganovich chilled him to the core. He set the rusted papers aside, fingers trembling, stunned by the final revelation.

There was even more on the encrypted disk—written by another dead old man. All the answers were there.

A sudden thought gripped Constantine. He knew a lot about Lazar Kaganovich ... *But who was Maxim Malinin?*

7

Every morning as he walked around the Novodevichy Convent, the pain in Ilia's foot pulsed where the toes should have been. All these years, his mind denied that a part of his body was no longer there. He had lost the toes to frostbite in a Moscow bombed by the Germans and swept by the cold. He remembered the air raid shelters, and his father and brothers who went to the frontline and never returned. It was the cold and the self-sacrifice that had won the war. If not for the Battle of Moscow stopping the blitzkrieg, the world would never be the same. It had made Stalingrad and Kursk possible, but the Germans had met their doom in 1941; from then on victory had come down to throwing enough Soviet bodies at Hitler's armies.

Ilia was a survivor who should not and *would not* have survived, if it were not for God's mercy.

In Moscow, he'd once had a home and a loving family—before an air raid that took away everything except his life. Struggling on his crutches, he towed himself to the Novodevichy Convent.

The Convent, too, was a survivor.

Over the five centuries, these walls had seen the fall of two dynasties of Russian czars. After the revolution, in 1922, it was shut down, the nuns driven out by cutthroats. By 1939, it remained as one of only 400 churches in all of Russia; the other 80,000 had been vaporized.

And it survived the war—the waves of German bombings that rained on Moscow.

The Great *Patriotic* War was a term coined by Stalin intentionally as homage to the original Patriotic War that ended in victory over Napoleon. His years at a seminary had taught Stalin that when tragedy came, the people would not turn to communist ideals to save them. To win, the people needed patriotism.

They needed God.

And God's help.

Thus, Joseph Stalin, demolisher of churches, brought religion back. But there weren't enough priests. A seminary was opened at the Novodevichy, officially titled as a "theological institute" that offered quick Christian education. The Novodevichy had become the largest repository of Orthodox texts, and Ilia's mind consumed them eagerly.

The gates of the Novodevichy were still the same as when he had passed through them for the first time. He had joined the Church after Stalin's death, at a time when Khrushchev persecuted religion with renewed fervor. Ilia remembered the cloudless morning ... the elation of touching holy books.

With passing years, Ilia had learned about the Kremlin collection—and the atrocities of the Bolsheviks. And he also saw that his clerical brethren did not always share his motives of entering priesthood.

The Convent stood as it had for centuries, while the Communist empire crumbled. Yet the age of democracy brought heartbreak instead of change. He had fought against the repressive system from the outside, and now found himself *inside* it. He felt that atheists governed the Church.

His post as Metropolitan of Kolomna was symbolic. The Novodevichy was where everything had started for him. But it was less of a monastery and more of a tourist landmark. In effect, by this appointment Ilia had been ousted from the politics of the Church—a trade-off that equally satisfied the Holy Synod and Ilia himself. He still led his private crusade against the aftermath of Bolshevism—as before, covertly. New declassified documents, more facts, hidden crimes of the Soviets against the Church emerged. At times, he thought his investigation would yield no tangible results, until a human rights group approached him to offer assistance. A *liberal* group, come to think of it! Free Action. They claimed their mission was searching for truth, fighting the governing bureaucracy that did everything to shut them down. At first Ilia treated them with cautious skepticism, but the findings they shared with him were too convincing, too important to discard. And they shared Ilia's cause: a final denouncement of Communism.

And then a brilliant student appeared at Sergiev Posad.

Ilia's monastic vow of celibacy did not prevent him from having a son like Constantine. But his heart was full with anguish at the guilt he felt for making the child part of his dangerous search. Old fool! Dear Lord, *forgive* me! What madness had he thrown Constantine's pure, innocent soul into?

Now, as he walked along the Novodevichy's courtyard, with every step the Metropolitan's cane tapped lightly against the ancient stones. Solitary sounds in the endless vacuum of silence. The early morning was as desolate as his heart. Perhaps everything *was* pointless, he wondered. His personal quest was not worth the cost of threatened lives.

A sharp whisper startled him.

Ilia halted. His hand gripped the cane tighter.

"Your Eminence!"

Abruptly, a touch brushed his shoulder, pricking his nerves.

Ilia turned to see a man standing right behind him like a wraith. The collar of his brown leather jacket was pointed up to hide a part of his face, but Ilia recognized Herman Weinstock, his only ally, the leader of Free Action.

The manner of his approach bewildered the Metropolitan, but before he could demand an explanation, Weinstock bowed deeply, holding out his palms, his right hand placed over his left.

"Bless me, Lord."

As his perplexity evaporated, Ilia put his right hand into the man's outstretched palms, and Herman brought his lips to it, kissing the wounds of Christ.

Drawing back his hand, Ilia asked with concern, "Herman, what has happened?"

As he rose, Weinstock's eyes were level with his, burning. He was of medium height, a timid middle-aged man of great physique, but always hunched and constrained.

"Lord, I have good tidings. We have received a message from Constantine. He is here, in Moscow. He wants to see you."

Ilia leaned against the cane to support his weight, his legs suddenly weak. Gasping, he held his chest where pain lanced from his heart.

"Are you all right?"

Weinstock reached out to hold the Metropolitan, but wincing, he motioned that he was fine.

"Constantine! Thank God!" Ilia breathed. "When?"

"Tonight. He wants to see you tonight."

Ilia's body sagged over his cane.

"God is with us."

Weinstock nodded.

"But the venue he has chosen ..."

"Yes?" Ilia frowned attentively.

"It may be unsafe. And we have no means to change it," said Herman Weinstock. "If you allow ... I can suggest a plan."

8

No disaster compared to the stampede occurring in Moscow Metro at rush hour. Constantine worked his elbows, making his way along the seething throng of humanity. He could have evaded the flood of evening commuters, but his timing was chosen consciously, intended to decrease the chances of being detected by the subway's security cameras.

The Metro was high-tech, as the busiest in the world should be, but besides all the modern equipment, little ever changed. It was also the world's deepest, designed to withstand air raids with ease. As an impossibly long and steep escalator took Constantine down below, he examined the exquisite interiors of Kievskaya Station. Its décor bloomed with magnanimous use of marble, chandeliers, statues, and paintings. The sheer grandeur worthy of a museum was breathtaking—as any display of Soviet dominance was meant to be. Each time Constantine entered these so-called "palaces of the people," he was fully apprehensive of the price that the luxury had come at. Lazar Kaganovich, the foreman of the Metro's construction, had subjected laborers, most of them volunteers, to conditions worse than those in the Nazi camps. He knew that some of the marble under his feet had been recycled from the wrecked Cathedral of Christ the Savior.

Thinking about it, Constantine concluded that Moscow was a city of cemeteries. Even in Moscow's very heart, next to the marvelous cathedrals, the Red Square was a burial-ground with Lenin's undead corpse open for public display. Over a hundred urns containing Communist ashes were entombed in the Kremlin wall. The Donskoy Monastery, infested with the bones of Beria. The desecrated Novodevichy Convent, and another fortress-come-cemetery, the House of Government—a funeral pyre ...

At the other extremity of Kutuzovsky, invisible behind dense growth and even denser security checkpoints dotted across the occupied hectare of land, was Stalin's Blizhniaya Dacha. The place where the Master had died.

The dacha's stretching, barn-like corridor and gray rooms existed as fresh images in Constantine's head, brought up by the writings of Kaganovich.

Despite the musky dampness coming off the congestion of bodies packed in the train, Constantine shuddered.

Beyond the cursed dacha was the site he'd picked for the rendezvous with Ilia.

Kuntsevo Cemetery.

9

When Constantine returned to broad daylight, the air was thick with approaching rain. By the time he entered the cemetery, the skies were overcast, which satisfied Constantine. The visitors to the graves of Kuntsevo were few, and the rain would discourage those who bothered to remember their dead. He was glad that the plastic zip-up folder containing the papers and the disc was waterproof.

Unlike the celebrity-filled Novodevichy Cemetery, the graveyard at Kuntsevo was mainly reserved for military commanders, with a few notable exceptions. The Cemetery's most prominent corpse was Soviet Premier Malenkov.

There was a haze of old mysteries surrounding the Kuntsevo, courtesy of the KGB. As Constantine walked towards the designated part of the cemetery, he passed a plaque which carried the name of one F.F. Martens. In fact, it was none other than Kim Philby.

The grave that Constantine reached at last was just as deceptive in presentation. Engraved in the cold marble surface of the slab were the letters RAMON IVANOVICH LOPEZ. An inscription in a smaller type underneath declared that the remains, when alive, had been honored as a Hero of the Soviet Union. Only the claim about the dead man's medal was true—but not his name nor the reason for the highest decoration in the Soviet military. This information had been classified once, but now it was commonly known that Lopez was the alias of Ramon Mercader, the agent who had rammed an ice pick into the head of Leo Trotsky on a fine August day of 1940 in Mexico City.

Constantine was early—more due to agitation rather than caution. His effort of scouting the area was intense but naïve in terms of professional countersurveillance. Still, at least he did his best to prevent any sloppy or arrogant ambushes.

No less nervous, Constantine found cover in a tight space blocked between a bronze monument and the body of an ancient oak. Peering out from his concealed position, he had a direct line of sight at Mercader's grave and every alley that led to it.

Constantine waited.

The seconds stretched until time froze. He couldn't stand it anymore!

He had to tell the truth to the Metropolitan!
The truth!

Impatience clawed at him. The wait was maddening—and then panic snowballed. *Maybe he isn't coming? Could it be that they got him . . . ?* That was too horrible to contemplate.

First drops splattered on a tombstone nearby, and then the walkway was dotted with moisture. Just as a soft drizzle began, a solemn figure appeared at the designated spot, in front of Mercader's grave.

Ilia!

Constantine wanted to rush out to him and—

He willed to restrain himself. He dared not attempt to be reckless—not when everything hung in the balance.

So near and yet so far.

Something churned inside Constantine as he looked at a man that was everything to him now, unable to reveal himself.

The Metropolitan stood motionless, propped against his cane like a living statue, only the wind moving his plain black cassock. Dressed like an ordinary priest, he appeared defenseless. His eyes gazed in the direction of promise and hope, waiting for Constantine to appear any moment now. Ilia, the closest person Constantine had to a father, resembled an obedient child left alone by a parent, the roles crazily reversed.

Constantine scanned the vicinity. No one. It was as if the cemetery had become completely deserted, that he and Ilia were the only two people in the world.

Wait. Diligence and discipline—were these not the virtues instilled by Ilia? *It could still be a trap,* his senses screamed. *Be patient—or die!*

Turning away from the forlorn figure of the Metropolitan, he concentrated on the alleys. Still empty.

Mentally, Constantine started a count, to mark the time and draw off desperation. With excruciating slowness, seconds turned into minutes. Finally, he decided the longer this stalemate continued, the higher the chance of someone actually appearing, either by accident or intent, when he made his move—and what would he do *then*?

Constantine broke away from his cover and made a dash. Ilia's face lit up with a mixture of astonishment and relief as he recognized the man who approached him.

"Constantine! My boy—"

His voice trailed off as he was overcome with emotion. There was so much one had to tell the other. A myriad of questions and answers passed between them, but they did not need to voice any, understanding reflecting in their eyes as they looked at each other wordlessly.

Gently, Constantine took the old man's elbow and guided him along an alley, away from the open area.

Constantine's descriptions were ragged as he recounted the meeting with Malinin, getting to the core, the reason behind everything.

The Kaganovich diaries.

As he told Ilia about the papers, Constantine asked: "Do you remember Stalin's words to Molotov shortly before his death? At the map?"

The Metropolitan nodded. Those words were of a kind that was never easy to forget.

When Stalin surveyed the borders of Soviet territory after the war, he turned to Molotov and said:

From the clutches of capitalism, the First World War freed a single country. The Second World War established a socialist camp of several countries. Our next step is to free the entire world.

"A nuclear Third World War was Stalin's dream, Father! It wasn't madness of a sick, dying old man. Everything was *real*. The purges were building up, the names in the notepad marked and crossed. *Jews.* He was targeting Jews—those he'd spared years ago with great foresight. He would punish their alleged plot, their sympathizers and associates, their Zionist controllers in the newly-formed State of Israel, and the guardians of that state—Americans."

Ilia's voice was an urgent whisper. "Then you're saying that those men in the Politburo ... "

"They killed Stalin. *Poisoned* him at the Blizhniaya Dacha. Khrushchev, Malenkov, Beria, Molotov, Kaganovich—they all took part in the killing of their caesar." Constantine paused, the handwritten confession still fresh in his memory. "Finally there's proof."

Ilia crossed himself. "So it's true," he said, shaking his head in bewilderment and stroking his white beard.

Suddenly, out of nowhere, a shadow materialized.

An athletic man, clad in leather, was blocking their way. He projected a deceptive impression of mediocrity, someone easily ignored elsewhere—but not *here*, and not *now*!

"It's okay, Constantine," the Metropolitan said calmly. "This is Herman Weinstock of Free Action. He was the one who received your note."

Constantine vaguely recognized the name. Weinstock was the mastermind of his escape to France.

"The area is secure, Your Eminence," Weinstock said. "We are alone here. My people have taken positions around the cemetery to warn of any danger."

"God bless you and your deeds," Ilia said in acknowledgement.

"It doesn't mean we must stay here long enough for the danger to *come*. It would be safer to leave—as soon as possible. I have a car waiting outside. Do you have the documents with you?"

Constantine's heart spiked.

"*What* did you say?"

"The documents. Are they with you?"

It wasn't the interest alone that rattled Constantine. Everything came together: the context of the words, the edge in the voice, the stance, the burning eyes. The face—emotionless, forgettable—was a mask scarier than the black balaclava of the monster who'd assaulted him on that dreadful night—or was it the *same* man? The eyes, my God, the *eyes* . . .

Several moments of the abrupt stupor produced an irritated scowl on the mask-like face of the stranger.

"Really, we have no time to waste. This place is dangerous. You're only making things difficult for yourself," Weinstock said, reaching inside his bomber jacket, whipping out a gun and pointing it at Ilia.

Before Constantine's reflexes could work, the muzzle spat out a flash. The Metropolitan collapsed.

The gun shifted to Constantine's face.

"Get *down*! Put your hands on the ground! Right *now*!"

Constantine did not follow the commands barked by Ilia's killer. He stood petrified, reeling from a horror that returned to ravage his sanity! His eyes were on the old man's inanimate body. *Father Ilia had just been killed!*

Trancelike, Constantine turned to Weinstock. The killer's features were twisted with rage, hand drawn to deliver a blow. The motion was lightning-fast, practiced. But regaining clarity and decisiveness, Constantine made a swifter move. Just as the gun-wielding hand swung to impact against his skull, Constantine sidestepped the strike, and lunged out in a low stance, knees bent at right angles. His elbow, snapping out like a battering ram, stamped into Weinstock's solar plexus.

A grunt of pain and shock accompanied the loss of balance. Even before Weinstock hit the ground, Constantine broke into a run.

He rushed along the long alley, searching for an opening. A searing white flash blazed, followed by a crack. What he momentarily feared as a gunshot was a rainstorm. The squall unleashed its full fury in an instant, lashing down at everything below the black skies.

And then more thunderclaps sounded as the ground at Constantine's feet erupted—*real* gunshots, aimed at him! He zigzagged and dove sideways for cover.

Somewhere behind, the killer's voice shouted, "*Stop* him!"

Shadows moved, blurred by the driving rain. A pincer formation of three men, one closing in, the others flanking.

There was no way out, but for one. Constantine jumped over the low fence that bordered off the graves, wet earth squishing under his feet as he darted past granite headstones and wooden crosses. He tried to visualize the cemetery's layout, needing an avenue of escape, a direction to choose.

It didn't matter. His pursuers limited his choices, surrounding him, *cornering* him. His shirt and jeans stuck to him, wet and heavy from the rain. Mud filled his shoes.

He stopped and glanced around. No route was left open by his enemies. They were circling around him, tightening a noose. But their ranks were still broken too far apart, having been forced to regroup by Constantine's unexpected maneuver.

He found a weakness in their line, and charged headlong. One of his pursuers froze, taken aback, seeing that the quarry was running straight at him. The man tried to meet him with a rising knee, but Constantine flung himself into a crashing tackle, elbow out. Knocking into each other, Constantine was the one better off, his hit connecting, his opponent barely conscious as they landed.

Constantine rolled, hurrying to rise.

Bodies—running, skidding in mud—piled on top, smothering him.

Constantine screamed like he never had in his life. A hand clamped down his mouth, trying to silence him. He bit. Now it was the hand's owner who screamed. Someone else punched Constantine, and he let go, jarred, an ugly taste of blood in his mouth. He was subdued. Powerful tentacles twisted his arms, fingers dug into his jaw. Four of the bastards were holding him up, presenting him to Weinstock, their leader, the natural-born killer who had destroyed his life a year ago.

Constantine shrieked, "You son of a *bitch!*"

Weinstock smirked. "Fool."

Then, savagely, he slammed the pistol butt against Constantine's head.

10

The house in Bykovo offered all the comforts, but not the burdening presence, of civilization. Heeding Klimov's advice, Sokolov came here for a few days of peace and quiet, to wait out for the governmental upheaval to die down as the EMERCOM chief handled the backlash of their mission in Sochi. For once, Sokolov was beginning to appreciate his work leave.

Bykovo. The village conveniently placed on the mid-point between Moscow and Zhukovsky had all the peace and quiet one could ever ask for. Eugene Sokolov's home was secluded, tucked away in the woods, only a driveway connecting the plot of land to the estates of other cottagers. A microcosm created by his father, whose touch lived in every item belonging to the two-storied log house. It was all that he had left of the past. Due to the proximity to Gene's work, it had turned out naturally that he would occupy the house, and their family's apartment in Presnya had become Constantine's. And so it was, until his brother's disappearance.

Constantine ...

An entire year, not a single day of which had passed without Gene thinking about him. He would sometimes imagine that he was still there, near him, but it was so only in his memories and dreams, not reality.

Sokolov had received no help from the authorities, who added Constantine as one of the 100,000 Russian names that ended up in the missing persons list every year.

His own search became pointless as time progressed. He did not know why or where Constantine had disappeared, but he hoped that one day his elder brother would return. Even if it would take another five—or fifty—years, they would find each other.

Before then, his days would be tarnished by gnawing futility, the pain of not knowing the answers.

There was only one way to clear his mind from the torment—incessant workouts.

On the second floor of the dacha was his bedroom and study; the rooms below had been completely converted to accommodate his private one-man dojo, screened off from the rest of the floor by sliding *shoji* partitions. Bright sun rays passed through the wall-sized glass door that opened into the backyard where his Land Rover Defender was parked—it was an EMERCOM staff car, for he couldn't afford his own. Either wall was covered with frames—paper scrolls with the quotes of Sosai Mas Oyama on one side; on the other were blown-up black-and white photographs, the first pictures Gene had ever shot in his life—a portrait of his family. His parents and his brother. All gone.

The environment inside these walls felt like a living being, interacting with him. Years ago, the dojo was the place where Constantine had saved him from disability. After the shots fired in Beslan, he was bedridden for two months. The complete lack of motion had caused his muscles to atrophy. His normal life was on the line. Recovery would be painful, he knew, though he hadn't known just *how* painful. His legs caused the worst suffering. He started his daily warm-up with prayer and meditation, sitting in Japanese *seiza* style, the traditional kneeling position. Placing his weight on his heels, with feet and knees on the floor, the simple pose was torture. The pressure on his shins and ankles was crushing. Stretching exercises followed. Joints cracked. Stiff ligaments protested. Every cell in his body hurt.

After that, the real work-out began. He practiced his punches and kicks, first cutting through air, then battering a bag. Every strike reached an imaginary target—a masked gunman, or a black-clad woman with a bomb belt. Sometimes he would move outdoors, especially when he needed ample space for kata. Then came the weights, and his routine was finished by push-ups and sit-ups.

He had wanted to give up a thousand times. Each time when he knew he couldn't take it anymore, Constantine would prod him on, reassuring him, making him believe that he could return to normal life.

Four-hour sessions, one after another, day after day. It had been hell then, but he had recovered. He had been second dan before Beslan—and earned the fourth afterwards. He'd had to pass the toughest test in martial arts and overcome a hundred opponents to get it.

He'd done it all to punish—and prove—himself, to heap self-accusation—and reach ultimate redemption. On that horrible day in Beslan, he'd carried a six-year-old girl in his arms, running out of the burning school. And then the shots came, and the slug passed through him. *She* had died, yet *he* was alive! He would have given anything to have it the other way around. Convinced that a trained soldier would have done better in his place, he'd set out to surpass any soldier, to achieve physical perfection.

He'd accomplished his goal, purging the mixed poison of guilt and vanity, but above all else he had done it for his brother, the only person for whom his life had any worth.

As usual, Sokolov dressed in his karate uniform—the rustling, starched-white *gi*, and his black belt. The belt bore his name, sewn in golden katakana, a mark of his achievement. Now he entered his dojo with a new sense of strange emotional turbulence, similar to what he had experienced after Beslan.

Asiyah. The helpless, comatose young woman that so reminded him of the child he had failed to save. Thinking about Asiyah, remembering her face, he felt her longing for his protection. Leaving her, giving her away to the FSB was *wrong*. An inexplicable uneasiness was swelling inside him.

He tried to push it aside. He had other thoughts to occupy his mind—rational contemplation. The mystery of the Black Sea disaster intrigued him. *What* agent, chemical or otherwise, caused the killings—perhaps that would be known via the EMERCOM lab tests. But the essential questions were *who* had done it and *why?* Was it a show of force? A sample of a new destructive weapon? Then the choice of instrument for political assassination was unusual. He was vying for answers, and again he mentally returned to Asiyah. What could *her* role be in it?

Sokolov found himself pummeling the punching bag with more force than was necessary. He paused, grabbing a towel to wipe the sweat off his face, wondering what had come over him. Two hours of his work-out had gone in a blink. He felt a strange premonition ... No, it was a sound he heard.

Outside, car tires scratched against the gravel road, coming to a stop. Throwing away the towel, Sokolov opened the Japanese wall screen and walked past a small dining area to the front entrance, just as the doorbell rang. He glanced out the window.

Sure enough, a dark blue sedan was parked on a small clearing between his house and the pine grove.

Sokolov opened the door. Two uniformed grunts in gray suit-and-tie attire were waiting on the porch. Short hair that screamed former military—or active.

"Eugene Sokolov?" The statement-question came from a black-haired man with stained teeth. Both of them were of medium height, and he was the shorter of the two, reaching Sokolov's shoulder level in height. His right hand was bandaged.

"Correct. And who might you be, gentlemen?"

"FSB," said his partner. He had a flat, moon-like face and ginger hair. To add weight to his words, he emphatically produced his ID, holding it so that a pair of moon-like faces now stared at Sokolov, one real, one photographed. Captain Something-or-other.

"And you?" Sokolov turned back to the short, dark man.

Incomprehension crossed his face.

"Are you also with the FSB?" Sokolov clarified.

"Of course." The bandaged hand produced a similar badge from the inner pocket of the grey suit. Displaying it, he rose slightly to the balls of his feet, as lesser men tend to do.

Sokolov peered beyond the threshold. The car's engine was running. Apart from the driver waiting behind the wheel, another man, no doubt also FSB, was standing next to the car, smoking, ready to act as backup. Their strength in numbers was certainly alarming, as was their possible intent.

"If you dropped in for a friendly inter-service chat, I suggest you address my boss, the EMERCOM Minister. But he won't be too friendly, I assure you," Sokolov said nonchalantly.

"Mr. Sokolov—"

"*Major* Sokolov. I outrank both of you."

The round-faced Chekist was unperturbed. "The matter which brought us here is extremely serious. It concerns your brother."

Lightning struck Sokolov. It was electric rage.

"*What about my brother?*"

The Chekist's tone was official, reciting a procedural cliché. "Your brother, Constantine Sokolov, is wanted for the murder of Metropolitan Ilia."

Constantine? Murder?

"Impossible," Sokolov breathed.

"You should know otherwise, since you were his accomplice."

Sokolov's hand clutched the lapel of the grey suit.

"It's a *lie*! And you know it!"

Astonished, the Chekist uselessly tried to pry away the fabric of his jacket from Sokolov's death grip.

"You will tell me *everything* you know, *right now*!" Sokolov said coarsely. His arm trembled with fury.

The short man reached inside the suit again, and Sokolov knew this time he would show something more convincing than his ID.

"We are authorized to use force! Proceed with us to the car!"

He was pulling out his gun, and the smoker stepped forward to assist his colleagues.

Never letting his hostage go, Sokolov scythed the short chekist with a low round kick. The hit smacked inside his shin, wrecking his leg. He buckled, crying out in pain.

Seeing this, the smoker attempted to imitate the brutal kick, aiming it against Sokolov.

Sokolov used the attacker's motion against him, countering the inept challenge with a well-placed heel strike to his ankle. The smoker sank to the ground, yelping, clutching his knocked foot that was swelling rapidly.

Metal cracked, clasping around Sokolov's hand that held on to the moon-faced chekist.

The bastard handcuffed him!

"We can still do it the easy way or the hard way!" the round-faced man said, yanking the arm joined by the cuffs to Sokolov. "You choose."

"The hard way," Sokolov replied, propelling his unchained arm in an elbow uppercut.

His strike met the man's nose, smashing cartilage.

Groggily, the smoker was rising to all fours. Sokolov axed a high front kick that went through his jaw. The force of the kick almost lifted him off the ground, and he rolled on his back, out cold.

While the man handcuffed to Sokolov was busy holding his bleeding nose, Sokolov seized the wrist he was locked to.

He crisscrossed his forearms over the wrist and corkscrewed suddenly. The bone crunched, breaking. The chekist screeched at the top of his lungs.

"*Freeze!*"

It was the driver, wild-eyed, aiming a gun. His hands were steady.

Sokolov pulled his handcuffed would-be captor—now captive—to act as a human shield.

"Go ahead! Shoot!"

"Put your weapon away, you idiot!" yelled the short man with the bandaged hand, failing to get up. "We must get him alive!"

"*Where's my brother?*" Sokolov demanded.

"We don't know, dammit!" barked the short man, and blood shot out of his forehead, half of his scalp gone.

The driver, with his inadequate pistol, attracted a volley of tracers that sizzled through him.

An ambush! The sound of gunfire was coming from the woods!

The round-faced man who was shackled to Sokolov gasped as bullets pierced his lungs. Reeling, the man crashed down, and Sokolov dove for cover as glass shattered and splinters flew.

He had to get inside the house—behind the walls and whatever protection those wooden logs could offer. Sokolov crawled, but the bulk of the dead man arrested him with the handcuffs. Sokolov tugged him by the chain, dragging him along the floor, as well as trying to keep his own head low.

Inside, the bullets were devastating walls and furniture, scattering broken fragments across the floor. Sokolov pulled the corpse in and cleared the doorframe, hiding in relative safety under a window sill where the wall seemed to absorb the onslaught of gunfire.

There was a strange swooshing sound, and an object streaked through the empty window above Sokolov, leaving a trail of smoke as it landed across the room.

Sokolov rolled into a ball, shutting his eyes and ears.

As the projectile exploded, everything around him burst into flames.

11

The incendiary grenade unleashed a voracious tempest of fire. The wooden walls and floor boards went ablaze instantly, enveloping Sokolov. The pungent black smoke made him gag, his eyes watering. Intensifying, the heat waves baked his skin.

He was still shackled to the corpse!

Sokolov tore away the keychain from the man's belt. Releasing his hand from the bracelet, he scrambled away from the wall.

Sokolov sucked in air, suddenly dizzy. If he didn't die like a thrashing human torch, it would be due to the noxious smoke suffocating him sooner than that. The oxygen was fizzing out quickly—he already felt the effects, his thought and action retarded.

Air! It was coming inside the house to *kill*, not save. The wide open front door served as a lethal passage for a draft that spread the fire with double speed. Sokolov kept on crawling across the floor, not daring to rise, as the smoke was clouding up.

The flames spared nothing. Above the kitchen, the automatic sprinkler did little to extinguish the firestorm, but it still improved his odds of survival. Upon activation it sent a signal to the nearest fire brigade. And the little sprouts of water fell like manna—he tore off a sleeve of his gi and soaked it under the tiny shower. The wet fabric, pressed against his face, would reduce the intake of poisonous carbon dioxide.

Sokolov saw that the wall leading to the dojo was gone. The easily combustible shoji paper of the partition, the fastest to burn, was turning to ash. Sokolov grabbed the first solid object his hand managed to find—a lamp—and wrecked it into the burning frame of the screen, clearing his way as he leapt inside, half-crouching.

Being the farthest from the epicenter of the explosion, the dojo was still intact, but the smoke and the heat transformed it into a gas chamber.

Everywhere, the dry timbers of the house cracked, threatening to cave in and crush him under an avalanche of burning wreckage.

There! The thin wall-length window was all that separated Sokolov from the backyard.

Yanking the handle, he fell out, chased by a thick pall of black smoke.

Outside.

He choked and gulped at the same time, his heart banging like crazy, oxygen surging into his blood.

He stumbled into the backyard, where the Land Rover was parked.

The Land Rover was his only asset.

Around him, the forest was menacing. Sokolov had no way of knowing how many shooters were hiding in the trees, or whether they had moved in to surround him. Who were his enemies, and what was their training?

If they had dispersed, a blasting gun could emerge right before him at any instant. But going out in the open would spell immediate death, as proved by the four corpses from the FSB.

He needed to create a distraction!

His keys were gone in the fire. The Defender was locked—but a set of keys was inside, he remembered.

The chance stimulated him.

Hurrying, Sokolov failed to notice the cut on his arm as he broke the glass, released the lock and opened the door. Just as he'd hoped, the keys were there. He snatched the keys—but did not start the car, fearing that a sudden engine noise would alert the killers early. He wanted to stall until the last moment.

Nestled far in the back of the Land Rover, a full canister of gasoline helped him create a weapon. He poured the sharp-smelling liquid around the interior generously, covering every surface. As he emptied the canister, he unlatched the removable driver's seat, accessing the auxiliary gas tank. It had a capacity of forty liters, complementing the main eighty-liter tank of the fuel-hungry Defender. Sokolov unscrewed the cap off the top of the tank and replaced the seat.

He got behind the wheel and started the engine, which chugged to life with a half-turn of the ignition. From the glove box, where he kept emergency items, he took out a box of matches.

He shifted into first gear, releasing the clutch ever so slightly, until the heavy four by-four rolled into motion.

Sokolov lit a match, throwing it on the rear passenger seat as he dove out.

Landing on the grass, he saw the Land Rover lumber away, the interior flickering with flames.

Clearing the side of the house, the burning Defender reached the lawn, a timed bomb that was aimed at the source of the gunfire. As the killers realized this, a staccato of shots came at the car, piercing the aluminum, hammering glass, going for the tires. The Land Rover swayed like a drunk, but held its course.

There was no stopping it.

The bursts of automatic gunshots ceased.

He saw them running into the forest, at least two men in jungle fatigues, their complexion dark, Asian.

The Land Rover slammed into the trees. By this time, the fire had burned through the thin cushion of the passenger seat, and attacked the open gas tank.

Exploding, the 120 liters of gasoline blew chunks of metal off the Defender's frame, hitting a row of trees with the blast force of a napalm strike.

Stunned, standing there with his house and his car burning in front of him, Sokolov realized that the gunmen were Orientals. Who the hell were they? Why did they kill the FSB officers?

He could not let them escape. He had to chase them.

Sokolov slid into the woods.

12

The forest never brimmed with sunshine, muting it through its dense canopy, but now visibility was slashed to just a few meters, as a toxic mist drifted from the burning trees. The murky air could be either a foe or a friend. One misstep could lead to an injury. Treacherous roots covered the forest floor. A terrain of bumps and holes, covered with moss and wild grass, fallen branches, pine cones, and dead stumps, demanding calculation in every step. Sokolov was familiar with the forest of his childhood, but his enemies were not—and that made it twice as deadly for them. A cough forced by the smoke, a misplaced foot snapping a dry twig, grass rustling under body weight—all would betray them. Not only their location, but their numbers—which they themselves would not be sure of. The haze blinded them, and the possibility of exposure silenced them.

There was one advantage on their side that outweighed Sokolov's knowledge of the territory: they were armed. For the enemy, disclosed position equaled loss of stealth; for Sokolov such a mistake would lead to loss of life.

His senses tuned to pick up the faintest scrape in the distance, so other sounds became exaggerated, like the thundering drum beat of his heart, fueled by adrenalin. This, in turn, heightened his sense of danger.

His bare soles stung as Sokolov moved across the ground, invisible like a wraith. He had to force them out, immediately. *Divide and conquer.*

Sokolov felt a large rock under his foot, grabbed it and hurled it into the thicket with all his might. It landed, hitting something hard with a thump.

Sokolov registered the unnatural sensation. The sound—or a sudden lack thereof. A gentle rustling sound which he had taken for a leaf rolling in the breeze had suddenly stopped. A man had been moving, and on instinct, startled by a threat that was the flying rock, he had *halted.*

In a few moments, the almost imperceptible pattern of sound resumed. That was it. Sokolov locked in his memory the source of the soft rustling, and its direction.

Sokolov crept—anxious, feeling an influx of strength. A human shape came into focus—a man's back.

Sokolov was on him like a raging demon—which he was, having escaped from burning hell.

Sokolov wrung his right arm around the man's neck, the rigid side of his left hand slashing across the locked head, rendering him unconscious.

The man sagged in Sokolov's arms and he set the shooter on the ground.

Another shooter sensed that something with his partner had gone terribly wrong.

"Hey!" a voice yelled. The partner made no reply.

Nervous shots railed through the mist, short bursts traveling in every direction, hopeful to ward off a lethal blow. That convinced Sokolov that there was only *one* of them left. There would be no shooting unless a man was suddenly alone, driven by fear, showing no concern for hitting teammates by friendly fire.

The volleys ended, and the sole shooter broke into a run. Motion caught the eye, and Sokolov spotted a silhouette moving rapidly, dodging trees. Running deeper inside the forest, the man escaped the hanging mist, out into clear air.

But his ankle snagged against a crooked root, and he tripped.

Sokolov covered the distance in two leaps, and pounced. His heel crushed the man's wrist and kicked aside the automatic rifle; his knee plummeted down into the man's ribs, Sokolov's entire weight converging in a single point.

The Asian screamed something in his native tongue.

Sokolov forced him up and slammed him against a century-old pine.

He pulled out the Asian's belt and used it to tie his hands behind the tree trunk, in a manner that would aggravate the pressure in case of resistance. Then Sokolov searched him. The camouflage suit held spare ammo, a small encoded radio, a handgun, a lighter ...

And three photographs.

Tiny, laminated prints.

Close-ups.

Eugene ... Constantine ...

And Asiyah Kasymova.

Sokolov jabbed the picture of his brother into the man's face.

"*Answers.* Your life depends on them. Who are you, and who is *this*?"

"I received an order," he replied in accented Russian. "To kill the man on the photograph. We were told he could come to you, or you could lead us to him."

The arrival of the FSB men had interfered with those plans, Sokolov thought.

"Who gave you the order?"

The assassin shook his head in defiance.

Sokolov held up the photograph of Asiyah.

"And what about *her*?"

The man was silent. Sokolov repeated his question, this time pressing the handgun against the assassin's head, but his Oriental eyes showed no fear.

"I don't understand," the Asian answered.

Sokolov knew he would not extract any information. The man had stated the obvious, and nothing beyond. Sokolov would never resort to torture. Otherwise, all questioning would be a waste of time. He knew enough, anyway. The girl was marked for death. He was also willing to bet that these killers were Kazakh.

He had to move. Find a way out of here.

Somewhere outside the forest, sirens wailed. By some grim irony, they belonged to the firefighting brigades of EMERCOM. A tempting lure, illusory salvation that hindered immediate action. If the FSB, and someone comfortable with hiring assassins, were chasing Constantine and himself, he couldn't use any official routes.

Sokolov picked up the automatic rifle and disappeared.

13

Sokolov waded through the the woods, his mind rebelling against the insanity.

Death all around him. The gunshots, the flames, the *killings*—it was Beslan all over again!

Sokolov suppressed the thoughts. *Not now*, for goodness sake! Act! *Move*! Asiyah may still be alive!

And his brother! Dear God, *he* was alive! He was near, perhaps agonizingly so. Nothing mattered more than this knowledge, no matter how crazy the circumstance. Now there was more than hope to hang onto—he had *certainty*.

Rescuing Asiyah or finding Constantine—a choice he would loathe to make, but there was *none*! He had no means of finding his brother, no direction, no starting point—except for her. Somehow, *she* was the connection, the other target of the hit team. Everything was combining into a bigger picture that he could not see—yet.

He cleared the forest where a rural road dissected it. There was a single car parked off a curb, fifty meters ahead. It was a 5-Series BMW sedan, white in color but tinted gray by dust. Only the rear number plate stayed reasonably clean.

The plates. Instead of the ordinary white, they were blue, belonging to police vehicles.

What was this car doing here? He could hardly imagine a patrol car failing to react to gunshots within walking distance. There could be only a single explanation for any car to be found parked anywhere near the place.

It was the transport of the two assassins.

As he advanced toward the BMW, Sokolov discerned the shape of its single occupant, the driver, arm dangling out of the open window, cigarette wedged between fingers. When Sokolov was close enough to hear the soft idling of the engine and see the driver's tense features reflecting in the side mirror, the man flicked away the cigarette, his eyes following its glowing trail. It was then that he noticed Sokolov looming in the mirror, and reached for his gun. Twisting in the seat, he arched his body through the empty window to get a point-blank shot as he raised the gun, which—with a shock to his wrist—dropped to the road. Sokolov had knocked the weapon from his hand, striking with the butt of the Kalashnikov before he slashed it at the man's head.

As Sokolov opened the door, the driver's senseless body fell on the asphalt.

Sokolov searched him, finding a pair of handcuffs. He dragged the body around the car. Opening the trunk, he saw an arsenal that could benefit a small army. Five handguns and assorted boxes of rounds, three Kalashnikovs with sawed-off stocks and plenty of banana clips. Hardly typical police inventory. Sokolov was becoming proficient with handcuffs. He stuffed the body into the trunk, and shackled a wrist to a leg, slamming the trunk door closed.

Back at the driver's seat, he went through the contents of the glove box. Two fat billfolds of cash, another handgun, and—thankfully—a cell phone!

The phone was turned off. Sokolov took it apart to take out the SIM card. The model was a GSM device. He knew for a fact that all mobile networks were monitored by the FSB, and a SIM card logging into the network would be traced.

Sokolov threw the SIM card away and switched the phone on. Without the card inserted, the handset operated in emergency mode, meaning that instead of the conventional GSM signal that became unavailable, it used *any* radio waves to make emergency calls, and nothing else.

But it was the only call he needed.

EMERCOM.

The phone software booted and Sokolov dialed 112, the international number of distress. It had to work even if the handset had been reported stolen, and the unit's IMEI identification number was blocked.

He watched the icons appear on the phone's screen when a message came up.

The call went through.

An operator replied. Identifying himself as per special procedure, Sokolov demanded an encrypted line with Klimov.

A few seconds later, Klimov's voice boomed through the speaker.

"*Gene*! What happened? I have a firefighting crew chief on another line claiming he's at your place, finding bodies!"

"My house burned down. In fact, I was inside when it happened."

"Are you hurt?"

"I'm all right ... fine," Sokolov said between breaths. The effects of the clash were still catching up on him. "Where's Asiyah?"

"What?"

"Asiyah Kasymova. Where is she?"

"What's going on, Gene?" Klimov's voice was stern, but still full of concern.

"I've had an encounter with a team of professional assassins. One of their other targets was Asiyah. She may be in lethal danger as we speak, or she may already be dead. Is she still in FSB custody?"

"Yes, in the Central Clinical Hospital, as far as I know. Under the authority of their witness protection program. If she is in any danger, I'm sure they'll take care of her."

"The hell they will! They can't even take care of themselves. Those dead bodies in my house are FSB officers."

He could hear Klimov mutter a curse.

"The FSB attacked me. And someone else hired the men that burned my house. Now I'm wanted by both camps. I want you to contact Frolov and tell him to move Asiyah to a different location as soon as possible. I'll call you again soon," Sokolov lied.

"Gene, wait, hold on! I don't like the sound of your voice—are you sure you're okay? Can you reach the paramedics? Where *are* you?"

"Don't worry about me, my friend. And don't go searching for me—I'll find you myself when the time comes. For now, I'm dead as far as you're concerned. You don't know any of what I've just told you. I'm missing and presumed dead should anyone inquire. It's all connected with the mess in Sochi, so you and the guys better watch your backs as well. Take care."

Sokolov killed the connection.

The Central Clinical Hospital. It was all he'd wanted to hear.

He had utmost faith in Klimov, knowing he would do everything in his power to help. But even if the FSB followed up the warning, he could not rely on them acting efficiently. Regardless, there was only one thing he could do.

His mind was riveted on reaching the hospital, filled with desperate energy.

Fearful of electronic eavesdropping, Sokolov pried off the battery and hurled the disassembled phone through the window. From his anti-terrorist training, Sokolov knew that intelligence services could use any mobile handset to spy on its owner. Logging into a radio network, the IMEI identification also left a unique footprint, which could be used to hack the device and gain remote access to it. Although mobile carriers around the world did not advertise this Big Brother feature, a cell phone could be secretly used to feed audio and video streams through its microphone and camera to any computer—even if it was fully switched off. All that was required was the battery to be in its place.

As the phone broke into pieces, Sokolov engaged the roof-mounted blue siren, and sped away.

The ersatz police-car shell of the BMW belied raw power under the hood. Instead of a sluggish 520 model, it turned out to be an authentic high-performance M5, one of the world's most coveted sports cars. The BMW's engine growled, voicing the urgency that swelled inside Sokolov.

All too soon, the sky had grown dark. Sokolov winced as he saw storm clouds clash in the sky. Midsummer showers in Moscow were as fierce as they were frequent, bringing calamity to the poorly-maintained roads. A fat blob of a raindrop smacked against the windshield and streaked down before it was erased by the wipers that engaged automatically. And then the rain scattered more drops over the glass, drumming out its force.

He took the fact that the FSB was keeping Asiyah at the Central Clinical Hospital as a mixed blessing. On the one hand, it was a civilian institution that would be easy for him to reach. But as such, it was located near Moscow's heaviest traffic route, loaded with commuters that could well keep him stranded for hours. Making it in time could well be hopeless.

The thought forced a new feeling, but it wasn't panic. A clinical calmness associated with a rescue mission.

Resolve.

His foot pressed the accelerator harder.

14

Dazzling lights clashed in her head, whiting out the images of death, tipping her mind back into consciousness.

Before she opened her eyes, she became aware of distinct sensations. She floated in a cloud of numbness that gave off a faint smell of antiseptics coming off invisible surfaces.

When Asiyah finally did open her eyes, the overhead lights stabbing her temples, she discovered that she was alone.

It *was* a hospital. She lay in a white-walled room, fluorescent lamps above, a narrow bunk below her. Drab polka-dot pajamas were her clothes, right sleeve rolled up, an IV line connected to her arm. Hurriedly, she tore off the catheter, rubbing the purple bruise it had formed, panic swelling. What had they pumped her with? Definitely sedatives, but what kind? Amobarbitals? Had they performed chemical interrogation?

It didn't matter. She had been trained to withstand the so-called truth serum. Narcoanalysis was error-prone, the hypnotic effect probing the imagination more than memory. Regardless, she should have been dead by now—and yet, she was *alive*, which only meant that her captors still wanted something from her.

She calmed her breathing, overcome with sudden exhaustion. Her bones seemed to be aching. Her hands and feet felt so cold that she shivered. She wanted to close her eyes and go back to the comfort of sleep ... No. Must get up.

Pushing off the bunk, she attempted to raise herself, but her vision spun in a merry-go-round, and her knees buckled. She grabbed at the bed.

Slowly, her mind thawed off. Focused, she looked around the room.

There was a chair next to the bed, a folded blue robe placed on it. Donning the robe, she felt the extra layer of clothing give her some warmth. As she rounded the bed, she saw the security camera. Suspended under the ceiling, it was observing her from the far corner of the room. A door and a window were the only two links to the outside world.

The door's electronic lock, activated by magnetic keycards, had a red light blinking below the handle, an alarm likely primed.

Feeling stronger, she crossed the room to reach the window, holding the sill for support. Outside, she could see the foliage of trees. Birches and pines, a familiar blend of century-old plants, so good for recovering heart patients.

She *knew* this place! She had been here before, when her father—no!—don't call him that!—that *monster* was receiving treatment here.

The acres of forest, the alleys and benches, vivid in her memory from the long walks with him. A complex of several buildings scattered around. Straight ahead, cardiology ... the main facility to the right ... the maternity ward and pediatric care ... And the room she was in was located in the psychiatric ward.

It was the Central Clinical Hospital.

Moscow.

She murmured a grateful prayer, and plotted her next move. Her thoughts raced, her mind sharp, life returning to her body.

15

She would make them pay for their complacency. Without knowing it, they had provided her with weapons. Made of stainless steel, the IV stand was light enough to carry, weighing around three kilograms, but heavy enough to cause damage.

Wheeling the IV stand near the window, she contemplated her plan.

The window was three or four levels above the ground. Any attempt to use that avenue of escape was suicidal.

Perfect.

Mustering strength, she gripped the pole two-handed, like a hockey stick, the stand's low center of gravity resting on the floor. Lifting it, she banged its wheeled base against the reinforced glass of the window. Both the pole and the window rattled loudly. The armored glass was undamaged. Undaunted, she repeated the motion, this time with more force, shrieking as she struck.

"Let me *out* of here!"

She faced the camera, her cry hysterical, the metal in her hands smashing its lens.

There was audible commotion in the corridor outside the room. A rush of feet.

The lock clicked, and a man burst inside. Though he was wearing a lab coat over his suit, it hardly disguised his muscular bulk, all the more making him look like a guard instead of a doctor. Holding a shock baton ahead of him, he moved in to restrain her.

Asiyah struck him with the pole. He raised his arm to parry, but the steel shaft thudded, deflecting off his shoulder as it broke from Asiyah's grip, and knocking the baton from his hand. The baton clattered on the floor. Before he could recover and attack her, she snatched the shock baton and discharged several hundred thousand volts of electricity into him.

Asiyah's peripheral vision caught a second guard rushing through the doorway. The man lunged, grabbing at her. She zapped him, and he went down for good.

The short eruption of violence was over. Asiyah walked to the door, staggering.

Carefully, she peered out, eyeing the corridor in either direction.

It was empty. But not for long, she knew.

From one of the guards, she claimed a lab coat, and a master keycard. Locking the room behind her, she opted for the elevator instead of the staircase. The risk was justified. She knew she would not manage the stairs. She had to travel a long way down.

The elevator car was spacious, designed to hold a gurney and accompanying medics. Asiyah was quick to get in, pushing the button for a level *below* ground. Only when the doors closed and she felt the downward drag, did she let out a sigh.

Because the patients could not be taken outdoors for transfer from one building to another across the vast territory, especially during winter, a system of subterranean tunnels connected all the facilities of the Central Clinical Hospital. She intended to use one of them.

Asiyah would hardly be allowed to leave the psychiatric section through the front door unchallenged, but if she could reach the main building, her chances of escape increased, security virtually nonexistent. Leaving the hospital grounds was an entirely different matter, but she chose to tackle problems as they appeared.

16

Gliding through Kuntsevo, the black Lexus sedan headed for the Central Clinical Hospital. The two Asians inside it, shielded behind the car's tinted windows, kept their eyes on the road. Both men mentally prepared themselves for action, trying to curb the thrill that preceded it, just like in their days during military service.

Because its primary function lay in servicing top-level government officials, the Central Clinical Hospital was traditionally under direct authority of the Kremlin, being the most elite hospital in Russia, and among the best medical institutions in the world. And as such, it maintained strict security procedures, unchanged for decades. Formidable walls outlined the perimeter, entry possible only past guarded checkpoints. The first control measure was a separate exit from the highway that led to the main entrance. It was a view that had become familiar since it was televised in news flashes during Yeltsin's frequent illnesses: a patch of forest broken by a concrete fence, and a guard booth before the gates.

When the Lexus drew up to the barrier, the FSO officer admitted the car to the hospital's territory without question, paying attention to the car's special number plates, registered with the parliamentary staff of the State Duma.

The hospital was a town in itself, the tiny streets eerily deserted because of the downpour. The route was straightforward, following the road to the main compound, an oval-shaped structure with splayed-out wings. When the driver parked the Lexus in front of the medical unit, the passenger retrieved a handgun and attached a suppressor to the muzzle. Satisfied with his weapon, he hid it inside his leather overcoat, and stepped out of the car. Hurrying through the falling rain towards the entrance, he pulled up the collar of the coat to cover his face, a protection from glances as much as the weather.

Behind the palatial front door made of solid wood, the lobby of the main building was just as substantial, a Stalinist luxury that had been built to last. It would have looked spacious even when crowded, but there were not many people around, with only a few medical staff passing by silently on their errands.

It was easy to go unnoticed.

As though he had been a frequent visitor, the assassin did not linger at the information display, familiar with the floor plans. Flicking away specks of water from his coat, he traversed the lobby quickly.

Beyond the thick leather sofas, he reached the elevator he needed and pressed the call button, making sure nobody would accompany him on the way down—to the tunnel that led to the psychiatric ward.

17

Scraping inside the shaft, the elevator came to a stop. Asiyah stepped into the tunnel. Underground, the silence was total bar the hum of ventilation and the buzz of overhead lamps.

She was alone. It was a slow day at the hospital.

The tunnel was a white-walled corridor like any other, except for its length. It stretched infinitely like an abandoned subway shaft. Somewhere at the other end was another row of elevators. She did not see any surveillance cameras around, but that was no reason to shorten her stride. The lamps glared in the floor tiles, casting a sequence of white orbs that her leaden feet padded over.

The tunnel opened, she could see, into a foyer. It was a nexus that connected the main elevators to other underground hallways that branched from it like wheel spokes. For a moment, Asiyah was confused.

Which way to go?

Then she saw the elevators that joined the tunnel with the main building above. There were several cabins, the system designed so that at least one elevator was always available at either level to save precious seconds.

She strode towards a cabin in the middle, the indicator above showing that it was at the underground level.

She had no chance of reaching it.

When she was still a few meters away, another elevator opened.

She was taken aback, the initial numbness of exposure giving way to terror as she saw the Oriental man inside.

There was a menacing quality about him. She hadn't a doubt in her mind that the man was there to kill her. His own surprise at seeing her lasted only a split-second before lethal composure took over. He moved forward, fixed on her.

At once her survival instincts kicked in, shaking off her sluggishness. Every nerve cell became supercharged. The assassin started toward her, drawing his gun, his motions well-honed. At point-blank range, she was a target impossible to miss.

Before he could level his gun at her, she lunged, acting upon training over instinct. In the tunnel's confines, dodging sideways or running in retreat would have spelled instant death. The adverse movement *towards* the man made her opponent vulnerable. Asiyah eliminated the distance separating her from the killer, cutting down the time he had to make his shot, stifling his freedom of movement, the proximity so horrific that she could hear him suck in air when she struck him.

Thrusting the shock baton like a fencer, she jabbed the electrodes into his chest.

With the electric impulse disrupting the signals coming from his brain to the body, the assassin went instantly limp, paralyzed. His hand released the gun and he crashed back into the elevator cabin like a slain beast.

He lay immobile, eyes empty. The elevator doors engaged to shut—but, finding resistance against his numb legs, rolled back wide open.

Asiyah felt she had done enough to escape from the tunnel, and wasted no time. The second elevator was still waiting.

As she pushed the call button, she caught glimpse of the assassin regaining movement. He was still too stunned to to get off the ground, but he was trying to reach the gun at his side. Beating him to the gun was out of the question—she had to flee.

She darted inside the empty cabin and punched the button to go up.

Fear scalded her as she saw the door slide shut, creeping with agonizing slowness, as if conspiring with the killer to stall her escape. If he reached the button for the elevator, nothing would save her. Punches and kicks were useless against a gun.

The door sealed, and she pleaded for it to stay that way. Only when she felt the drag of the elevator rising did she remember to breathe again.

18

Sokolov was driving along the rural road that twisted through the forest, squeezing every bit of power from the car. It was an unfamiliar route to Moscow compared to the one he normally used from Bykovo, but the dashboard GPS screen provided navigation, plotting the shortest distance to the Ring Highway.

Moscow was shaped like a spider's web, originating from the enclosure of the Kremlin, weaving out exponentially, and secured by the outer circle of the Moscow Ring Highway—a gigantic race track that confined the city limits. On the map, the M5 was a blinking dot outside the southeastern edge of the web. A dark-colored, forested mass of land spanning between Kutuzovsky and the *western* part of the Ring was the Central Clinical Hospital.

Once he made it to the Ring, he would have to travel all the way along the circumference to the other extremity.

But first he had to get there. He pressed the accelerator all the way to the floor. The M5 howled and charged forward like a predator in full stride. A knot was tightening in his stomach as he navigated blind turns on the narrow road. Thankfully, the road was almost free of other cars. Whatever few sluggish vehicles he encountered forced him to veer off to the opposite lane and overtake, risking a head-on impact with an oncoming car, or a slide into the trees off the slick surface. And yet, he could not slow down. He tricked himself into thinking that the only way to overcome this was to finish the section quicker, so he attacked the turns, and the stretches between them, more aggressively. The BMW gripped the road tightly.

Instinctively, he referred to the GPS screen to monitor his position, as if his willpower would have any effect on distance. The first part of Sokolov's race ended as he turned onto the Ring. It was a sizeable highway of twelve lanes, halved by a concrete barrier. Sokolov fused into the stream of traffic, and charged along it. Siren shrieking, he piloted the BMW along the track of the Ring like a jet fighter, shifting to the left, overtaking. The motorists yielded, fearing the authority of the blue siren, and fell behind in puffs of minute spray their wheels kicked up.

As the lane cleared for him, Sokolov picked up speed, careless about all perils. To him, everything was trancelike, secondary to his goal. He looked with detachment at the green digits ticking off the M5's velocity on the HUD, as the car shot through vanishing scenery. Going at 140 ... 150 ... 160 kilometers per hour ... Water cascaded across the windshield. Rain bombarded the road. The needle of the BMW's speedometer passed two hundred, and it was still too slow! The isolated comfort inside the car warped the sense of speed, and danger. The mind adjusted to cruising velocity, and assured itself of complete safety, coupled with the narcotic urge to go faster.

All he cared about was time, his eternal challenger.

Amid distant trees, on the crest of a hill, he could make out the rooftop of the cardiology center, prominent at the edge of the hospital compound. The Central Clinical Hospital took up a park area located between Kutuzovsky and the Ring, neighboring Kuntsevo.

Sokolov took the exit that led to it.

Driving past the concrete fence that surrounded the Hospital, Sokolov glimpsed a break in the stretch of trees, and the main gate disappearing in the side window of the BMW. Alluring as it was, arriving at the heavily guarded checkpoint would have ended his effort right there. Unable to take a direct approach, he followed the perimeter of the Hospital, turning right, to a street cutting through a residential area that neighbored the medical facility.

There was another entryway—formally numbered third, yet functioning in a primary role, used on a daily basis by authorized vehicles that needed to be admitted without delay.

Even if he had no fixed appointment with any of the doctors, there was a way of getting past security.

For all the spaciousness within the compound, outside it was squeezed for space by residential blocks that grew tightly around it. Creeping through narrow driveways between houses, Sokolov separated from the main street and found refuge behind a set of high-rises, in a small yard made even smaller by a chain of parked cars. He stopped the BMW near a children's playground, which the shower made deserted, and got out.

The rain lashed his face and soaked the grimy rags of his gi. Sokolov rounded the car and opened the trunk. The man inside was still unconscious. Sokolov removed the handcuffs and dragged him out to the front of the car, placing him in the passenger's seat and strapping him with the belt.

Returning behind the wheel, Sokolov eased the BMW around the corner and activated the strobe lights as he pulled up to the hospital checkpoint.

He stopped the patrol car at the barrier. A security guard emerged from his booth, spurred further by Sokolov blasting the horn.

"I have an injured officer here!" Sokolov yelled through the open window. "Open the gate! Move!"

Sokolov's commanding demeanor generated the required effect. The guard had no reason to question Sokolov's order, seeing the condition of the BMW's second occupant, who probably required urgent medical assistance. Whether or not they were entitled to it was up to others to decide, so he did his routine job and let the police car through. He knew better than to act wise.

Sokolov floored the pedal, sending spray around, leaving the guard fuming at his recklessness as he blazed by. It never occurred to the guard that it wasn't the passenger's life that Sokolov wanted to save.

19

Asiyah could not tell if it was only her heart or her entire body shaking. She anticipated facing another gunman when the elevator reached ground floor. Instead, the lobby was empty, but for a receptionist and a guard who showed no interest in her. As she crossed it, she felt her spine tingle in the spot she thought a bullet would hit if the assassin caught up with her.

She rushed to the gargantuan front door and pushed it, slithering through the opening.

The unbounded view gave her a hint of freedom. Tumultuous black clouds were cast in golden outlines by the sun concealed behind them. A gust of wind swept the treetops and slanted the rain to touch her face. The air was crisp with ozone, clearing the moldy sensation left in her by the hospital. Across the alley, the compact parking lot was neglected.

She ran down the front steps, scanning the parked cars. She hoped to find one that would be easy to steal. There was always the likelihood of someone leaving the keys in the ignition, or keeping the vehicle unlocked. The leaden sky pelted her with raindrops. Asiyah hurried, though getting soaked wet was the least of her concerns. She glanced over her shoulder to make sure the assassin was not behind her. Just then, the light came on inside the farthest car in the lot as its door opened. A man emerged from the dark Lexus sedan.

The ground exploded at her feet, water spraying.

The assassin's backup fired at her as he moved in, his shots missing narrowly.

With a knock, Asiyah fell to the ground, finding cover behind the nearest car. Keeping as low as possible, her back pressed against the car's body, she wormed away from the impacting bullets, grazing the skin on her hands against the rough paving. Dirt clung to her clothes. In the storm's din, she could not hear the approaching footsteps, but she knew that the man from the Lexus was coming for her. All he had to do was get her in his sights. She was trapped.

Even if she had no place to run, she wasn't about to give up. Reaching above her, she found a door handle with her fingers and yanked. No use. She was going to try smashing the window when the gunman loomed over her.

There were no last words before the end, no prelude or drama. The killer simply pointed the gun at her face. He was a few meters away, too far for her to attempt struggling.

At first, Asiyah didn't know whether it was the effect of the drugs or the coming of death, but in that moment everything around her flashed blue. Louder than the storm was a guttural shriek that grew wildly. But it was no hallucination of hers. The assassin turned to the source of the shining and the roar, when suddenly a powerful light beam focused on him, blinding.

He swung the gun from Asiyah towards the advancing car. Before he could scream, the braking vehicle slammed into him.

Impacting laterally, the car's bumper smashed his knee, and in the same instant the bonnet hit his thigh. The assassin's entire body wrapped around the front of the car, his head striking at the edge of the bonnet and the windshield. In a squeal of wet tires, the car jerked to a stop, and the assassin's body rolled down and smacked on the ground.

On impulse, Asiyah backed away, trying to get up. Her body lagged in response. She had no strength to raise herself. Clutching his leg, the assassin gurgled, yelling, then fell silent.

Asiyah set her eyes on the car—a white BMW police cruiser, coated in cascading water droplets, blue lights flickering on its roof.

The driver's door flew open, and a man hopped out into the beating rain. He did not even remotely resemble a policeman. The kind of martial arts uniform on him was stained black with soot, a sleeve torn off. As he neared her, his captivating blue eyes looked into hers.

"Asiyah."

He knew her name, strangely.

"Asiyah, I'll get you out of here." He bent down to reach for her hand. "You'll be safe."

He held out his open palms and helped her up, walking her away quickly from the car and the assassin's body. He guided her to the empty Lexus, which still had its engine running, and opened the rear door. Climbing inside, Asiyah spread across the seat, feeling dead. She huddled against the heated leather, the warmth and dryness almost dizzying. She shut her eyes, she wanted it all to be gone, the death, the broken bodies. She felt the car's wheels roll. Someone cared for her, someone wanted to save her from this madness, even if she didn't know him.

The Lexus picked up speed, the rain splashing harmlessly outside, wipers swaying. She believed she would be alive now, and with that, something snapped inside her, making her unable to stop crying.

20

Sokolov directed the Lexus to the hospital's main gate. In the back of the car, Asiyah lay sobbing, tears seeping through her fingers as she covered her face. Sokolov felt for her, but he knew it to be the mind's response to extreme stress, an emotional release that was necessary. He would have feared more for her if it hadn't come. Sokolov himself was shaken. He struggled to hold the steering wheel steadily, as if it still carried the aftershock of the impact that had resonated up to his shoulders when he ran over the gunman. Turning to the main building, he had seen the assassin pointing the gun at Asiyah, and at that moment he knew there was no other option left but to hit him. Under the circumstances, the killer's injuries were minimal, the reduced speed meaning he had suffered broken legs at most. His life was not in danger—the hospital was the best place to be hit by a car, anyway. Sokolov had little concern or pity for the killer, but it was not the kind of experience he would ever want to relive. The thump a human body made against a rushing mass of metal turned Sokolov's stomach no matter what. He forced the remembrance of that sensation away. Now he had to finish his job—get Asiyah to safety.

Impatiently, he honked the horn at the main gate of the compound, and only when he merged with the traffic in the street did his tension begin to ease. The first hurdle had been cleared. Sokolov needed to find a temporary stopover to get hold of his senses and contemplate further action. He followed the highway away from the hospital and took the first exit at Kuntsevo. The full-fledged tropical storm had reduced to a drizzle. Going deeper into the back alleys of the residential district, the Lexus made its way through a maze of sleepy apartment blocks. Generic Soviet-era high-rises, weathered by decades, stood alongside their newer siblings that boasted superior design and floor count, but shared the same concept. In front of each house, the narrow driveways were made almost unusable by parked cars crowding either side of the curb. As the Lexus crept past, its tires rustled over pools, stirring the rainwater. Sokolov eyed a tree-shaded opening in front of a stretching iron fence, and brought the Lexus to a stop. The fence surrounded a squat, rectangular building. Between the building and the fence, in the spacious enclosure, was a children's playground with basketball hoops, which the rain made look forsaken.

Sokolov pulled the handbrake and silently let out a breath. He realized that the place he'd parked next to was a public school. Regardless of the memories, the location would suit him just fine. It was a quiet spot, far from the main traffic, and deserted because of the summer holidays. No one would trouble them here for the moment, and it would be easy enough to ditch the car—which they would have to do as soon as possible. There was no way of knowing if the Lexus was equipped with a homing device that the killers might follow. Also, he had to do something about Asiyah's condition; if she remained immobile, they would have no chance of survival.

"Who are you and what do you want?"

It was the first time he had ever heard her voice, which was softly melodic even when her question was cold and demanding. Sokolov craned his neck and looked back to see her sitting upright, her gaze fixed on him. The tears on her face had almost dried, leaving transparent trails that highlighted her perfect cheekbones and jawline. Her eyes were deep cosmic black, sucking him in with their burning intensity. There was not a trace of confusion or panic there, and it pleased him. She handled the stress well.

"My name is Eugene Sokolov. I want to save your life."

She tried not to show it, but Asiyah's eyes glistened, her brows arched slightly as if the reply had caught her by surprise, as if no one had ever said such words to her before.

"Why?"

Sokolov could not easily rationalize an explanation, but he knew that for her the question was logical, and extremely important. Her mind was trying to cope with the madness that raged around her, unaccustomed to the notion that someone would want to end her life.

"I command an Extra-Risk Team of the Russian EMERCOM. My team reacted to the crisis in Sochi." He avoided mentioning the *Olympia* or any specifics that could be too vivid. "You were unconscious when we found you. We took you to Moscow and put you under special supervision. But then ... I learned that your life was at risk, so I came over to investigate. Don't worry, everything will be fine now." He did his best to reassure her, speaking calmly. "I will get you to the embassy. From there you will safely travel to Kazakhstan, under protection."

"No. It's out of the question." Her voice was barely above a whisper, but its force was piercing. "I can't go back to Kazakhstan." As she spoke, moisture filled her eyes and streaked down her cheeks, but her voice never quivered, not a muscle moved. "The person who blew up the *Olympia* was my father, the President of Kazakhstan, Timur Kasymov. He arranged for the Russian President to rape me. After that, they would have killed me and dumped my body in the Black Sea. I escaped. *I killed* Nikolai Alexandrov and escaped. Sounds crazy, but it was self-defence, I broke his neck. So you see, I don't think I should go back to Kazakhstan."

Her hypnotic black eyes remained locked on his, tears cascading, the words ringing in Sokolov's ears, cracking with their meaning. He had never been so stunned before.

Leaning closer to him, she said, "I didn't ask you *how* you decided to rescue me from those assassins. I asked you *why*. Why did *you* come? Why didn't you leave it to the police? Or the FSB? Who *are* you, Eugene Sokolov, and why do you care for me?"

Sokolov had attempted to shield her from revelations that could be too shocking for her, but in fact, she had hit him with a truth that was far more frightening than anything he could conceive. And what she told him *was* true, without a doubt. The dead President, neck twisted, was a residual image before his eyes.

He would not lie to her. He *couldn't*. Sokolov decided to tell Asiyah everything. She had confided in him fully, bared her soul for him. And she needed no false protection of half-truths, she had been too hardened by what she had gone through. From the beginning, she questioned him to assess him, not seek comfort. She needed to look into his psyche, test his motives, determine if she could really trust him with her life.

"I did not leave the matter to the FSB because I know they are involved. They practically forced your arrest after Sochi. FSB agents showed up at my house this morning to detain me, but they were killed by assassins who were sent after me. That's how I knew you were in danger. But the same people who tried to kill you and me are hunting for my brother."

He told her the rest. Constantine's disappearance a year before; the alleged murder of the Metropolitan; the mysterious connection with Sochi. He told her about Beslan, about the demons of guilt and the memories she brought back.

"From the first moment I saw you, I felt I couldn't let anyone harm you. So now you know *why* I did ... what I had to do."

"Yes, now I know," Asiyah said softly. "It's everything I needed to know."

They were both drained emotionally by their mutual confession, but it had served to expel the burden each of them carried. Sokolov felt as if he had also emptied himself of tears. In the silence, they sensed their inexplicable bond.

"Where do we go now?" Asiyah asked. "We need to get rid of this car."

"I have a plan. There's the one place no one would bother to look."

Sokolov pressed a button on the steering wheel to activate the hands-free function of the car's cell phone. Using it was not much of a risk—had the Lexus been bugged, their whereabouts would already be known anyway. Sokolov dialed Klimov's personal number. Only Klimov's wife, members of the Government and Sokolov knew of its existence.

Sokolov began without preamble. "It's me. I need an ambulance at ... " He peered through the window to read the street name. He did not need to tell Klimov it was urgent.

If anything, Klimov was prepared.

"You should have it in a few minutes," said the Minister and broke the connection.

As they began to wait, a familiar restlessness took over Sokolov, the kind always associated with a mission. The oddity was that this time *he* was the one waiting for the arrival of EMERCOM.

21

When the ambulance appeared, it came to a halt a few meters away from the Lexus, right in front of the school building as Sokolov had indicated. The Lexus was empty. Sokolov and Asiyah watched from the other side of the street, hidden from view. If the ambulance was not what it seemed, they would run away. He didn't take anything for granted anymore.

The vehicle itself was ordinary—a white van, red stripe painted across—but for one exception. Stenciled below the windshield in mirrored lettering was the word *Centrospas*, the name of EMERCOM's special medical unit.

"Is that the car your friend Klimov sent for us?" Asiyah murmured.

"I hope so."

A moment later, the ambulance inched forward, then stopped again. The passenger's door swung open and a man got out to scan the area. He kept his hands tucked inside the pockets of his blue-and-orange coat as he turned his shaved head as he scanned every direction. He froze when he caught sight of Sokolov and Asiyah in the distance, and banged his fist against the side of the van, yelling something to the driver.

"Thank God," Sokolov said. He took Asiyah's hand. "Let's go, this is our ride."

She followed him towards the ambulance. "Are you sure?"

"It's my pilot and best mate. He was the one who found you in Sochi. The Minister picked the right escort for us." In fact, Zubov was the last man he expected to see.

The driver, Sokolov noticed as they neared the ambulance, was Mischenko.

Sokolov made quick formal introductions.

Beaming, Zubov pulled the van's sliding door open. "Happy to see you both alive and well. Hop in."

"Shouldn't you two be on vacation?" Sokolov asked as he helped Asiyah inside.

"We were vacationing in Klimov's office when you called his private number. Let's say we volunteered for this."

Sokolov knew them too well—they would have rushed to his help regardless of Klimov's decision. Also, from a security standpoint, Klimov did not have to involve anyone outside Sokolov's own team, so there were hardly any other suitable candidates.

With concern, Zubov scrutinized him from head to toe.

"My goodness, you look like you really need first aid, Gene."

That made Sokolov suddenly feel self-conscious. He was abominable. The wet cotton of his gi clung to his skin. He had dirt and soot on him, cuts from the glass shards, and red burn marks.

"Don't worry," Sokolov smiled wearily. "I feel much worse than I look."

In the back of the ambulance, Sokolov sat next to Asiyah. Zubov climbed in last and shut the door. Mischenko put the car into gear, his feet feathering the clutch and accelerator. The engine rumbled, setting the ambulance into motion, rocking gently on the uneven pavement. For a second, a chilling deja vu of the Beriev leaving Sochi flashed in Sokolov's mind.

"Where to, Gene?" Mischenko asked.

"Back to the Zhukovsky airbase."

Mischenko glanced at him in the mirror, grinning. Then the big man flicked on a switch that gave life to the shrieking siren and accelerated like a street racer.

Holding on to his seat as the ambulance steered around corners, pushing his feet against the floor for support, Sokolov realized just why Zubov always complained about Mischenko's style of driving.

22

Even though the tone of his voice was measured, Victor could barely hide anger as he recounted the details of his failure. The skies outside the private office of Director Frolov were as dark as the Director's face. Victor felt the waves of fury emanating from the source that was Frolov.

His fury was silent, brooding, a fierce emotion that triggered extra mental strength that Frolov needed to calculate the complications. Asiyah Kasymova and Eugene Sokolov had vanished. The officers attached to Sokolov were dead. The hired killers, maimed and senseless, knew too little and were of no use.

And the vital information Asiyah possessed was now lost.

When Victor had finished, Frolov allowed a few moments of silence before he spoke.

"Are you saying that you lost your best operatives?"

"It is so, Comrade Director ... "

"But the killers who eliminated them were themselves helpless against a single man?"

"Yes." Victor's face was a stone mask.

"Eugene Sokolov, Major of the EMERCOM. No special forces training, no combat experience, no odds."

"He has a reputation in martial arts, but still ... I never believed in him as the right candidate. Neither him nor his brother. But as always, your judgment was perfect."

"That was to be expected. It's all in their blood, Victor. All in their blood. Cossacks are the deadliest enemy anyone could face." Frolov's mouth twisted in a sardonic half-smile. "I'm not claiming full credit for that judgment, however. Other great men before me have noted this. Napoleon said, 'Give me Cossacks and I will rule the world.' He had first-hand experience fighting them, of course. Napoleon's army encountered sophisticated guerrilla and special operations tactics that saw the French chased all the way back to Paris. Eugene and Constantine have this blood, never forget that. Every Cossack is a warrior. Even the name of the rule in the Don State was unique—*Voisko*. Not Duchy or County, but *Army*. A land of armed men who had never been slaves and had no slavery. Cossacks were the backbone of this country we call Russia. It sometimes scares me to think that they could have reclaimed their territories and left us with nothing."

Frolov did not exaggerate. The Cossacks had expanded Russia's borders from Fort Grozny in the Caucasus to Fort Verny in Central Asia and beyond, to the Asian continent's eastern limits, exploring Siberia and venturing on the Alaskan coast almost a hundred years before Bering. All land from the Urals to the Pacific was their gift to Russia, one that they had presented freely as they sought no conquest beyond their homeland in Southern Europe, along the banks of the River Don. Every major city from Vladikavkaz to Vladivostok had Cossack founders. When the Bolsheviks came, the Cossacks had indeed almost succeeded in defying their rule—and toppling it as they fought back. But ultimately, the Cossacks, like all of Russia, lost.

"Each of my predecessors, every man behind this desk since Dzerzhinsky, has busted his guts trying to break them."

The history was personal to Frolov. It had changed his life, sending him on his chosen path of distinction by making him part of that history.

Ever since 1917, "decossackization" had gone for years, claiming millions of lives. The Don's resistance continued until the late 1930s, when finally the Cossacks appeared to have been subdued by the collectivization, the famine and the extermination wreaked by Stalin.

But it was not to be. Their Scythian spirit was always too strong.

On June 1st, 1962, the workers of Novocherkassk, the Don's capital, organized a rally against a thirty-five percent lowering of wages, and an equal increase in food prices. Nikita Khrushchev gave the order to shoot down the peaceful demonstration and punish everyone responsible for the show of dissent. The procession of fourteen thousand workers was mowed down by tanks. People in the streets were chased by automatic fire.

Then the KGB instigated a hunt. For those who took part in the demonstration. For those who didn't.

Those who knew anything about it.

And those who didn't.

Men and women. Old and young.

Not a home had been passed, because the murderers were afraid of their victims—and it was the worst kind of fear, triggered by instinct, rooted in the core that carried remembrance of Cossack whips, of the blood washing the Don's banks as the shocked armies of Bolshevik revolutionaries were hacked by the unyielding Cossacks during the genocide against them that went down in Russian history under the name of Civil War.

The KGB did their job expertly. The thousands of bodies were transported to the wilderness and buried. The executioners were sworn to secrecy; violation was punishable by death.

Even now. The top secret status of the massacre was still in action. Fifty years on, the relatives did not know where the dead were buried, or how many were killed.

Decades later, Frolov remembered everything as clearly as if it had been yesterday. He had been a young KGB officer then, zealous, decisive. He pulled the trigger, and shoveled the earth, and carried the bodies—for several days, losing count of the dead, until the killings became mechanical and tedious.

Eugene and Constantine had lost their grandparents in 1962, so there was a remote possibility that Frolov's own hand had shot them. He didn't care much to think about it.

Frolov picked up the glass prism from his desk and held it up, watching the refractions of light as he titled it. His voice became cold, each word clipped.

"Sokolov is a true warrior. I know what he's like, I saw this quality in men like him, his ancestors. We have his brother's freedom. He'll come to us, and he'll stop at nothing. From the beginning, it was clear that we needed to have them both for the mission to succeed. Now that Eugene is with the girl, it's absolutely vital. So everything is going quite well, Victor—the loss of your men can be considered a test of his capabilities, a bargain that I'm comfortable with. Eugene Sokolov will be our greatest asset, and Constantine is proving to be our greatest lure."

23

The hot water scalded Sokolov's entire body, stinging the cuts, bruises and burns. He let the steaming jets soothe his aching muscles, keeping no track of the time he spent in the shower. Like many times before, he treated this simple comfort of civilization as a luxury, knowing that he may not see it again all too soon. He relished it, the relief that the water gave him being as much emotional as it was physical.

A cloud of vapor preceded him as he stepped out of the shower. He toweled himself and wiped the mist off the mirror, getting a clear look at himself. He was thankful there were no serious injuries.

He returned to the room. His bedroom. By design, it emulated the normalcy of a home between missions, so that the impression could alleviate the minds of EMERCOM crews from the shock of human catastrophe they faced, a change from the bunks and tents, ruins and wreckage. It helped heal the mental scars. Asiyah more than anyone needed the benefit of the psychological effect. When they arrived back at the base, as secretly as possible, they had placed Asiyah in Mischenko's vacated room, the best one available, next door to Sokolov's. He left her in the hands of EMERCOM's top psychologists and physicians. Only when Sokolov realized Asiyah was in absolute safety, and that she needed rest and privacy after her ordeal, did he return to his own room and get down to putting himself back into shape.

For many years Sokolov had thought of this room as his second home. Now it was his only home.

His fresh clothes lay on the bed—underwear, socks, a blue EMERCOM tee-shirt and jeans. Dressing, he grabbed the remote from the bedside table and switched on the television. News headlines would be on in a few minutes, and he wanted to see if the fire and the shootout at his house had made the story.

With the TV jabbering away in the background, Sokolov allowed himself to sprawl across the bed and close his eyes.

The news flash caught his attention. What he saw on the screen rattled him so much that he bolted from the bed, afraid that he might be hallucinating.

With a look of feigned concern, the anchorman announced that Metropolitan Ilia of Kolomna, Father Superior of the Novodevichy Convent, had been hospitalized after suffering a heart attack. His condition was thought to be stable, and he was due to resume his duties after undergoing several weeks of treatment and monitoring.

On archived footage, the Metropolitan was a serene, full-bearded old man, standing tall in his clerical attire. The brief clip was the first time Sokolov had seen Ilia. Then the picture changed to that of a church official voicing his hope for Ilia's speedy recovery and commenting on his fine record of service.

Sokolov knew that Constantine had spent some time attending courses at the seminary in Sergiev Posad, but he was oblivious to the fact that his brother and the Metropolitan would know each other personally. Even more shocking was the claim that his brother had murdered the Metropolitan.

And yet, despite what the FSB officers had told him moments before their own deaths, the Metropolitan was reported to be alive, more threads adding to the tangle. If the news was to be believed, Ilia was not in perfect health, away from everybody's eyes, but he was alive. This could mean a number of things. For example, someone was laying the groundwork for a further announcement of the Metropolitan's death, so as to make it as low key as possible. Someone was covering up.

Sokolov sat at the edge of the bed, staring blankly at the screen.

There was a sharp knock at the door.

"Come in."

It was Klimov.

"You look like you've just seen a ghost," he said, entering the room.

"I may well have."

Sokolov recounted the events surrounding Ilia, beginning from the allegations against Constantine. Then he switched to another news channel, catching a recap of the same "heart trouble" story.

After Klimov finished watching the brief report, Sokolov muted the television.

"What do you make of it?" Sokolov asked. "Where is the divide between truth and lies? Is Ilia dead or alive?"

"I'm at a loss here." Klimov shook his head. "The Metropolitan is a prominent figure, one of the top officials in the Orthodox Church. I can tell you that if he *had* been placed in any clinic, I would have been among the first to know. I'll run a check on this for a confirmation."

"I would appreciate if you did. But so far, until there *is* a confirmation, the whole story seems like a hoax."

"In that case someone is going to all ends to hide his death. But why?"

"*Fear*, Danya. Someone is very afraid. Constantine couldn't have murdered the Metropolitan. Perhaps he was there when it happened. It's not his *death* that they want to hide—I'm sure it will be announced soon enough—but the very fact of *murder*. Whoever staged all this will attempt anything to make sure Constantine's name isn't dredged up if the media learn he's the prime suspect."

"You mean someone from higher up put a hand to this televised announcement? Like the FSB?"

"They are the only ones capable of this deception, and the ones interested in it. They're chasing Constantine, and they know that someone wants to kill him. But it's only a small piece of the jigsaw. What Constantine got himself into is bigger than this—and it stretches far back. A *year* ago. At the time when he vanished. So the FSB doesn't want the connection between the Metropolitan and Constantine to be known to anyone. They don't want those who are after him to know where to look. Perhaps even where they *should* have looked."

"All of it is merely speculation at this stage, of course," Klimov said.

"I'm ready to grasp at any sort of speculation when my brother's life is at stake. And not only *his* life. I don't have any other starting point, I'm afraid."

"Yes, you're right, Gene. Damned right. If I learn anything about the Metropolitan or your brother, you'll know it." Klimov drew a long breath. "Looks like we're hitting dead ends on every front."

"What do you mean?"

"We ran a chemical analysis of the hair sample you brought. It did *not* show a high concentration of any known poisonous substance. Same in Sochi after autopsies on the recovered bodies.

Something killed them all before they drowned, without leaving a trace. And that makes it even more frightening."

"No explanation to the symptoms?"

"None whatsoever."

"Did the FSB experts have their say?"

"They're clueless, apart from at least one cause of death that is certain. But it is an exception that is of little help to us in solving the rest."

"And what sort of exception is that?"

"The President. Someone broke his neck."

24

Sokolov sat alone on the bed, facing the glowing television, watching the recurring footage of the Metropolitan every time it appeared. In his mind he held the three pictures of the assassins' targets—the photographs of himself, Constantine, and Asiyah. Now he had to add a fourth print alongside those—the image of Ilia that he saw before him. Four lives thrown in a battle for survival by someone's pathological whim. Ilia was most probably dead. The rest of them were pursued by the world's most fearsome security agency on charges of murder. Not only this bedroom at the EMERCOM base, but everything in Sokolov's life would be temporary as long as he was on the run. Until he settled all accounts. More so if Constantine was also dead, he thought as dread squeezed him.

"Eugene."

She called his name in a tender voice.

He had not heard her approach him, so quiet was her step—or so unfocused was his mind that he did not register the intrusion despite his extraordinary hearing.

He stoop up sharply and turned in her direction.

Asiyah stood in the middle of the room. The door behind her was ajar. She was dressed in a white sleeveless shirt of the standard EMERCOM ladies' variety and blue baggy pants. Her black hair glittered with freshness, still a touch wavy. Her skin was lustrous. Her eyes were full of satisfaction at him seeing her like this—not the miserable rain-soaked girl but a gorgeous woman.

"Eugene," she said decisively now, "we must find your brother."

"Please sit down," he offered, and she settled on the bed next to him. "Why are you saying this, Asiyah?"

"Timur Kasymov, my father, is alive, and he needs to be stopped. He is a monster. The men who tried to kill us were sent by him. He blew up the *Olympia* and he is planning to go down in history as a mass murderer. If he wants to kill your brother, it means that somehow he crossed my father's path, and he will not rest until your brother is dead. We must not allow it to happen."

She looked him in the eye, letting him understand that no matter how crazy she sounded, it was not the aftershock overtaking her. Her delivery was rational, her voice firm, calculated to make sure they both knew she was right. The enormity of her words was something that Sokolov now accepted as normal in the context of the last few days.

"I know, Asiyah. I'm going to find him. I'm setting off tomorrow."

"You don't understand. *We* must do it together. I want to go with you," she said without hesitation.

"It's better that you don't put your life at risk," he said in refusal.

She glared at him.

"As if my life isn't at risk already!"

"I can't allow it."

"What makes you think you have this right?"

He was the one stung by the words now, and the truth behind them.

"I will not burden you," Asiyah said. "I need to *do* something to escape this madness! I *cannot* just sit in a different prison cell, waiting for someone to kill me! I'd be safer near you, saner, too. If you left me, wouldn't you be thinking all the time whether I'm still alive or not? Wouldn't it distract you?"

"It would," he admitted. "All the time."

"Then let me stay near you. Your friends can't stand watch at that door forever and risk *their* lives."

Inwardly, Sokolov had to concede that she was right when she said that her safety would last only until the FSB produced another search warrant. And he couldn't protect her if he was far away from her.

What truly amazed him was her energy, only a few hours after their escape.

"You don't know what my father is like. You weren't aboard the *Olympia* when she capsized in flames. You may come across a clue only I can interpret. You need me, Eugene ... and *I need you,*" she let out in a whisper.

If he had any doubt, she dispelled it.

He could not be a hypocrite, telling her that she would be better off locked up. And he could not deny her logic. They were in this together.

Sokolov nodded and placed a hand on her shoulder.

"Get some rest, Asiyah. We're leaving early."

25

"Comrade Director, we have a breakthrough."

The encrypted line was reserved for matters of extreme urgency.

"We have deciphered Constantine's disk," Victor said. "The information it contains is staggering."

Frolov gripped the handset, feeling sweat moisten his palm. For several years, that disk had been the holy grail of his work.

"The amount of data Malinin collected on his former employers equates to thousands of pages. I am preparing a full report, and it will take some time to process all the data we have obtained ... but there are facts that I felt obliged to bring to your attention at once."

"Yes? Go on."

"The truth is, all this time we have been chasing phantoms. The Fourth International is a ruse. An elaborate ploy set in motion at the start of the Cold War. It does not exist ... at least not in any tangible form."

The words meant that a giant hand swept all the pieces from the virtual chess board that Frolov had meticulously set up. It would be a different game now, with a new player—and new rules. Which side held the advantage remained to be seen.

"I want that report to be lying on my desk the moment you've finished it. Anything else you can tell me?"

"Asiyah Kasymova."

"What about her?"

"She is not who we always thought she was."

PART IV

1

The Caucasus mountain range rises like a dragon's back between the Black Sea and the Caspian. Its peaks and gorges form the most daunting fortress on earth, conquered only by boisterous flora—dense and jungle-like. Several kilometers higher, the scenery travels to a different world: a kingdom of eternal cold, of snow so thick that a man could be buried and never found, where the sun casts blinding glitter but brings no warmth, and the wind murders silently.

No peak in Europe can match these impregnable mountains. Crowned by ice caps, they stand together like ancient giants—immovable, unavoidable, and unforgiving.

The Caucasus is impossible to discount—it invades your vision, and overwhelms your senses. Only here can a man draw inspiration from proximity to absolute greatness and feel unease realizing the insignificance of humankind against so powerful a backdrop.

Over centuries, the North Caucasus has seen as much death and violence as the Middle East, and then some.

Up above, in the peaks that overlook the Black Sea, a single glacier secretes water, drop by drop. The drops become a trickle as they slither down the rocks, and the trickle is joined by rivulets, to form a stream. Crashing against the craggy terrain, the stream charges down. The Caucasus shapes it, guiding it along the gorges, giving it force until—loud and wild—it becomes a river. A mountain river just like any other, one that rushes downhill, sweeping away pebbles, shifting rocks, adding strength to its thunderous current. But more trickles and streams join it along the way. By the time this water mass reaches the base of the Caucasus, it becomes known as the Terek, the most important river in the region. From its origin around the area of Vladikavkaz, the Terek flows east, along the base of the Caucasus range, some six hundred kilometers until its delta unites it with the Caspian Sea.

For centuries, the Terek was the divide between the mountains and the valleys of the Caucasus. The land north of the Terek belonged to Cossack settlements. South of it, the mountains were populated by the indigenous tribes of highlanders, too numerous and varied in ethnicity to count.

Across the Terek, opposite the Cossack town of Grozny, the mountains were home to the Chechen and Ingush villages. The Chechen highland was made up of rock, mist and desolation. They prolonged their meager existence only through shepherding sheep, or raiding the valleys north of the Terek to pillage Cossack homes and kidnap women and children for sale in the Turkish slave markets. Decade after decade, the Cossacks fought back, and a volatile balance had been kept.

All it would take for the Caucasus to explode was a spark. The kind of spark brought by the Bolsheviks.

The Reds saw Cossacks as the greatest threat to their rule. Genocide had been predetermined.

To wipe out the Cossack population in the Caucasus, the Bolsheviks turned to the Chechens and the Ingush, arming their bands, reinforcing them with three Red Army divisions. The Bolshevik who had arrived to take charge of the slaughter was none other than Joseph Stalin.

Attacking, the Bolsheviks and the Chechens contested each other in savagery. It took three days to kill twelve thousand people. It took three years to kill the rest.

Another three years were gone, but the land of the Cossacks was still void, as dead as the people, filled with too much blood.

In time, people returned to the valleys north of the Terek—other people, new people, those reformed by the holy light of the Revolution.

For their endeavor, the Chechens had been granted the land of the people they had massacred. But the Bolsheviks were never good on their word. They pushed the Chechens back into their mountains, to shepherd their herds as they had done for centuries. They wanted the land of the Cossacks for themselves.

It was a land rich with oil.

2

When Stalin's empire faced its darkest hour, and the country's entire military capability strained to fight Hitler, the eastern ridges of the Caucasus facing the Caspian Sea became exposed. As Stalin saw it, the Chechen bandits returned to their old ways. At first, they sabotaged the war effort by deserting from the Red Army. Later, they began to raid the now-Russian valleys north of the Terek, behind the front line. Fearing that the Chechens would side with Hitler, Stalin decided to solve the problem once and for all. He could not afford to fight two enemies on either side of the Caucasus.

Joseph Stalin had his own methods in dealing with problems. In 1944, he ordered that the NKVD deport the Chechens to another territory.

Every Chechen.

Stalin picked the most isolated location he could think of: Kazakhstan.

The Chechen population was packed into trains at gunpoint and sent off in a matter of weeks. When they arrived, the people discovered that their new home was a barren steppe that stretched as far as the eye could see. It was Stalin's cruel irony: From the cold mountains to the deserted, flat Asian ground. Not to the lush valleys of the Terek, but to a similar fate suffered by the people in those valleys.

Of the 400,000 exiled Chechens, at least 150,000 either perished during the deportation itself, or died from starvation in the next five years.

Like any social organism, the Chechen community in Kazakhstan adapted and survived. They accepted the environment, but not the treatment. The infertile Kazakh land was only capable of nurturing the seed of hatred planted by Stalin. A half-century later, it exploded—following another insane act concocted by a

Soviet leader. Mikhail Gorbachev decided to bring the Chechens back to Russia. To a place they had never inhabited—to the land *north* of Terek, the former Cossack stronghold which was now given a new name.

Chechnya.

In 1992, a twenty-year-old Ahmed Sadaev left his Kazakh hometown of Karaganda, and headed to Chechnya. The young Chechen republic was being run by gangs that specialized in trafficking drugs, smuggling arms and trading slaves. Shortly, Sadaev formed his own gang that terrorized Chechnya's dominantly Russian population. An all-out war against Russia broke out in 1995, turning Sadaev's bandits into freedom fighters. The black-market business boomed, making Sadaev one of Chechnya's toughest commanders. Soon after he met Oleg Radchuk, who had already made a reputation for himself, and their partnership thrived. Sadaev's gang was feared by the federal soldiers, Chechen rivals, and local populace alike.

Such credentials paved their way to Shamil Basaev's guerrilla cell of Islamic terrorists. "The Gynecologist", as Basaev would soon become known, was looking for experienced fighters as he prepared to stage a big "action" against the Russians. Their target was a hospital in Budennovsk,—a small town near Stavropol founded by Cossacks in 1667, known as Holy Cross, later renamed by the Bolsheviks to glorify one of their cutthroats.

On June 14, 1995, the Chechen terrorists took 1,600 hostages, and occupied the hospital's maternity ward. Federal forces surrounded the building, and Moscow began negotiations with Basaev that resulted in humiliation and shock.

Twenty corpses of women and children spewed blood at the feet of Shamil Basaev. For the rest of his life Sadaev would remember the way it felt, clenching the knife as he gutted pregnant women, ramming the blade to the hilt and slicing down.

As the army stormed the hospital building, a helpless Yeltsin promised Basaev immunity and agreed to all of the terrorists' demands. The Alpha Group of Russian Special Forces had already secured the first floor of the hospital, but the assault was called off. After killing thirty soldiers and policemen, and over a hundred civilians, Shamil Basaev and his butchers simply walked away. Back to Chechnya. Moving behind a human shield of another 140 hostages.

After the hospital massacre, Sadaev ascended to the ranks of terrorist elite. But his fame also exposed him, stripped him of his safety. His moment of glory entailed a manhunt by the vindictive Russians. Most of all, Sadaev was afraid of the Cossacks who would not stop until they had his head. It would be a matter of time before he was found inside Chechnya. Sadaev returned to Kazakhstan through Georgia, with Oleg Radchuk at his side.

Shortly after they came to Kazakhstan in 1996, Timur Kasymov employed their services. Under President Nazarbayev, the Kazakhstani security service KNB conducted national purges in its ranks, sacking Russian personnel. As a result, the force was understaffed, most notably the operations division. The then-head of that division, Kasymov, did not miss the important cadres arriving into the country, and he quickly hired both Radchuk and Sadaev, giving them new identities, making them disappear from the radar of the Russians. The Chechen and the Ukrainian proved their worth against the regime's political opposition. Kasymov never asked what they did to the bodies. Only the result mattered.

A growing bond of crimes drew them closer together. It was cemented by mutual fear that spawned a perverse kind of absolute trust: each of them knew that betrayal would equal self-destruction. And so their status quo endured the years—the boss and his henchmen, always together. Ultimately, they became the praetorians of the country's ruler.

Neither Sadaev nor Radchuk held any official capacity in the President's staff, but their positions in Kasymov's personal hierarchy were so high that none was required, their actions beyond anyone's control but the President's.

They were trusted with something far more important than even Timur Kasymov's life.

They overlooked the Project.

3

Ahmed Sadaev's boots crunched with each step as he walked down the road amid a gray sea of sand. He still thought of the desert around him as the sea, for it had once been that. Not anymore. There was dust and salt under his feet. What once gave life had become parched, eroded—dead. Not a living thing within a hundred miles.

The military complex had been rebuilt in the middle of this wasteland, able to withstand any dust storm, but the day was cloudless, and there was no motion in the acrid air. According to the forecast from the meteorological station, fair weather would last all week, but the lethal winds usually defied prediction.

Sadaev was proud of the complex. It was his fiefdom, and at times he permitted himself to think that he was the master of it. But indeed he was not. He was merely the keeper. The real master—the khan—was arriving to inspect his property, his achievement.

And what an achievement that was! The complex was the core of their project, its very reason. Without it, nothing would have been possible. And it had been restored from ashes, given new life that would *bring* death! Death to the infidels who had conceived the complex in the beginning, and who had killed the sea, turning it into desert! *Renaissance*. The name was so appropriate. The cycles of life and death, revolving in one place.

Air rippled with the heat, distorting the faraway outline of a white private jet as it descended for landing.

With the sun scorching, perspiration drenched him, and he was glad that he'd left the car's engine idling. He climbed behind the wheel of the Mercedes Geländewagen and drove away from the compact cluster of buildings, to the airfield, two kilometers northwest.

Originally intended for use by the Iranian armed forces before elevation to cult luxury status, the G-wagen was not at all incongruous with the backdrop of dunes and withered shrubs that formed the desert terrain. As part of the reconstruction, the road to the airfield had been restored. The gravel airstrip, previously good enough for Antonov An-2 aircraft, had also been rebuilt up to the President's high standards.

But the airstrip's unorthodox shape could not be helped. Built on what was now a plateau, with a limited patch of level ground, it was a star shape of four runways intersecting in the middle. Between 2,000 to 2,500 meters in length, each was more than adequate for a private jet, and acceptable for most passenger liners.

It had taken a minute for the salt dust to settle after the Learjet had touched down. When it did, Sadaev pulled up the G-Wagen to the opening door.

Two passengers emerged. The first one was Oleg Radchuk. The other was their khan, Timur Kasymov. Sadaev praised Allah for giving vision to this great man. The destruction of the *Olympia*, Sadaev's personal triumph, was but a small step in his master's grand design.

Radchuk opened the rear passenger door for Kasymov and joined Sadaev in front. Sadaev put the G-Wagen in motion, turning around for a return run to the complex.

Sadaev did not need to look in the rearview mirror to know Kasymov was gazing at him.

"Is everything going as planned, Ahmed?" Kasymov asked.

"Like clockwork, Mr. President," Sadaev said. "After the successful trial, we are ready to take the project to the next level."

"I'm afraid we must put the second phase on hold, Ahmed. We have a change of plans."

"Bad news from our diaspora in Moscow?"

"Couldn't be worse," said Radchuk. "They have failed to eliminate the targets. We presume that Asiyah is now in the clutches of the FSB."

Sadaev tried to keep his hands steady on the wheel.

"The FSB? How?"

"It's the EMERCOM man, Eugene Sokolov," Radchuk replied. "She's hiding with him now. He was the one who led the rescue team in Sochi. And his brother turned out to be Malinin's courier in Europe."

"I don't believe in such coincidences," Kasymov said. "Both of those men are deep-cover FSB agents on a mission against me. I am certain they are not even siblings. It's impossible that one man could be partial to both of our recent failures. Now the entire project is teetering on the brink of collapse. Now Asiyah is off limits. I have called off the search for her. We must prepare for uninvited guests. I want you to increase security of the complex, Ahmed."

"How long will you be staying, Mr. President?"

"For as long as it takes to defeat the enemy."

4

The night deserved to be named such only due to a dark smudge passing over the sky. Though Moscow was too far south to qualify for the notorious "white nights" of Russian summers, the brief interval between sunset and sunrise was a frustrating prank of nature. Asiyah noticed that past eleven p.m. the sky retained its brightness. Then, shortly before three a.m., she saw the glint of a new dawn etching the eastern horizon. Staring through the window, she watched the yellow beam of light thicken across the horizon, setting ablaze the dark blue of the sky, growing steadily in proximity to the wisps of clouds. A perfect reversal of the sunset she witnessed aboard the *Olympia*. Muttering a curse under her breath, she got up. In the bathroom, she stood over the basin and looked at her gaunt face in the mirror. Asiyah opened the tap, cupped water and splashed it on her face, feeling strength return to her body.

Her fresh clothes were EMERCOM surplus, simple and effective. She could not remember being so comfortable in a long while.

From the fridge, she grabbed a can of ice coffee. The coffee tasted like acid because of her tense nerves. Her life would be decided in the next twenty-four hours. She had to help Eugene find his brother. If Constantine had managed to disappear without a trace for almost a year, she could well use that knowledge to vanish herself as well, beyond the reach of any intelligence service in the world, and begin a new life.

There was a firm rap at the door, which she answered. It was Sokolov. She found it unusual to see him in civilian attire—an untucked black polo, black denims, and a pair of leather Nikes.

He smiled. "I should have guessed that after that dirty wet *gi* and strict uniform, seeing me dressed normally would be a bit of a surprise."

"Oh, I . . . " Asiyah pressed her hand to her face, self-conscious. "Did I actually have that look on my face? I'm so sorry."

"I actually practiced that line." Sokolov grinned with mock shyness and Asiyah laughed.

She knew that Sokolov was a good psychologist, and while his trick was basic she could not help but fall for it—a few light-hearted words made her feel at ease instantly.

"Glad to see that you're up and raring to go."

"You said we'd hit the road early, but I still didn't expect it to be *that* early."

"Do you need some time to get ready?"

"No," she said. "No. I could hardly wait for you to come."

As Sokolov led her through the base, she saw that no one slept—people went on with their work just as a few hours before. EMERCOM functioned like a well-oiled mechanism, the personnel on duty always ready to go from stand-by to full action.

Outside, the air was pleasantly warm, a precursor of the heat wave that was about to crash on Moscow after yesterday's thunderstorm.

"That's our car," Sokolov said, pointing at a vehicle parked ahead of them.

"Oh? Not an ambulance this time?"

"Afraid not."

In fact, it was a Land Rover Defender. Gleaming white, with orange and blue lines painted across the body, the letters EMERCOM stenciled above the Ministry's emblem of a triangle within an eight-pointed star.

Sokolov and Asiyah climbed inside. The car had the highest clearance Asiyah had ever seen, which made her feel like she had boarded a bus. Sokolov turned the ignition, and after a brief hiccup the engine emitted a mighty roar and came to life.

"Hope you can handle this beast," Asiyah said.

"Sure. I had one just like it," Sokolov said.

"What happened to it?"

"Well, it slightly . . . crashed. And burned. But this thing is reliable as long as you don't try to set fire to the gas tank under your seat."

"I see."

Sokolov navigated to the highway and cruised along. Even at such an ungodly hour, there were other cars always in sight.

"Looks like we sure beat the traffic," Sokolov said.

Starting from six a.m., every major road would be congested as commuters headed to their downtown workplaces from the suburbs. During rush hour, Moscow came to a standstill.

Sokolov adhered to the speed limit, flickering the headlights whenever a slower car was in front of him. Seeing the huge EMERCOM vehicle, the motorists moved out of the way to a different lane.

"We're not exactly inconspicuous," Asiyah said.

"It's an advantage," Sokolov said. "I doubt that the people who wanted to kill us will be on the lookout for an EMERCOM staff car. There are dozens of EMERCOM cars out in the streets of Moscow. Ordinary traffic police would not want to meddle with another government agency. Same with the FSB—would they risk putting out an alert on us? They'd rather keep things quiet. They'll be waiting for us, but they don't know where we would be coming from. Besides, we might find use of the Defender's off-road capability where we're going."

"We're not driving to Moscow?"

Sokolov shook his head. "There's no point. Showing up at the Novodevichy would be useless. It's not the place to find the answers. Every door would be closed for us, because the Metropolitan is not yet dead officially. The FSB must have scoured the place already for all the papers, every bit of evidence connecting Ilia with my brother. Moscow is a trap."

"Where *can* we find the answers, then?"

"Up north. We must begin at the beginning, Asiyah. The place where Constantine first met Ilia. The Trinity St. Sergius Lavra. All the answers are there."

5

After his parents died, a young man named Bartholomew left his home to become a monk. He went deep into the forest that spanned from his hometown of Radonezh all the way to Pereyaslavl, and chose the most desolate spot for his hermitage, as far away from the world as possible. There, in a place so forsaken that even the nearby river was shallow and muddy, he built a cell for himself, and a tiny wooden church to pray in the name of the Holy Trinity. His elder brother Stefan joined him in his quest, but after some time Stefan could no longer endure the strict life in the forest and left for Moscow, so Bartholomew remained alone.

Taking his monastic vows, Bartholomew changed his name to Sergius. For seven years Sergius lived in total seclusion, away from the world, but knowledge of his endeavor began to spread, and twelve other monks followed him into the woods to build twelve more cells and seek his guidance. By that time, Sergius had turned thirty.

It was then, in 1344, that the Trinity Monastery was thus founded.

People came there en masse, from peasants to princes, and the Monastery grew both in size and fame, for the principles set by Sergius were simple—love, humility and hard work. This spiritual core defined the Russian nation, uniting the lands around Muscovy. With the blessing of Sergius, the combined forces of Russian armies crushed the Mongols in the Battle of Kulikovo, stopping the Golden Horde from destroying Moscow.

Centuries passed. The Trinity Monastery evolved. Stone churches appeared, their beauty made eternal as marvels of Russian architecture, new buildings growing until the late nineteenth century. Christian life centered around it, blossoming with iconography, theology and reshaping monasticism. It went far beyond the convention of a monastery both physically and religiously, at the same time becoming the model to inspire every cloister across Russia. As such, the monastery achieved the honor of the Greek title Lavra, meaning *alley*.

Even by today's standards, the trip from Moscow to the St. Sergius Lavra was not the quickest, requiring to cover seventy kilometers to the northeast of the Russian capital. Driving from Zhukovsky, Eugene and Asiyah made it in two hours, justifying their early start.

The dense woods surrounding the Trinity monastery ages ago had since succumbed to civilization—the homes of the early pilgrims had expanded in numbers, developing into a a village, and eventually a town which became known in the late nineteenth century as Sergiev Posad. Still, even today the nature was rich in green, blending in throughout the town as a testament of the locale's past. As if welcoming the strangers who came to see the Lavra, other churches were dotted around Sergiev Posad, each of them splendid on its own.

Sergiev Posad had one main street running through the town, with tiny alleys branching off it occasionally. Parking on the square in front of the Trinity St. Sergius Lavra was not allowed to avoid congestion, so Eugene left the Land Rover at one of the special parking lots, three hundred meters away.

The view of the Lavra was mesmerizing—the white fortress wall of stone and the constellation of domes rising above it, sharing the golden glow with the sky.

Sokolov increased pace, a sense of foreboding clinging to him like a ghostly mist. The road under his feet, Sergiev Posad's main driveway, was called the Red Army Prospekt. All around him, signs provided directions to Karl Marx Street, Kirov Street, Soviet Square ... The town's street names defiled the town's purpose. It was a mystical unity of the murderer and the slain victim, a circle of beginning and end. Thousands of monasteries had originated from the Lavra, and the road leading to it eulogized the people who destroyed them. But there was a difference from the time when Stalin had renamed Sergiev Posad as Zagorsk to honor some long-dead Bolshevik. These Communist signs now announced defeat instead of victory, like dust-covered runes marking a pagan crypt. Symbols of an extinct past, but harrowing symbols nonetheless.

The life teeming in Sergiev Posad proved socialism's demise. Lazily, cars were filling the Red Army Prospekt. English lettering advertised shops and hotels to the foreign tourists who seemed to outnumber local residents. A McDonald's stood on a street corner, competing for early customers with a sushi bar across.

Because the Lavra was a functioning Orthodox Christian site, a lady needed to adhere to a proper dress code in order to be permitted access. At a stall right of the entrance, Sokolov bought a traditional Russian kerchief to solve the problem. Asiyah used it to cover her head.

Sealed off by a wall measuring fifteen hundred meters in perimeter, the Trinity Lavra was a small island left to itself, preserving the fundamental canon intended by St. Sergius when he abandoned the distractions of the world. The entrance to the Lavra, known as the Holy Gates, was a tall archway leading through a gateway church—a tower the lower part of which was a frescoed gallery, and the upper part was a church rising over it, crested with a golden onion dome. By this design, visitors to the Lavra passed through a church via the tunnel in the middle, witnessing images of angels and saints portrayed on the curved walls.

Asiyah squeezed Sokolov's hand, the effect not lost on her. Sokolov himself felt as if entering the gateway church outside the Lavra, and exiting it *inside*, surrounded by frescoes of the Holy Trinity, was similar to going through change, crossing the line that left the world behind.

Outside the gateway church, the main churches of the Lavra opened before their view, stone walkways connecting piazzas before each of them, lawns and young trees enjoying the vast open spaces in between. Cathedral of the Dormition, the Lavra's largest church, was directly in front, a small crowd of people gathering at its entrance. It was a larger version of its namesake in the Kremlin, but it did not obscure the other churches around it. On either side of it was a narrow bell tower spearing the sky, and a tiny church of the Holy Ghost. Farther behind, Sokolov eyed the Trinity Cathedral, a 1422 stone replacement of the original wooden church built by St. Sergius, its golden dome jutting atop a low turret. To the far right was the Monastic Square, an enormous plaza that linked the low-slung buildings stretching along the Lavra's walls, visible beyond the trees. Located centrally was the monastery itself, two stories of it lined with windows belonging to monastic cells, the church it housed having its golden dome extending through the slanting roof. Next to it was the Lavra's Academy, which had evolved from the Orthodox seminary established in

1742, and a separate wing for the colossal library. The other buildings constituted a tiny hospital, an administrative building, and a guesthouse where pilgrims could stay at no cost.

Sokolov's heart thumped. Behind these great walls of white stone, his mind and soul touching the ancient Christian glory that he saw before him, he felt the confidence that he was also within touching distance of his brother. Constantine was somewhere nearby.

Asiyah followed his gaze.

"Do you think your brother could have stayed here as a monk?"

The thought, however obvious, was eerie for Sokolov to accept. Constantine becoming a monk? He was not comfortable imagining it, but after all the madness Sokolov had gone through in the last few days, the notion was not unbelievable.

"A monk. A priest. I don't know, Asiyah. Perhaps he might have stayed in one of those rooms meant for pilgrims."

"For more than a year?"

"With Ilia's influence, why not? Sheltering fugitives does not go against the Lavra's tradition, anyway. A young Peter the Great sought refuge here hiding from enemies, if I remember correctly."

"It makes sense," Asiyah said. "Assuming that your brother was hiding at the Lavra, he would be immune to police searches or identity checks. Not to mention that in a place as big as this, there is always the leeway to escape. A warning could be passed quickly if someone started nosing around. No one would ever hunt him down here."

Sokolov nodded. "Let's go. We need to find a person who knows everything about the Lavra."

They started toward the Trinity Cathedral. Other visitors going by granted them no more than passing glances; Eugene and Asiyah fused well with the crowd. There were lonely old ladies clutching their prayer books, scornful of intruders; younger women strolling in twos and threes; men arching their heads, captivated by the lavish architecture. And the foreigners. The tourists had not yet flooded the Lavra like they would closer to midday, but Sokolov registered camera flashes and hushed voices in Arabic and Chinese, German and Italian.

All the same, Sokolov kept his check, not knowing where the danger could arrive from.

Sokolov crossed himself curtly as he opened the thick wooden door. Contrasting with the beating sunshine, the air inside the church was cool from the stone walls and reigning shadow. It carried the smell of melting wax, as candlelight highlighted the cathedral's icons and frescoes in the semidarkness.

Most of the icons were created by the hand of Andrei Rublev, painter of the *Holy Trinity*, the single most famous icon in Christianity which he had created for this church, currently being preserved in a controlled environment behind bulletproof glass at the Tretyakov Gallery. Rublev himself was a mystery. Nothing was known about him, not even his appearance. Only his genius that matched eternity.

The Rublev who painted the frescoes and icons of the Trinity Cathedral had a grimmer vision than the master who created the *Holy Trinity*. In a country torn by gory feuds, the faces of saints were filled with more suffering.

"It's so beautiful here," Asiyah whispered to him. Her voice was full of reverence, her wide black eyes eager to absorb the art that inspired awe beyond the boundaries of religious denomination.

Sokolov followed her towards the iconostasis. For a few moments, neither of them wanted to say or do anything.

The longer Asiyah regarded the icons, the more stunned she became, until tears rolled down her face freely. Concerned by her reaction, Sokolov held her hand gently.

"Are you all right? Did something go wrong?"

"I don't know what happened to me there," she said. "But it made me feel different somehow."

Her fingers wiped the moisture away from her cheeks.

"I ... " she needed a breath. "I never thought these images could move me so much. My father always said that the Russians were heathens, worshipping their wood and paint."

Hollow clicks on the stone floor—footsteps.

"That is not quite correct," said a gentle voice behind them.

Sokolov turned his head sharply. A few paces behind them was a priest. Over his cassock he was wearing a bright pheloneon—a heavy cope necessary for service. He was middle-aged, his hair untouched by gray, his black beard trimmed neatly.

"We do not worship the icons," he explained, smiling. "Even in a church, the human eye requires to rest somewhere. So is it proper for a person thinking of God to have his gaze lingering on something too earthly, like a cracked wall or an old chair? In fairness, it is better to set one's sight on a depiction of a biblical event which reminds us of God. This is the real purpose of an icon."

"I understand now," Asiyah said.

"But I apologize for the intrusion."

Sokolov was afraid that the priest might leave.

"No, please," he said. "I must ask you a question."

Aware of the pleading urgency in Sokolov's tone, the priest drew nearer.

"Is there any way I could help you?"

"Yes," Sokolov said. "Father ... ?"

"Father Mikhail."

"Father Mikhail, I am looking for someone."

Sokolov hesitated. Perhaps it was not such a good idea after all. A one-in-a-million shot that could bring him to nothing—or even destroy whatever little hope he had.

As Sokolov struggled for words, the priest encouraged him to go on, giving him full attention.

"It's my brother, actually. About a year ago he disappeared, left us without a word. I don't know anything about his fate. I haven't been able to find him anywhere, and the police have been of no help. But ... but I know that he attended some courses at the Academy here. He was fascinated by the Lavra. So I began to wonder that he might have become a monk. Could he have stayed at the monastery? Could he *still* be in the Lavra?"

Father Mikhail's expression changed at the last question. He looked at Sokolov with sympathy, as he himself was now trying to pick his words carefully, touching a personal matter that was so sensitive.

"You see, when someone makes a decision to quit the material world and dedicate one's life to serving God, it is sometimes difficult to accept for the family. In any case, it is a brave decision— a selfless act that we cannot interfere with. I understand how much pain and confusion it may be causing you, but *if* your brother chose the path to God, you should be just as selfless, and try to take it with humility. And after all, you must realize that your brother may have gone elsewhere. I do not mean to suggest the worst, but everything is in God's will, and your brother is in His hands."

The words were sinking in bitterly.

"But you have come here for my help, and I will do everything in my power. Tell me your brother's name."

"Constantine Sokolov."

The priest's hand trembled slightly. He looked into Sokolov's face, and then cast his gaze at Asiyah, who also appeared to be a bereaved family member, emotion glittering in her eyes.

"Constantine Sokolov?" the priest said at length. "Yes. I know him. He was expecting you to come searching for him here. I can help you. Follow me."

6

In the most distant area of the Lavra, next to the northern tower, the monks preserved the flowing springs that were deemed holy. It was this fresh water that St. Sergius had discovered by God's grace to survive, with the muddy river unsuitable for basic needs. Now located behind the main building of the monastery, it was a site that few visitors to the Lavra ever ventured to—even though it was not closed to the public.

Father Mikhail guided Sokolov and Asiyah towards the monastic section of the Lavra. It was only then, as they were reaching the northern tower, that they realized how enormous the territory of the Lavra really was. Even the booming din of the grand bell—and the supporting chimes joining it to reverberate around the Lavra—now sounded duller.

"You will have your rendezvous at the clearing behind the monastery, near the springs," the priest said.

From there, Father Mikhail left them on their own.

Sokolov and Asiyah followed the paved alley and rounded the corner behind the monastery, to find the springs.

There, on the grassy knoll, a man was sitting on a rock, peering at a gushing stream. He wore the plain cassock of a monk, which suited him well, and his feet were bare.

Sokolov could not believe his eyes.

"My goodness ... " Sokolov murmured. "You're alive ... "

For a few moments, there was nothing Ilia could say in reply.

7

The Metropolitan sat motionless, his eyes locked on his visitors. Only when Sokolov and Asiyah approached to face him did the elderly cleric speak.

"You are Eugene? Constantine's brother?"

"Just what on earth is going on?" Sokolov demanded. "Why all this?"

"I have chosen seclusion in this monastery as punishment for the hardship Constantine had to suffer because of me. I brought it upon him for one year, now I am taking it back—for the rest of my life."

Sokolov studied Ilia, and his rage vanished. Ilia was a broken old man. Under the sun, the bald skin on the top of his head had turned pink. His eyes were red-rimmed, a mesh of wrinkles on his face, lips trembling. He did not look like he had much life left in him. In lieu of Sokolov's anger came bitter emptiness.

"I want to know what you did to my brother. And why he is charged with your murder."

"You have many questions that are not easy to answer. Just like Constantine did when he came to me for help. Your brother's discoveries came along with threats, so he had to leave the country, secretly. He did it to protect *you*, Eugene—from the knowledge of what he got himself into, to keep *you* out of harm's way." The words sounded like an allegation.

"What could he possibly have been involved in that required such extreme measures? And where did he go?"

"He found something that could shake the Russian Government at the very top. All the way up to our President. I don't know what exactly. Only later did I learn that he spent twelve months in France. The man who helped him hide there was Hermann Weinstock."

"Who is Hermann Weinstock?"

"He is the leader of a human rights group called Free Action. His political activities are banned in Russia by the authorities. When Constantine was forced to return to Russia, it was Hermann who arranged my meeting with Constantine. Your brother had something important to tell me. But something went wrong. Hermann sensed that we were under surveillance. So I had to fake my own death. It was a stage show for the watchers hunting after Constantine. As a distraction, Hermann pretended to have shot me and kidnapped Constantine."

"This is madness!"

"True, but it was the only way to make them think I was dead so that they could not find your brother! The link had to be severed!"

Ilia's eyes became wild, reflecting paranoia.

"So this man Weinstock is the last person who saw my brother?"

Ilia nodded.

"How do I find him?"

"I don't know."

"What do you mean?"

"He was the one who always got in touch with me. I never contacted him. It was his means of protection against his enemies, instrumental to his survival—and Constantine's."

"But now we can't find him. "

"It's a double-edged sword, yes. You must understand the logic," said Ilia. "This way no one can use leverage against Constantine. I cannot betray him because I don't know where he is, and because I'm dead anyway."

Sokolov refused to accept that he hit a dead end.

"What about Weinstock's organization? Free Action?" he persisted.

"It exists only on paper. It has no office, no tangible assets, no staff, *nothing*."

"But in that case, what does Free Action do?"

"Free Action fights against the re-emergence of old fascist regimes."

"That is something very abstract," Sokolov pointed out.

"For a real-life example, you don't need to look further than the EU. The manifestations can be very basic and very complex. As basic as youth marching in the streets and chanting Nazi slogans."

"I'm struggling to follow you."

"I will explain everything in detail. I am very old—I remember things no one is supposed to remember. You do know of the annual parades of SS veterans in the Baltic states nowadays? The death squad members celebrating their murderous exploits, dressed up in their full Nazi uniforms and cheered on by the governments of Estonia, Latvia and Lithuania?"

Sokolov nodded.

"Have you ever asked yourself *why*? Why is that allowed to happen in the twenty-first century? Why does the European Union turn a blind eye to Nazi sympathizers in their midst?"

"I have no idea."

"It's a matter of embarrassment, my boy."

"They're embarrassed to face the fact?"

"No! Quite the contrary. They don't want to be embarrassed by this fact anymore. They want to forget it. Forget the guilt of the Second World War. They want that moral pressure of history out of their way. Right now Germany is the driving force of the European Union. They don't want to be reminded of Hitler's crimes several times each year, of reputable German companies using slave labor from the camps. They want to make it seem that everything was not so bad after all. Dilute the emphasis. Mix black and white into shades of gray. After all, the Americans nuked Japan, and Stalin wasn't such a nice guy anyway."

"And what is the reason behind this policy?"

"That is the key question. You see, it is not only Germany that wants to wash off the stains of guilt. It's all of Europe. The Axis powers—and beyond. You should take a look at the tombstones across the continent, and the lists of Wehrmacht divisions in order to understand the reality. You will find every European nationality present on the map fighting alongside. Germans and Austrians. Italians, Belgians, French, Dutch, Hungarians, Croats, Greeks, Ukrainians, Danes, Albanians, Romanians, Bulgarians, Czechs, Slovaks, Norwegians ... All were volunteers strengthening Hitler's war machine. The Waffen SS was sixty percent foreign. Throw in the Swiss with their dubious neutrality, even the Vatican, and there you have it. So it turns out that Hitler was the first man who truly unified Europe in the twentieth century."

"That is a terrifying thought."

"A thought no one wishes to face. And it's made even more terrifying when you remember that Hitler did in fact bring about the dream of another man. Leo Trotsky. What Trotsky called, in his own words, the *United States of Europe*."

Sokolov was beginning to feel sick.

"As much as we enjoy blaming Americans for everything that goes wrong, there is one thing that they did perfectly right," Ilia continued. "When they established West Germany, they instilled upon the Germans a collective sense of national guilt for the crimes of the Nazis. *Every* German was deemed responsible, not only those who worked for the Gestapo, as we are now told. This sense of guilt lasted over decades, becoming remembrance for future generations. Not so in East Germany. It was not the case under Soviet rule. A society that accepted Communist ideology was sinless. Especially if this ideology was forced on the populace by those who defeated the Nazis. The West were the bad Germans, the East were good. And through this initial defiance, a neo-Nazi state was preserved. New flag, old methods. Gestapo morphing into Stasi, swastikas changing into hammers. I'm sure you know this first-hand, Eugene, from your time in the DDR."

"Indeed, I do."

"I don't blame the people for their failure to condemn their past. It is only natural. But where does this road lead to? What *did* rise from the wreckage of the Berlin Wall? Did West Germany incorporate the DDR, or was it East Germany that slowly devoured the *Bundesrepublik*? Imagine for a second that the preserved Stasi regime made its way to the top hierarchy of the unified Germany. And hence to the summit of the new European Union, which expanded through new members from the Soviet Bloc. You will get an abomination."

Sokolov wondered how deluded Ilia had to be in order to believe such a conspiracy theory. And what sort of power did Hermann Weinstock wield over the old man in order to indoctrinate him so feverishly?

Ilia added, "That is why I always felt we should have had our own Nuremberg. We wasted the chance in the nineties to get rid of the Communist stigma, and I'm not sure if it can be possible now."

"A Nuremberg trial of the Communists was never possible," Sokolov objected. "*Everyone* was Communist, to a certain extent. Did you expect the whole country to exercise self-flagellation? For it to become the world's largest prison again?"

"I do not mean the Nuremberg trials literally, with charges against every Communist leader. I'm implying the broader sense, the emotional cleansing. The collective guilt of the post-war

Germans. Not persecution, but *confession*. Russia wanted a return to God, but it did not have a communion, did not defy the Devil. Is there anything shameful in saying that evil is evil? Yet there are many people left in this country who would jump at your throat if you mentioned the crimes of the Bolsheviks. Will we eventually forget it all, like Europe tries to forget the Nazis? I do not know, and it scares me, Eugene. Those magnificent skyscrapers will stand for the future generations to marvel at, as will everything that Stalin built. No one cares how many people died constructing the Egyptian Pyramids as one gazes at them with delight. I pray that people don't forget all the blood and the terror that our country suffered."

"Oh, but it happens all the time," Sokolov replied. "People *do* forget. Even those who love to hate the Communists often glorify the man who made their rise inevitable. The man who single-handedly primed Russia for self-destruction, dooming the Romanov dynasty when he murdered his only son. Czar Peter, dubbed the Great for drenching himself in blood, waging catastrophic wars, decapitating the Church, creating serfdom and a behemoth bureaucracy. A great villain in Russian history is now being hailed as a great hero. Not that I really care, but it's nothing new. I can get over it. Every day, I have other things to occupy my mind. Real lives depend on whether or not I'm good enough at what I do. And when I clash with death, I really don't give a toss about historical conspiracies. Right now, I'm trying to save my own brother."

For several seconds, Ilia sat wordlessly, humbled.

"Yes, you are right, my boy."

Sokolov had to press Ilia one more time. Everything revolved around Weinstock and Free Action.

"I need to find Hermann Weinstock. There has to be a way to reach him in case of an emergency."

"There is none," Ilia said apologetically. "It is better that way, Eugene. When the time is right, Constantine will come back, with God's help."

Futility gnawed at Sokolov, making him desperate. He curbed his temper. All throughout his EMERCOM missions, he had learned never to give up hope.

"Do you know any other people who share Weinstock's ideas? How does anyone get involved with their group? They should attract supporters somehow, spread their political views."

Ilia hesitated.

"Like I said, to my knowledge, Free Action does not operate in Russia directly. And you cannot sign up to join them. They only approach the potential members they deem worthy."

For Sokolov, it was another turn of the screw.

"But," Ilia continued, "Herman could barely contain his excitement about a convention he was organizing. A meeting of Free Action members coming from all over the country to discuss their strategies. He called it a turning point."

"Do you know where and when it's taking place?"

"This week. I'm not sure about the exact schedule. As for the venue, it was some place called the Rainbow Hotel ... or the Rainbow Resort—something like that. I can't remember."

That mere half-chance gave Sokolov a spike of emotions that left him exhilarated.

"Thank you for your help, Holy Father."

"What I've done is not much in the way of help, I'm afraid. But I will be praying for God to shine His light on your path. Mind that you may not even find Weinstock at that event of his. It really is a shot in the dark."

Sokolov bowed in appreciation and prepared to leave. There was nothing else to learn here.

Asiyah had been listening intently to their conversation, not uttering a word until that moment.

"There is one thing I need to ask you about," she told Ilia. "In case we *do* find Weinstock."

"Yes?" The lines on his forehead deepened as he gave her his full attention.

"What does he look like?"

8

"I know about the convention," Asiyah said when they returned to the Land Rover. "What the Metropolitan said is true. Alexandrov mentioned it over dinner aboard the *Olympia*."

Sokolov was disoriented. "How could it be?"

"Alexandrov was annoyed that real opposition was making its presence known. He said that he could ban a rally, crack down on the media, but he couldn't take away people's privacy. He was forceless to stop anyone from meeting for discussion. I remember that bit clearly, because my father then joked that Alexandrov should bust them on charges of extremism, for being extremely low-key. Free Action is real, Gene, plotting something behind the scenes."

Sokolov had already engaged the GPS navigator mounted on the Defender's dashboard. Consulting it, he discovered that the establishment which Ilia had mentioned was in fact called the Rainbow Country Club, located twenty kilometers north of Moscow, isolated on the riverbank of the Moskva River. From the map, he followed the link to the club's homepage using the built-in web browser. Over the wireless connection, it popped up instantly. Sokolov tapped EVENTS on the touchscreen.

"There," he said. "We've got it. The event held by Free Action is listed. It's referred to as a conference on political science, booked for the whole week. Started two days ago."

"Thank goodness," Asiyah said. "But today we may already be too late. Or far too early."

"We have only one way to find that out."

"Right. Let's go."

Sergiev Posad was left behind. Sokolov followed the course forty kilometers to the southwest plotted by the navigator.

He did not want to think about failure. He had fought the odds through sheer determination when everyone but his teammates had given up. But he wasn't leading his friends on a mission now. Throwing himself at the unknown, he was taking Asiyah with him. His responsibility for her was even greater.

Yet, his gut feeling told him that Weinstock would show up at the event. After the left-wing parties crumbled in Russia, mostly down to their own failures, the democrats have been trying to regroup. But their internal squabbles always prevented them from challenging for the Kremlin, or even the Duma. No matter how delusional, the liberals always believed they could mount another challenge. So Weinstock would be taking this gathering very seriously. He needed it to gain momentum throughout the country. If you can't go to the people, make the people come to you, and listen to what you have to say.

Asiyah switched to the web browser, going over the description of the Rainbow Country Club.

"Damn, even I didn't always have such luxury," she laughed. "Just listen what they've got there. A luxury spa and saunas, tennis courts, indoor and outdoor swimming pools, and a nightclub—that's the boring stuff. What I'm really impressed with is the hunting lodge, a skeet-shooting range, a nine-hole golf course, and a horse-riding school."

"Sounds like a great place to visit in any case."

The navigator's female-sounding voice announced an imminent exit from the highway, and Sokolov followed the directions. A minute later, the road wound through a village that boasted picturesque cottages, restaurants, plazas, and manicured lawns stretching along either side of the smooth pavement. For years, Moscow's suburbia had relished the influx of cash that turned crumbling villages into stylish towns of glamor and exuberance, basking in their vicinity to the capital. Beyond the village, which was no more than a blip in the landscape, the straight rural road continued to cut through the fields and forests surrounding it once again.

Looming ahead, where the road curved, was a high fence.

Sokolov slowed the Land Rover down, creeping along the concrete wall revetted with stone. According to the map, it was their destination. But the wall simply ran on without end. Puzzled, Sokolov peered ahead to see a large wooden sign indicating an entrance. The Rainbow Country Club.

"Is this it?" Asiyah asked.

"Should be. Matches the picture on the web, too."

The gate was a mock-up of a medieval drawbridge, right down to a miniature moat under it. There was no security in attendance, but the lack of human presence was made up for by an abundance of surveillance cameras. As Sokolov drove deeper inside the grounds, the masonry of the fence quickly disappeared from view, the area within apparently limitless. What surprised Sokolov most was the fact that he had never known about a resort that took up acres of land, including a sizable chunk of pine forest and the riverfront.

The Rainbow Country Club was a testament to Moscow's burgeoning workaholism and its rewards. Small businesses and large enterprises adopted Western management techniques eagerly. The most popular of those was expanding a corporate culture and unity among the employees beyond working hours. It was the common belief of Russian HR managers that teamwork had to be built by means of the company staff sharing weekends together, strengthening congenial ties through barbecues and pool parties. The practice caught on well; after all, collectivism remained a tradition.

Like many other countryside resorts dotted around Moscow, the Rainbow Club possessed all the prerequisites of successful stress relief. Located on the riverbank of the Moskva, lost behind dense greenery, it was a retreat from the hectic urban bustle.

The quiet natural surroundings seemingly belonged to a different planet altogether, yet at only twenty kilometers north of the city limits, it was an unbeatable choice from a logistical point of view.

More often than not, business facilities at such resorts were the most crowded. The managers could never detach themselves from their jobs, and the resorts essentially turned to variations of offices in colorful settings, the weekends differing from weekdays only by the view outside, much longer hours, and the midnight cocktails with the boss.

For the purposes of Free Action, the venue was perfect. It could accommodate every visiting member and allow them to hold their meetings in complete privacy. By all appearances, it was just another corporate group on a get-together picnic. They could stage lectures and seminars, watch motivational videos, receive instructions and duffel bags full of untraceable cash. Then these activists would go back to their towns across the country, to use the new directives and resources and bring in more supporters. Boys and girls who are susceptible to indoctrination. And no one would ever have a clue about what was going on covertly behind these walls.

Ingenious.

Going past private bungalows, the tennis courts and the swimming pool, Sokolov parked the Land Rover in front of the hotel building. Its facade was designed to resemble a romantic castle—conic spires, towers that were too compact to intimidate, stone tiles colored in pastel beige. A lavish fountain was spewing jets of water before the entrance. Flowers bloomed along the sidewalks.

No one welcomed them. The windows were tinted, rendering it impossible to see anything from outside. The loudest sound he could hear was the stillness of the air. They had not encountered any human presence so far. No porter attended the revolving glass door. Sokolov felt it strange for a place of such size to have so little activity going on. Unless someone was overly sure that no activity be spotted. He shrugged it all off. No time to play mind games with himself.

As he swung the door, Asiyah huddled next to him in the same enclosure. She did not want to be separated from him. They crossed the threshold of the hotel in step.

It was far from deserted, they saw.

A sudden gust from the air conditioning chilled Sokolov after the blazing sun. Live piano music was playing softly. At the front desk, the lone receptionist was busy checking-in a new guest, the weight of a leather laptop bag slung over his shoulder wrinkling his expensive suit as he fumbled with his papers and credit cards. Several clients chatted over drinks in the lobby. The marble floor reflected a giant chandelier suspended over it.

Asiyah squeezed his hand, directing his attention to a large plasma screen in the corner of the lobby which displayed an announcement.

Special Guest Speaker
Herman Weinstock
Conference Hall

Sokolov drew a breath. His objective was a few paces away.

No title or position, no topic of his speech, no association to politics was mentioned anywhere in the notice.

The start of the event was listed at just under an hour ago. He did not want to think that they might have missed Weinstock by a few minutes.

Sokolov and Asiyah traversed the lobby. Frantically, his eyes darted around the notice boards which showed directions to the ground floor services.

Restaurant ... Gift shop ...

Business center ...

Conference Hall.

They proceeded along the corridor, facing the tall double door of the Conference Hall. A metallic voice echoed from within it, amplified by a microphone but muffled by the thick walls so that the words were barely comprehensible.

Sokolov stepped closer, his hand hovering over the door handle.

He had no idea what would be waiting for him behind that door. His fingers were colder than the chrome he touched as he pulled the handle. The door was not locked. He pushed it ajar, peering at the audience in attendance. The speaker's voice flowed clearly now at him through the narrow crack of the opening.

"*I must emphasize that it's absolutely unacceptable ... Now, proceeding to the next diagram ... Hold on a second ... Ah, here it is ... As you can see, the figures shown ...*"

A low, gruff voice.

But Sokolov was unable to see the speaker. As the door was at the back of the hall, he could only glimpse the last rows of chairs in the audience, men and women listening intently to the unseen orator at the other end of the hall. There was no way Sokolov could get a look at the man he hoped to be Herman Weinstock without revealing himself.

He turned to Asiyah, and she nodded in agreement

Sokolov pushed the door and slid inside the hall, Asiyah at his side.

The conference hall was almost full, with around fifty attendees, and some of them turned their heads, responding to the intruders. Sokolov felt the admonishing stares leveled at him. Middle-aged faces; men and women; hard, cynical, lacking any warmth. The room was cavernous, rendering clear acoustics. Light flooded in through a row of double-hung sash windows overlooking the distant riverbank.

Herman Weinstock was just as Ilia had described him. Average height and build, a short haircut. He was dressed casually, wearing a turtleneck sweatshirt, jeans and loafers. His face was chiseled from stone, with heavyset features and piercing eyes.

Ilia's precise tags helped Sokolov identify an otherwise forgettable man that he would never give notice to in a crowded street.

For an instant, Weinstock seemed jarred when Sokolov and Asiyah entered. He paused his narration in mid-sentence. Sokolov's breath was cut short as he and Weinstock locked eyes. It lasted a beat too long, and Sokolov fought the urge to break away from the intense eye contact. Weinstock's flash of alarm was replaced by hostility and then an assumed calmness. Again with abruptness, Weinstock resumed his lecture, picking up his monotonous pace as if nothing had distracted him.

The only unoccupied chairs remained in the back rows, at the other end of the hall. Sokolov would not back away now. He intended to take it all the way through. Suffering the attention of every pair of eyes in the room, they walked all the way around the back. They took their seats and the bobbing heads quickly shifted their focus back to the man addressing them.

Hidden behind the crowd, Sokolov studied the people around him. This was the inner core of the Free Action setup. All of them were accustomed to pounding slogans into the brains of ordinary laymen, In this room Weinstock was doing the same to them. Many attendees were making notes of Weinstock's speech. In the corner of the room, a video camera was mounted on a tripod, one of the participants recording the event for future generations.

As he talked, Weinstock held the microphone lazily at chest level so that his voice, while audible anywhere in the hall, was not overly loud. Next to him, atop a small table, was a laptop hooked to a projector, showing a pie chart on a white screen. Watching, Sokolov struggled to understand how anything about Herman Weinstock could have impressed Ilia. Weinstock's ramblings about the deficiencies of the Russian government were tepid, as if the limelight put him off balance. His language was simple and straightforward. Not only did his statements lack eloquence and passion, making Sokolov think that Weinstock did not actually believe in what he was saying, but the man had trouble following his own logic, as if his mind was elsewhere. It was shocking.

"There's something wrong about all this," Asiyah murmured. "I can feel it."

Sokolov held Asiyah's hand. It was as much as he could do to reassure her. And himself. No matter what, Sokolov was determined to come up to Weinstock and use any means to learn what he had done to Constantine. Until he had finished delivering his lecture, in front of witnesses and cameras, all Sokolov could do was wait, and try to learn the most about Weinstock from his speech and body language.

It was then that Sokolov spotted a possible explanation to Weinstock's edginess. As Weinstock cast his glance around the audience, more often than not his attention lingered on Sokolov and Asiyah. There was no mistake about Weinstock deliberately studying them. Their arrival had unsettled Weinstock. Scared him enough to make his lecture irrelevant. It was the reaction of a man fearing for his life. Weinstock had recognized a threat.

But not the other members, Sokolov's inner voice told him. The people around him no longer paid any attention to the two outsiders; as compact as Free Action was, the supporters probably did not know each other well enough to get paranoid over seeing a couple of unfamiliar faces joining a meeting. Weinstock alone was rattled, and there was only one reason for such a reaction—Weinstock knew exactly who Eugene Sokolov was and what he wanted.

Weinstock knew they had come because of Constantine.

Anger swelled inside Sokolov.

"And that concludes my presentation," Weinstock finally said. "Questions and comments are welcome."

No questions were posed.

As if puzzled by this, Weinstock searched the faces of the attendees, inviting discussion. Crossing his arms, he turned to Sokolov and Asiyah.

"Perhaps our trespassers wish to speak up?"

His grey eyes crackled with malice. An inevitable confrontation simmered. With each passing moment, more pairs of eyes from the crowd followed their leader's scathing look, turning to the intruders they had almost disregarded. Sokolov forced himself not to be intimidated by those eyes Weinstock had—his true weapon.

A deathly silence hung in the conference hall, an ominous veil of some calamity about to strike.

Sokolov cursed himself mentally. Barging right into the vipers' nest had been crazy in the first place. Now his recklessness endangered Asiyah. To protect himself, Weinstock could turn the crowd against them. Outnumbered, there wouldn't be too much of a fight to put up.

Without warning, the door burst opened and camouflaged figures surged inside the conference hall like ants. Their blue-gray fatigues and black balaclavas identified them as OMON, Russia's fearsome police unit

"Everybody down! *Your faces to the floor!* Now!"

Gasps and obscenities rippled through the crowd. The OMON troopers spread out, threatening with their batons. Their compact AKs added weight to the shouted orders. Frightened by the onslaught, several Free Action members raised their hands in submission, and sank to the floor, knowing better than to ask questions. Most were too stunned to move, and in the eyes of the troopers, needed encouragement. One OMON goon, with the build and the attitude of a bull, shoved a woman down to the floor and smashed his baton against the neck of a man next to her. The OMON emphasized the point, dishing out punishment to those nearest to the exit, pushing them away. Chairs toppled. Cries filled the room.

An enraged neighbor of the hurt woman threw himself at the policeman, and the two crashed on the floor. From the middle of the audience a well-trained group organized quickly, crowding an aisle to block access to Weinstock. Others stood up and challenged the OMON squad, hindering their movement. Batons sliced the air angrily, crunching against human bodies. With chairs flying the opposite way, punches and kicks breaking against body armor, it all turned into a mad brawl, the OMON winning in violent hits, but losing in numbers and initiative.

Sokolov's senses fired up. Seizing the chance, he backed away from the crowd, shielding Asiyah with his body.

"Keep your head low," he whispered to her. "Stay right behind me."

They moved to the empty corner of the conference hall, away from the immediate skirmish.

With the situation going out of control, an OMON man trained his Kalashnikov on the mass of people.

"*Back off!* Everybody down, you scum!"

Through the slits of his balaclava, his mouth was twisted with rage, eyes ablaze, making his face a hideous mask.

That did enough to subdue the resistance. Advancing through the conference hall, the OMON would get to Eugene and Asiyah before long.

Sokolov saw the barrel of the assault rifle pointed at them.

The memory of Beslan was spinning in his mind, a vertigo of perverted reality. He was reliving an even uglier version of the nightmare. *This* time, as he put his body between Asiyah and the shooter, the *police* acted as terrorists, herding hostages in a confined space. The Kalashnikovs—and the black masks—were identical. And Asiyah, the girl he had vowed to save, was next to him. What maddened him was seeing the OMON fighting civilians—with all the ferocity of 1993, as he imagined his father at the barricades, clashing with the same riot police. It galvanized him into action.

Before anyone could react, Weinstock grabbed his table and tossed in at the window.

Glass burst into fragments, the frames broke off their hinges.

"Gene! He's trying to escape!" Asiyah said.

She ran in tow as Sokolov dashed forward. Chasing Weinstock, Sokolov cared less about catching him than using the escape route he had created for himself. Saving his skin, Weinstock gave them the only chance out.

Seeing their charge, Weinstock yelled, "They are the ones who brought in the cops! Get them!"

Ignoring the policemen, three of Weinstock's loyal men cut into Sokolov's path.

With amazing dexterity, Herman Weinstock hopped over the window sill, and then vanished, running to the riverbank across the field. Two OMON troopers pursued him—clearly, their orders stood to catch Weinstock alive.

Trusting their comrades to arrest the leader of Free Action, the others were busy standing over their prone captives, frisking and handcuffing them. The troopers hesitated, but saw no reason to interfere as three brutes started a fight with a solitary man and a girl. If anything, it was amusing entertainment.

Before his attacker—a bearded, square-shouldered thug—could swing a punch at him, Sokolov axed a front kick, belting the foot into his face. Caught on the chin, the man staggered and fell. Sokolov's foot was still in the air when—with one powerful motion—he hooked it sideways and slammed his heel against the head of the man's partner, knocking him senseless.

Sokolov opened himself up for a counter from the third man, and prepared to block his strike, but Asiyah drove her boot into the man's gut, and following up with another roundhouse to bring him down.

Not missing a beat, Gene and Asiyah ran for the window.

The dozen-strong OMON squad would no longer watch idly.

"Hold it right there!"

One trooper pressed the stock of his Kalashnikov to his shoulder and aimed. There was no question about the seriousness of his intent. The OMON only shot to kill.

Now or never. Putting his body between Asiyah and the line of fire, he hoisted her to the empty window sash. Asiyah jumped clear.

When the gunshot came, it boomed around the hall, rocking him, deafening.

9

Asiyah tumbled to the grass lawn.

Diving through the window, Sokolov landed near her. Adrenalin buzzing, he recovered quickly, getting back to his feet. Although visibly shaken, Asiyah did not appear to be hurt as she picked herself up.

The shot had missed. Sokolov knew he did not owe his life to poor marksmanship. The thunderclap of the Kalashnikov was a warning—to stop *them*, and to alert another OMON trooper standing watch outside. He was alone—whether his comrades had gone after Weinstock, or he was waiting for backup, Sokolov hardly cared.

The trooper hacked with the baton. Sokolov met the strike with a sharp block to the man's wrist and punched with such power that he felt his knuckles fracture the jawbone.

Asiyah tugged his shoulder, and he followed her, together running away from more danger.

They were out in the open, charging through a grass field. Sokolov expected OMON to ambush them any second, or a bullet to sizzle into his spine. Asiyah set the pace, Sokolov running hard to keep up with her. He knew they had to take cover somewhere, veer off the direct course.

To their right, an impregnable mesh of netting screened off the boundaries of the golf driving range.

To their left was a pine grove, part of the woods maintained at the Country Club for game hunting.

"Go for the trees!" he called to Asiyah, but indeed, he needn't have. Swiftly, she had already changed direction, her vision and thinking as quick as his.

They dashed to the grove like Olympians pushing for the finish line. Stopping as they penetrated it, Asiyah pressed against a tree, exhausted.

"Anyone chasing us?" Asiyah said.

"I don't think so," he said. "But it won't be for long. Soon, the OMON will be crawling all over the resort."

Asiyah nodded. "I saw Weinstock heading to the riverfront. We still have a chance of making up the head start he has on us."

"No, Asiyah. It's out of the question," Sokolov said bitterly. The chance to find Constantine had disappeared together with Weinstock, cut off by the arrival of the OMON. He could not risk going forward any more. It was time to retreat. "I need to get you someplace safe. There has to be a way out."

"Weinstock *is* the way out! I'm sure he planned for every contingency. He has an emergency route out of here." Asiyah threw up her hands. "We have no choice, Gene. Nowhere to run, and no place to hide. The OMON have sealed off every exit, and they may start sweeping this grove any minute now. Whichever way you look at it, we must follow Weinstock's trail. You know that as well as I do."

"You're right," Sokolov admitted. "I think I know why he's moving towards the river. Weinstock wants to reach the fishing boats."

Asiyah shook her head. "He's one cunning bastard."

Sokolov gathered his bearings.

"Let's take a shortcut."

10

Sokolov led Asiyah through the woods, recalling in his memory the layout of the Rainbow Country Club that he had seen on the website. They would surely not beat Weinstock to the boat jetty, but they could cut the gap in time before he escaped. Topped up, a typical twenty-foot bowrider had a range of around three hundred kilometers—enough to reach the expanse of the Volga. If it blasted away even at 30 mph, any chance of catching Weinstock would dissolve together with the spray setting in its wake.

The grove had thickened into a mix of birch, pine and asp. Sokolov strained to listen to the sounds around him. A squirrel scampered up the trunk of a birch and disappeared in the canopy. Birds chirped a short exchange that faded in the air. Sokolov kept his guard for other sounds—of things lurking in the shadows. He was much less worried about being attacked by wild boar than ambushed by the OMON. The animals were locked up in their pens somewhere, waiting to be drugged for slaughter by rifle-wielding tourists. In reality, the forest was as fake as the medieval castle, an arena for exotic amusement, too carefully planned and laid out. Ugly stumps jutted where trees had been sawed down, nature sacrificed for perceived symmetry. The footpaths were too straight, the landscape too accurate in geometry. It was not the untamed forest of Sokolov's childhood, and that made it even more dangerous. A human environment designed for amateur hunters to trap their game. Even Asiyah, a city girl, stepped noiselessly over the twigs and roots as she waded along. Sokolov felt he would struggle to detect an adversary from afar, which could just as well work in their favor, making them invisible. He was grateful when the passage ended.

They reached a clearing, fifty meters ahead of the riverbank. The slow current of the Moskva, ripples on its surface, washed the artificial slope of a sandy beach.

They did not find the motor boats, or the jetty. The river's edge was barren.

But they found Weinstock.

Sokolov ran up to him, forgetting all caution.

Then Weinstock did something that Sokolov least expected.

He started laughing.

A snickering that grew into a booming cackle.

"Sokolov, you're an idiot. I have you now. You ran away from my little masquerade with the OMON, but you walked in right where I wanted you. There troops will be here soon. You're surrounded."

Weinstock leered at him with contempt.

Sokolov raised his hand to strike, but if he unleashed his full fury, he knew he'd kill Weinstock. Instead, Sokolov unclenched his fist. In a knife-hand chop, he slashed across Weinstock's face with the ridge of his open palm, drawing blood. Weinstock lurched back. Blood oozed from the gash on his lower lip. And again, he laughed. A full, throaty laugh, sinister in its absurdity, Weinstock's teeth colored red with blood.

"Where's Constantine?"

"*Look!* Over there!" Asiyah called, and he turned to see her gesturing towards the river.

Squinting from the sunlight, Sokolov peered at the opposite shore. Gliding through the water, a yacht materialized from afar. As she approached, Sokolov could make out the yacht's name. The *New Star*.

He would have marveled at the beauty of her hundred-foot black hull, or the sleek white superstructure—if not for what he saw happening on board. Sokolov stood paralyzed in numb shock.

On the deck, a man was returning his gaze. Sokolov could discern enough of his features to recognize him as Saveliy Frolov, the Director of the FSB. There was a second man standing at Frolov's side, and Sokolov did not need a second look to know who the man was right away. Sokolov's heart knew the answer only from his posture, the breadth of his shoulders, the color of his hair. But he also saw his older brother's face. Constantine's face, fair-skinned, youthful, the handsome features rigid with mute bitterness.

And he could clearly see that Director Frolov was holding a gun to Constantine's head.

It was all over. The world inside him turned upside down. He had found his brother, but he had never wished it to be this way.

Asiyah screamed.

Sokolov pivoted to witness an OMON trooper grab Asiyah from behind.

His mind went berserk, but Sokolov didn't have a chance to move a muscle.

The blue flash of a taser held by Weinstock was the last thing Sokolov remembered.

11

Sokolov returned to consciousness. He bolted upright to see that he was inside a chamber. Brilliant lights from the ceiling and bedside lamps stabbed his eyes, reflecting off the polished surface of wooden paneling around him. He sprang to his feet, getting off the springy mattress of the king-sized bed. A seascape painting took up the wall above the bed. On the opposite wall was a flat display matching in size and symmetry but showing dead blackness. The carpeting felt wooly—his feet were bare. He was still wearing his street clothes. The mirrors hanging on the walls visibly increased the size of the confines. As he cast his glance around the room, a hot wave of despair filled his chest.

He was aboard the yacht. The *New Star*. He pressed his face to the single window to his right. The water surface was glassy, with ripples rolling on it. On the shore, the distant rooftops of village homes glistened in the sun, disappearing together with the birches lining the riverfront as the view glided past.

Sokolov charged at the door, twisting the knob violently, ramming with his shoulder, kicking. No use—he was trapped.

He faced the window again. Ever since losing his Breitling in the fire, he'd felt a vital part of his wrist was missing. The sun's position had shifted past zenith now, so he could tell that the yacht had been traveling away from the Rainbow Country Club for at least an hour. Anxiety flayed his nerves raw. Was Constantine aboard the *New Star*? Or was Eugene being taken away from his brother, shut off in this cabin while Constantine was being spirited away to a new location? And Asiyah. Dear God, where was Asiyah—was she *alive*?

He turned from the window sharply, his eyes darting around the room, his mind seeking a way out. His fury against the surroundings turned into bitter rage at himself, if not disgust. Even a man trapped under wreckage would claw at the debris until his hands were caked in blood and lost all feeling. But there was nothing Sokolov could do. He felt utterly worthless, and he considered his futility as betrayal of Asiyah and Constantine.

They were important. They needed him. He channeled his emotions, preparing for a fresh start. He had to make the most out of his defeat, but he had to accept it first. From there, he had a chance to turn things around and get the upper hand. Giving up was the easy way out. For some reason, he was held captive on the yacht, alive. It was his only advantage, and he was determined to use it—and save Asiyah and Constantine. The FSB wanted something from him. Even if he had no idea what it was, he could not waste his chance to claw his way out.

As if on cue, the lock clicked and two men entered the cabin before the door sealed again. Sokolov assessed them, his back pressing against the cold glass of the window. The first man was Frolov. Ramrod-straight yet light on his feet, Frolov passed through the room and sat on the edge of the bed, crossing his legs. It was the first time Sokolov had seen him up close. A short, stocky man, his thin grey hair combed over his skull. Sokolov noticed the capillaries on his bulbous nose. The flabby skin on his neck hung like a turkey's snood. Over the decades, coffee and cigarettes had colored his teeth almost orange. Frolov enjoyed the triumph, a sneer slackening his jaw. His puffy eyes were going over Sokolov with careful interest, as if deciding whether a long-awaited trophy lived up to the hype.

Staying behind Frolov, acting as his guard was the man he knew as Hermann Weinstock.

"Are you afraid of me so much that you can't face me alone? You brought your leashed dog to protect you?"

Weinstock's neck flushed red, but not a single muscle twitched. Frolov remained silent for a moment. He had expected to intimidate Sokolov with his presence, but Sokolov's unexpected response put him on the back foot. Sokolov did not scream, sulk, protest, or plead for mercy—he acted like he was the one in complete control.

Frolov spoke calmly, but his voice had a hard edge to it.

"Not at all. My assistant—his name is Victor—is here to keep you from doing anything foolish, for your own sake. So I'm not afraid of you, Eugene."

"I see no other reason for it, Frolov."

"*You* are the only reason. Everything would have been a lot simpler if you had just agreed to follow my people from your house in Bykovo. Other factors came into play, of course, and you disappeared. From then on I had to draw you out—all the while keeping you from those who tried to kill you. I knew you had to make your move, eventually, because of your brother. My men kept watch at a number of locations that you were likely to appear at: your old apartment, the Novodevichy Convent, the Lavra ... Fortunately, you chose the most direct route, and found Ilia at the Lavra. That old deluded fool did what he had to without even knowing it."

Sokolov felt sick with the realization. The magnitude of Frolov's deception seemed limitless. He was caught in a labyrinth of lies without a waypoint. How far-reaching was Frolov's control? All the way to the attack against Constantine. The manipulation of Ilia. But to what detail had the lies been planned? As far as placing a fake news report in the national media, intended for just one man in the multi-million audience? As deep as having the President worry about a phony political force to give credence to the mirage? Lies seemed planted everywhere Sokolov looked—from allegations of Ilia's murder to the staged bedlam of the OMON raid.

"You *led* me?"

"No. I did not bring you here. *You* came here through your own will. And you had to overcome a lot of obstacles on your way. *You* went to the Lavra to find answers. *You* followed the trail to the Rainbow Country Club. I did not make you enter the hotel. I did not force you to open the door to the conference hall. Chasing Weinstock was your own decision. Each choice was a mark of your bravery and determination. A test of your character as you went deeper into the rabbit hole. I have to say you justified my trust in you. Losing you would have been stupid because it also meant losing Asiyah. But you have come here, giving her to me."

Frolov was just messing with his head, Sokolov told himself. Frolov was trying to make him feel guilty for failing Asiyah.

"Asiyah won't be any good to you. She was at the wrong place at the wrong time. Let her go."

"Do you really think she is innocent? Far from it. She deceived you in ways you could never imagine. She used you, and she doesn't care about your fate anymore. I would even say she is quite comfortable right now."

Could it be that Frolov *knew* that it was Asiyah who killed the President? Nothing seemed impossible any longer. Or was he talking about something else? It didn't matter. Sokolov was tired of the mind games. In *his* mind, Asiyah *was* innocent.

"I don't believe a word you're saying," he said.

"Without lies, there is no value to truth."

"So what is your truth? How did any three of us cross your path? What do you want from us?"

"Your help."

"What sort of help are you talking about?" Sokolov demanded.

"I think you will be more inclined to hear out the details together with your brother."

"Where *is* he?"

"Constantine is aboard the *New Star*. He is in the master cabin next door."

Frolov picked up the remote and powered on the widescreen panel.

Backing Frolov's words, a still view of the other cabin filled the large screen.

Video cameras. That explained Frolov's apt arrival after Sokolov had regained his senses. Could it also mean that the *Olympia* had been wired as well, and the FSB had obtained recordings?

The picture showed Constantine. He had his back turned to the ceiling-mounted camera, standing frozen before a similar television screen. There was no audio. Eugene was grateful to see Constantine, alive and well.

Frolov produced a plastic card from his pocket and held it up. "This is the keycard for his door. You can liberate him," he said with a cruel smile. "Or maybe not. Don't you think you've suffered enough because of him? Perhaps you shouldn't be so eager to see him, after all. You will find nothing but more pain—for yourself, and for Asiyah."

Eugene Sokolov snatched the keycard from the FSB Director's fingers and stormed out, brushing Victor aside on his way.

12

The deck was empty. There were no guards in sight, but none were required. The *New Star* was a different kind of prison, restricting farther than the deck's boundaries.

Running away was never an option for Sokolov in any case. He was focused only on the door to Constantine's cabin. Sokolov held the small piece of plastic so tightly that his fingers turned white, fearing that the most precious item he'd ever had might suddenly disappear from his hand.

He slipped the keycard into the slit of the lock, but his fingers quivering, it did not open. Sokolov cursed, anxiety rising at the thought that the key was fake.

Then he heard movement behind the door.

"Constantine! I'm here to get you out!"

Nothing. No response from the other side.

Sokolov thrust the keycard sharply in and out of the slit again, and this time he heard the click of the lock mechanism. Grunting, he tore at the handle and rushed inside.

Right in front of the door, Constantine was facing him.

Overcome with emotion, Constantine gazed at him as if Eugene were an apparition, but his face lit up, seeing his brother after so long. Eugene placed his hands on his brother's shoulders, and Constantine embraced him so tightly that Eugene's breath was cut short. It felt like Constantine was never going to let him go, and Eugene did not want him to, holding his brother just as hard in return, feeling his warmth and his heartbeat.

"I'm so sorry, Gene ... I'm sorry I pulled you into all this ..."

"Everything will be fine now," Eugene said. "Don't worry, we'll make it out. We're together now."

He felt his own eyes becoming moist.

They remained that way for a few silent moments longer; the younger brother comforting the elder.

"I need to get away from this cabin," Constantine said. "Need some fresh air. And I don't want those bastards to be watching us. Let's go outside. I will tell you the whole truth. I hope you can forgive me, brother."

13

Constantine shifted his weight against the rail, not looking at the water below, the sun-filled sky, or the picturesque scenery. His attention centered on Eugene alone, just as Eugene was studying only him, compensating for the lost time.

Eugene tried to pick out the physical details that had altered in Constantine—the hair that was longer than usual, or his stronger physical shape—but then there was something that Eugene couldn't distinguish, only feel.

The overall difference in his brother was intangible but noticeable, like two snapshots of the same person taken a year apart. Constantine was a year older; a year different. A year of each other had been robbed from their lives by Frolov.

"You've changed," Constantine said. The mischievous twinkle in his eyes was unchanged, though.

"I was about to say the same."

"Much worse, eh?"

"Different."

"I do feel a lot different. And a lot worse."

Constantine sighed, recollecting.

"I think our quarrel was the starting point, Gene," he said. "Do you remember it?"

He remembered. Constantine had always held a grudge against him after he had joined the EMERCOM, feeling that Eugene served the government that had killed their father. In Constantine's mind, it was betrayal.

Eugene had countered, saying that back in 1993 the opposition leaders wanted to pull Russia back into Communism, conning ordinary people to die for them. Besides, Eugene wasn't working for some butcher government, he was saving human lives.

In the end, one such argument reached a breaking point. Tempers flared, and Eugene responded to the accusations with an analogy of his own.

Our father was the one who truly betrayed us. Mother begged him to stay with us, to keep away from that madness, but he wouldn't listen. He couldn't swallow his pride. He went there and got himself killed.

It had become the mark of their alienation.

"My stupidity and stubbornness is to blame for everything," Constantine said. "As the elder brother, I should have made amends. But I guess I couldn't swallow my pride, either. I went soul-searching then. I ended up attending lectures at the Theological Academy. It was there that I met Metropolitan Ilia. He was a very kind and considerate old man. I shared my pain with him. Eventually, he confided in me that he could learn something about the man who destroyed our father."

"And that man turned out to be President Alexandrov."

"How do you know?"

"That was what Ilia told me as well."

Constantine flinched.

"*What*? Ilia?"

"Ilia is alive."

"Are you sure?"

"In fact, I met him a few hours ago."

Constantine fell silent for a moment.

"How could they stoop to such treachery ... making me believe ... What did Ilia tell you?"

"He seemed less than sincere about the details, especially when his own involvement was concerned, but I could fill in the blanks myself. He also told me that your life was in danger and you had to hide in France. But why didn't you ask *me* for *help*?"

"I could not allow myself to make you suffer from the mess I started."

"You didn't start it—the FSB did, unbeknownst to you or to Ilia."

"Still, I was stupid enough to walk right into the FSB's path. Of course they couldn't pass up the opportunity to use me. Now I know that most of the information they gave me on Alexandrov was fake, but I fell for it then. Just as Ilia himself had fallen for the dirt about the top clergy's affiliation with the KGB. Anyway, they had to get me to France, and they did," Constantine continued. "Ilia had been searching for the whereabouts of the Kremlin collection, and the only man who had the relevant documents wouldn't pass them to an outsider. His name was Malinin, an emigre living in London. So their common paranoia for FSB agents led them to employ me as a conduit—exactly as the FSB planned all along."

"Bastards," Eugene breathed. "They used you and Ilia in their scheme twice, switching the roles. First they lured Malinin to Ilia through you, and then they lured me to you through Ilia."

"But *why*, Gene? What do they want from *you*?"

"Whatever the reason, it's not your fault. It's all part of their sick plan, which has something to do with the girl I rescued."

"The girl I saw on the riverfront? Who is she?"

"Asiyah Kasymova. She is the daughter of the President of Kazakhstan."

"Kazakhstan? It can't be. Oh no, it can't be. How did it all happen?"

Eugene recounted the events beginning from the destruction of the *Olympia* and his mission in Sochi.

When he finished, blood drained from Constantine's face.

"Do you know what's going on?" Eugene asked.

"Some of the things I've learned from Malinin's documents and the disc while I've been on this yacht can provide an explanation. But I believe there could still be more questions than answers in this affair, and I feel that Asiyah is the missing piece of the puzzle."

14

Eugene found his own cabin to be empty. Frolov and his bodyguard were gone. With no one to challenge, he would have to search the *New Star* to find Asiyah—if she *was* indeed aboard the yacht. Frolov had never given any proof to back his words, and in reality she could be anywhere between the Lubyanka and the hands of the OMON goons. The thought made Sokolov sick to his stomach.

At a hundred and ten feet long, the *New Star* was in no way the biggest among luxury yachts, but still there were four guest cabins, a large dining salon, and a second lounge on the upper deck.

They found Asiyah in the salon. It was an oblong compartment dominated by a dining table. With the sunlight flooding in through a row of windows, every lacquered surface of the cherrywood interior gave off a sheen.

Asiyah sat alone at the empty table which was big enough to seat ten. Her hands were placed atop the pastel silk tablecloth, and her posture was rigid, her body unnaturally tense. She was immobile, her eyes closed, as if lost in prayer or meditation.

Eugene was both elated at seeing her and perturbed, not knowing what to make of her condition. As he and Constantine came closer, he was at a loss whether he should call her name.

Then suddenly their intrusion startled her, and she turned her head. She gasped, her eyes showing surprise at seeing someone other than whom she had expected—or feared.

Her eyes held Eugene, and he was powerless to utter a word.

On impulse, she sprang to her feet and pushed away the chair. When it seemed she was ready to rush into his arms, she caught herself in mid-stride, freezing as she regained her poise, making the moment all the more embarrassing. Eugene did not know if it was Constantine's presence that held her back—or the awareness of the cameras—or maybe he had imagined the whole thing, simply wanted her to run to him and hold him tight.

She lowered her eyes, and then looked up again at the two men in front of her, and clasped her hands together nervously.

"Hello, Eugene. I never thought I'd see you again. I'm happy that you and your brother are safe," she said earnestly.

"What have you been doing here, Asiyah?" Eugene said.

"I've been sitting here ever since that Weinstock bastard got me and threw me in here. All this time I've been trying to get my mind off this damned yacht. This damned dining room, and the damned water. I feel like I'm on the *Olympia* again, and it's driving me crazy."

The thought made him feel a surge of the same fear he had experienced inside the sunken yacht, and he could only imagine how much worse it was for her.

"But it's only a minor nuisance," she said. "It doesn't matter. It's all over for me. They won't let me live. There's nothing else they can do except put a bullet in my head. I hope they let you go, but I'm as good as dead."

"It's not over. Nothing is over yet, Asiyah. We're still together. We will all make it out. I promise you."

A few moments passed before she said, "I'm afraid you're wrong this time. There isn't a chance. You need to worry about yourself and Constantine. You don't know what you're up against. Just forget about me."

Her last words made Eugene want to cry out, telling her to keep fighting, but there was nothing he could do as he saw her dejection.

"Asiyah," Constantine said. "Maybe what Frolov is going to tell us will change everything. Maybe we should all still keep the faith?"

"Do I have a choice?" she said, uncaring.

A coarse laugh sounded.

"You don't!"

Frolov's voice boomed from behind as he entered the salon. His bodyguard was nowhere to be seen, but it didn't mean Frolov was vulnerable. There was nothing to come out of it had any of them threatened him. Frolov crossed the room and occupied a plush sofa at the other end so that all three of his captives remained in view.

"So much for the introductions," he said. "I'm sure we're in for a very amusing conversation. There will be plenty of interesting facts to hear from everyone—but most of all, from Ms. Kasymova."

"You're mistaking me for someone else, Mr. Frolov," Asiyah said calmly, but her eyes flashed with malevolence. An almost palpable wave of cold emanated from her now, accentuated by a morbid beat of silence. "There is nothing I can tell you."

"Maybe not at once," Frolov said. "I can't force you to talk, but I can force you to listen. Much of what you hear won't be news to you. You won't be able to feign innocence all the time. And eventually I'll have you cornered." Frolov chuckled. "Now all of you sit down so I can begin."

Warily, Eugene and Constantine occupied the nearest chairs. Asiyah assumed her previous position across the table, closing her eyes again, blocking the madness out. Frolov gave no attention to her attitude.

"Before Asiyah cooperates," Frolov said, "I'll start from a different angle—that of the only other person who links everything. Dead men speak no tales so I'll do it for him. The missing treasures, the Sochi disaster, and the assassination attempts each of you has survived are all related to one another by the enigmatic Maxim Malinin."

"And how did that come about, may I ask?" Eugene said. "Who was Malinin anyway to start all this?"

"Malinin was not the man who originated these catastrophic events. He had played an active—albeit minor—role in the conspiracy, and remained a watchful bystander since. But information can be either a blessing or a curse. And the knowledge Malinin possessed was the kind that he would be killed for sooner or later. When he felt the heat rising, he decided not to wait for some freak accident happening to him, and disappeared. But the people from his past had always kept an eye on their own. You see, Malinin was a former member of the Fourth International."

Ilia's horrifying words haunted Eugene.

"So it's *real*? What Ilia told me is true?"

"It's real, but what Ilia told you is definitely not true. None of the drivel that we fed Ilia bears any resemblance with reality. Do you seriously believe we could allow him to go babbling state secrets? But the Fourth International does exist ... and at the same time, it doesn't. It is a phantom, one myth hidden within another, rooted in the Second World War and then reborn from the ashes. The Fourth International no longer has any members, it has *nothing*, but yet it wields unimaginable power.

That power is information. Revealing just a portion of it would have been enough to destroy them. It all began in Kazakhstan and it will all end in Kazakhstan. That is the location of the Kremlin collection."

"The treasures? All the death and destruction was wreaked for relics?" Eugene's voice rose in incredulous outrage. "For *gold*?"

"The treasures are not the reward but the means," Frolov replied. "There's something else apart from the icons. A bigger treasure. A mystery dating all the way back in history to the beginning of modern Russia as we know it. A Russia emerging from decades of bloodshed and unrest, tyranny and mass murder, to become a superpower built on human bones."

"Again, the revolution?" Eugene muttered under his breath, but he was wrong.

Constantine shook his head.

"Three hundred years ago, in the reign of Peter the Great. And it's not about the gold. It's amber," Frolov said. "The Amber Room."

15

The Eighth Wonder of the World.

It was the most apt description for the Amber Room.

Six tons of amber were rendered into panels of awe-inspiring beauty. The Room consisted of three full-sized walls, their surface measuring fifty-five square meters—each centimeter adorned with carvings and ornate mosaics. Its rich patterns accented by gold leaf and mirrors made the Room a glorious masterpiece in its own right.

Few beholders could remain immune to the amber's bewitching qualities. Whenever light filled the Amber Room, the sun saturated it with flowing radiance. The walls flooded from inside with waves of captured sun rays, as if the amber's energy longed to break free.

During his visit to Prussia in 1716, Peter the Great was so mesmerized by the Amber Room's luxurious brilliance, that Friedrich Wilhelm I gifted it to the Russian czar.

By 1770 the Room took final shape, refined, expanded and enriched by Russian craftsmen. It remained in Tsarskoe Selo, a small town south of St. Petersburg, until 1941 when the town fell to the looting Nazis. From that moment on, nothing had ever been learned about the fate of the legendary masterpiece, its mystery becoming a part of the legend.

Frolov began. "After Germany and the Soviet Union signed their non-aggression pact in 1939, Stalin wanted to honor the growing ties with Hitler, as well as amaze him, by presenting a stunning gift. He chose no better souvenir than the Amber Room, which had previously found its way *from* a German king to a Russian czar. Stalin thought the nice touch would be appreciated."

Stalin wanted to give the Amber Room to the Nazis? Eugene wondered as Frolov talked.

"Lazar Kaganovich didn't like the idea. He convinced Stalin that something as valuable as the Amber Room would be of good use to Stalin himself, and Hitler could manage fine as he were without it. However, Stalin would hear none of it, especially not from his subordinate. He was adamant about treating his new German partner with opulence never seen before. Of course, at the same time the idea of keeping the Amber Room appealed to him. So it got him thinking, and soon Stalin found a way out of the dilemma. He came up with the most obvious answer. Create a copy of the Amber Room for Hitler and keep the original. It was a daunting task, no doubt. But not impossible. Nothing was impossible in the USSR if it was an order from Joseph Stalin. If He wanted to *create* the Amber Room *again*, it had to be done." Frolov rose, pacing the salon.

"There was only one man capable of standing up to the challenge," he continued. "Kaganovich summoned Russia's greatest art restorer of the time—the quiet genius who lived in a tiny wooden house, behind the walls of the Novodevichy Convent. The famous architect, Peter Baranovsky. Ironically, he was Kaganovich's nemesis. It was Baranovsky who had saved St. Basil's Cathedral from destruction by the Bolsheviks, and now he was called upon to do work for the very barbarians he hated. Together with his apprentices, Baranovsky was assigned with recreating the Amber Room, sworn to secrecy, and dispatched to Tsarskoe Selo. He pushed himself right to the limit, working day and night until he suffered a heart attack. Nonetheless, two years later he completed the work. He had produced an exact replica of the Amber Room. He finished it on June 20th, 1941. Just two days before the war. By that time it was already too late to think about presents. When the war broke out, Kaganovich personally oversaw the evacuation of valuables, most notably from Leningrad and Moscow. In particular, he ordered that the authentic Amber Room be dismantled. The newly-created copy was installed in its place. On July 6th, a train running from Leningrad to Tashkent carried the treasure away from the doomed city. And when the Nazis ransacked Tsarskoe Selo, they took the *copy* of the Room back to Germany, not knowing that the real one had been removed. Lazar Kaganovich had high hopes resting on the passage of the train from Leningrad, serial number FD-382. Disguised as a freighter of heavy machinery for relocated factories, it carried four carriages filled to the brim with the most precious artifacts looted by the Bolsheviks, including the Amber Room and, indeed, the object of Ilia's search, the Kremlin collection."

Frolov poured himself a drink. "Sadly, the war eroded Lazar's infallible loyalty to his master. He was overwhelmed by the uncertainty of his future, fearing that his lifestyle, the foundation of his existence, could now be shattered. Stalin's judgment of Hitler had been so erroneous that it led to an inevitable tragedy. Kaganovich believed that the war was hopeless, and, obeying his self-preservation instinct, he intended to scamper off the sinking ship. He was going to defect to the USA. Having all of Russia's sacred riches aboard a single train was too much of a temptation and too great of a chance to ignore. The train would never reach its final destination. The trick, of course was actually pulling it off; someone had to hijack the train for him. Kaganovich couldn't rely on anyone in the mighty NKVD which was headed by Beria, his lethal foe. Picking the wrong cadres for the job meant instant death, but dealing with personnel was a skill Kaganovich excelled in. The NKGB, which was NKVD's sister department created in February of 1941, had continuously warned Stalin about Hitler's impeding invasion, and some intelligence officers there became disgusted with Stalin.

"Kaganovich discovered such NKGB officers and coerced them into effecting his scheme. Kaganovich placed one of them, a man named Yehlakov, to command the cargo's protective detail, and instructed Yehlakov to seize the train once it reached the desolate Kazakh steppes, where the rest of his rogue NKGB team would meet them. Among those NKGB officers was an infiltrator of the Fourth International. The original Fourth International, created by Trotsky to undermine Stalin's rule in Russia. Even after Trotsky's death, the secret organization operated from across the Atlantic. Heavy firearms were unattainable at the time, as everything was given to the front, so the welcoming committee, fully comprised of Trotskyites, had smuggled American machine guns. They got their revenge for being annihilated in the 1930's, capturing enough financial resources to ignite a permanent global revolution. As soon as Stalin learned that the train had disappeared, he banished Kaganovich from his duties and eventually replaced him with Beria as his closest servant. The debacle also spelled the liquidation of the NKGB," Frolov added some historic insight from his own realm. "It was merged with the NKVD on July 20th."

Eugene and Constantine exchanged glances. Frolov studied

their reaction.

"Amber Room became lost to the world, but in reality it remained hidden. The Trotskyites had no capability to take the cargo out of the country. They were behind the most strictly protected border in the world, where everyone was scrutinized as a potential saboteur. The ingenuity of their plan was that they wouldn't have to do anything to get out. Hitler would do everything for them. Operation Barbarossa implied the capture of Moscow within forty days of the invasion. As soon as Moscow fell, Russia would plunge into chaos, so the Trotskyites could bring their stash out and escape with it freely. Unfortunately for them, the Battle of Moscow was won—Hitler was pushed back and their hopes were crushed. The cargo remained locked in at the secret location in Kazakhstan. In the coming years, the Fourth International disintegrated—its agents inside Russia eradicated, the cell across the Atlantic dwindling and finally perishing after the war. They had never had any chance to carry out the plan even when the treasures were in their possession, and their secret outlived them.

"But the Fourth International survived, becoming a entry in the CIA database. American intelligence services had been monitoring its activities, and when it crumbled, they took over what was left of it, incorporating all the information of its inner workings. Over the years, the project which is now a mass of digits in a computer in Langley has evolved into a network of the CIA's assets in Kazakhstan. However, the Amber Room is still a huge factor affecting its functions. For example, the spooks in charge of running the Fourth International played a decisive part during the collapse of the Soviet Union. Only months before the country fell apart, they learned that the aged Lazar Kaganovich was about to reveal the story of the Amber Room. Had the real location of the Amber Room been unveiled, Gorbachev would have attempted to keep Kazakhstan from breaking off by force. A lot of blood would flow in the ensuing conflict—not to mention the CIA's own plans for the region being disrupted by these complications. Ever since the start of the perestroika, the CIA had a growing number of 'agents of influence' working in Moscow, particularly among the higher-level apparatchiks. One such man was Maxim Malinin, a Communist staffer and part-time employee of the KGB. We still have a file on him archived somewhere." Frolov smiled. "Malinin had always been a scumbag, doing the kind of work for us that I personally take no pride in—spying on his colleagues, reporting dissent overheard in conversation, sliming his way up the career ladder. Always filled the profile of a traitor, and so he'd been subverted by the CIA in the late 1980's when he travelled to Canada as a member of some visiting Soviet delegation. Malinin was acquainted with Kaganovich, and he had no remorse when he killed the old bastard in cold blood. In return Malinin was awarded with a rich life in England, and a consultant's position within the revamped Fourth International."

Constantine frowned.

The FSB Director took a sip from his glass and went on.

"The obvious question is, Why didn't they extract the treasure after Kazakhstan became independent? A new country like Kazakhstan would not part with such an earth-shattering discovery. And for all his nationalism, President Nazarbaev always leaned towards Russia as his ally instead of the U.S. Nazarbaev was an old Soviet hard man by nature, one they couldn't risk dealing with. The CIA decided they needed their own man as the Kazakhstani President—and they got Timur Kasymov. A new breed of the ambitious Kazakhstani elite, successful in business, eager to take his country forward."

At the mention of her father, Asiyah's gaze bored through Frolov, but she remained silent.

"Kasymov always conveyed the image of a leader who prized the support from across the Atlantic. At times he was a bigger proponent of any White House policies than the White House itself. By the time Kasymov came to power, the Amber Room and the treasures had long since become secondary for the Fourth International. Much more important was the location. The same place chosen by the Trotskyites more than fifty years ago to stash their loot has become the venue of the world's most highly classified military program. That was why Timur Kasymov had to stop Malinin from telling the world where to look for that train's cargo yet again. So he killed Malinin for the same reason Malinin himself had murdered Kaganovich. The irony."

Indulged in his own speech, Director Frolov eyed his captives with satisfaction.

"One may be forgiven for thinking the treasures are cursed. But if there is any curse, it must be lying on the patch of land where the relics ended their journey. The final destination where the conspirators hid the cargo and never retrieved it. A sea that will never be such, and an island that has grown so large that it ceased to exist. The place is called Renaissance Island in the Aral Sea. Or at least what has remained of both."

16

The Aral Sea was a tragedy more devastating than even Chernobyl.

Technically, the Aral was an inland sea, isolated from the World Ocean like a gigantic saline lake. With a surface area of 68,000 square kilometers, it was the fourth-largest lake in the world. A prosperous fishing industry supported thousands of people in the Aral community, making it an oasis in the middle of the steppes. But very soon, the Aral Sea would become a wasteland.

In the 1930s, Soviet leadership began to undertake a staggering project to irrigate the cotton fields of Central Asia, and they thought of no better way to do it than to draw off the water from the Amu Darya and Syr Darya—the only two rivers feeding the Aral Sea. Construction of the numerous canals intensified to divert the rivers. The madness reached its peak until the water flow into the Aral Sea stemmed completely in the 1960s. From then on, the Aral had begun to shrink. Disappear.

Evaporate.

The rate at which the sea had shallowed was shocking. In a few decades the Aral had lost a water mass equal to the combined amount of lakes Erie and Ontario. The drop of the Aral's water level accelerated with such ferocity that it defied belief—going down by twenty centimeters each year, then sixty and then all of ninety centimeters.

When the Aral Sea was first explored in 1849, the Russian expedition discovered Renaissance Island, positioned in the sea almost centrally. Although it was the largest island in the Aral, it measured a mere two hundred square kilometers in size. Renaissance Island had been a heavenly spot overgrown with shrubs, a sanctuary of untouched wildlife. The island's bays teemed with fish. Herds of wild Saiga antelopes grazed freely. When the edges of the Aral Sea rapidly contracted on every map, water levels plummeting, the island conversely multiplied in size. As a result of the Aral's shoaling, Renaissance Island effectively became a peninsula in 2001, it's southern tip meeting with the main landmass. By then, the Aral had reduced to a quarter of it's original area, having already split into two separate pools of highly-saline water. In a few more years, the two basins divided further into pools and pockets of water, only ten percent of the sea left. The island had merged with the desert around it.

Man's barbaric incursion into nature had destroyed the ecosystem of an entire region. All the sealife in the Aral had died when the salt reached an extreme concentration. The flora along the coast had perished as well, trees and bushes gone forever, the land barren. The climate had changed, suffering dramatically—the summers taken over by scorching dry heat, the winters lingering, becoming colder. Winds ruled the Aral now, creating dust storms that carried the salt and toxic pollution for distances up to five hundred kilometers, destroying crops far out. Villagers had abandoned their homes, tens of thousands of people driven away by the salt-filled environment. Years later, many would be diagnosed with lung disease and cancer.

The death of the Aral Sea could not be undone. There was no reversing the impact.

All this time until 1992, even as the Aral Sea was diminishing, Renaissance Island was the site of a Soviet military base called Aralsk-7. For almost forty years, Aralsk-7 was the country's most highly classified research facility."

Every student in the EMERCOM Academy knew of its history, and Eugene Sokolov was no exception. Aralsk-7 stood at the forefront of the Soviet Union's germ warfare program.

Although such developments were banned by the relevant 1972 UN Convention against the research, production, and stockpiling of biological weapons, both the U.S. and the U.S.S.R. were locked in the WMD race. A nuclear war was impossible and unwinnable. So a biological war was actually *preferable*—and more likely than anyone could imagine. The Americans never shut down their own experiments, at locations such as Fort Detrick. The Soviets, in their time, built the world's most extensive bioweapons system, with dedicated R&D centers all around the country. The most notable facilities for research and manufacturing were located in Sverdlovsk and Sergiev Posad, while the main testing site was Aralsk-7, Renaissance Island, the Aral Sea.

Aralsk-7 mainly dealt with anthrax, smallpox, and bubonic plague. There was enough stock to kill anything in sight ten times over, but when the base was closed down in 1992, all of the biological agents had been disposed of. An American inspection team visited Aralsk-7 in 1994 to confirm that the site presented no danger. All the rumors about the anthrax spores spreading from the island never went beyond local lore.

Frolov was making it seem that every trail led to Kazakhstan—and therefore, to Asiyah.

The FSB Director explained, "Aralsk-7 was established only in 1954. But Renaissance Island had been used by the military much earlier. In 1936, the first secret expedition arrived on the island, assigned by the Red Army Medical Institute to study germs. A precursor of sorts to the work to be carried out years later. A group of a hundred scientists worked on the island for a little more than a year. Then in 1937 they were called back and most of them arrested on charges against the security of the state. It was 1937, after all." Frolov snickered, finding it funny. "So it appears that those accusations were justified in hindsight. Trotsky had built extensive connections during his exile in Kazakhstan. It may have been that one of the hundred specialists on the island was in fact a Trotskyite agent. Someone who made Renaissance Island known to the Fourth International. So in 1941 the rogue team had a stopover site at their disposal. The island was empty; from there the transfer of the valuables out of the Soviet Union would be made."

"In other words, you're trying to convince us that Renaissance Island is the place where boxes chock-full of ancient artifacts have been lying untouched for more than half a century?" Constantine asked, his voice sardonic. "And that none of the several hundred—or thousand—people who constructed and operated Aralsk-7 ever noticed it right under their noses?"

Frolov was unfazed.

"The fact is, they didn't hide it on Renaissance Island proper. Renaissance had an archipelago of tiny islands dotted around it, some of them used for underground storage. I find it perfectly possible that the Trotskyite mole inside the original Red Army expedition could create a cache on one of the nearby islands without anyone knowing. Naturally, it would never be found later, when all the activity was focused around Aralsk-7."

Constantine exhaled. "So what is happening there now? What's so important going on in the Aral?"

"Asiyah knows," Frolov said. "She knows everything. Do you want her to speak up?"

Asiyah snapped, losing her calm. She faced Frolov, her intense glare reflecting the anger boiling inside her.

"That is the most pathetic stream of garbage I've ever heard coming from anyone's mouth. It's preposterous. How can any sane person believe any of this? And more than that, you're trying to put me as someone ... *responsible* for this? I need to *acquit* myself?"

Frolov raised his eyebrows.

"Why are you so stubborn, Asiyah? You're only making matters worse for yourself."

"What do you want from me?" she murmured tiredly.

"All I want from you, Asiyah," Frolov said, "is to elaborate on what I have already learned from *you*. You *talked*, Asiyah. You talked under the drugs, and you said a lot. Now I simply want the full story."

Eugene did not know whether Frolov was bluffing or not—he could not see beyond the old man's wicked smile. But what he did see, was the look of sheer terror in Asiyah's eyes.

"No," she said quietly. "No. You're lying, Frolov. It's impossible. You want to turn my friends against me, but it won't work. Don't believe him, Gene."

"Fine," Frolov said. "You think I don't have any hard proof to back my words? I know that you're a biophysicist. I know that there was a ship passing *Olympia* at the time of the explosion which is named *Isebek*—and which belongs to a company registered in your name. But I can pretend you have nothing to do with anything. Have it your way. You want to go back home? Well, I can deliver you right to the doorstep of the Kazakhstan Embassy. Can you imagine what they will do to you? Death will be the easy way out, Asiyah. Your father won't care if you revealed any of his secrets, because he will assume you did. And he wants to kill you in any case. So why don't you have your revenge against him? Do the damage. Expose him. Don't let him triumph."

"And if I do tell you everything?"

There was no way back for her now.

"I will do everything to punish Timur Kasymov," Frolov said.

Asiyah lowered her eyes.

"It's all I need."

17

Asiyah never took her eyes off Sokolov as she spoke. To her, he was the only person in the salon. She was doing it for him alone, to restore his faith in her, so that he would understand that she hadn't used him.

"They called it Project R," she said. "But that's beside the point. The project has had many names since it began, and has gone through more agencies than anyone can remember. R stands for Renaissance because the island proved to be the only place where it could be carried out. Not only technically, but rather politically, geographically. Only the project's essence is important. It is a quest to develop the most horrifying weapon in the history of mankind. What gives life shall be forced to bring death. For that reason alone, it was too dangerous to conduct it anywhere else. The shroud of secrecy had to be absolute, and it can be only attained by dictatorship. And when the project started, no one could predict the effects on the area around it in the event of anything going tragically wrong. So the choice fell on the Aral Sea. Aralsk-7 had to be rebuilt."

"The entire military compound? Recreated?" Frolov asked.

"You might be amazed, but it didn't need to be recreated. The Soviet Army knew how to build things that lasted. The structures of Aralsk-7 were designed to withstand a nuclear attack. Over the years of neglect, the base had been ransacked by the remaining locals living nearby, that much is true. All that could be torn off and dragged away was stolen—the equipment, the furniture, the wiring, pieces of metal, everything. But the walls still stood. As solid as ever, withstanding the test of time and the onslaught of the environment. And no marauder could reach the main sections of the base. So in essence, Aralsk-7 needed a renovation boost. I can say that the overhaul it received made it look better than new. My father spares nothing to achieve success. He established a state of the art research facility."

"Researching what?" Frolov inquired.

"Water," Asiyah said.

"Water?" Frolov said in bewilderment. "As simple as that?"

"Do you think water is simple?" Her tone was mocking. "I reckon you never went to school, Mr Frolov. Otherwise you wouldn't have made such a ridiculous comment."

She smiled at her own audacity. From the corner of her eye, she could see Frolov's twisted face, his neck coloring red. Yet even facing such humiliation at her hands, Frolov remained silent. He could not retort in any way, could not punish her immediately because that would stop her from giving out the information he needed so badly. *She* was in control now, and it freed her. She felt as though she was lecturing again, back in her academic element, and it was a much more efficient method to block away all the madness around her.

Constantine chimed in. "All I remember from my science class is that water is H-two-O and that it expands at four degrees Celsius although it shouldn't do so when cooled. For me even that is pretty complicated."

"Correct," Asiyah said. "So why does that happen? Why does it shrink on melting? What *do* we know about water? The most abundant substance on planet Earth which shapes our lives every day is a mystery. What *is* water?"

"Water is an anomaly," Eugene responded. "It is unlike any other substance in the universe. No other compound can be found in all three states—solid, liquid, and gas—in our natural environment. As ice, water is the only solid substance that can melt when compressed, and at the same time liquid water *freezes* when compressed at high pressure. And water has atypically high melting and boiling points, at 273 and 373 degrees Kelvin. The speed of sound increases within water. Water has a higher density at its surface than its bulk. Ice has a bigger variety of crystalline forms than any other solid. Water possesses capillary action that defies gravity and carries such force that a growing flower can break through concrete. There are dozens more odd characteristics which I can't remember off the top of my head, like changes in viscosity, conductivity, and so on. It's not something new. Aristotle was the first to notice that hot water freezes quicker than cold water."

"Very impressive," Asiyah said.

"My NBC Defense training didn't count for nothing," Eugene said. "By the way, if you add ions of silver to it, water becomes the most potent anti-bacterial and anti-fungal treatment available."

"All of these qualities have less to do with water's chemical composition than its *physical* attributes," Asiyah explained. "Or, in particular, the hydrogen bond. As you know, the water molecule is V-shaped, with two atoms of hydrogen covalently attached to the oxygen atom. However, the oxygen atom has a net negative charge while the hydrogen atoms have a net positive charge. Through this dipolar nature of the water molecule, each hydrogen atom becomes attracted to an oxygen atom of a neighboring molecule. This is known as hydrogen bonding. A water molecule can form four hydrogen bonds, with four other molecules, donating two and accepting two connections. The hydrogen bonds between the five molecules arrange themselves in clusters. These clusters determine the water structure by the means of bond strength and direction. Increasing temperature reduces the clustering—which explains many of the unusual properties. This is why water expands as it reaches the freezing point—the clusters rearrange to a crystalline shape of ice which is lower in density. The strong hydrogen bonds also mean that more energy is needed to break them down—hence the high melting and boiling points. But hydrogen bonding is more than the reason why ice can float on water. It's the reason life can exist on our planet."

"All life came out of the water," Eugene mused. "Water content measures over half of our body mass, as high as ninety percent. *We* are made up mostly of water. It accounts for the regulation of body temperature. Every living organism must have water for nutrition. Without water, dehydration will kill any person in one hundred hours. It's common knowledge. But what are the inner workings by which water gives life?"

"Life *is* water," Asiyah said. "No other substance has the required properties to give and sustain life, both chemically and physically. Enzymes require water molecules to work. Without water, the DNA double helix would not form its spiral. Without water, proteins—the foundation of life—could not be active. But it is not the water itself that makes life possible. Water can be found in outer space, or on other planets, but the chemical formula is not enough for life to emerge. The fragile balance of life rests on the strength of the hydrogen bonds. A different bond strength, and water would only be liquid in sub-zero temperatures. It's a delicate act. A different bond strength, and metabolism could never happen. If the hydrogen bonding between water molecules were stronger, the molecules would not be free to hydrate proteins and DNA. And if the bonds were weaker, biomolecular interactions would be impossible within DNA and proteins. Cells depend on water chains to exchange information."

"Information?" Constantine repeated.

"Water maintains structural information about the cluster's behavior. It is the key to a major breakthrough in understanding it. Hydrogen bonding passes information from one water molecule to another. This way, clusters are persistent. Whenever the lifetime of a single molecule's bond within a cluster expires, the cluster shifts, attracting other units and keeping its structure. And a water molecule responding to a solvent can relay information to all the other molecules in its cluster even though the molecules are not covalently attached. So molecules can sense each other over distances of several nanometers, and act in synergy to rearrange clusters."

"What does that mean?"

"Water can gain additional properties when affected by external factors. Different clusters are formed. Water can then retain its new structure and carry this information. So while it is still chemically the same, the physical activity of structured water is radically different."

"Can the effect really be achieved?" Constantine asked.

"The method is being widely adopted. In agriculture, the use of structured water brings astonishing results. Plants absorb structured water more efficiently, become stronger, yield more produce in a shorter time and require no fertilizing. Another real example is homeopathy. In an experiment, human antibodies were diluted in water to such a low concentration that it passed below the Avogadro number, meaning that there was no likelihood of any molecules of the diluted substance remaining in the water. However, exposed to an allergen the water responded with a strong immune reaction—much stronger than the original content of the antibodies which should have dissolved into nothingness. This experiment went against every law of conventional chemistry. It demonstrated the water sample's ability to assume the qualities of a solute."

"How was that possible?" Eugene asked.

"We still don't know why water acts this way. We're only beginning to acknowledge that it does. In a sense which is more metaphysical than physical, I might say that ... " Asiyah hesitated. "Water possesses memory. This ability is short-lived ... At first it was only a few nanoseconds ... But it was there to see. It was factual. We have conducted thermoluminescence studies that showed similar results using a salt solution. Like I said, water structure reacted to the solute, spreading the information of salt molecule presence through the hydrogen bonds, and the altered formation of the clusters remained even when the salt dissolved to be chemically gone. As the research went on, other ways to influence the water structure have developed. We subjected water to energy fields—electrical, and magnetic—deriving a range of new physical attributes."

"Wait," Eugene said, grasping her words. "If a given amount of water could be structured to act as a cure, like you said—then couldn't the reverse be done?"

"You mean," Asiyah said, "is there a way to use water as a weapon?" She let the question hang in the air. "Yes. In basic terms, it's a reaction that triggers a kill switch. The signal travels through the hydrogen bonds, changing the water structure to cause death. For example, it affects human blood, which is ninety percent water."

"The hemorrhaging," Eugene Sokolov said somberly, picturing the gruesome images from Sochi.

Asiyah nodded.

"It flashes through in a nanosecond. What happened in Sochi was an amount of dead water hitting the entire coast like a gigantic ripple. Of course, the effect weakens over distance, passing through billions of changing hydrogen bonds in a short time. Even so the sheer size of the affected area surpassed every estimation. People exposed to the water within several kilometers from the source could experience instant side-effects to their health."

"What did you call it?" Frolov asked. "Dead water?"

"An ugly pun which I coined for lack of a better colloquialism," Asiyah said. "It is the ultimate weapon. Massive mortality with no counter measures. A weapon of mass destruction available in infinite supply that no treaty can control, no inspection can detect. And we haven't begun to tap in on the full destructive potential of dead water. The scariest thing is that we have no idea about its capabilities."

"Then why did you ever get involved in it?" Constantine said.

"Believe me, I did not end up participating in the project by my own choosing. I originally specialized in global warming, but water *dominates* any study of climate. Water covers over seventy percent of the Earth's surface. The ocean is a heat reservoir that controls the temperature on the planet, keeping it from great fluctuations. The Gulf stream carries warmth to northwestern Europe. As rivers, lakes and oceans freeze over, the ice insulates the water below from further freezing and saves marine ecology. In a way, global warming has increased the awareness of water's mysteries, water structure being the most important of all. You should remember that the research of water structure is no secret to the scientific community—it has been going on for *decades* across the world. But as always, there are forces seeking military application to every discovery. I am sure you are no stranger to using the dark side of technological progress, Mr. Frolov."

Frolov scowled. "What I would certainly never do is outsource a new-age equivalent of the Manhattan Project to a foreign country, like the CIA and DARPA did."

"That is not the case," Asiyah said. "The project was run by hundreds of institutions around the U.S. and Europe. Aralsk-7 is a vital yet isolated and depended part of it. If anything, its functions resemble those it carried out within the Soviet WMD system—testing, and production on a minor scale. The project is still years from mass introduction."

"And if the Aralsk complex is taken out of the equation?" Frolov said. "How far back would that set the entire program?"

"In that case, real results would be pushed to at least a decade."

"Then it should be done as soon as possible," Frolov stated as if on cue.

"What are you talking about?"

"Aralsk-7 must be shut down again. It is the only site belonging to the dead water project within our reach, so we must attack it."

"Air strikes performed against a sovereign country will cost you dearly," Asiyah warned. "It won't go unpunished."

"Not at all. Military action against Kazakhstan is out of the question. But I don't want to destroy the complex. I am planning to capture it."

Asiyah laughed. "I cannot believe it. It's a suicide mission."

"Is it, really? I suppose the facility is heavily guarded?"

"Adequately. Security forces are kept to a minimum due to secrecy—but there is enough firepower to repel any attack."

Frolov smiled.

"We'll see. And you, my dear Asiyah, will be able to see for yourself. On location."

Asiyah's eyes grew wide.

"You will accompany the assault team," Frolov continued. "After all, you know your way around the place, and they will need someone to guide them."

"Is this some kind of sick joke?" Eugene said.

"I'm in no mood for merriment. Soon you won't be either—because you're going along, too."

Frolov crackled with ill-hidden satisfaction.

"You will also lead the group to take over the base. If I remember correctly, you have the required anti-terrorist training—*and* experience. You are an expert in NBC Defense, so your knowledge is crucial to the mission on hand. You have also proven your capability to overcome the most daunting obstacles as evidenced by you sitting here in front of me." Frolov paused. "And of course, when the actual operation starts, you will be a bit more motivated than anyone—with your brother still staying aboard the *New Star*."

"You'll keep my brother *hostage*?"

"I would not employ so crude a term ... *Hostage*? I prefer to call Constantine my guest. But if you insist ... Let's just say that your brother's freedom will depend on your own success."

"You can't be doing this ... " Asiyah whispered in disbelief.

Frolov shrugged.

"In the end, is that not what each of you wanted? Eugene will get back to reunite with Constantine. And you, Asiyah, will get your revenge."

18

In his cabin, Eugene sat on the edge of the bed, staring ahead listlessly. Behind him, Constantine was leaning against the wooden wall paneling. They both appreciated being near each other after so many months. The experience was bittersweet, poisoned by the new horrors facing them. The silence between them was now more comforting than the agonizing words.

"Please," Constantine repeated quietly. "You must understand."

"Don't start it again. I will have none of it."

An ember of an argument had been smoldering between them for the last couple of hours. It did not break out openly because neither brother would allow it to ruin their reunion. But their disagreement became impossible to contain as they brooded over it. Each of them perceived the impeding point of no return.

"I beg you, Gene. Don't do it. You can't let Frolov have his way. Look at what he's done to us!"

"It's not about Frolov! It's about putting an end to all this!"

"By getting yourself killed? It's madness!"

"There *is* no other way out." Eugene rose to his feet and faced his brother. "What is the alternative? At best, the two of us will be charged with multiple murders and go through hell for the rest of our lives. And Asiyah will go back to her father to be killed. Have you thought about *her*, brother?"

Constantine threw up his hands. "Do you think she can stand any chance in there? Storming the base?"

"I don't know. But I'll do everything to protect her. I'm willing to take the shot. Siding with the lesser evil. Frolov can have his way. But I'll be damned if I let Timur Kasymov have his."

Another heavy silence fell.

"They will kill you," Constantine murmured. "If you die, I will never forgive myself."

"Nothing is going to happen to me," Eugene retorted.

"My God! You sound just like him ... You always thought our father betrayed us when he left ... but you used the same words he said when mother begged him to stay!"

This realization gripped Eugene numbly.

He stormed out of the cabin—to keep a cool head and stop the damage of the clash from escalating beyond repair.

And to escape the truth of Constantine's words—his chilling analogy.

He walked out to the deck and headed aft. At the stern, he found Asiyah watching a patrol boat that followed the *New Star*'s wake in the distance. The boat had taken them to the yacht, Sokolov reckoned, and now it was making sure they stayed aboard.

"They've taken every precaution, haven't they?" he said.

"God knows I wouldn't ever think of jumping overboard again." Asiyah sighed. "I guess you despise me, but no more than I despise myself now."

"No," he objected. "You're wrong. I care about you. More than ever."

His own candor surprised him, but he felt he was right to say it.

"Even after you learned that I had been hiding my involvement?"

"Back in Zhukovsky, you said that your father had to be stopped. It was the truth. The truth which still stands. Nothing has changed. I promised to get you through this nightmare, and I will. You have nothing to feel guilty about, and I hope I don't, either—no matter how much Frolov wants us to believe otherwise. We haven't failed each other. We're still together."

She looked at him with affection, his words convincing.

"Thank you. I feared that you wouldn't understand. I ... " Her voice trailed off. "My father made it look like I was fully behind his plans. All the lies, the paperwork, the finances—everything was done on my behalf. And then I was used blindly to participate in the research, until it was too late to stop him when I discovered his real intentions."

Sokolov was pained to see Asiyah tormenting herself when in fact she had been in the complete control of a monster who had abused and enslaved his own daughter, a girl powerless to fight back or disobey. And yet, she was carrying the responsibility for the actions of a madman, feeling that she had done too little to prevent it.

"The CIA would have made sure your father succeeded, regardless of your part, Asiyah."

"The CIA played a much lesser role than it might appear. It wasn't really a case of the CIA controlling my father. Quite the opposite—he was controlling *them*. The Renaissance project came about by way of a man named Clayton Richter. He was the CEO of Seton Industries, a huge American company that had construction interests in Kazakhstan. He established strong ties with my father as his company was rebuilding the capital's infrastructure. But Richter was also a CIA agent. What Richter really wanted to get was a stake in the Caspian oil reserves. Father would not let him into the Caspian unless he received access to a top-level research project. The military use of water structure had always stayed on the back burner even inside DARPA, considered too far-fetched to yield any significant results. So they let my father into it, albeit cautiously. Seton Industries unofficially received first option to develop the Caspian oil beds as soon as all territorial disputes ended. And my father took on the Renaissance project with unparalleled enthusiasm. He contracted Seton to rebuild the Aralsk base covertly. It was my father who financed the water structure research all over the world, including the U.S.—not the American government. And the money he spent on it was insane. The CIA believed they still had full control ... but when the first positive results came, father crossed his CIA partners. He severed all the ties—literally. Clayton Richter was killed."

The revelation carried frightening possibilities.

"Asiyah, what does he really want?"

"My father wants to challenge the United States of America. He dreams of reuniting Russia and Kazakhstan—to take over *Russia*. With President Alexandrov gone, he feels he will have no rival in the elections after the referendum. And he intends to use the Kremlin collection—and the Amber Room—as the means to become the President of Russia. He feels it can be a political chip, a symbol of reunion guaranteeing him to ascend the throne. He is obsessed with it. And worst of all, he is dead serious about fulfilling his dream."

Sokolov shook his head in disbelief.

"Does your father think he's on a divine mission? Did he brand himself as a Special One chosen by fate?"

"You're almost right, but it's much worse. He believes he is *Tore*."

Sokolov gave her a quizzical look.

"What does it mean?"

"*Tore* is what the Kazakhs call a Genghisid. A direct descendant of Genghis Khan," Asiyah explained. "He even resorted to DNA testing to confirm the genealogy."

"Confirming it as true?"

"Don't be so surprised. Genghis Khan's eldest son Jochi had offspring of forty boys, at the very least. And his grandson Kublai Khan, the ruler of China and the founder of the Yuan Dynasty, had twenty-two sons. There are approximately sixteen million Genghisids in the world today, so it's not uncommon, and many Kazakhs like to think of themselves as Tore. Some of them have valid grounds for that, including my father. But only the spear side qualifies, of course, and it's one of the reasons my father hates me. He believes it is his destiny to restore the might of the Golden Horde. The true Golden Horde, guided by radical Islamism. He will trump everyone who considered him a pawn in their game—the Americans, the Russians, the Chinese, the Iranians—and command the world's only superpower. Russia will be the first step, and from then on he will have an arsenal to go further. Including a new-age weapon in his possession. If I'm going to die, Gene, I must die trying to stop him."

Sokolov let out a breath.

"Frolov may be a motherless bastard, but he's right," he said. "We have to go there. Destroying the base, we will destroy Timur Kasymov."

"To hell with Frolov. We must do it for our own sake."

Asiyah turned away, lost in thought. As if musing aloud, she spoke in a calm, detached voice.

"He thought he'd done enough to kill me, you know? When I come back I'd love nothing more than to see the look on his face as I crush his dream."

"You sound certain that he will be there, at Aralsk-7."

"I am sure he went there straight after *Olympia*. He thinks no one can find him there. He will feel invincible, but I will prove him wrong. I will kill him."

PART V

1

Not only did all Russian roads lead to the capital, but every waterway seemed to as well. Heading back to the city along the Moscow Canal, the *New Star* approached the canal's starting point, the North River Terminal—an architectural triumph of cascading arcades that culminated in a clock tower.

The North River Terminal served as a gateway to a network of rivers connecting Moscow to five seas—the Baltic, the White, the Black, the Caspian, and the Sea of Azov. The entire system of the Moscow Canal, incorporating locks, terminals, hydroelectric power stations, and gigantic water reservoirs was a feat of engineering that stretched for 128 kilometers. And it was a lifeline that Moscow would have died without. By the 1930's, the Moskva River had dried up into a muddy creek. Knowing that the city was doomed, Stalin had ordered a canal built joining the Moskva and the Volga, bringing the water of the great Russian river to the walls of the Kremlin. It had taken almost five years to complete, using the manpower of one hundred thousand inmates of the gulags—ten thousand of which had died building it, their remains buried in that soil forever.

Victor escorted Eugene from the yacht without so much as letting him say goodbye to Constantine. Again he felt that he was separated from his brother completely. Even if they kept Constantine aboard, there was no guessing where in Russia the *New Star* herself would vanish to without notice. Only now, worse than before, Constantine too would not have any knowledge of his brother's fate.

A glossy black Mercedes S 600 was waiting for Sokolov and Asiyah; Victor got behind the wheel. As the car sped through the city, Asiyah said, "Where are you taking us? The Lubyanka?"

Victor did not reply.

Looking outside, Sokolov let his memory absorb the streets

and the people who walked them, the buildings and the trees, saying goodbye while he had the chance.

He loved Moscow, and he loved his country. Bitterly, he reflected how much Frolov had misjudged him. Did the FSB Director think that he would only defend Russia through leverage against him? Perhaps it was the only way Frolov operated, the notion of patriotism lost on him in favor of personal power and control, measuring others by the same yardstick. But Sokolov still remembered what service to his country meant, and these were not empty words to him. He had chosen a profession of saving lives, but he had always known that one day, to save lives he would have to go to war. Sokolov admitted he had been preparing himself for something like this, the ultimate test of his worth to his country. His worth after Beslan. As a man holding a military rank, and as a Cossack, he considered fighting for his country to be both duty and honor. The Frolovs of this world would never understand that.

And there was no mistaking that war was the only course of action to stop Kasymov.

The Mercedes made its way east of Moscow to a sleepy suburbia of villages, lakes and residential blocks. In a town named Balashikha, the car turned to a road that cut through fields and a receding forest. The road ended in a thick concrete wall which was topped by a coil of barbed wire. The wall was gray and weathered, bearing no signs or markings denoting the nature of the installation it enclosed. Considered by some to be a military base, it had far too many surveillance cameras peering at the outside world to really be one. Rising beyond the wall, visible through a shield of trees, were the rooftops of several low buildings, a sandy-yellow tower over a dozen stories high, and, incredibly, the dome of a small church.

The gate opened and the Mercedes drove inside, without any security checks. The road continued past the church to a multi-level garage, four hundred meters away. Killing the engine, Victor got out the car and his passengers followed him to the sand-colored headquarters. It was an imposing structure that looked like two different chunky high-rises wedged right through each other down the middle and stuck at right angles. Other buildings, three or four stories high and shaped like blocks of concrete, were interconnected around the towering axis, forming tiers and appendixes that sprawled a hundred meters wide. Taking up the space between the headquarters and the garage was an unpaved running track and an obstacle course two hundred meters long.

"What is this place?" Asiyah asked.

"The home of the Alpha Group," Sokolov said.

"This place is called the FSB Special Purpose Center," Victor said drily.

In 1974, KGB Chairman Andropov authorized the creation of a counter-terrorist force, which was assigned to the Seventh Directorate (Surveillance) and called the A Group. The first live combat mission carried out by the highly secret unit came five years later in Afghanistan, an operation to storm the Tajbeg Palace in Kabul and kill President Hafizullah Amin. Following that success, the A Group—or Alpha, as the media later named it—went on to specialize in hostage rescue and fighting terrorism primarily within Soviet borders. To conduct black ops in foreign countries, the KGB set up a different unit in 1981, known as Vympel. The two groups had been classified even inside the KGB, so for years neither Alpha nor Vympel had known anything of each other's existence. After the fall of the Soviet Union, the KGB's special forces had been incorporated into the FSB, becoming Directorate A and Directorate V. And in 1998, they had been united by FSB Director Putin to function within the Special Purpose Center.

Sokolov had always held Alpha and Vympel in high regard. Their job, like his, was saving lives, and they defended Russia with valor, even if they received their own share of betrayals from the government. Yeltsin had disbanded Vympel in 1993 after their refusal to storm the beleaguered Parliament. And he had humiliated Alpha in Budennovsk, saving the terrorists instead of the hostages.

Two officers came out to greet the arriving visitors. Both almost matched Sokolov in height, and dressed in black battle uniforms they carried a no-nonsense air about them. Victor quickly made the introductions. Colonel Ivan Grishin, a mustached man with piercing brown eyes, had no insignia but for a sleeve patch which showed the letter A over the traditional sword-and-shield pattern. Major Cyril Petrov, his blond hair cropped, his lively eyes set in an angular face, belonged to Vympel.

"We've been waiting for you," said the Alpha man. "Given the constraints of the timescale, we have our work cut out for us."

2

The progression of images that appeared on the wall-sized screen mesmerized Sokolov. A slideshow as vivid as the one Victor was presenting had an even bigger effect in the near-empty briefing room, with a silent audience of only five people. It was the death of the Aral Sea, and the history of Renaissance Island.

The sequence opened up with a topographic map of the Aral Sea dated 1957, showing a huge water mass of over a thousand cubic kilometers, Renaissance Island just an irregular speck in the middle of it. Pictures taken from reconnaissance aircraft gave a measure of its vastness. Suddenly, the idyllic view was replaced by satellite photographs that carried a sense of foreboding. The photos were grim—Sokolov looked at them like a doctor examining a radiographic set in the knowledge that the patient was doomed. First came the black-and-white shots from the sixties, and within a decade, the difference became noticeable: the jagged coastline evening out as it nibbled up the sea around the rim, Renaissance Island becoming more prominent.

The sea's ailment spread like cancer, and indeed by the time it metastasized it was too late to stop it. The tumor that was Renaissance Island grew as the sea around it shrank. The rate at which it was happening on the screen was truly shocking, ever more rapid in the final years. Now in maximum detail, color and resolution, the Aral Sea was all but dead—ashen in pallor from the salty wasteland that had devoured it, the tiny pockets of water a shallow green. Renaissance Island had also dematerialized, joining the mainland as a peninsula, an isthmus, and then dissolving in it as a lifeless canyon.

As the last photo stayed on the screen, no one spoke.

On his laptop, Victor switched the slideshow to a still picture with a top-down view of the original Aralsk-7 base.

"This is our objective," he said. "Major Sokolov, would you

please give us a run-down on the layout, from your professional viewpoint?"

Sokolov cleared his throat.

"As you can see here, the standout feature was the airfield which had four runways crisscrossing in a wind rose fashion of sorts. About two kilometers east from the airfield were the military quarters, designated on all maps as a town named Kantubek. It consisted of the barracks, command posts, and utility buildings such as the mess hall, weather station, hospital, library, boiler plant, and the like. The actual bioweapons complex stood separately further south—the main laboratory block and support facilities, about a dozen buildings in all, surrounded by a fence. So Aralsk-7 had a compact arrangement, the airfield and two stations all located within a couple of kilometers of each other. The only exception was the open-air polygon where the chemical battalion conducted aerosol testing, which had to be placed as far away as possible, on the southernmost tip of Renaissance Island."

"How much of the infrastructure has survived?" asked Major Petrov of Directorate V.

"This is what it looks like now," Victor said, bringing up another picture of Aralsk-7. "Shot taken from a Persona-N1 satellite."

Despite the myth created by intelligence agencies and sustained by pop culture, spy satellites were not the all-seeing wonders that could hang in space indefinitely, watch over the planet, and raise the alarm as they zoomed in on a terrorist suspect. In reality, satellite reconnaissance was essentially an upgraded version of aircraft reconnaissance. Orbit, speed, weather conditions and optical diffraction accounted for the basic drawbacks that it suffered from.

On this occasion, the shots offered clear detail, although the ground resolution was limited to large-scale views of Aralsk-7 and Kantubek.

If anything, the rundown condition of Kantubek matched expectations. Even an overhead perspective conveyed a sense of abandonment. The town's buildings stood damaged by decades of neglect. Sections of the barracks roofing had collapsed. Paint had eroded. Brown rust had smothered every metallic surface, making the settlement blend with the desert landscape, the roads and walkways swept by sand and salt.

The same could not be said of Aralsk-7. Even an expert in imagery intelligence could not determine whether the buildings had been deserted for thirty years or merely thirty days. The difference hardly caught the eye. After all, given the nature of the compound's activities, it was expected to last much longer than ordinary Soviet housing, and it had also been spared from plundering.

But when another picture appeared next to the current image, the difference became striking. It was a photograph taken some years *earlier*, revealing Aralsk in as much ruin as Kantubek. The comparison of the two pictures laid side-by-side made the renewal of the complex apparent. Every building had received an overhaul, looking solid with a new coating of white and gray paint. The layout of Aralsk-7 remained unchanged, for the most part. There were around twenty buildings in total. The three-storied laboratory was the largest, standing on the northwestern edge of the complex. The rest were research and support facilities of smaller sizes, arranged in a grid. A few of the buildings from the Soviet era had vanished, the area becoming more compact. Gone was the old metal fence enclosing the complex; a thick concrete wall now ran along the perimeter. Three other low buildings were located further south, outside the defensive barrier.

"All of Aralsk-7 has been rebuilt to last another hundred years," Asiyah commentated to her silent audience. "The old buildings were reinforced and refitted. Some were demolished and exact replicas constructed in their places. The area has remained unchanged, measuring roughly three hundred by four hundred meters, plus the barracks of the security force, a hundred meters away, converted from the quarters of visiting Soviet inspectors. What we are seeing on the screen is a new complex altogether."

"And now it's up to us to put an end to whatever is going on there," said the colonel from Directorate A.

It was a statement of fact, a professional acknowledgement of the job at hand. The two officers from Alpha and Vympel needed no further explanation regarding the nature of activity at Aralsk-7 beyond knowing that it posed a threat to Russia's security.

The reply of their superior hardly came as a surprise to either man.

"The first phase of your mission involves seizing the compound and destroying the opposing terrorist force. Ms. Kasymova's role is to guide you inside the main building to extract every shred of documentation, every computer and all the equipment that can be transported. Major Sokolov's role is to deal with any biological hazard you may encounter, as well as keep an eye on Ms. Kasymova in case she has second thoughts about assisting us. Then you will proceed to the airfield north of the complex and await extraction."

Two new photos were projected on the screen.

"Also, it is highly likely that during the mission you could find these individuals," Victor continued. "You must eliminate them. Ahmed Sadaev, Chechen extremist involved in several acts of terror including Budennovsk. His partner, Oleg Radchuk, a Ukrainian mercenary notorious for his brutality against hostages."

The last photo was a carefully-staged, official portrait of a man taking an oath, right hand placed on a ceremonial copy of his country's constitution.

"And finally, someone you have probably recognized. Timur Kasymov, the President of Kazakhstan," Victor announced. "I repeat, these targets must be identified and killed on sight."

3

For Sokolov and Asiyah, the following days consisted of incessant briefings and physical training.

Major Petrov of Directorate V oversaw their drills.

He declared, "I will not allow either of you to be a hindrance to the mission, so you must qualify if you want to wear the uniforms you've been issued."

Qualification equated to passing a series of fitness tests, starting with runs on the track outside the headquarters. A hundred meters in under 12.2 seconds, three kilometers inside eleven minutes, followed by a session in the gym.

None of it was as strenuous for Sokolov as his own karate training regime, but he was impressed with Asiyah's fitness level. She took on hundreds of push-ups, pull-ups and sit-ups as if her slender body was primed for each exercise, tuned by years of practice. Gracefully feminine, she could still give any Alpha or Vympel man a run for his money in terms of agility and endurance.

Even more impressive was Asiyah's performance at the shooting range. Reasonably comfortable with firearms, even though he abhorred their use, Sokolov did not fare too well, the grouping of his shots chaotic. Asiyah outclassed him, displaying marksmanship with every weapon Petrov gave her, from various handguns to a Kalashnikov.

As far as briefings were concerned, Sokolov's active input was limited to assessment of the hazards they would face. The rest of the time, he absorbed the strategy and tactics explained by Grishin to his men, as Sokolov's role would largely come down to fighting alongside them. Using existing diagrams of Aralsk-7, Asiyah guided them through the layout of the rebuilt compound.

Sokolov noted that the plan shared many similarities with the legendary Operation Storm-333, the assault on Tajbeg Palace, not least because of the common objective to eliminate a foreign president and former ally deep inside Central Asia. Palace was really a misnomer for what Tajbeg truly was—a fortress. A three-storied stone mansion with walls thick enough to deflect artillery rounds. Set atop a forested hill, Amin's stronghold had been inaccessible, a single road leading to it through minefields, any approach visible from high ground. And yet the Alpha assault team of sixty men had broken inside Tajbeg, overcoming a force that numbered twenty five hundred guards. The operation had resulted in the death of Hafizullah Amin and loss of five Alpha members, as they seized the palace killing over two hundred Afghan soldiers.

The lab complex on Renaissance Island had also been designed to withstand heavy bombing, and the island was now a hill. But compared to the textbook scenario of the Tajbeg Palace, the FSB team could have a key advantage working in their favor. The bulk of the enemy force on Renaissance was concentrated away from the actual installation. The three barracks could be cut off easily. The isolation of the Aral Sea meant little chance of reinforcements arriving.

"What is the composition of the force protecting the complex?" Colonel Grishin asked Asiyah. "I expect we might face our former brothers in arms, so to speak. Is that correct?"

For a few brief years before the Soviet breakup, the 14th Regional Division of the KGB's A Group had been located in Alma-Ata, Kazakhstan. After 1991, Kazakh President Nazarbayev had transformed the unit to act as his personal bodyguards, forcing the Russian majority of the Alpha servicemen out of the country. Renamed "Arystan"—or "Lion"—the Kazakh A Group had been given over to the KNB. Decades later, the FSB Special Purpose Center and the Kazakh presidential detail had very little in common, save for the initials in their names—but they shared their history and their roots, and the prospect of meeting each other in battle was a touch perverse.

"I don't believe so," Asiyah replied. "My father tasked the Lion team with protecting his residence in Astana. The security force in Aralsk-7 is made up of an entirely different contingent of troops, fanatically devoted to him alone."

"What contingent is it?" Grishin inquired.

"Militants. Radical Islamists."

The colonel frowned. "Haven't we seen enough of that scum already."

"They go through terrorist camps set up all over the country," Asiyah continued. "Expertly trained in hand-to-hand combat, assassination and guerrilla warfare. Above all, they've been conditioned to sacrifice their lives for Timur Kasymov's cause. They wear black bandannas and call themselves *batyr* after the Kazakh medieval warriors."

"How are they recruited?" Sokolov asked. "Are they all from Kazakhstan?"

"Most are ethnic Kazakhs, yes, but not necessarily. I also saw Russians and Ukrainians, and Chechen instructors at the camps. But the biggest source of new trainees comes from orphanages."

"Orphanages?" Grishin repeated.

"Children are easy to recruit, indoctrinate and force into combat. The Batyr units are made up of graduates aged sixteen, but some fighters are as young as fourteen. Those in the camps are even younger. Around eleven or twelve, boys and girls."

Sokolov muttered a curse under his breath.

"It shouldn't come as a surprise," Asiyah said bitterly. "The use of children is not my father's unique invention. It's widespread all over the world, especially in Africa and Asia. In fact, Ahmed Sadaev brought this practice over from Chechnya, where he saw such units fight the Russians. It's barbaric, yes. But then again, some countries pretend to be civilized when they turn eighteen-year-old kids into cannon fodder. Is there really a difference?"

"And they are actually guarding Renaissance Island?" Grishin asked.

The real question is, Sokolov thought gritting his teeth, are we actually going to kill children?

"Yes," Asiyah said. "No fewer than a hundred are on duty at Aralsk-7 at any time, but the functioning barracks can accommodate two or three hundred."

"Have you actually seen any of them in action?" Petrov asked.

"More often than you may think, believe me. I acquired my combat skills in one of those camps. In fact, I was among the top graduates."

4

Before the departure, Sokolov prayed and lit a candle at the unusual chapel of the FSB Special Purpose Center. It was called St. George's Church, built to honor the memory of the Alpha and Vympel men who had died on the battlefield, forty-five in all, their names engraved on a granite monument. Ten names from that list belonged to the men killed in Beslan, caught in the crossfire between the terrorists and the Russian 58th Army tanks that hit the school.

Sokolov cast aside his memory of the tragedy, and the premonition it could evoke. Focusing solely on the upcoming mission, he walked off to pick up his gear. After the final check on his uniform, armor and weapons, he joined the assault team leaving the Special Purpose Center.

Chkalovsky Military Airfield was only five kilometers away, allowing instant deployment. At Chkalovsky, Sokolov saw their aircraft, recognizing an old friend.

It was an Ilyushin Il-76 freighter, a beauty to behold. Sokolov eyed the familiar lines which had earned the plane its affectionate nickname of "Swallow"— the powerful arrow-shaped wings set high atop its thick fuselage, driven by four large turbofan engines, and the sweeping T-tail. The Il-76 was a workhorse that operated without fail in any weather conditions, using any airstrips and carrying forty tons of cargo across five thousand kilometers. Over the years, not a single plane had crashed due to technical breakdown.

Sokolov almost smiled, thrilled at the reunion. The image of the Il-76 had always accompanied him, first throughout his life at the air force base in East Germany, and later during his service in EMERCOM, which used Il-76s to deliver humanitarian aid.

This particular version, an Il-76MD, had an even greater capacity and range, and was equipped with jamming capabilities, essential for raids behind enemy lines. With the cargo ramp at the rear of its undercarriage opened, three military vehicles were being loaded inside. Resembling BMPs, the original Infantry Fighting Vehicles, these units were in fact designed for air delivery by parachute, and called Airborne Fighting Vehicles, or BMDs. When burdened by the military hardware, the number of paratroopers the Ilyushin could take aboard was reduced from 160 to 21.

Colonel Grishin commanded a group of nine Alpha men, and an equal number of fighters from Vympel, including Major Petrov. Together with Sokolov and Asiyah, the assault team made the required total exactly.

Like Sokolov, they wore desert battle dress uniforms and body armor, devoid of any insignia. Tactical goggles accompanied their helmets for protection against a sandstorm. Each FSB fighter carried a full arsenal of weapons—new standard-issue Yarygin PYa pistols, Kalashnikov AK-104 rifles, and enough grenades to blow up the entire island. Asiyah and Sokolov each only had a Yarygin handgun, and an AK-104—a shorter modification of the AK-74 with the full stopping power of 7.62mm ammunition.

On the hot tarmac in front of the Ilyushin, nothing gave away the tension of the FSB fighters who appeared nonchalant as they awaited boarding. Sokolov tried to remain calm, but Asiyah was nervous, her eyes full of anxiety, transfixed on the BMD vehicles. With their turrets and caterpillar tracks, they looked like adequate substitutes for tanks, but Asiyah's expression conveyed her failure to imagine these beasts being parachuted from transport aircraft.

"Eugene," she said. "Are you sure it's safe?"

"Everything will be fine," he replied, hoping that it really would be.

"I still can't believe we're going to drop out of the plane inside those things," Asiyah murmured. "Whoever could conceive such idiocy?"

Petrov winked. "Don't worry, the method is foolproof. You'll be so comfortable that you won't notice the landing. Even if we fall into whatever water is left in the Aral Sea, the BMDs are amphibious."

Once the BMDs had finished loading, the assault team embarked, boots clanging as they walked up the metal ramp and along the main cabin floor, passing the vehicles. On either side of the cargo cabin, a row of integrated jumpseats lined the wall, and the FSB fighters picked their places. Sokolov pulled a seat down and occupied it, pressing his back against the hard interior of the fuselage. Asiyah took the one next to him. Grishin and Petrov faced them opposite.

The ramp closed, and Sokolov felt a knot tightening in his stomach as he anticipated the lift-off. The Ilyushin's four heavy engines whined, warming up, and the freighter taxied to the runway. The noise of the turbofans rose to a roar as the Ilyushin charged down the airstrip, and then its nose pitched up.

"Hold tight!" Sokolov told Asiyah.

The jumpseats lacked belts or any other means to secure passengers, and the unfamiliar lateral pull could come as a surprise. Sokolov grabbed the side of his seat, but the thrust of the Ilyushin produced so much power that he had to plant his feet firmly against the metal floor to keep from sliding sideways. Asiyah clutched her jumpseat, but the steep burst of the plane made her lean close to Sokolov for a second.

"ETA is three hours," Colonel Grishin announced to the team as the airlifter climbed to its cruising altitude.

In the windowless cabin of the Ilyushin, all that Sokolov could do was focus mentally, just as he would en route to any other assignment. The hum of the engines made conversation strenuous, and there was nothing to discuss anyway. For all the planning, no one really knew what to expect once they hit the ground.

Sokolov thought of the irony that accompanied the mission. The Ilyushin would be matching the route flown from Chkalovsky countless times. The airfield acted as the main transportation hub for the adjacent Star City, the Russian space camp, and most of the flights originating from Chkalovsky were bound for the Baikonur Cosmodrome in Kazakhstan.

5

From Chkalovsky airfield, the Il-76MD set course south to Karshi-Khanabad airbase in Uzbekistan. The base had been used until 2005 by the U.S. during the war in Afghanistan, and then utilized by Russia ever since the Americans had left. The Ilyushin's passage would be routine throughout the flight, but for a section above the Aral Sea, where it would briefly drop altitude. On paper, the official Kazakh-Uzbek border lay across the Aral, even dividing Renaissance Island between the two countries, but in reality, the border stayed neglected, like the entire region.

Thirty minutes before the Il-76 began to descend, Grishin ordered the assault team to assume positions inside the BMDs.

The idea behind the creation of the BMD was delivering a specialized vehicle to accompany paratroopers, thus giving them superiority on the battlefield. Unlike a simple personnel carrier, it had to be highly mobile, and at the same time provide heavy firepower and protection—a complete combat system. Light aluminum armor allowed for both defense and maneuverability, and firepower was something the BMD packed in abundance. The current, fourth-generation BMDs were equipped with a twin 100mm and 30mm cannon and two mounted Kalashnikov machine guns with 4,000 rounds of ammo, which created a firestorm.

At some point, the BMDs designers found it logical that the airborne troops be dropped off already *inside* the vehicles for extra efficiency. Rising to the challenge, the Russian Airborne Corps had honed the procedure to such perfection that parachuting crews inside BMDs had become the standard method of operation.

But every other country in the world deemed it too dangerous to merely attempt.

That thought alone made Sokolov psych himself up.

Each BMD-4 could take on a crew of seven, so the assault team members broke into three even groups. Following the Alpha men into the first vehicle, Sokolov climbed through the rear hatch. Loaded with men and equipment, the interior was tight, but he quickly strapped himself in his seat. Securing the straps on his ankles, his knees, waist, and shoulders, he imagined that he resembled a death row inmate who was personally preparing himself for execution in an electric chair.

Sokolov felt pressure in his ears. Descent. Fifteen minutes to the drop.

Colonel Grishin entered the BMD through the turret hatch and assumed position in the commander's seat, flicking switches and checking the communications equipment. On his command, the crew tightened their straps and reported their status.

"Ready!" Sokolov said, repeating after the Alpha fighters, the straps digging into his limbs.

This is it, he thought, adrenalin surging.

Seconds stretching, Sokolov waited for the signal, bracing himself, jarred when it came—a siren blasting inside the Ilyushin.

"Get ready!" Grishin commanded again.

As instructed, Sokolov tensed his muscles—arms, legs, and neck—and pressed himself against the seat to avoid injury.

The ramp began to open and the entire plane shook violently, as if it were about to crash. Then the turbulence subsided but a thunderous howl of the air current filled the Ilyushin, together with the screaming voice of the turbofans. Sokolov strained his muscles, expecting the worst.

Sokolov then felt a pull as the BMD rolled along the floor railing, propelled by the launch system.

Suddenly there was nothing underneath but a chasm that sucked them in.

Expelled from the Ilyushin, the BMD fell down like a sedan hurtling off a bridge. The vehicle angled sharply from its normal axis, accelerating towards the earth nose-down. Gripped by pure fear as the BMD rotated, Sokolov's heart thumped, his breath cut short. To his vestibular sense, the world was somersaulting, the vehicle going past ninety degrees in an attempt to swing upside down. He clenched his fists harder. The BMD possessed the aerodynamics of a brick and weighing fourteen tons, it plummeted like one.

A jolt went through his body as the canopy ripped open. Only seconds after release, the parachute had deployed. The BMD straightened. Encapsulated, Sokolov felt like he was dropping inside a high-speed elevator.

"At ease!" Grishin's voice barked in the comms device.

He slackened his grip on the seat. But his nerves stayed taut, the rate of descent too rapid for comfort. He would not be safe until his feet were back on solid earth.

The BMD floated down for what seemed an eternity. Finally, the word LANDING lit up on the electronic display before Grishin.

"Attention!"

Sokolov contracted his muscles again, hoping he would still be alive when they struck against the ground.

Ten seconds later, a cloud of smoke covered the BMD. Hanging underneath the BMD was a probe released by the parachute system. Upon contact with the surface, the probe engaged rocket thrusters located beneath the parachute, cushioning the BMD's fall.

After the final impact came stillness. Sokolov exhaled. They had arrived.

"Is everyone all right?" Grishin asked his men, who replied in the affirmative. "Sokolov?"

"Fine," Sokolov said, unbuckling the straps, eager to get out of the BMD as the field manual required. His first airborne experience was something he wished he never had to relive.

He put on his tactical goggles, pushed open the hatch above him and slid out of the BMD. Kicked up by the vehicle's drop, a billow of particles was settling down again, and Sokolov tasted the salt carried by a sharp wind. The late afternoon sun hung low in the blue-tinted sky, where the tiny speck of the Ilyushin was all but invisible, flying deep into Uzbekistan.

He jumped down on the arid soil, his boots stepping on sand mixed with grain of sediment. He crouched down, feeling the heat that radiated off the ground, and found a strange pebble under his feet.

But the white, round object was no pebble. It was a tiny seashell. A relic of the Aral.

They had made landfall on a plateau, in the middle of the desert formed around Renaissance Island, some thirty kilometers south of the island proper. Sokolov saw the waterless sea of grey sand stretching into infinity. Along with the rolling sand dunes, the desert landscape was streaked with ridges of salt and sediment turned into rock. The view was clouded with whirling dust, and the distorted quiver of warm air.

The other two BMDs were nowhere to be seen. Could it be that Asiyah and the Vympel team had crashed? The thought made Sokolov anxious.

Grishin's crew wasted no time preparing the BMD for action, as they discarded the parachute system and released the protective covers encasing its tracks. The powerful diesel engine rumbled, and as the driver raised the ground clearance to its maximum, the fighting vehicle resembled a deadly beast awaking from sleep.

Following the Alpha fighters, Sokolov climbed back into the troop compartment.

Grishin radioed the commanders of the two other BMDs, who reported successful landing. Relief washed over Sokolov as he learned that Asiyah was fine. On the satellite navigation screen, Sokolov saw the position of the vehicles. Having launched at eight-second intervals, the BMDs had dispersed in a straight line, spaced within a kilometer. Grishin peered through his periscope, watching the other BMDs pull up from behind a dune, sand pouring off their tracks.

As soon as the group assembled, they moved out towards the objective: Aralsk-7.

6

The BMD column raced across the rugged terrain, as if challenging a stage in the Dakar Rally for record time.

Time was all that mattered now, the decisive factor of lighting and weather conditions. The assault team operated within a limited bracket, when the sun was no longer scorching at fifty or sixty degrees Celsius, but nightfall was already fast approaching. At dusk, the temperature would drop to near freezing, and the intensifying wind would bring frostbite, and possibly a dust storm. Even with night vision equipment, the darkness would slow them down in unfamiliar, hazardous surroundings, and hand the advantage to the enemy.

In the sand behind them, the caterpillar treads left a wake of furrows over a pattern of wind-blown ripples, as if the sea were still there. But the Aral was far deadlier than any sea, or any desert. Jagged reefs protruded from the former sea floor, concealed by a shroud of sand.

It was extreme territory that welcomed no man, after what mankind had done to it. The BMDs were lost in the several million hectares of desert, but they were intruders nonetheless.

Inside the rumbling BMD, Sokolov expected a collision with a dune or an outcropping at any second, but the driver navigated the route expertly.

An hour later, they reached it.

Renaissance: no longer an island, nor even a peninsula, but a mesa, the highest point of the Aral Desert.

The plateau they had parachuted on was part of a natural slope that extended from the southwestern tip of Renaissance, elevating gradually to rise thirty meters above the desert. Driving uphill, the BMDs came atop the flatbed of the island's overgrown mass. It was the most remote part of Renaissance, the venue of the testing polygon, accessible from the settlement by truck. The land here differed from the desert surroundings below—there was no sand on the hard, cracked earth, only a thin layer of gray salt dust covering the even surface. Beyond the edge of the polygon, the southern shore of the island had turned into a cliff. The rocky canyon yawning deep down at the base of the cliff had once been a harbor teeming with fish. Now all life had vanished from the Aral Desert. Even the anthrax spores had been long dead.

Beyond the polygon, the scenery remained flat and empty. The island's vegetation had withered. Only mounds of brown bunchgrass dotted the flat ground, along with dry, skeletal twigs of the occasional saxaul shrub.

The barrenness became even more pronounced as it contrasted with the single trace of human presence.

The man-made landmark appeared out of nowhere, running like a scar on the island's body.

It was a gravel road.

7

After the rough ride through the desert, the surface of the road seemed smooth, but it did little to calm Sokolov. Behind him, the 450-brake-horsepower turbodiesel whined at full throttle, echoing his apprehension. His cold fingers slid over the polymer handle of the Kalashnikov. If worst came to worst, he would have to fire the rifle through the gun port near him, just like the other Alpha shooters in the back of the BMD.

The driver's voice sounded in Sokolov's headset, carried via the UHF radio which enabled communication both internally and between all three vehicles.

"Ten kilometers to target."

Cruising at top speed, they would reach Aralsk-7 within ten minutes.

It took less than five for the complex to become visible.

Sokolov glanced over to the commander's position in front, where Colonel Grishin was surrounded by an array of equipment: panoramic daylight and night-vision periscopes, one rearview periscope, target tracking screen, rangefinder, satellite navigation, 6x zoom scope and firing controls.

Thermal imaging rendered the view on the screen in gray hues. Against the lighter tone of the sky, blocky outlines appeared on a north-easterly bearing. Growing in size, the shapes split into two clusters as they became more defined. The larger one belonged to Aralsk-7. Standing separated from it was the Batyr camp.

Grishin turned to the scope.

"Target identified," the colonel said. "Time for some recon in force. Commencing fire."

The turret rotated automatically, adjusting slightly to the right. On the screen, the Batyr barracks were locked in the crosshairs. The numbers underneath were decreasing by twenty meters per second as the rangefinder measured the distance, now going below 4,000 meters.

It was well within the range of the 100mm cannon.

Whirring inside the turret, the autoloader slid a shell from the revolving carousel of the projectile ring, and slotted it home.

Grishin pressed the fire button on the control stick.

The BMD's main A270 cannon thundered. The deep, sharp crack resonated above the engine noise loudly.

Through his own periscope, Sokolov saw the hit. The high-explosive shell impacted into the concrete wall of the Batyr structure, erupting in a cloud of smoke and dust.

The autoloader whirred again, and the next shot blasted, six seconds after the first, finding its mark, registered in another distant explosion.

Thirty-two shells still remained in the conveyor.

As the range between the BMD and the complex diminished, the cannon fired with greater accuracy, recalculating aim through a ballistics computer. The shells kept pounding, tearing away chunks of the barracks. Sokolov could now see that a section of the first Batyr building had been destroyed into rubble. Black smoke and tongues of flame rose from the blackened facade. In a cacophony of artillery fire, the other BMDs joined in, each of the three choosing a separate target to pummel. The barrage was relentless. The projectiles followed each other, ripping through the barracks before the roar of the previous impact died away.

Experience told Sokolov that the blast waves and collapsed ceilings had doomed anyone inside. But he saw motion. As the cannons were completing their destruction of the Batyr barracks, Sokolov saw that a few had managed to escape. Indiscernible figures, trying to survive like all living things. Disorganized, injured, some began to flee while a small group opened aimless fire. Out of range, the bullets could not reach the BMDs, and before the enemy's resistance had any chance of being effective, it was drowned in a chattering of heavy weaponry.

The loud cracks belonged to the 30mm guns working rapidly. What gave the BMD's 30mm cannon its power was the monstrous rate of fire, expending an arsenal of five hundred rounds in just over a minute.

A single burst could cripple a tank. Used against infantry, it resulted in decimation.

Human bodies tearing apart, scythed down. The weapons required no extra accuracy; even hitting the ground, the shells exploded and the fragments killed anyone in the vicinity.

Abruptly, the gunfire died down, and the sound of the diesel was again the loudest noise that Sokolov could hear inside the vehicle. It was the most harrowing silence he could remember. They had destroyed the Batyr force without ever slowing pace.

The BMDs stopped before the gravel road ended, a few hundred meters from either the burning barracks or the main compound.

"Move out!" Grishin commanded.

As the hatches opened, the FSB fighters disembarked with lightning speed. Sokolov needed no extra encouragement to leave the confines of the armored vehicle. Never before claustrophobic, he pulled himself through the opening with such urgency, as if he were breaking water for a gulp of oxygen.

Instead he felt as if he'd entered a sauna, the dry air almost too hot to breathe. The sun blinded him temporarily, the vastness of the sky overwhelming. Together with Grishin and his Alpha men, Sokolov hurried to jump from the BMD's side to be shielded by the vehicle. His feet touched down on the arid earth carpeted by patches of desert grass. Petrov also had led out the Vympel fighters. Sokolov caught a glimpse of Asiyah for the first time since they had been inside the Ilyushin.

The assault team reassembled into two groups. Only the driver and gunner remained in each of the three vehicles. Protected behind the armor, the assault team would follow as the BMDs made their way towards the compound, and break off to storm each building.

The BMD rolled forward, and Sokolov jogged alongside the others. After the shock of the parachute drop and the cramped drive through the desert, his legs felt like jelly. Unable to stop, he ignored the feeling until his limbs recovered. Keeping his head down as instructed, he gathered his bearings as much as he could.

They were moving away from the ruined Batyr camp far to their right, the sight of the ravaging flames unsettling him. How many had died there? Were they children? He pushed the thoughts aside as the view receded. He failed to spot any survivors. The threat from the compound's security had been eliminated. Even so, it was somehow reassuring that Vympel team was defending their rearguard.

Aralsk-7 loomed ahead.

Up close, the pragmatic design of the complex impressed. It was huge yet nondescript. It did not dominate the view, spreading out over huge territory instead of towering over it. The compound's wall ran for hundreds of meters, and the twenty or so buildings beyond barely had their rooftops visible. The tallest laboratory building was only three-storied, but it stretched so wide that at midpoint it protruded from the boundaries of the complex like an appendix. Such odd layout was irrelevant decades ago, security taken care of by gunboats patrolling the Aral Sea. Now, however, it was the weakest spot of Aralsk-7 defensively, presenting the assault team with a direct route to the objective. Any sentries or scientific personnel left inside the complex were cordoned off by the fence, making the mission easier. Once the team captured the main building, they would have the advantage to proceed inside the area and secure the rest.

The side elevation faced them with three rows of windows and the blocky finesse of industrial Soviet architecture. Vympel continued towards the entrance, Major Petrov leading the line, Asiyah going last behind the second vehicle. Alpha stayed a hundred meters behind.

"Begin assault, begin assault!" Grishin radioed.

The Vympel team did not make it even as far as the laboratory's metal doors.

Explosions rocked the laboratory building.

Flames lashed through the shattered windows of the first floor. Fragments flying, the Vympel men were knocked to the ground. The size of the BMD saved Asiyah from fragments but she, too, fell down.

Further away from the epicenter, Sokolov ducked instinctively, deafened, holding up his AK. He felt a gust of heat blowing past. Next to him Grishin was yelling orders.

Sokolov realized that the blasts were not so much intended to demolish the laboratory as to cause a raging fire inside. Already the entire first level was devoured by flames.

Within seconds, new detonations sounded distantly as other facilities beyond the fence exploded.

As the flames crept up the first level of the lab, gunshots flashed from the third floor windows. From the vantage point, shooters pinned down the stunned Vympel team.

"Return fire!" Colonel Grishin shouted. "Group V under attack, return fire!"

The Alpha men aimed for the top floor, AK bursts suppressing the enemy. The BMDs joined in, their PKT Kalashnikov machine guns thrashing out tracers across the face of the building.

The shots from the lab did not abate, as if there had been a replacement ready for every gunman hit by Alpha. Slugs rained down in every direction, dust bursting from the scorched ground. Petrov's group made it behind the shield of their BMD, but several prone figures lay helplessly before the laboratory. Some Vympel men rushed out to pull out their wounded teammates, but were held back by relentless gunfire.

"Use your cannons, grenades, whatever you've got!" Sokolov told Grishin.

The colonel faced him. He had to make a decision immediately.

"Save your men, Colonel!" Sokolov urged. "We've lost the lab!"

The blaze had now reached the second floor, but it would take some time until it reached the top. But the building was inaccessible now. Any equipment or data inside would be destroyed by the flames. Clearly, their most pressing goal was to eliminate the suicide shooters.

The BMDs recoiled as the heavy weapons thundered again. One by one, the shells bombarded the enemy positions, pulverizing every window and the exterior around them. The hits ripped yawning cavities in the facade. Smoke curled up as bright orange flames flickered inside. The Vympel troops lobbed a couple of grenades into the windows.

Sokolov watched the scene in numbed silence, as if revisiting Beslan.

Burning debris sailed down. No one fought back, and the barrage set off another fire on the third floor. The conflagration now engulfed the laboratory over all levels, spreading along its length at an astounding rate. It had to be pre-arranged, the incendiary rounds igniting a combustible substance inside. In any case, Aralsk-7 was finished. Several volleys from the AKs sounded, and then the laboratory was left to burn out on its own.

Sokolov dashed over to Vympel's BMD. Asiyah was still on the ground. Kneeling, he picked her up by the shoulders, and held her in a semi-sitting position.

"Are you hurt?" he asked.

"I'm okay," she said. "Don't worry."

To Sokolov's relief, she could hear him and she breathed normally as she talked. The main cause of mortality after high-order explosions was damage done by a shock wave of over-pressure impacting the body. The supersonic impulse of compressed air led to ruptured lungs, eardrums or eyes, brain concussions and even internal hemorrhaging. But the blast wave had lost its strength over the distance to the BMD, the pressure well below the dangerous threshold. Pulmonary traumas could kill within a span of seconds or hours, so Sokolov thanked God that Asiyah was unscathed.

She quickly got to her feet.

"It's not over yet," she said with alarm.

Sokolov turned.

He couldn't believe his eyes.

From the other end of the complex, a crowd charged at them. The black mass of figures flooded from around the corner at the far side of the destroyed compound, heading in the direction of the BMDs. As far as Sokolov discerned, they numbered over fifty. Their individual silhouettes were tall physically, but still had to bulk up in muscle. He knew who they were.

Batyr soldiers.

Children.

Sokolov grabbed Asiyah and they ducked behind the vehicle as bullets zinged past their heads.

Quick to react, the FSB assault team fired back, the sounds of the AKs and PKTs overlapping intensely. Still, the crowd advanced in some last-ditch attempt to overpower the assault team.

Their shots pinged all over the BMD's armor like pellets of hail, but could not hit the intended human targets.

The ranks of Batyr soldiers were up for slaughter. Moving in open ground, the distance at which they had engaged the assault team gave them no chance. Sokolov heard their screams, growing ever louder. Tracers streaked.

In a frenzy, the few survivors still went at Alpha, as though oblivious to the fallen. There was no stopping them, even if no more than a dozen stayed on their feet.

Black-clad bodies toppled, spilling blood. But the child soldiers were determined to break within point-blank range of Alpha, who were desperate to gun them down before it happened.

Hit by a volley, the last running attacker fell, his young face twisted by hatred.

Still, the tracers swept over the prone bodies, finishing off those that moved, making sure none ever did.

The scene was barbaric. The young soldiers had been turned into mindless killers, first robbed of their childhood, their humanity, and now their lives.

Corpses everywhere, the dusty soil blood-soaked. Now everything was truly over.

8

In the aftermath of the battle, Sokolov turned his immediate attention to the casualties of the Vympel team. Walking over to their vehicle, at once he saw three dead bodies lying on the ground. One of them looked like he had been killed by fragments, his face mutilated. Another had taken a slug in his throat, which had produced a grotesque blood stain on his chest. The third was riddled with bullets, hit in his limbs and armor, including a hole between the plates in his vest, which had proved mortal. Sokolov's job involved direct encounters with death, but the sight of wasted human life was not something he could get used to. But he never allowed himself to lose his composure, knowing that others depended on his actions.

Several men were standing near the bodies solemnly, the rest flocked around the BMD.

Cyril Petrov was sitting propped against it, pressing a hand against his bleeding left arm.

Next to Petrov, a lieutenant was working his way through the contents of a medical kit. He was sinewy, with an angular face and deep-set eyes. Polevoi was his name, Sokolov remembered.

"Let me handle it," Sokolov said. "Just find some gauze and peroxide. And give me your knife."

The lieutenant obliged.

Expertly, Sokolov cut off the sleeve of Petrov's uniform and examined the wound. Below the shoulder was an opening.

"How much did it bleed?" Sokolov asked.

"Not an awful lot. I don't think it damaged the artery," Petrov replied. "Just a graze. Nothing serious."

Sokolov nodded, satisfied, not so much by the answer as Petrov's condition. If he had lost too much blood, shock would be setting in, his systems shutting down. But the major showed no symptoms of it, his speech clear, his skin color, breathing and pulse all normal. In fact, only the soft tissues had been damaged. The bullet had gone through the outside of his arm, missing bone and vessels. The exit wound was spaced a few centimeters away. Both wounds were small, typical of low-energy shots. Petrov had been lucky.

"Anyone else injured, Lieutenant?" Sokolov asked Polevoi while he treated the wound.

"Negative. A few cuts and bruises, nothing penetrating. We were out quickly."

Sokolov glanced at Polevoi. Around the spot where bullets had hit his vest, the uniform was ripped to shreds.

"I'm glad you did."

Polevoi nodded gravely, grief over three of his teammates flashing across his face.

Sokolov finished with the wound, first applying pressure to stop the bleeding, then cleansing it with peroxide and gauzing it up. Finally, he gave Petrov a shot of antibiotics and analgesics.

"Now, Lieutenant, if you could come up with a makeshift sling, your commander's arm will be as good as new in no time."

"Thanks, Major," Petrov said.

"You're welcome, Major. Try to reserve your stamina and be immobile as long as you're comfortable. Sip water if you're thirsty."

Sokolov headed back to see the colonel, who was yelling over a satellite comms link.

"Requesting air transport urgently. Do you copy? ... I repeat, we have three 200's and a 300. Over."

The figures came from Russian military jargon. Cargo-200 stood for "dead" and -300 for "injured." Both dated back to the Afghan War, originating from the numbers of standard accompanying forms that had to be filled out to transport the respective casualties.

The colonel ended the connection and turned to Sokolov.

"How's Petrov doing?"

"He won't lose his arm, but that doesn't mean he can stay here for long. He needs to be properly diagnosed and treated in a hospital. There's still risk of contamination. He has a cavity in his arm that's filling with clot, with tissue damage around it. If the bullet's energy had fractured the humerus, then the antibiotics shot won't be enough against bone infection."

Grishin shook his head in disgust.

"I've already called for the plane to fly in, ahead of our estimated schedule. This whole damned mission is a failure. We've completed none of our objectives and lost personnel in the process! All we can do now is get the hell out of here quickly." He muttered a string of obscenities.

Sokolov could hardly disagree.

"Well, Major Sokolov, I appreciate your involvement. I hope we aren't going to suffer any more casualties, but I know you can be counted on. We will be setting out for the airfield once the advance team has secured it, so be ready for it."

"Colonel, don't you think that we should inspect the ruins of the barracks? There could still be survivors."

Grishin's face turned to a rigid mask.

"I strongly advise you against it, Sokolov. I pledged allegiance to my country and my men, so I will not allow you to put them in harm's way. If you believe you will be able to find a live terrorist, I see no value in taking prisoners. Anyone appearing within sight of our position will be shot. Do whatever the hell you want if you're looking for thrills, but don't expect us to be acting as your personal bodyguards or searching for you if you go missing. I have enough trouble on my hands already."

Sokolov knew that Grishin was right.

Grishin ended the conversation as if Sokolov weren't there. He was busy coordinating the operation of Alpha units he deployed within the complex.

His radio squawked, the troops reporting as they cleared the buildings. They had found that of all the structures in Aralsk-7, only four research buildings had been set on fire along with the laboratory. A total of twelve other support facilities had been vandalized, stripped down to bare walls. All evidence of the compound's recent activity had been destroyed.

When the Alpha men returned empty-handed, Grishin picked a group of ten men to take a BMD and head over to the airfield. Swiftly climbing inside or atop the vehicle, they drove off northwards.

Sokolov walked back, following the compound's wall. The BMD left a trail of dust in its wake. Aralsk-7 was smoldering. Lonely clumps of desert grass swayed briefly in a wind carrying the stench of diesel, soot and blood.

Sokolov stared at the laboratory, its face charred by the flames and pockmarked by hundreds of rounds. Three rows of disfigured eye sockets only emitted smoke

Out of frustration, Sokolov cursed aloud. He searched the surroundings again, but there was no need to confirm the sudden realization.

Asiyah was missing without a trace.

9

Slipping away unnoticed was easy enough, Sokolov concluded. All he had to do was follow the compound's perimeter, disappearing behind the laboratory, and continue until he reached the other side. Then he simply walked off into the desert. As the assault team prepared to withdraw, no one had taken notice of his disappearance. And, Grishin had warned, it wouldn't be long before somebody did.

He went onward until he reached what had been the island's eastern shore, now the edge of the mesa that sloped down to the bottom. From the vantage point of Renaissance he had a clear view of the waterless sea. Ahead, he saw a gigantic pool of white, spread over a pit in the sea floor like a frozen lake. It was a field of crystalized salt.

Scattered around the landscape were the hulls of sunken ships, eaten by rust. The Aral was their graveyard.

Sokolov jogged along the edge of the precipice, his eyes scanning the desert. The sun hung low in the gray evening sky, but the ground still gave off heat. He wiped a bead of sweat off his brow. He figured the air temperature had finally dropped below thirty-five centigrade. Bearable enough.

In his mind, Asiyah had only one possible destination. All he had to do was pray he could find her before she made it.

Then he spotted her, marching in the distance, her stride determined. He broke into a run.

He caught up with her a kilometer away from the compound.

He shouted her name.

She stopped in her tracks and spun around aiming her handgun. Seeing it was him, she lowered it.

"Is he there, Asiyah? Your father is in Kantubek, right? Is that why you're going there?"

She said nothing. Annoyance crossed her face. She hadn't planned on him interfering with her actions.

"Why, Asiyah? What do you want?"

"He's laughing at those idiots, you know. He's conned all of you. He even made Alpha finish off the lab, destroying everything they'd come for. It was a clever ploy, giving up the complex. Now the Russians are leaving Renaissance willingly. But I'm the one who's going to have the last laugh."

"But how can your father be staying in a derelict village?"

"My father planned to have a reserve base in Kantubek. It's his personal bunker, constructed beneath one of the buildings. He kept it so secret that I never knew if he had finished it, but I'm confident now."

"You've never mentioned it before," Sokolov said, incredulous.

"Why should I have, I had no proof it existed. There had always been speculation about an underground facility at Kantubek, some sources claiming it was as large as the town itself. We found nothing of the sort investigating the area, but the Soviets had put in some groundwork. At the time, it resembled an area for storage and air-raid protection, but it could be expandable. It was hard for me to judge. Besides, don't forget we were dealing with Frolov. His objective was the complex. If his shock troops had succeeded, this information would be beside the point."

"But now you're going there alone? It's dangerous," Sokolov almost shouted.

"I have no choice, Eugene. I'm doomed. I couldn't stay with the FSB team and I can't go back now. I'm sure Grishin wants me to answer a few questions as to why I led his men into an ambush. My innocence won't concern them. If he doesn't execute me on the spot, I'll disappear somewhere in the dungeons of Lubyanka. I have no future. But I have a chance of achieving my goal before I die."

"We'd stand a better chance if I came with you."

"Don't you understand?" she said in exasperation. "The sentries would kill you the moment you showed up. I must go alone because they won't dare hurt me. They would never take away that pleasure from their President. Stop trailing me. I don't want you to sacrifice your life for naught. Go to back to Grishin's men and fly to Moscow."

"I allowed you to be with me in Moscow when you felt you needed to. I'm begging you now to do the same."

"You saved my life by keeping me next to you. I can only save *your* life by keeping you as far from myself as I can. I'm settling the debt I owe you, Eugene. Accept it."

"You never owed me anything."

Asiyah had made the decision long ago, and no words could dissuade her from effecting her suicidal plot.

But he had no other leverage. Bitter futility choked him.

Sokolov turned back without casting another glance at her.

10

The only reason Sokolov stormed off was to get a head start on Asiyah. Pondering his options, he decided to take the initiative into his own hands. In truth, Asiyah's logic was valid. She had to avoid a confrontation with Grishin, and God only knew what fate awaited her in Moscow—to Frolov, she was an inconvenient witness he no longer had use of.

The revelation of a functioning installation in Kantubek was unexpected. Sokolov doubted that she had lied just to ward him off. But even if Kantubek was abandoned and she was heading there only to hide from the FSB team, she still had no escape from the Aral afterwards. On her own, she would never survive a trek through the desert to the mainland.

He'd be damned if he'd betray her. He would never leave her to die only because she wanted him to.

Reaching Kantubek was his first priority. Asiyah was traveling along what used to be the road from the research complex, taking the most direct path to Kantubek's southern outskirts. Sokolov chose to approach from the flank to the east of the airfield.

He was moving inland, and the terrain became tougher to cross on foot closer to the center of the island. In addition to the island's natural incline, he had to pick his way past rocks, troughs, mesh of dry grass and impeding shrubs that clung onto his uniform with their desiccated stems. He measured his progress relying only on the memory of the island's map and his sense of direction. Every second counted, and in the last five hundred meters he definitely hadn't made up any leeway on Asiyah.

His bending detour finally took him to the old gravel road, similar to the one that led from the polygon to the research complex. Over the decades of erosion it had deteriorated so much that it corrugated out of shape, slowly erased by the island. Wind had blown away pebbles, forming cracks, and strewn bigger stones over the road's surface. But despite the potholes, it was flat, straight, and free of large obstacles. Sokolov upped his rhythm, making up for lost ground.

The town came into view, drawing him like a magnet.

The clear, dry weather provided for excellent visibility. Even from afar, Sokolov could make out individual houses of the former Soviet settlement.

But all that could change in a blink. A hot gust came in, sweeping particles across the road, and died away.

The Aral acted as a cauldron for raging winds. During the active years of Aralsk-7, air currents tended to blow north to south, hence the southernmost location of the aerosol polygon in relation to the lab and Kantubek. But as the region's ecosystem suffered annihilation, the weather fronts became totally unpredictable in their strength, direction and timing. Stirring in the Aral, they produced dust storms that travelled thousands of kilometers. A storm could start in seconds, shrouding everything in an impregnable pall, and last hours—or end as suddenly as it came.

Getting caught by the storm in the open, he—and Asiyah—would be as good as dead. All the more reason to hasten towards the shelter that Kantubek provided.

Pebbles of stone and sand crunched under his boots. Sweat rolled down his nape, the shirt's fabric sticking to his back. The three kilometers he had to cover between Aralsk and Kantubek felt like ten, handicapped by the oppressive heat and his load of armor and weapons.

The road swerved, turning into Kantubek's main street.

Lenin Avenue.

An apt name, Sokolov thought, for a pathway traversing a ghost town.

The scene before his eyes could only belong to a vision from apocalypse.

The layer of pavement had disintegrated to crumbs.

Rows of rust-colored scrubs and bunchgrasses lined the road. Their rigid twigs shivered at a gust of wind. A solitary dead tree stood nearby, pointing out its skeletal branches.

The street's lampposts had broken off, lying across the road. Each had snapped above its base like a matchstick and toppled. The fallen concrete masts were only joined to their stumps by twisted innards of metal rods.

The surrounding houses had become meaningless monuments. Most were roofless, missing stolen or collapsed tiles, revealing naked joists beneath. Wooden window frames had rotted and fallen out. Years of extreme conditions had faded and stained the bricks.

Sokolov could not fathom that the ruins around him had once belonged to a quiet seaside neighborhood. One of these structures had been brought back to life by Kasymov to accommodate his sanctuary. The idea seemed even more striking than before, but he knew it was possible.

But where could it be located?

Unlike the restored Aralsk-7 complex, the town appeared as if no human being had set foot on its soil in decades. The last men who had left behind a visible mark were looters. Outside the garage of Kantubek's motor pool, two carcasses of military trucks stood slumped on their chassis. Their wheels had been removed and stolen. The bonnets had been wrenched open and engine compartments stripped clean. Any part that could be torn off had been plundered, down to rearview mirrors, headlights, and door handles. The rest succumbed to corrosion.

And where was Asiyah?

Sokolov noticed a triangular road sign. Rust had blotted it out, as if replacing the warning with a new alert signal. This was a place best avoided by strangers.

Sokolov paid no heed to premonitions. He unslung his AK and followed Lenin Avenue into the heart of Kantubek.

11

Asiyah recognized the graves.

It was an old burial ground for the animals—mostly primates—killed at the polygon during field tests up until 1987, when the practice ceased due to erratic wind patterns. In several locations on Renaissance Island, the Red Army soldiers had dug deep pits, dumped the cadavers and filled the holes with chlorine and sand. Once a row of sand mounds extended too far, another site was chosen. In total, there were four or five burial sites, numbering over a hundred animal graves. All were scattered in the vicinity of the lab or the polygon. This particular gravesite was located the closest to Kantubek. From then on, finding her way was a straightforward affair. She pushed on, aiming for the water reservoirs that appeared in view, now empty and rust-ridden, and then she suddenly reached the outer buildings of Kantubek.

Her physical and mental fatigue from the last few hours had evaporated.

She crossed the residential district. The two- or three-storied apartment blocks, warehouses, boiler plant, mess hall, and even the kindergarten embodied depression. It was a maze of ugly brick boxes, featureless in their plight.

The military headquarters could not be far away.

Adrenaline surged in her system.

Asiyah rounded a corner and faced a group of three Batyr teenagers on the prowl. Their Oriental complexions were darker than normal, tanned for months by the Aral sun. The youth in charge had intricate tattoos on his neck and arms. Following in tow was a burly guy with a headband around his shaved scalp, and the youngest of the three, whiskers shading the corners of his upper lip.

They were alone. She had them at her mercy.

Seeing her emerge out of the blue, the young soldiers froze. The leader swung up his AK-47, pointing it at her, but his eyes showed panicked indecision. His whiskered comrade followed suit, aiming his rifle at her. The burly teen just stood gaping at her in confusion.

"Put your weapons down," Asiyah ordered in Kazakh, advancing.

Fazed, the leader hesitated. A vein throbbed on his tattooed neck. Fully aware of Asiyah's identity, he struggled to cope with the complication. If they harmed the daughter of his President, death would be the easiest punishment dealt to him. The only solution lay in shifting the responsibility off his shoulders to someone higher in rank who could bring her in.

Yelling at the top of his lungs, the Batyr leader sounded the alarm.

The call for support barely escaped his throat.

In a smooth motion, Asiyah fired the handgun, feeling her wrist absorb the recoil. The bullet went through the teen's skull, cutting short his cry, and his limp body crashed to the ground.

She held the gun at the whiskered boy. He dropped the AK and froze like a statue.

"All you have to do is show me the way inside the bunker," she said.

The youths cowered, nodding their willingness to cooperate. They now knew Asiyah was not going to ask questions twice.

The whiskered boy opened his mouth to explain the directions, stopping abruptly.

Pain erupted in her right shoulder. From behind, an arm locked around the joint and yanked it back. The pressure was unbearable. Her fingers released the gun. She gasped, but a vise choked her, squeezing her windpipe as the attacker pressed her body to him.

"There you are, Princess," Oleg Radchuk whispered in her ear. His breath and his skin reeked. "We've been missing you."

He held the blade of a hunting knife against her cheek. The razor-sharp serrations of the knife's edge punctured the tender skin. Blood seeped. She was too frightened to breathe. The slightest motion would prompt Radchuk to draw the blade across her face, disfiguring her with a scar.

"Ah, we don't want to tarnish that pretty face too much, do we? Daddy won't be happy about that. Better let him decide what to do with you."

He shoved her down to the ground and pinned her with his boot. She felt unable to resist.

"Tie her up and bring her where she wanted to be," Radchuk told the child soldiers. "And then get that son of a bitch lying here out of my sight. Bury your worthless friend next to the chimps."

12

Sokolov heard the report of the handgun and sprinted towards the source of the sound at the farther end of Kantubek.

Asiyah. She had to be there!

Before he could cover a few meters, a rifle cracked, and the force of a sledgehammer pummeled his stomach. He fell flat on his back in the middle of the avenue, the wind knocked out of him.

It took him a moment to realize he had been shot.

Despite the agonizing blow, the polymer armor had saved his life after all. He eyed his vest, identifying a depression that matched the source of the pain. The slug had deflected off a trusty old titanium plate, but the effect hurt so much that Sokolov was hardly in a mood to celebrate.

Stunned, he began to pick himself up. But no sooner had he recovered than a dozen-strong swarm of Batyr soldiers converged on him.

He picked up his AK-104, but before he could level it, the first few soldiers that were onto him knocked it out of his grip.

Crowding him, they landed an avalanche of blows. Feet and rifle butts struck all over his body. All he could do was curl up, shield his face with his arms and let his armor and helmet take the brunt of the onslaught. He avoided the temptation of kicking out at them—it would only open him up to a sucker punch to the groin. And they could shoot him at any time. The hits came down with such intensity that he didn't have a breather. But they would wear out soon at this rate. As long he soaked up the pain, he had a chance to get out.

The problem was, they were not tiring. And simply battering him was no longer enough. With irate cries that reached a fever pitch, they were clawing at him. His helmet torn off, his handgun snatched from his side, they went for his uniform, trying to rip out a piece of fabric or yank off the bulletproof vest. Someone spat at him.

As far as Sokolov could predict, stoning would ensue.

"Enough! Back off!" a man bellowed.

The voice carried such authority that the mob instantly paused their lynching.

"I have a better use of this swine. Take him to the field."

Sokolov's curiosity made him glance up at his perverse benefactor.

Not the tallest of men, he still possessed an intimidating presence. Black-bearded, eyes burning wildly, he packed physique under the fatigues of a Batyr commander.

Sokolov remembered him from the photos. Ahmed Sadaev, the former Chechen guerrilla.

Quickly reminding him that his ordeal was far from being over, the Batyr mob picked him up. They half-dragged, half-carried him somewhere along the dusty streets and then threw him unceremoniously on the ground.

Getting up, Sokolov realized with dismay where he was.

The ground underneath him was flat and barren, only bits of debris and litter scattered about. Tillers of yellow desert grass carpeted the surface in lieu of a green lawn.

The goal posts and the spectators' stands had long since decomposed to metal framework.

It was the football pitch, whatever was left of it.

The child soldiers surrounded him, forming a wide circle. As they jeered at him, two men entered the pitch. Ahmed Sadaev, accompanied by a tall Slav stripped to the waist to demonstrate sweat-slicked muscles, his blond hair tied in a ponytail. It was Radchuk.

Sadaev and Radchuk entered the improvised arena. Radchuk toyed with a hunting knife, flipping it in his hand. The Chechen unsheathed his own weapon, and gestured at Sokolov with the long, jagged blade. This time the crowd cheered. Radchuk had a smug grin on his face. They were going to play with him until he bled out like a lamb.

Sokolov braced himself for the mismatched fight.

Ahmed Sadaev lunged at him. Sokolov sprang back, the blade slicing the air. The Chechen swung his knife again and instantly followed up with a kick that Sokolov parried, smashing the instep of his foot into Sadaev's side. Sokolov thought he'd put enough power in the roundhouse to topple an ox, but Ahmed only staggered, his fist already flying. The blow glanced off Sokolov's head. The hit would have fractured his skull had it connected properly. Pegged back, Sokolov was wary of the Batyr soldiers limiting his space from behind, ready to shoot.

Radchuk approached slowly, amused that the victim resisted. Holding the knife in a reverse grip, Radchuk took a swipe. Sokolov repelled it with a fierce strike of his forearm to Radchuk's wrist, opening him up for a counter. An elbow across his jaw and a kick to the ribs pushed Radchuk away, but not before Radchuk thrust out reflexively, stabbing Sokolov in the heart.

Radchuk bolted back, retreating.

"He has his vest on. You're a cheat, Ahmed, I scored a good kill!" said Radchuk angrily, gritting his teeth in pain.

"Don't be a sore loser," Sadaev replied. "You won't beat me."

It wasn't just a game, it was a contest between them.

Sokolov knew his odds of survival were getting slimmer by the second. Twice already he'd barely held them off. He was still alive only because the ritual was dragging on in its prelude. Once Kasymov's thugs got down to business, they would end it all very quickly. A single flick of a blade would be enough to sever an artery and kill him. Unprotected, his limbs were extremely vulnerable. Real knife fights were rapid and ugly, especially for an unarmed and outnumbered victim. Knocking the knife from Radchuk's grasp could have made a difference, but he had no time to rue the lost opportunity. Sokolov focused solely on the two attackers facing him.

The wind intensified, whipping up particles. Sokolov tasted salt on his cracked lips. Haze already descended on the more distant buildings of Kantubek. A dust storm was imminent. The adverse conditions would cripple his coordination. But Radchuk and Sadaev did not want to test the experience any more than he did.

"All right, Oleg," said Ahmed Sadaev. "Let's finish him off, it's getting boring."

"*Eeya*! *Eeya*!" the teenagers reacted in anticipation.

Nothing to lose now. Do or die.

The cat-and-mouse game turned into a violent melee.

Sokolov charged forward and feinted as they came for him. Radchuk slashed. Sokolov grabbed his knife arm and rapidly kicked his thigh, throwing him off balance, punched his face, breaking the jaw, landed a blow to his solar plexus, but failed to overpower him. Hitting out with his leg, Sokolov caught

Ahmed Sadaev as the Chechen's knife swung in a lethal arc, then ducked under Radchuk's hook, elbowing his ribs, kicked Sadaev again, and drove his knuckles into Radchuk's windpipe. He dropped the knife, and Sokolov tripped him, busting his ankle. The big Ukrainian went down to the ground and took Sokolov with him, snatching his leg. Radchuk clobbered him with his thick arm, swatting Sokolov away. Seizing the knife, Sokolov sprang to his feet. Radchuk was rising. He slashed the blade across Radchuk's throat and down his chest, carving open two deep slits. Blood flowed as Radchuk fell back. The wind howled, bringing a dust cloud that obliterated visibility to a couple of meters. The dust stung Sokolov's eyes. Ahmed Sadaev grappled at him, kicking, punching, slashing, missing Sokolov's spleen by a thread as he hit the border of a titanium pad, Sokolov stabbing his gut quickly. Impaled, the Chechen flopped, Sokolov twisting the jagged edge up, slicing through the abdomen as he withdrew the blade. Sadaev stared in wide-eyed shock, his entrails bulging out. Radchuk wheezed, paralyzed, choking on his blood.

Disoriented, the gory brawl vanishing from view, a Batyr soldier fired rounds crazily. Bullets whistled past. Sokolov fell flat to the ground and rolled sideways. He swept out a foot to hack the nearest Batyr troop. The teen tumbled, and his AK-47 fell into Sokolov's hands. Striking with the rifle butt, Sokolov rendered him unconscious.

Sokolov rolled again, lay prone and let out a volley into the dusty haze. On the other side of the pitch, a gurgling scream broke through the storm, someone hit in the crossfire. Murky silhouettes fled. Panic was spreading. Sokolov could not see farther than the tip of the AK barrel, squinting, the wind blowing particles in his eyes. He kept low, shielding his face with his sleeve. A few erratic shots sounded. Then the shooting ceased. Leaderless, isolated, they dispersed, seeking cover.

Sokolov crawled a few meters towards the border of the pitch, got up and darted for the streets of Kantubek, vanishing in the storm.

13

The sand gritted between his teeth and stuck in his hair. His eyes burned. Without his helmet and goggles, Sokolov stumbled blindly. He grabbed the canteen off his belt and splashed water onto his face and shirt sleeve. Breathing through the fabric of the sleeve as he pressed it to his nose and mouth, he used his free hand to shield his eyes as much as he could. He tried following the direction of the sandblast, keeping his back turned to the wind. It tore at Sokolov's uniform, sneaking sand under his clothes. A coarse gust of desert air scratched his skin.

He coughed spastically, suffocating. The wet cloth filtered grains of sand, but gave no protection against the finer particles of dust he was inhaling. Running harder, short of breath, he sucked in more of the dust-filled air, but didn't slow down. The effort was less dangerous than continued exposure. Sokolov had to take shelter from the storm.

Reaching the nearest house, he groped his way around it and pressed his back to the brick wall, hiding from the force of the wind.

He stood behind the building for a few moments, gusts breaking up against it. Sokolov's heart still raced after the fight on the football field. He had pulled off a miracle to escape, but he needed another one to save Asiyah.

Running in short bursts, he moved from one house to another. The ruined buildings came back into view as the dust cloud dissipated. The storm was subsiding.

Sokolov expected the child soldiers to be lurking in the eerie mist ahead, but no one shot at him as he changed position.

He walked past Kantubek's ghostly buildings, anxiety mounting. He stumbled upon the military structures—headquarters, barracks and mess hall—bunched compactly around the parade ground. Kantubek ended beyond that point, Lenin Avenue exiting to the waterless seashore. None of the buildings could be distinguished as a secret presidential base. None were even guarded.

Where had the Batyr troops gone? Were they no longer willing to sacrifice their lives for their President? Or did they have no one else to protect—or fear punishment from—once Radchuk and Sadaev were dead?

Was Kasymov really in Kantubek?

Sokolov cast his hesitancy aside. Asiyah knew exactly what she was doing. One of these wrecks disguised Kasymov's bunker. The gunshot he had heard was proof enough.

It had to be the military headquarters building. If the Soviets had chosen to improve Kantubek's defenses, the safety of commanding officers would have been their highest concern.

Then he saw a black stain on the ground in front of the headquarters. A pool of blood drying in the heat.

A few paces away from the blood stain, a Batyr soldier's corpse lay sprawled on the road, dragged there and left behind once the storm had broken out.

Sokolov approached a windowless opening in the wall and looked inside. The room was empty.

He pulled himself up and slipped through the decomposed window frame, AK at the ready.

There was nothing but bare walls. Everything had been pilfered, from furniture to doors to wiring. Only broken plaster, rubble, and dust remained.

Scanning each room through the sights of the AK, he inspected the ground floor.

He came to the stairs leading down to the basement.

Whether he was right or wrong, there would be no second chance to find Asiyah.

He raced down the flight of stairs.

The lighting was dim, but he saw two figures in the far corner of the basement as they turned sharply and raised their rifles.

Sokolov held down the trigger, gunning them down. The torrent of bullets hammered flesh and ricocheted off concrete, bodies falling, sparks flying.

Sokolov stepped over the corpses. He did not look at their faces. Youths or not, it didn't matter. He was beyond caring. Kill or be killed. The remorse would come later, he knew.

He turned his attention to the object that the sentries had been assigned to guard.

A metal vault door.

It was purely mechanical, with no electronic elements that could fail due to a power shortage.

He turned the spindle handle, hearing the bolts inside click as the vault door unlocked and swung open the three-inch-thick bulletproof steel.

Beyond it, a spiral stairway led deeper down.

Sokolov descended, taking two narrow steps at a time. The stairway was steep, and he pressed against the wall, expecting to face new guards behind the turn.

But the stairway ended in another vault door.

He had passed the zone sealing the subterranean base from the outside world.

Sokolov slung the AK-47 over his shoulder and spun the handle with both hands, and pushed the massive armored door, revealing a hallway.

Fluorescent lights bathed the white-tiled corridor in a brilliant glow.

Startled, a masked sentry grabbed his rifle a second too late. Sokolov dashed to him up close, cutting his arm with the hunting knife and then crashing the hilt against the back of his head. The man dropped on the tiles, out cold.

Pulse ringing in his ears, Sokolov looked around to see that he was alone and proceeded down the passage. He walked silently, the only audible noises being the hum of the lamps and ventilation, as well as vibrations coming from a remote power plant that provided the electricity.

Sokolov had no time to admire the engineering, but it was evident that this facility had been built recently, decades later than the ruins above it.

Metallic doors with porthole windows were located on either side of the corridor. Each was marked with an unintelligible sign. Lacking their own alphabet, the Kazakhs had adapted Cyrillic, so Sokolov couldn't understand the words even though he could read them.

It was all irrelevant. The corridor ended in a pair of wide sliding doors which bore no lettering.

But there was light spilling through the portholes.

14

Asiyah had never suffered so much pain.
She was lying bound and gagged on the floor and Timur Kasymov was giving her a savage beating. His lacquered shoes kicked all over her body. Her arms, legs and back numbed.

The strength of the blows ebbed away until Kasymov drove a foot in her stomach and delivered a final strike to her head. A swell of nausea picked her up and fireworks exploded in her brain.

Kasymov stepped back, panting with exertion and rage.

"I gave you life. And how did you repay me? You betrayed me! After all that I've done for you."

The gag stifled her cries. She squirmed, but the plastic restraints dug into her wrists.

"You couldn't do anything right," he continued. "You destroyed my dream. Did you come back to ask forgiveness? No, you've done everything to stand in my way. Even now, you can't die properly."

Standing over her, Kasymov spat in her face.

"I own you. I can do whatever I please. But I have no use of you. You're not my daughter. You're a worthless little whore. I banished your new masters from my land, and I'll get rid of you."

Then he took out his handgun and pulled the slide, chambering a round.

"There is no other way to rectify you."

She looked past the gun barrel. She didn't want it to be the last image of her life.

She wouldn't hear the shot when it came, nor would she feel anything.

Her vision floated.

The seconds stretched infinitely as she waited for it all to end.

But she knew she had already died because what she saw the next instant was impossible.

A burst of white light flashed in her eyes, and emerging from it was Eugene Sokolov.

Then her mind plunged into the black abyss.

15

Sokolov pressed a switch and the doors parted.

He was awestruck with the scene appearing before him.

In the bright lighting, the amber panels gave off a dazzle. Covering the surface from floor to ceiling and wall to wall, the ornate mosaic glowed in honey-colored shades of orange and yellow, accentuated by golden cornices, frames and chandeliers that lit it.

It was the Amber Room.

But Sokolov was jolted by a different sight.

Asiyah was lying motionless on the floor.

Next to her, Timur Kasymov dropped to his knees, hands held behind his back.

"Thank God!" Kasymov cried. "Please save us from these monsters! They kidnapped me and my daughter and held us captive here! You must—"

In mid-sentence, Kasymov whipped out his gun and fired at Sokolov.

The bullet missed. Sokolov's AK blasted, hitting Kasymov in the shoulder, blood spraying down the silk shirt. Kasymov crashed down with a throaty grunt.

Holding the Kazakh President at gunpoint, Sokolov hurriedly came over to Asiyah and checked her pulse.

She was unconscious.

He took out the gag and cut the plastic straps fastened around her hands and feet.

He took her in his arms, overwhelmed for an instant by the chamber around him.

Taking a closer look at the wall surfaces, Sokolov realized that the panels held more golden ornament than the actual amber. The room itself was much smaller than the palatial original, the frescoed stucco ceiling suspended lower, the walls too narrow.

The installed sections of amber had deformed, irregular contours complemented with decorative filler. The bits of amber fitted together had been misshaped by the decades of extreme heat. A few patches had discolored turning brown or white.

Although authentic, the amber mosaic had recreated the Room as a hideous copy of itself. A decomposed corpse that had been exhumed, dressed in rich clothes and jewelry and a pretense of being alive.

But once dead, it could not be reborn. The remains of a three-hundred-year-old relic could not be brought back to its glory.

Soft and brittle, the fossilized resin that was amber would eventually crumble into dust.

The Amber Room had not escaped the curse of the Aral after all.

As he carried Asiyah out of the Amber Room, he cast a final glance at her father.

Kasymov groaned. His shoulder shattered, the wound bleeding, he was prostrate with shock, helpless. His arm was useless and the agony rendered him unable to twitch a muscle. Life was draining from him quickly, a red pool of blood spreading from the ruptured subclavian artery.

"Help ... me ... "

Kasymov gaped, croaking through the torment of each breath he took.

Could anything be done to ease his suffering?

Sokolov decided it would be best to leave the President alone with his treasure.

16

Carrying Asiyah in his arms, Sokolov emerged from the headquarters building. Outside, the weather had calmed. There was a stillness in the crystal-blue sky, without the slightest motion of the wind. Only a tinge of salt in the air remained from the dust storm.

He rounded the corner cautiously and saw a BMD driving down Lenin Avenue, the Alpha troops riding mounted atop the vehicle's roof.

Spotting Sokolov, Grishin ordered the driver to stop and hopped down from the BMD.

"What the hell's going on, Sokolov? I thought you got lost in that storm, but all of a sudden we had to eliminate a bunch of enemy troops running to the airfield from this dump of a town. I knew you were up to something. What's up with the girl? Care to explain yourself, Major?"

"There's nothing for me to explain, Colonel. But now that you're here, I wouldn't mind a hand."

Grishin smirked but let the matter go.

Together with his Alpha troops, he helped Sokolov ease Asiyah into the compartment through a hatch.

Sokolov followed Grishin inside the vehicle to hold her safely as the BMD drove back to the airfield.

On the horizon, the evening sun hung above the gray rim of the Aral desert, setting the entire sky in a fiery tint that blazed with all hues of amber.

EPILOGUE

1

Completing the One-Hundred-Man Kumite, Sokolov had endured an ordeal of incessant full-contact fighting. It still lasted all day even though it took Sokolov less than two minutes to defeat an opponent. Each new competitor stepping up to spar against him was fresh, while Sokolov had no chance to recover, his stamina sapping with each bout. A single loss for Sokolov would have immediately ended the test in failure.

By the time he had won the hundredth round, four hours and four minutes since the start of the challenge, Sokolov could barely stand on his feet. All of his fingers had been broken by continuous punching, his body bruised and battered. Physically, he was devastated. But mentally, he was overcome with the kind of euphoria that nothing could ever match. The ruthless Kumite was a test for the mind as much as the body. Going past the limits of human ability, no one could cross the 100-man mark without extraordinary power of will and dogged determination. Only a select few had the attributes to succeed, and he earned his place in that bracket.

But now, Sokolov had survived the Renaissance assault without so much as a scratch, and yet felt crushed emotionally. Nothing took as heavy a toll on the psyche as war. He would get over the impact of the senseless killings, he knew. A single thought comforted him.

Homecoming. He would be back with his brother now.

The Ilyushin landed on the bizarre crisscrossing runway and took the assault team back to Chkalovsky before sunset. Throughout the duration of the flight, Sokolov remained silent, cradling Asiyah. She came to just once, and looked at him with her deep hazel eyes.

"Am I dead, Eugene?" she murmured in delirium. "I hurt so much ..."

He administered a shot of analgesic and she slept until the plane touched down.

He had believed he could exorcise the demons of Beslan from his mind, but Renaissance filled him with the same futility.

It was some kind of a recurrent sick joke. He was bringing Asiyah to Moscow again, this time against her wishes. Again, there was no other choice for them both. He had saved Asiyah from death, but what did it mean for her life?

At Chkalovsky, Sokolov disembarked the plane as Grishin's team unloaded their gear and the bodies of their comrades.

Two men had been waiting for the Ilyushin's arrival. Constantine, who had come to see him. And Victor, who had come to get Asiyah.

The FSB security detail took Asiyah, placed her in their car and drove away.

Sokolov knew he would never see her again.

But he also knew he had to move on and return to normal life.

He had his brother back now. He had his job.

In the days that followed, as he and Constantine moved back to their apartment in Presnya, Sokolov encountered a strange impression of limbo. The FSB showed no interest in him. They didn't call him up for a debriefing—or interrogation. They acted as if nothing had ever happened. Seemingly, Frolov disappeared from their lives as abruptly as he had invaded them.

When a call finally came a month later, it wasn't from the Lubyanka.

Eugene and Constantine received summons to appear in the Kremlin.

2

The early morning light spilled over Frolov's desk as the FSB Director was reading through a stack of documents. He had already finished with the reports from Colonel Grishin and Major Petrov, the transcripts of Asiyah Kasymova's questioning and memos from a team of experts he was sending to Renaissance to inspect the bunker. The last folder was the most exciting: a progress report from the special operatives in Astana. They were preparing to stage a coup that would bring about the ascension of a loyal Kazakh general and allegedly force Timur Kasymov to flee the country. Frolov ascertained that the plan was advancing as scheduled. Now nothing could prevent the reunification referendum from going through. He locked away all the papers and tapped his fingers cheerfully on the empty desk.

Victor ushered a visitor.

Asiyah Kasymova entered Frolov's office.

She was wearing an elegant business suit that combined well with her makeup. She had mended well, according to the doctors. Luckily, no bones had been broken, no organs seriously damaged.

"You look wonderful, mademoiselle. How do you feel?"

"Worse than I look, thank you, although much improved from five weeks ago. I don't believe my incarceration in one of your fine medical institutions can benefit my health any further. So, Comrade Frolov, have you invited me here to announce my release or my death sentence?"

Frolov grinned. Not only did that woman have poise, she had enough daring to jibe him.

"You are fully aware that I can do neither, Asiyah. Killing you would be a waste, and releasing you would be sheer idiocy. You are too valuable and too dangerous. We have failed to retrieve any sort of data from Aralsk-7, let alone equipment. Starting our water-structure weapons technology from scratch will take years, provided the government can find financing, which is unlikely. We will need your knowledge and assistance then, if ever. But if you go to the Americans ... Your expertise will give them a boost in a new arms race and we will never be able to close the gap. And back in Kazakhstan, you may well be killed because you know too much. An accident or a mugging, that kind of stuff. There's only one decision to make. I can't let you leave Russia. What I want to offer you is a choice."

"A choice?" Asiyah raised her thin eyebrows. "A choice of prison?"

"Almost, but not quite. You can point your finger at any location on the map of Russia you want to choose as your place of residence. Any city, town or village that tickles your fancy. We will provide you with a new identity, money, housing, cars, anything you want. You will live in luxury. I only need your cooperation in the future." Frolov held up his arms. "Well?"

"Sounds attractive, but I need time to think it over."

"No. I must have your answer right now. You know you're in no position to bargain."

"Any town?"

"Yes."

"In that case," said Asiyah, "there is one place that I have very fond memories of."

It was Frolov's turn to be surprised.

"And what might that be, my dear?"

"Sochi."

3

ST. George's Hall was the largest in the Grand Kremlin Palace. Built under Nicholas I, it was meant to embody Russia's glorious military history. The Hall's white walls soared seventeen meters in height to form a curved ceiling, supported by eighteen massive pylons. Etched in gold on the marble plates of each pylon were the names all the Knights of the Order of St. George. Along its sixty-meter length, six crystal chandeliers illuminated the Hall, hundreds of lights reflecting in the polished floor woven from twenty species of wood. The walls were adorned with bas-relief sculptures and marble plaques bearing the names of Russian regiments.

At the window facing the Moskva River, encased in glass, was a silver composition depicting the Cossacks whose names were synonymous with the greatest Russian triumphs: Yermak, the discoverer of Siberia, and Matvei Platov, the vanquisher of Napoleon.

Being almost empty today, St. George's Hall gave the impression of being even more spacious than usual. Only twenty chairs were arranged in rows for the participants of the upcoming ceremony.

The ceremony itself was top secret. Neither the names of the attendees nor their accomplishments would ever be disclosed.

They were the members of the Alpha and Vympel teams who had assaulted Renaissance.

And alongside them, Eugene and Constantine Sokolov.

The brothers sat calmly in their silk-upholstered chairs, enjoying St. George's Hall's splendor, aware of the occasion that necessitated their presence.

Each was about to receive the Gold Star Medal, the country's highest decoration, and the accompanying honorary title, Hero of the Russian Federation.

Eugene had put on his midnight-blue EMERCOM full dress uniform. With a fresh shave and haircut, Constantine was sporting a black suit and tie.

Apart from being a secret, the ceremony was also a mystery.

Minutes before it commenced, the details of its protocol remained unknown.

Who was going to address them? Eugene wondered.

Would it be the Prime Minister? The Presidential Chief of Staff?

The Kremlin had released press statements announcing the President's heart problems, successful surgery and imminent recovery. Knowing that Nikolai Alexandrov had been dead for over a month, he expected other headlines to hit the news agencies soon—a sudden deterioration and unfortunate passing of the nation's leader.

He felt a hand brush against his shoulder from behind.

Turning, he saw FSB Director Frolov standing over him.

"Congratulations," Frolov said quietly. "Thanks to you, we have uncovered the location of the lost treasures from that train. Apart from the Amber Room, we found all the icons and artifacts also stored in the bunker, including the Kremlin Collection. Sadly, you will never be able to claim credit for the discovery, which is set to be made officially at an archeological dig somewhere outside Kaliningrad. But it's a job well done, all the same."

Eugene was unperturbed by the man's praise.

"Comrade Frolov, where is Asiyah Kasymova? What did you do to her?"

"Sorry, I don't follow you. What are you talking about, Comrade Major? Who is she?"

Eugene did not show his anger, but when Frolov winked at him, he wanted to grab the old rat by the neck and crush it. He mustered all his will to rein back the swelling rage.

"Take it easy, he's not worth it," Constantine muttered.

With a smug grin, Frolov proceeded down his row to an empty seat.

There was no time to mull over Frolov's treachery.

The announcer called for attention.

The ceremony got underway.

A pair of FSO guards dressed in historic 1812 costumes of the Preobrazhensky Regiment pulled open the Hall's immense gilded doors as a gray-haired man walked briskly down the red carpet.

"The President of the Russian Federation . . ." the announcer's voice boomed.

It couldn't be . . .

" . . . Nikolai Petrovich Alexandrov."

Stunned, Eugene Sokolov was the last to stand up as everyone around him rose in applause.

President Alexandrov strode to the rostrum. Smiling, he motioned for his guests to sit down as he began his address.

"Dear friends . . ."

His mind reeling, Sokolov did not hear the President deliver his speech on the fight for freedom and democracy, their acts of courage, and the warriors who had sacrificed their lives on the altar of peace.

Was it an illusion, his eyes deceiving him?

It was impossible.

"Am I hallucinating?" he asked Constantine.

"It's him, Gene," his brother replied.

One by one, the announcer called up the names of the honored guests and the President conferred their new decorations on them.

Colonel Grishin, ramrod-straight and full of pride for his troops.

Major Petrov, his arm supported by a sling, but his head held high, his gait measured as he approached the Supreme Commander-in-Chief.

The men of Alpha and Vympel with whom Sokolov had trained at their base in Balashikha.

When the sound of his name reverberated around the marble vaults of St. George's Hall, Eugene Sokolov felt his blood rush.

He walked to the rostrum, his eyes boring into President Alexandrov's face.

I saw you dead! I could touch your drowned corpse!

Alexandrov did not seem to notice Sokolov's intense gaze. He picked the Gold Star Medal from a cushion held by a guard and pinned its tricolor badge to Sokolov's chest.

Sokolov shook the President's extended hand. It was warm and fleshy.

"Well done, Comrade Major," Nikolai Alexandrov said.

Alexandrov's eyes sparkled. Sokolov detected a slight puffiness around the eyelids, the result of recent cosmetic surgery.

"Thank you, Mr. President," Sokolov said firmly. "I'm happy to serve my country."

4

After the ceremony, Eugene and Constantine took a long walk. Crossing the Cathedral Square, they exited the Kremlin through the Trinity Tower and strode along the Alexandrovsky Garden. The Gold Stars on their lapels glistened in the sun.

"His corpse was right next to me, I saw it at the wreck of the *Olympia*."

"It could be an impersonator, Gene. A double."

"Then or now?"

"We'll never know."

"That's all it was from the beginning, then. A deception."

"Yes, but not the only one. I think I've come to understand what happened back in 1993. The shooting of the Parliament. We were lied to that it had to be done to keep Russia from a return to Communism. We both know it was impossible, there was no going back, not in 1993. But was there a way to go forward from it? Imagine what would have happened if there had been a nationwide trial against the Soviet regime? A full-scale Civil War would have broken out. Our rulers were too scared to take the responsibility, so the shooting was a stage show played out between Yeltsin and the parliamentary leaders, at the expense of thousands of lives. A symbolic denouncement of the past in front of the television cameras."

They reached the wrought-iron gates at the entrance of the Garden, topped by imperial eagles, and walked out to Red Square. Opposite the Garden's fence stood the equestrian statue of Marshal Zhukov, the mass murderer of his own soldiers. Looming ahead, adjacent to the Kremlin's wall, was the blocky pyramid of Lenin's Tomb.

"So you're saying we'll never distance ourselves from Sovietism?" Eugene asked.

"I'm sure we will, we already have. Such fundamental changes require either a lot of blood or a lot of time. It may take decades, a generation, but Russia will gradually recover. There are a lot more people who view history adequately than we think. The ghost of that mummy lying here will no longer haunt us. We're living in the age of a Russian renaissance."

Arriving at the other end of Red Square, they came to the bright-colored domes of St. Basil's Cathedral. The clock of the Kremlin's Spasskaya Tower chimed once, marking a quarter-hour.

"I don't know what to believe anymore," Eugene said. "What if the Amber Room aboard the train in 1941, the one I saw in Kantubek, wasn't real? There could be *two* copies, one taken by the Nazis, the other stolen by Kaganovich, and all the while Stalin kept the real Amber Room hidden somewhere else. Like you said, I don't think we'll ever know."

"It's not inconceivable," Constantine mused. "Suppose that all the blood, from Kaganovich to Kasymov, had been shed over a fake ... In that case, Joseph Stalin has tricked everyone once again."

Made in the USA
Lexington, KY
06 December 2018